P9-DCW-393

PRAISE FOR CHRISTINE CARBO

Mortal Fall

"Compulsively readable . . . Carbo paints a moving picture of complex, flawed people fighting to make their way in a wilderness where little is black or white, except the smoky chiaroscuro of the sweeping Montana sky."

—*Publishers Weekly*

"Carbo doesn't do superficial. She gives her characters weight. And like her debut, *Mortal Fall* provides a story with dual tracks—the investigation into murder and the rugged journey of the soul."

—*New York Journal of Books*

"[Carbo] writes with a sense of simple realism that comes from being a local. The grandeur and beauty of Glacier isn't over-written, nor ignored . . . the perfect mystery to read beside the lake. . . ."

—*The Missoulian*

"If *Mortal Fall* were just a beautifully written, sharp-eyed procedural, that would be reason enough to read it. But Christine Carbo offers so much more in this fine second novel. It's a study of flawed, compelling characters and the ghosts that haunt them. It's also a fascinating look at the relationship of humans with the too-rapidly changing landscape of Glacier Park. And finally, it's the tragic story of the forces that can shatter a family. This novel works on so many levels, all of them masterfully crafted."

—William Kent Krueger, *New York Times* bestselling author of *Manitou Canyon*

"*Mortal Fall* is a terrific read. With a masterful hand, Christine Carbo guides her readers through an intriguing mystery full of complex relationships and smartly developed characters. Her rich descriptions immerse you in the grandeur of Glacier National Park as this riveting story unfolds. Christine Carbo should be a part of every mystery lover's personal library."

—Allen Eskens, author of *The Life We Bury*

"Carbo brings subtlety and sensitivity to the smallest of moments . . . those willing to soak up the character-driven context will find much to enjoy here."

—*Booklist*

The Wild Inside

"[S]tays in your mind long after you've put the book down. I'm still thinking about it. Prepare to run the gamut of emotions with this fine treat of a story. Then, in the years ahead, be on the lookout for more from this fresh new voice in the thriller genre."

—Steve Berry, *New York Times* bestselling author of the Cotton Malone series

"Fans of Nevada Barr will love this tense, atmospheric thriller with its majestic Glacier National Park setting. *The Wild Inside* is a stunning debut!"

—Deborah Crombie, *New York Times* bestselling author of *To Dwell in Darkness*

"An intense and thoroughly enjoyable thrill ride. Christine Carbo's literary voice echoes with her love of nature, her knowledge of its brutality, and the wild and beautiful locale of Montana. *The Wild Inside* is a tour de force of suspense that will leave you breathlessly turning the pages late into the night."

—Linda Castillo, *New York Times* bestselling author of *The Dead Will Tell*

"The brutality and fragility of Glacier National Park's wilderness provides the perfect backdrop for this well-crafted, absorbing novel about the barbarities and kindnesses of the humans living on its edge. Christine Carbo is a writer to watch."

—Tawni O'Dell, *New York Times* bestselling author of *One of Us*

"Grizzly bears, murder, mauling, and mayhem mix in Carbo's debut novel. Ted Systead's past and present intersect in an unexpected—and chilling—manner against the incongruously gorgeous backdrop of Glacier National Park."

—*Kirkus Reviews*

"Sharp, introspective Systead is a strong series lead, and Carbo rolls out solid procedural details, pitting him against Department of the Interior bureaucrats. The grittiness of the poverty-wracked area surrounding Glacier plays against the park's dangerous beauty in this dark foray into the wilderness subgenre. Put this one in the hands of those who enjoy Paul Doiron's Mike Bowditch novels and Julia Keller's Bell Elkins series."

—*Booklist*

ALSO BY CHRISTINE CARBO

The Wild Inside
Mortal Fall

THE WEIGHT OF NIGHT

A NOVEL OF SUSPENSE

CHRISTINE CARBO

ATRIA PAPERBACK

New York • London • Toronto • Sydney • New Delhi

ATRIA
PAPERBACK

An Imprint of Simon & Schuster, Inc.
1230 Avenue of the Americas
New York, NY 10020

This book is a work of fiction. Any references to historical events, real people, or real places are used fictitiously. Other names, characters, places, and events are products of the author's imagination, and any resemblance to actual events or places or persons, living or dead, is entirely coincidental.

Copyright © 2017 by Christine Carbo

All rights reserved, including the right to reproduce this book or portions thereof in any form whatsoever. For information, address Atria Books Subsidiary Rights Department, 1230 Avenue of the Americas, New York, NY 10020.

First Atria Paperback edition June 2017

ATRIA PAPERBACK and colophon are trademarks of Simon & Schuster, Inc.

For information about special discounts for bulk purchases, please contact Simon & Schuster Special Sales at 1-866-506-1949 or business@simonandschuster.com.

The Simon & Schuster Speakers Bureau can bring authors to your live event. For more information, or to book an event, contact the Simon & Schuster Speakers Bureau at 1-866-248-3049 or visit our website at www.simonspeakers.com.

Manufactured in the United States of America

10   9   8   7   6   5   4   3

Library of Congress Cataloging-in-Publication Data

Names: Carbo, Christine, author.
Title: The weight of night : a novel of suspense / Christine Carbo.
Description: First Atria Paperback edition. | New York : Atria Paperback, 2017.
Identifiers: LCCN 2016049055 (print) | LCCN 2016057439 (ebook) | ISBN 9781501156236 (softcover) | ISBN 9781501156243 (e-book)
Subjects: LCSH: Government investigators—Fiction. | Cold cases (Criminal investigation)—Fiction. | Missing persons—Investigation—Fiction. | Glacier National Park (Mont.)—Fiction. | Wilderness areas—Fiction. | Forest fires—Fiction. | BISAC: FICTION / Crime. | FICTION / Mystery & Detective / General. | GSAFD: Suspense fiction. | Mystery fiction.
Classification: LCC PS3603.A726 W45 2017 (print) | LCC PS3603.A726 (ebook) | DDC 813/.6—dc23
LC record available at https://lccn.loc.gov/2016049055

ISBN 978-1-5011-5623-6
ISBN 978-1-5011-5624-3 (ebook)

For Mathew,
Congratulations to my 2017 graduate!

"Where guilt is, rage and courage doth abound."

—BEN JONSON

– GLACIER NATIONAL PARK –

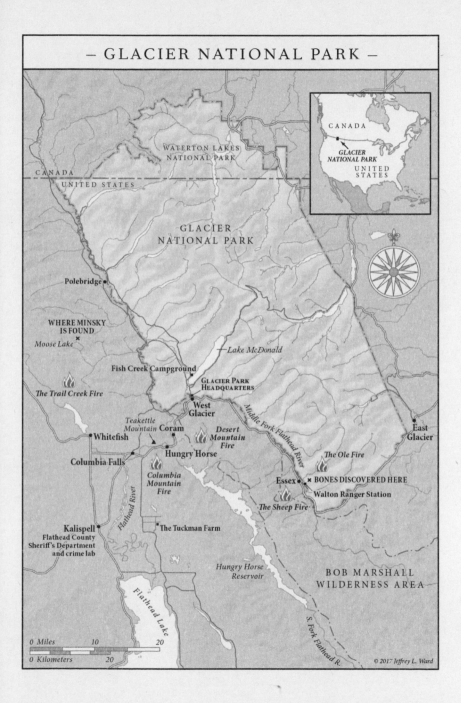

CANADA

GLACIER
NATIONAL PARK

UNITED
STATES

WATERTON LAKES
NATIONAL PARK

CANADA
UNITED STATES

GLACIER
NATIONAL PARK

Polebridge •

WHERE MINSKY
IS FOUND
Moose Lake ×

Lake McDonald

Fish Creek Campground •

GLACIER PARK
HEADQUARTERS

The Trail Creek Fire

West
Glacier

Middle Fork Flathead River

East
Glacier

*Teakettle
Mountain* Coram •

Whitefish •

*Desert
Mountain
Fire*

The Ole Fire

Hungry Horse •

Columbia Falls •

*Columbia
Mountain
Fire*

Essex • × BONES DISCOVERED HERE

Walton Ranger Station

Flathead River

The Sheep Fire

Kalispell •
Flathead County
Sheriff's Department
and crime lab

■ The Tuckman Farm

*Hungry Horse
Reservoir*

BOB MARSHALL
WILDERNESS AREA

Flathead Lake

S. Fork Flathead R.

0 Miles   10   20
0 Kilometers   20

© 2017 Jeffrey L. Ward

THE WEIGHT OF NIGHT

1

Gretchen

I'D LOVE TO tell you the person I am now has nothing to do with the
girl I was when I lived in Sandefjord, a quaint port town on the southern tip of Norway. I was born there, a place where the sun glinting
on the navy-colored, foamy bay made you feel alive, and the crisp air
gusting in from the North Sea ensured you never forgot your strong-
blooded, Nordic roots. I lived a typical, healthy life with my family—
skiing, sledding, skating—until everyone: my mother, my father, my
grandparents, my aunts and uncles, the neighbors, my classmates, my
teachers . . . quit trusting me. *I* quit trusting me.

It had been exactly five years and two months since the last time
I had gone through a phase of my dreaded sleepwalking habit, when
I was twenty-five. I have had what professionals call a REM behavior
disorder—a condition that takes sleepwalking to absurd levels—since
I was a child. Unlike most people who frame each day with an awaken-
ing from sleep and a submission back into it, I learned that the bracket
on the slumbering end of my frame was seriously flawed. After a busy
or stressful day when most people relish the thought of snuggling
into their beds, wrapped in warm covers, their heads sinking into soft
pillows and sliding blissfully into a world of dreams where time ceases
to exist, I fear going to sleep—sometimes dread it.

But I had begun to think I might be over my syndrome—that
I'd succeeded in prying myself away from my younger self, that
treacherous girl, like I was a toy comprised of two plastic parts held

1

together only by stubborn glue. Unfortunately, I was wrong, and my disorder began rearing its ugly head again one warm summer morning in August. Later, my doctor would say it was the heat and the particle-filled air that acted as a trigger, but I came to see its resurfacing as much more fated—a deeper prompt forcing me to dredge up raw, unwelcome memories.

I woke up at my usual six a.m. alarm and noticed the light covers—a sheet and thin blanket—tangled and pushed to the bottom of the bed. I gave myself the benefit of the doubt. After all, it had been a hot night. All summer the temperature had hovered upward of ninety-five degrees and half the Northwest was on fire. Montana was no exception. Fires burned to the east, west, north, and south of the Flathead Valley, and the ones raging in and around Glacier National Park had started more than four weeks earlier. Now the thick smoke blanketed the mountains and choked the valley, making each day feel like an apocalyptic event lurked around the corner.

I'd closed the windows the night before because it seemed better to suffer the heat than to inhale the dense, toxic air. A fly had furiously buzzed along the windowsill, captive in the stagnant room. For a good half hour, I listened to its maddening buzz and its random, annoying flights. After I tried to swat at it when it flew too close to my face a number of times, it settled somewhere on the ash-covered sill and left me alone. I finally drifted off listening to the whir of the ceiling fan. Of course, I thought, such circumstances would give *anyone* a restless night. I'd probably just kicked the covers down to get some air.

I swung my feet to the wood-planked floor, pleased to feel the smooth slats under my soles, and sat for a second rubbing my arms. The morning light filtered through the smoky sky and stretched across the golden floor like gauze, turning it a sickly yellowish orange. I looked out the window, hopelessly wanting to see something wet—some freshly soaked pavement, leaves dripping with moisture, or soil darkened by rain. It was bone-dry, the grass in the small yard turned beige, the leaves on the tips of the bushes tinged yellow. The pine trees in the side woods appeared diseased with reddish-brown needles, many already fallen and desiccated on the forest floor as if it were fall. There was no relief in the forecast.

I picked up my phone from the bedside table and checked for messages. There were none, so I headed to the bathroom to shower and get ready to go into the lab. Nothing too pressing was going on, but I needed to finish some paperwork on a deceased man—a young firefighter, in fact—from the day before. He'd been found separated from his crew, sitting still against a tree as if he were simply enjoying a peaceful moment in the forest, watching swallows diving in and out of branches or listening to the chickadees sing their songs, before continuing on his way. Only, in these fire-infested woods, there would be no birdsong. The ME determined that it was his heart—an arrhythmia—but we'd been called in before the ME made that determination just in case there was foul play.

I'd almost forgotten about my bedcovers when I looked in the mirror one last time, checking that my shoulder-length blond hair was secured neatly away from my face and that the small amount of blush I'd applied wasn't on too thick. Not out of vanity, I just hated too much makeup. My fair skin didn't take it well, so I picked up a tissue and gently wiped my cheekbones to dab up any excess color and lighten the effect of the already faint pink powder.

There were certain things you picked up from your mother whether you wanted to or not, and I could still hear her words: *Amerikanske jenter bruker for mye sminke.* American girls wear too much makeup. After moving to Seattle from Norway at age eighteen, I went for months painting on as much cover-up and thick mascara as possible just to separate myself from the au naturel Nordic girl that my family knew. Just to ensure that when I looked in the mirror, I could almost pretend I was *Americansk* and not notice the ghostly, nearly translucent skin and the treacherous blue eyes staring back, constantly questioning who I was and why the hell I was alive.

Eventually, I couldn't fight reality anymore and gave up one day after looking at myself and realizing I loathed the disguise just as much as I hated the girl underneath the raccoon liner, deep rosy blush, and mauve lipstick. That was the last time I wore heavy makeup.

I threw the tissue in the trash and headed to the kitchen to make some coffee. When I stepped into the living room, I stopped immediately. The shelves on the other side of the room stood vacant except for two cast-iron book weights formed in the shape of easy chairs. My books weren't there. All of them, probably fifty—paperbacks, hardbacks, and all my forensic texts—had been taken down. Instead, four rows of stacked books, each slightly crooked, rose in columns before the fireplace. I glanced at my small dining room off to my right. Two dining chairs stood peculiarly on top of the oak table.

What else had I done? I, of course, considered whether I had left the house or not, perhaps walked down the street in my underwear in the middle of the night—maybe even peed on some of the neighbor's bushes. But, even though I work in forensics, it doesn't take a super sleuth to check out the scene. I had taken a look around, filled in a few blanks, and discerned I'd done nothing crazy.

All my doors were locked, my key still hidden in its jar above the refrigerator, unmoved since I'd set it there before going to bed. My doors require keys for both entering and leaving. Since I'm not particularly tall, no more than five-four, I would have had to have grabbed either a chair or my footstool to reach above the refrigerator. All signs indicated that I'd only set the two chairs on the dining table and not messed with the other two. This I could also tell by a slight film of dust that had collected on the floor, since I hadn't eaten at my dining room table in months. And my footstool with its worn red, blue, and gold embroidered flowers and wooden lion's feet was exactly where I'd left it: near my closet in the bedroom with a pile of dirty clothes draped across it.

When I purchased the house, the locksmith thought I was crazy for wanting key locks that worked both ways, but as I mentioned, I don't trust myself. Not since I was exactly fifteen years and three months old. My parents used to try to convince me that there were plenty of people in the same boat—those who felt like they couldn't maintain control at certain times: alcoholics, drug addicts, people with anger-management issues. But my issue was different because I had always been fine during my waking moments. It was the nighttime that posed problems. Besides, I could see in their worried expressions, their furrowed brows and tear-filled eyes, that they didn't entirely believe the logic themselves, especially my mom. She wanted to, but ultimately, she couldn't. No one predicted that something as innocent as sleep could be lethal for me, for my family.

I pushed down the sickening feeling that rose inside of me. I marched over, grabbed each chair, and scooted it back under the table where it belonged. "Shit," I mumbled out loud to no one. Herbal tea, I thought, something without caffeine. I need herbal tea before I put away those damn books.

2

Monty

I'VE ALWAYS KNOWN that Glacier is a magical place: sculpted by glacial snowfields, shaped by bitter wind, wrought by hammering rain, carpeted by heavy snow, and scorched by fires. And even in the worst of circumstances, its beauty, cut over a billion years by remarkable forces, has a way of shining through.

It's what I loved most about it, and so have millions of visitors each summer: how you could have had the worst day, week, or even year of your life; gotten your ass chewed out by a boss or a parent; or had an awful fight with your wife, friend, or kid, but the second you entered Glacier, you could begin to feel the angst, the worries, the fears fall away, dissolving against the serrated edges of the peaks.

But not on this particular day. Because of the dense smoke swathing everything in a murky haze, not an ounce of Glacier's exquisiteness had been able to shine through in the past few days.

After a morning of meetings about the spread of the fires and the trail and campground closures, assigning area patrols to ensure that all hikers and visitors continued to be safely evacuated from certain backcountry sites, my boss, Joe Smith—chief of Park Police—sent me to the southern border of the park, to a small town called Essex. It was sandwiched between two fires blazing in or near Glacier National Park, one on the west side of the town named the Sheep Fire because of its proximity to Sheep Creek, and one on the park side called the Ole Fire because of its closeness to Ole Creek. Essex was now being evacuated.

Essex had been on the *Set* mode of the *Ready, Set, Go* evacuation model for the past two days, and reached *Go* today as Sheep and Ole began to charge the ridges closer to the town. Joe Smith and Sheriff Walsh from Flathead County had ordered residents to vacate under authority of an Incident Commander who'd been called in once the fires were deemed a Type One Event. Eugene Ford, Glacier's superintendent, had signed a delegation of authority to the IC to lead the Incident Command Unit, a system that works as an umbrella structure over all the various organizations to prevent it from becoming one huge train wreck. Glacier, its rangers and Park Police, the county sheriff's office, the Forest Service, the Hot Shot crews, the equipment and hand crews, and so on would all temporarily answer to the IC. Currently, pilot cars were leading lines of vehicles out of the area and soon the road would be closed to all travelers.

When I finally arrived in Essex at the Walton Ranger Station, not far from the Burlington Northern Santa Fe railroad, another Park Police officer working the area, Tara Reed, met me. Dressed in a Park Police uniform identical to mine—navy trousers and a light blue shirt—Tara had long dark hair streaked with a rich silver that gave her an exotic look, and wore it pulled back in a braid. She was maybe in her early forties, with olive skin and warm eyes framed by soft laugh lines. I'd known her since I joined eight years before. She was one of the first to grab a cup of coffee with me, show me around, and fill me in on what was what, who was nice, who was cranky, and who was screwing whom, figuratively and literally.

"Shit, it's brutal out here," I said as I put my hard hat on, just as she had. It was safer that way, with debris flying from the trees that the men were felling.

"Definitely not the kind of summer we long for," she said, her voice raspy, not from the smoke. Her voice always had a husky quality. "I'd take rain over this any day."

"Chief just wants us to check on the area where they're breaking the line—make sure there are no tourists or hikers still around, making their way back from Scalplock Peak or Essex Creek to Izaak Walton Inn or something."

"I doubt anyone's out here since those areas have been closed, but I guess you never know."

She and I walked over to where the crew was creating a fuel break from the Essex Creek trestle to Dickey Creek. We passed a backhoe closer to the railroad, its large forklike hand grabbing trees by their roots and yanking them up, wakes of soil falling in all directions. The steady, loud grate of its motor and the screech of its brakes every time it paused to back up or shift directions pierced the normally quiet woods.

It looked like a war zone, and I knew it was grueling, dirty, and sweaty labor. At least fifty men with red hard hats, beige heavy-duty work suits, and supply packs on their backs were heading out, each with a Pulaski—a tool that is a combination of an axe and a shovel—over his shoulder. Another thirty or so scattered about trying to clear all potential sources of fuel—dry brush and deadfall—from the ridge below the flames. I knew from the earlier meeting that some of the men had been going at it since three a.m. and would continue to do so all day until it got too dark to work safely, or the fire activity became too dangerous to continue.

We went through the woods, planning to sweep from the creek and back up to look for anyone not belonging to the fire crews. The Ole Fire had crossed one of the ridges to the east of Essex and there was a strong column of flame building two hundred feet upward on the next one over. It raged and glowed eerily through the dense smoke less than a quarter mile from us.

Tara coughed, then said, "That's the ops manager for the fire crews." A medium-height, stocky man of about forty came toward us. He reported to the IC as well.

I held out my hand. "Officer Monty Harris," I introduced myself.

"Hutch Wilcox," he said, removing his glove so we could shake. His hand was rough, callused from digging lines, clearing trees and brush, and assisting the helicopters as they captured and hauled water from the middle fork of the Flathead River. A smeared line of soot ran across his right cheek toward a thick eighties-style mustache.

"Thank you for your hard work out here," I said. "It's mind-blowing what you do."

"It's just, well, what we do." He wiped the grit off his face with the back of his hand. "More and more of it each year, it seems. And they're burning more intensely."

"Just making sure the area is cleared out for your men. Not that this area is all that welcoming to tourists right now."

"Definitely not, but I appreciate the extra caution. I've been on the lookout too, but haven't seen anyone other than my men around." Wilcox motioned to his crew. Near the rear of the line of men setting up to dig a fuel break, I recognized a firefighter named Carl Benson. I'd met him the last time we had a big fire season. Carl was about six feet and all muscle, maybe 175 pounds, with a long mane of dark hair that he kept tied at the nape of his neck. He was known for his boundless energy and constant composure—a natural in the crazy world of wild-fire fighting. He seemed to regard it romantically, even, as if he were Captain Ahab and each fire a red, pulsing, vengeful creature moving through the sea of mountains like the great white Moby Dick.

"You can't fight it; you can only corral it," Carl was saying to one of the men working next to him as Wilcox, Tara, and I walked up. The kid, tomato-faced and scared, looked like this was one of his first shifts on wildfire detail.

"Hey, Carl," I said.

"Monty." He tipped his hard hat to me. "Good to see you. We've got some real doozies on our hands this summer."

"Dryer and hotter than hell," I said.

"This is Jimmy Taylor," Wilcox offered. "Second day out."

"We appreciate the hard work." I grinned at him. He looked like he could use a little encouragement. Jimmy and Carl left to take their spot on the fuel break line, and Wilcox headed off to talk to some others on his crew who were waving him over. Tara and I trailed Jimmy and Carl for a short stretch, since it was on the way toward the river.

"Remember," Carl told Jimmy while he hocked a loogie and spit it out, then held an index finger over one nostril and did a farmer blow. Sinus passages didn't stay in the best of shape when working fire season. "The triangle consists of three legs: heat, fuel, and oxygen. We're just here to break the fuel leg so that we steer the beast clear of town."

Jimmy didn't look like he was hearing a word Carl said and certainly wasn't answering. I figured that what Carl was explaining was completely obvious at this point in the kid's training, not to mention that he looked like he was simply trying to survive . . . trying not to puke or pass out from the heat. He was holding one thickly gloved hand across his stomach while the other carried his Pulaski.

"You okay there?" I asked him.

"I'm good," he muttered.

"I told him"—Carl shifted his heavy pack on his back—"not to try the Copenhagen last night. I warned him it'd just get him sick and now here he is. . . . But you just watch, he'll probably end up with a lifelong love affair with the stuff like the rest of us."

"Felt all right last night," Jimmy said.

I could picture it: Jimmy taking a little in spite of Carl's warnings—squeezing it between his fingers and gingerly shoving it in between his lower gum and his lip. I remembered the first time I had tried it when I was a game warden on the east side of the Divide, in a town called Choteau. Another warden had pulled a fresh can out, snapped it against the inside of his palm, and offered me a pinch. I had taken some under his squinting gaze and within seconds, my head became light as a butterfly, my muscles slackened, and I simply buzzed and floated for a short time. Luckily, I never made a habit out of it like some of the other game wardens.

Carl eyed the kid as if he was some oddity he wasn't sure whether to study or curse. Jimmy was sweating so much that his beige Nomex fire suit was drenched and had already begun to turn blackish gray. I didn't envy him at all. The work was grueling. This was no campfire with steady, lulling pops and crackles. We were talking about the kind of roaring giant that presses in on you, fills your head with its freight train of noise, and makes your gut vibrate. The heat from the flames in the distance surrounded us and the sound engulfed us. The temperature was at least 107 degrees where we were standing.

"Grab your Pulaski and take your spot next to me," Carl pointed to a dry patch of land in line with the rest of the crew. Jimmy wiped his watering eyes, which had developed crusty granules in the inside corners of each, and took his spot.

The drill was not complex, just exhausting: throw your pick in again and again until the workers could advance. I knew it well since I'd filled in a time or two when I was in college and needed some summer money. This is how it got done—an entire train of mostly men and a few women pitched trowels . . . moving the sequence forward until enough strikes made a nice six-foot-wide break, a canal of sorts that would not get crossed by the roaring monster heading their way. Hopefully.

Jimmy took his place and drove the axe side of his Pulaski into tall dry grass, rock, and dirt to cut the break up a sidehill. He was second from the back. Carl was last, the caboose bringing up the rear.

Tara and I left them to their work and headed toward the creek. A loud crunching sound marked each step we took through the dried foliage, reminding us why the forests were burning in the first place. Everything crackled like tissue paper. I could hear no birds, no squirrels, no chipmunks, only the fire booming in the distance and the sound of the loud backhoe ripping the smaller trees out.

We made our way down the bank of the creek for a stretch. It babbled quietly as if it didn't care about the blazing mountain. The rest of the forest felt subdued, as if the woods were on hold, waiting patiently to see what damage Sheep and Ole would bring. Many animals had already departed or burrowed deep underground.

Twenty minutes later we were back near the line where the men were digging. The sequence had already begun to make headway in clearing the ground, and I spotted the end of the line. Carl and the rookie were still bringing up the rear. I watched Jimmy throw his axe, watched it land, and saw him pause and lean over at his waist.

"Oh no," I said to Tara, "looks like he might lose it after all." We headed a little closer. Jimmy picked up his axe and went for another blow, only this time his swing was gentler and smaller. I wondered if he was too weak to take a full swing when he kneeled down next to the ground and started scraping at something. As we came closer, I could see a dirty, yellowed rock.

"Time," Carl yelled, meaning time to move.

Jimmy continued to scrape at the ground. Tara mumbled something, and I was just going to ask her what she'd said when Jimmy announced, "Look at this."

"What?" Carl asked.

"Look." Jimmy sank to his knees and brushed dirt off a round object and ignored the line as it began to shift to the northeast again. I could still see it in the dirt, and had a quick thought that the rocks out in this area were typically oyster gray, blue green, or reddish purple, maybe, but not tan.

"What's the holdup?" I asked, leaning forward to get a better angle.

Jimmy was brushing it off with his gloved hand, when suddenly he startled, jumped back, and fell on his butt.

"Jesus, boy." Carl laughed. "What's your deal?"

Jimmy pointed at it. Tara, Carl, and I shuffled in closer, stuck our necks out and peered down at the ground.

"Holy shit," Carl grunted as we stared at the exposed skull.

I knelt down for a closer look.

"Shouldn't we—" Jimmy stopped midsentence, rotated his body away from us, wrapped his arm around his gut, and threw up unto the brown grass at his feet.

"Shit, kid," Carl said, backing away. "I had a feeling that nothing about you would be easy. Leave it to you to be the only firefighter out here to find a damn skull in a fire break."

• • •

"You're talking human skeleton?" Joe Smith's voice came through my radio.

"Yes, I am."

"Are you sure?"

"I'm positive," I said. In Glacier and the surrounding wilderness, it wasn't entirely uncommon to come across some rotting animal bones, and skeletal remains of a bear's paws are often mistaken for human hands, but the skull and the fact that they were buried discounted that these were animal bones.

"Remind him that there aren't exactly many monkeys around these parts," Tara whispered.

"What have you done so far?" Smith asked.

"Tara and I roped it off and told ops to divert the line around it, closer to the fire. Everyone's got a hundred things going on with the state of things, but this is serious."

"Definitely serious," Joe said.

"And I'm worried about how close Ole is getting. We need a forensics team on it sooner than later. If Ole hits this line," I added. "I'm not sure what kind of a beating these bones will take."

"I'm not sure either. Probably wouldn't incinerate them, but might destroy any chances of mitochondrial DNA."

"How do you want me to proceed?"

"Call the county and get forensics on it. I know Walsh"—he was referring to the sheriff of Flathead County—"is busy with evacuations as I am. I'll contact him. This is going to need to go through the IC as well now, since it's under their umbrella, but we'll want to give them as much information as we can about how we and the county usually handle this type of a situation." When a human skeleton is found, it's standard procedure to report it to the law enforcement system that has jurisdiction, get someone with experience to carefully excavate it, then send it to the local morgue, where the coroner and forensic experts examine it and decide if it can be identified locally. If not, it gets sent to a center in Texas that identifies bones.

"I've spoken to Wilcox. He's here with me now. I'll let him know that we'll need the county up here as soon as possible to get this bagged and processed."

"Shit," Wilcox said as I signed off with Smith. He'd come over to check on the holdup when he noticed the end of the line wasn't moving. "A skeleton out here. Wild. Think it's some drifter from the trains?" he asked, seemingly delighted to be talking about something other than wind speed and direction. "Someone who died out here in the cold or something?"

"I have no idea. Although someone who freezes to death doesn't get buried under the soil without a little help."

I knelt down again to look at the bones. Tara followed suit. Even through all the noise, I could hear a wheeze in her breathing as I stared at them and she waited for me to say something. I didn't want to put her on the spot, so I didn't ask if the smoke was getting to her. I just pulled out some latex gloves and ever so gently nudged the skull to angle slightly upward so I could see its profile.

"When we were first heading this way," Tara said, "even when I could barely make anything out, I knew something was up because I could see that that wasn't a rock." She pointed to a partially exposed longer bone that looked like a femur.

I didn't want to disturb the scene any more than it already had been, and I realized we were going to need a proper FA—forensic anthropologist—but I wasn't aware of one in the area. I told Tara that there was *one* person, though. A woman named Gretchen Larson whom I'd worked with several times before. Most of us in the local law enforcement arena knew her, since she was the lead of the Flathead County forensics team. "She or someone in her unit can maybe process the area and transfer the skeleton to the appropriate anthropologist or at least know who to call in to do it." I looked up at the ridge and turned to Wilcox. "Do you think your lines are going to hold?"

"We're trying our best," he said, "but it's a hot one. Afraid I'm going to have to pull my men by evening if the wind shifts as it's supposed to by later today. IC has established Trigger Point A for Ole. Java Creek. And for Sheep—Dickey Creek." He was referring to the predetermined lines that the fires might reach, and if either fire reached either point— in this case Java Creek for Ole, which was in the park—it was time to pull the crews.

"Okay." I turned to Tara. "Until we determine otherwise, we'll need to treat this as a crime scene, which means no one gets by the tape." I tapped my pocket where my cell phone was, well aware that there was limited cell service in the area. I would need to walk back out to the lot, the one place we could get reception, because, strange as it seemed, the railroad tracks acted as huge antennas, and with the booster in my SUV, I could amplify the signal of my cell phone.

She coughed and nodded.

Suddenly she looked pale to me. I wondered if it was just the un- earthly light reaching through the woods like a specter and making me feel like I was in some alternate universe. "You okay?" I asked.

"Yeah, just a touch of asthma. I've got my inhaler, though."

"You should get out of this smoke, is what I think. I can get some- one else to guard the area. You've already been a huge help with taping it off."

"Don't patronize me, Harris." She smiled, adjusted her hard hat slightly, but didn't go anywhere, just stood looking toward the ridge. I followed her gaze to the tongues of flame in the distance and the thick, dirty, tumor-colored smoke stacking above us like thunderclouds, then glanced back down at the shallow grave. Ash particles the size of mos- quitoes slowly drifted around us and fell on to the grave.

Even though I felt smothered by the intense heat of the nearby wildfire, and troubled by the bones that lay at our feet, I was foolishly energized to be thinking about even the minuscule possibility of some kind of a case. "If you're okay, then I'll be right back," I told Tara. "Make sure no one enters while I go notify IC and call the county."

. . .

Tara and I waited for Flathead County's Crime Scene Team—for Gretchen and whoever else she was bringing with her—at the parking lot of the Essex train depot. The frailest of the sun's light filtered through the congested sky, but I could still feel summer's strong rays penetrate, making the air stuffy and warm. The fire, looming over the ridge, radiated its own heat through the entire area.

We sat silently in the Park SUV I was driving, keeping the door shut to block out the smoke, turning on the AC periodically to cool it down and drinking bottles of water. Tara read a magazine, and I noticed her breathing was much quieter than at the site. I was writing some notes and looking at the digital pictures I'd taken and thinking about the bones, about a person buried in a place meant to be hidden forever—a clandestine grave. Whoever had put the body there had not anticipated a fuel break line being dug in the exact same area. Who *would* think of that? Then again, no one would think of burying a body anywhere at all other than a cemetery unless they had something to hide. I wondered how long it had been there—not all that deep under, the railways not far away, vibrations running through the ground each time a train barreled through.

My radio went off as I turned the ignition back on along with the cool air when I noticed Tara begin to fan herself with her magazine. "Monty here."

"Harris," my boss's voice came through. "How's it going?"

"Officer Reed and I are waiting for forensics. They should be here any minute."

"You know," Smith said, "you're probably not going to have the leisure of an entire day or two to complete this thing, so you're going to have to keep everyone working quickly."

"I'm on it, sir."

"Good, 'cause we've got another problem: a missing camper—a thirteen-year-old boy. I've got Greeley and a few others searching for him. He was at the campsite—at Fish Creek—when the rest of the family went for a walk around Lake McDonald. Wanted to stay back and play his DS—some gaming thing—but when they returned, he wasn't there."

"How long has he been gone?"

"The family called pretty quickly after they returned and they were gone about two hours, so we're not sure. No more than two and a half at this point." Joe sighed and it came through the radio as an airy, hissing sound.

Immediately, out of instinct and because of the boy's age, I thought of my best friend from childhood, Nathan Faraway. When I was twelve, he had gone missing in the woods in the night. I'd be lying if I didn't say that this incident fueled a large part of my ambition to work in law enforcement. But, here in Glacier, the kid had most likely just gotten a little lost and would be found wandering down a nearby trail in a short while, or hanging out at some other campsite where he'd met a new friend.

"They should be able to find him," Joe said. "Probably just walked somewhere, then got sidetracked or turned around."

"I was thinking the same." I said, though I thought of his parents and how afraid they must be. Because it was Glacier, after all, where it was not uncommon for hikers and climbers to go astray or to slip off a boulder into a raging stream. Anyone could let their imagination roam to the terror of sharp-clawed predators, crashing streams, and jagged cliffs.

But I'm an optimist, probably borne from my less-than-*Leave-It-to-Beaver* family life. I grew up with a paranoid schizophrenic mother, an alcoholic father, and an abusive older brother. As basic as it sounds, I survived by coming to rely on the predictability of things: the recurrence of the seasons, the sturdiness of the mountains I loved to wander, the start of a new, blue-skied day, and the eventuality that I would pull off good grades and pass exams each time I'd thought I'd underperformed.

"But if we haven't located him by the time the excavation is complete, we'll probably need your help."

"Of course," I said. "And I'll keep you posted on how the dig goes." I signed off, hoping they'd find the boy soon.

3

Gretchen

On the way to work, I turned the music on the radio up and tried not to let my mind wander too much.

Up until that one horrific night when I changed my family's life forever, and became *Marerittjente*—Nightmare Girl—my sleepwalking was a source of amusement: something comical rather than a condition to be treated. It meant that I did things that were annoying or funny—like the time I almost peed in the chair in the sitting room (fortunately, my mother was still watching TV and stopped me beforehand) or the time I exited our front door and trudged down the street in the middle of winter. Thankfully, a neighbor was coming home from his railroad shift and saw me in my pink pajamas trudging through the snow in bare feet in what is called a state of parasomnia—the condition of being both asleep and awake at the same time.

The very first time I walked in my sleep, my parents thought there had been an intruder in the house. I was nine. I woke up on a Saturday morning and heard them murmuring in low voices. My mom stood in the middle of the room with her short, silky bobbed hair, one arm folded across her waist. My mom, tall and elegant, generally moved in a calm, relaxed manner, and rarely startled, but she looked a little more wide-eyed than usual. My dad was checking the windows and the doors to see if they were all securely locked.

"What's going on?" I asked.

My mom turned and tucked her blond hair behind an ear—a graceful gesture that I'd seen a thousand times. "You're up early. Why don't you go back to bed?"

"What's Dad doing?"

"Nothing, really, just wondering who rearranged the furniture and the books." I looked around the room to see two of our dining room chairs pushed over to face the front windows. Books that were normally in the bookcase were neatly stacked on the coffee table. Another pile of encyclopedias was stacked by the door and two more by the fireplace.

"Were you in here last night playing?"

I shook my head. *"Nie, Mamma."* No, Mom. I didn't remember anything, but a thick feeling of guilt washed over me, and somehow I sensed that I had, indeed, played some role in rearranging things. When my brother got up, he suggested that maybe we had a ghost in the house, and my parents laughed, saying they were certain there was a much more reasonable explanation and that we should go into the kitchen and have some *brod* and *gjetost*. Bread and goat cheese. We sat eating, oblivious to what would happen six years later.

My phone rang, jerking me out of my reverie. I turned down the radio and hit the speakerphone hooked up to my cell.

"Gretchen here."

It was Monty Harris with Park Police in Glacier National Park. Monty and I had become friends during a case in Glacier involving two dead bodies discovered in a ravine. Monty was careful and seemed safe—the type to drive the speed limit with two hands on the wheel, to change his oil when the sticker on the windshield said to, and to shave every day, even though he sometimes forgot if he got really busy and absorbed in a project. And most important, he was the type who didn't care about what others thought of him; he just wanted to get the job done right, for his own sense of order and justice. That part I could relate to.

He was calm and methodical, and he moved that way, his muscles corded and sinewy like an Olympic runner. He had gone through a divorce over a year before and other than the possibility of him still being on the rebound, I knew he was free as a bird. But none of that made any difference at all. We would just be friends. Even though I was only thirty, I was certain there would be no more men in my life. I had told myself a long time ago that I'd never let myself get close to anyone, ever.

I'd already been married once, after graduating from the University of Washington. It's how I ended up in the Flathead Valley, where Jim's family lived. I met Jim—tall, thin, and an odd mixture of charisma and bookishness—before I transferred from my school's business program to the forensic science department. But it wasn't the romantic story most people imagine: boy meets girl in college, boy walks girl to class, girl walks down the aisle. It was a simple transaction, a practical decision between friends. We both knew that when school was over, I had only one year to work before my visa expired, but that if we married, I could stay forever. We were just friends, and he did me a favor.

So yes, I'm the kind of girl who will get married to someone she doesn't love just to stay in America. In all fairness, though, Jim knew I wasn't interested in a close relationship or married life, and he didn't care. He enjoyed showing me around Seattle, around Washington and the rest of the Pacific Northwest and Canada. We took road trips to Vancouver, Victoria, Olympia, Portland, the Columbia Gorge. . . . We even drove all the way down U.S. 101 to Los Angeles and went to Disneyland. He insisted I would never understand America without going on the Tower of Terror and told me a story about how his uncle was one of the four engineers who'd designed the ride. And most important, he never questioned the fact that I wanted two hotel rooms, and not just because I wasn't romantically interested in him. He's still the only one in America, besides a handful of doctors, who knows about my condition.

When he decided he wanted to go to Montana for a year or so before finding a *real* job, I went with him too. But I didn't follow him because of our marriage. A position with the county's forensics department had opened up around the same time and I threw my résumé into the mix. I interviewed and was surprised when the detective division leader called me and told me I got the position. After we moved, we officially divorced. A year later, Jim moved to San Francisco to manage a financial firm—his *real* job. We still emailed each other occasionally.

"We've found some buried bones," Monty told me over the phone. "In fact, a skeleton near Essex, near the fire."

"A grave?"

"Yeah, I think we're going to need you or an FA down here to excavate and remove them quickly."

"We don't usually handle excavations, Monty," I said. "An FA named Lucy Hayes, who teaches at MSU in Bozeman, does contract work for the Crime Lab in Missoula as needed and has worked several cases for the Division of Criminal Investigations."

"She's in Bozeman?" Bozeman was in the southwest, a five-hour drive to the park.

"Yeah."

"Not enough time—the fire's too close. We need someone nearby, someone who can excavate the skeleton quickly."

"That close?"

"Afraid so. Can we just do it ourselves and send the remains to her?"

"Hmm." I paused to consider our options. A proper removal was time-consuming—chiseling the remains out slowly, getting soil samples, running metal detectors over the surface area. "Monty," I said, "you know that an excavation should be performed by someone who really knows their stuff."

"Ideally, yes, but I'm afraid we don't have the time to wait for an expert. The crew is trying to stay ahead of Ole and Sheep and keep them both from charging down the canyon and into Essex. Right now the wind is from the southeast, but the head of ops says the wind might change by evening and then they'll need to pull out."

I paused again before answering.

"Gretchen?" Monty asked.

"I'm here. I'm thinking."

"Okay," I finally said. "Given the circumstances, let me call my division leader and see if I can get the go-ahead." Commander David Ridgeway was the detective division leader, my supervisor, and I was the lead crime scene investigator for the Flathead County Crime Scene Team. "I'll try and reach Lucy as well . . . get some tips. I'll be there as soon as I can if he okays it, but it's going to take me at least an hour and a half to get there. I'll let you know after I speak to Ridgeway."

"I need you to use your siren to speed things up. Like I said, we're probably good until the evening," Monty said. "But we need to hurry."

"Will do."

"And Gretchen," he added. "Thank you."

"Thank me later after you see what kind of a job I do."

. . .

Getting into Essex didn't take as long as I thought because all the cars were heading in the opposite direction to evacuate. I recruited Ray Jones, one of the three members available from my forensics team, and we loaded up the County CS van with equipment and headed toward the Great Divide, which normally jutted majestically upward into a blue summer sky that stretched forever, but was now obscured by curtain upon curtain of smoke. The other two from our team were working a robbery involving medications stolen from a dental office. Plus, Ray hadn't worked the firefighter scene the day before, so he was rested up.

When we passed West Glacier, I saw a temporary camp set up for evacuees, and something about their displacement reminded me of the cold morning I was sent to an inpatient psychiatric hospital called Sandviken Sykehus in the city of Bergen on the southwestern coast, a port city surrounded by mountains and high, sharp fjords.

I remembered standing in my bedroom, the base of my window covered in a web of ice crystals, unsure what clothes to pack and whether to take my small worn panda or leave him behind. After all, I was fifteen, technically too old for stuffed animals. But Panda, with his worn, matted cream-colored fur and bent, ripped ear, was the one object I could cling to that would be a link to home. One of his eyes had gone missing somewhere along the line, but you could hardly tell because of the teardrop black patches surrounding them. But *I* knew it was gone, and in that moment I felt that lost eye must have been some kind of an omen. Panda was my comfort, with his large round belly, his one-eyed gaze that communicated unconditional acceptance and was so unlike my mother's anguished, accusing stares.

I still don't deal very well with the details of my actions that night long ago, but I make the best of it. I take my medication, am as careful as I can be, and basically live for my job. I try to do it well.

"Look at all these people," Ray said, jarring me out of my daydream. "I hope they don't lose their homes."

"Me too."

We drove in silence while Ray sipped from a can of Red Bull and tried to catch fire updates on his phone until we ran out of signal and eventually reached Essex. We drove along the southern border of the park, passing green pools of river water, barely visible rocky escarpments veiled by smoke, and stone-built tunnels where the Burlington Northern Santa Fe railcars normally snaked in and out, but were no longer allowed under the conditions. Monty had instructed me to go past the firemen's base camp and across the bridge and park at the ranger station to save time hiking to the area. We pulled into a turnout where other park and fire work vehicles sat. I looked toward the northeast and Ray followed my gaze. Through the dark, dense smoke, you could see the orange inferno looming over the ridge.

"Damn," Ray said, running a hand through his thick sandy hair, which he wore bushy around his ears, seventies-style.

I stared momentarily at the angry flames, my heartbeat speeding up, before looking back to the road curving through the canyon and the parking area ahead.

"Double damn," Ray whispered again.

Monty and another woman I assumed was Tara Reed were walking toward us. Monty held a bottle of water as he strode over, medium height and lean as ever, his dark hair cut short. He gave me a sincere, closed-lip smile that, when combined with the play in his eyes, communicated an odd mixture of matter-of-factness, slight mischief, and a tinge of bittersweetness, all at the same time.

I saw him last at an annual fund-raiser, a banquet thrown to raise money for the local search and rescue helicopter operation. I was wearing your standard little black cocktail dress and Monty had taken me in from head to toe almost as if I weren't wearing anything at all. Not that I had minded. It was a long time since I'd gotten that look from a guy, at least from one I bothered noticing.

I knew he felt a certain loyalty toward me because I had assisted him during the investigation in which the body of the biologist he knew was found. I could tell it had brought stuff up for him, so I had met with him a number of times to discuss the case. By the end, something emotional had passed between us. We'd never discussed it afterward, mainly because I made myself scarce after realizing we were getting a little too close. He didn't push it because he had a separation, and later a divorce, to deal with.

Monty stopped a few feet away from me as I opened the back of the van to unload our gear. "Hey," he said. His face looked all business at first, but then he gave me a crooked smile. I couldn't tell what it meant exactly. He had a way of not being intrusive when he looked at me, as if he was simply wondering what it was like to be walking around as a blond, blue-eyed Norwegian-American crime scene investigator with a slight accent.

"Hey," I said back.

"Thanks for coming so quickly. This is Officer Tara Reed. She was on the scene first, after the fire crew found the bones."

"Nice to meet you." I held out my hand and we shook. Then I introduced Ray to them both. Ray crunched up his can of Red Bull, threw it in the trash in the back of the van, then smiled his broad grin, and shook with them both. Ray was always affable and easy to work with.

I have to admit I was a little nervous about getting the excavation right. It had been a long time since I'd been on a case involving skeletal remains. The first one was during an internship for the Seattle Police Department's CSI Unit. Some teens had broken into an old shipyard for fun on Halloween night and discovered a rotting corpse in an abandoned schooner. Apparently some aged drifter had decided to make it his home. I remember the sounds of rats scurrying around and the reek of mold, rotting wood, and dust as we collected evidence and labeled bones, but at least no excavation had been necessary.

I was well aware that this was a different matter and that the deteriorating effects of soil would need to be reckoned with. And I was also well aware now, as I was then, that the remains had once been a human body—that there could be a family out there still clinging to the hope that they would someday discover what happened to a missing family member. The worst, always—no exceptions—was the not knowing. It was the one thin prospect I could console myself with over the years—that in my case fifteen years before, there'd never been the agony of the unknown, just the cold, hard definitive blow of disaster. I refocused on Monty's dark, serious eyes, then Tara's green ones, and told myself not to be nervous. I was working with competent people.

"Thanks for coming," Tara repeated to us.

"You're welcome. Sounds like an interesting case. I've got everything we need here," I said, pointing to the back of the van.

. . .

We hiked toward the intense heat to the shallow grave, the hot, chalky air enveloping us. Monty had handed me a hard hat, which I obediently put on. The temperature struck me and took my breath away. I had been near it the day before to work the scene where the young firefighter was found, but not this close. My team had been a good two miles from the blaze.

Tara had been coughing on and off as we walked, and suddenly she started hacking so hard that she stopped, hunched over at the waist, and covered her mouth. Monty, Ray, and I paused and looked at her. Ray, who was chewing on a toothpick, shoved it into his pocket, his hazel eyes intense. As a CSI, he knew better than to drop anything on the ground, ever.

"You sound bad," Monty said to her. "We've got this." He motioned to the three of us. "You should go back."

"No." She snuck out one last cough, cleared her throat, and managed to contain another. "We're running out of time. You're going to need all the help you can get."

She was right, of course, and I could see Monty weighing it out in his mind. She was carrying some of the equipment—just a bag and a folding shovel that we could easily take ourselves—but it wasn't supply-hauling help that we needed. It was setting up grids, getting soil samples, and the meticulous scraping and sweeping of dirt that would be time-consuming.

Normally, the discovery of a hidden grave would bring Sheriff Walsh on-site, but he—along with Monty's boss, Chief of Park Police Joe Smith—both had their hands full with helping the evacuations under the Incident Command Unit that had come in for the fires. As I suspected, when I called Walsh, he had suggested I consult Lucy in Bozeman, which I did. She threw as much procedural information as possible my way, and I had put together a to-do list. I already knew that great care must be used in recovering remains from a grave, since the exhuming itself destroys the context within it. She reminded me of just how precise we needed to be in recording all the layers of soil.

I wouldn't typically need Monty's or Tara's assistance, but given the urgency, I appreciated the extra hands. From working with Monty before, I knew he could handle himself around a crime scene. Tara seemed smart and careful too, so I was glad she wanted to stick around.

"Your cough sounds bad and more frequent," Monty said to Tara.

In my pack I had the biohazard bag and suits, my camera, some water, and a shovel. Ray was hauling a large, folded army-green tarp that we would use to arrange the tools at the site and to eventually lay the skeleton out on before stowing the bones in bags. Monty was carrying the metal detector and the excavation case that I'd taken from the lab. It held containers for soil, picks and chisels of various sizes, brushes, and more. He was also carrying his own camera and wearing his tool belt. He held out his hand to take the folding shovel from her.

"I'm fine," Tara insisted. She almost looked like a child, hiding the spade behind her back. "Look, Harris, if I get any worse, I promise to go to the car. And," she said, "I have my inhaler with me. Ventolin," she added, as if the name made it more official.

Monty glanced at me and I shrugged. It was his call, not mine. First, it was under Park Police jurisdiction, but since this part of the park was contained within Flathead County, we handled forensics and cooperated with Park Police.

"Damn." He sighed. "You're like a stubborn child. But I'm dead serious—you begin wheezing again like you were earlier, you go immediately."

"Fair enough," Tara said.

When we reached the scene, I paused and took in the upturned heap of dirt about ten feet away from the fuel break line that had been dug. It looked like a murky patch of water that had been disturbed by something rising from the darkness underneath. Beyond it, the stretch of forest looked punished. Thankfully, the area we needed to work had been left alone as much as possible.

A pile of bones lay before us in a mixture of dirt, brittle clumps of cheatgrass, and dried foliage. I could see the skull, slightly tilted to the left as if it were keeping an eye on the ridge, waiting to see if the fire could be corralled. One yellowed rib bone curved out of the soil and one smooth length of a femur protruded out of some shoveled ground.

Sweat already ran hot and slick down my neck. I handed out gloves and biohazard suits to Monty and Tara. Ray had his own.

"Okay." I exhaled. I looked at my watch: 2:30. We need," I called out, "to grab as many samples from each layer in each grid as possible and mark 'em all."

Monty and I began photographing the scene as we found it. After we determined this was only a single site—thank goodness—Monty asked about the parameters of the grid we needed to set up in order to screen dirt from each level within different areas of the site.

"Do about a square meter," I told him. "And alphabetize and record the layout." Then I turned to Ray. "You're in charge of setting out all the equipment and helping Monty with the grid. After, you'll help me with the excavation."

Tara was unloading the plastic containers for the soil samples. "Thank you," I said, "for getting on that so quickly. You'll collect soil samples with the geologic sieves and document which grid you've collected them from. And Monty—" I turned back to him. He was already grabbing the plastic stakes and the twine to mark the outside perimeter of the area. "After you're done with the grid, you'll need to run a sweep with the metal detector and bag anything at all of interest."

Everyone went right to work, with only a few questions. I began taking additional photos while Ray and Monty set up the grid. We collected everything we could find on the surface to bag, label, and photograph, which wasn't much except some rocks and a few pieces of old trash that probably had no connection to the actual time period that the body was buried. After getting numerous soil samples and performing a thorough sweep with the metal detector, we began the slow process of excavating.

After several hours, I was kneeling down, examining the skull, measuring the total length of the skeleton and recording the terminal points of each measurement. Ash floated around me like a lazy snow. The muted sunlight, blocked by the smoke, tried to filter through and smudged everything a grayish yellow. I carefully brushed off the dirt on the apex of the skull. I was no expert, and I wasn't positive, but it seemed that neither the sagittal nor the coronal suture had yet fused, and in the pit of my stomach I felt that this might be a relatively young person. Plus, there was a significant fracture along the temporal and frontal area that gave me pause. I removed one of my gloves for a moment and rubbed the back of my neck, stiffened from hunching over and looking down for so long.

To me, the bones looked like they'd been buried for some time, at the very least five years, maybe for over a decade, but I wasn't sure. Determining how long depended on many factors, including the soil's moisture and acidity.

I grabbed another glove, put it on, and continued to carefully log the measurements, then went to work on the remaining shreds of clothing by chiseling around them. I already knew not to, but Lucy had warned against using a brush or whisk broom on fabric since it might destroy fiber evidence. There was no remaining hair on the head, but I was careful to get thorough samples of the soil under the skull in case any minute hair fibers remained.

Monty brought the metal detector over, and we ran it over the site again. As he neared the center of the grave, toward the pelvis, it beeped. Monty kneeled down and gently probed the soil where the signal had been. I also moved my gloved fingers carefully through the dirt, going a little deeper.

"There's something here," Monty said, his finger scraping around a small object. After a little more work, he pulled out a flat, oval item the size of an egg. "Hmm," he grunted, holding it before him and examining it like a surgeon. "Belt buckle?"

"Let's see." Ray held out his gloved palm to take the object and brushed it lightly off. "I can't make out any markings, but yeah, it looks to me like a belt buckle. They'll be able to confirm in the lab under the right lights and with the right chemicals to remove the grime."

"There could be some interesting markings that might signify the time period," I said, holding out my gloved palm to take a closer look.

Ray set it in my hand. It felt light, unsubstantial, and perhaps cheap. I couldn't make out any details either; too much grime and dirt coated it. Strands of a thick fabric still hung from the sides, and I could see that it was a woven cloth belt, not leather. I handed it back to Ray and he labeled it, put it in an envelope, and bagged the envelope in plastic.

I turned back to my work, kneeling down and continuing to carefully scrape around the minute bones of each hand with a chisel. After what felt like forever, I cleared the soil away with a medium-size brush and removed and laid each set of hand bones on the tarp, labeling them left and right. We had already cleared the leg, feet, and arm bones, placing them in paper bags, marking them by numbers, and storing them in plastic containers. We had photographed and mapped all parts prior to pulling them out. It was a tedious process and the heat and smoke weren't helping. The T-shirt and chinos I was wearing under my suit were drenched. My knees, shoulders, and back continued to ache from being in a kneeling position for so long, and a headache was shooting up the back of my skull.

I looked at my watch: 6:40. It had already been over four hours. A smoke jumper flew over, and a stream of pink retardant the color of candy made a line through the shrouded sky and began to disperse over the dim ridge. They had been flying above us all afternoon, but I'd been in such deep concentration that this was the first time I'd taken note. I'd read somewhere that they'd recently changed the dye they put in the retardant from burgundy to bright pink so it was easier to see against the smoke.

I glanced at Monty as he watched the plane circle back. I stood and stretched, pulling my shoulders wide when his radio crackled. I watched him hold it up to his mouth and talk to someone. There was something about the seriousness in his expression that made me nervous, made my skin, still damp from perspiration, begin to tingle and give me a slight tremor of chills in spite of the heat. I began to work faster, my lungs beginning to burn. I looked at Tara, putting away some samples. "You feeling okay?" I called to her.

"Yeah," she said, but didn't offer anything else, just looked back down to complete what she was doing.

I looked at Monty. "How's it going over there?"

"Going well," he said, putting plastic containers with sealed lids in a canvas duffel bag large enough to carry the containers out. "That was just Wilcox. They're watching the ridge closely because the wind is supposed to change soon. If it hits the trigger points on either Dickey Creek or Java Creek, everyone has to get out. Tara and I are going to wrap up with the soil samples and all the labeling. If we have to get out of here quickly, I want to be ready."

I nodded, but was beginning to worry that we would have to clear out before we got the job done properly. The enormity of it was overwhelming. Patience and time were invaluable to the process. As a CSI, I was well schooled in the art of persistence, but this seemed like an entirely different beast, one that was much more complex than the typical crime scenes I usually worked. I couldn't believe I was actually wishing for rain, something that would typically compromise an outdoor crime scene. But at least it would slow the fire's progress, and we could cover the grid with a tarp to preserve the evidence. "Rain, damn it, rain," I whispered under my breath.

Ray and I continued scraping at the lower ribs, which were still buried, when I heard Monty's radio crackle again, setting my nerves on edge. He had walked away from the site, and answered as he headed toward a birch tree with its papery white bark and its mixture of dried yellow and green leaves still clinging to life. Normally there would be a demarcation of shade, but not today, not in this smoke. Nodding and talking, wearing that white suit, Monty looked like an apparition in the dim light.

Beyond him, in the distant forest, I noticed some beige shapes meandering through the trees. The crew, I thought, hiking through, perhaps making their way to another spot or to the parking lot. I could hear Tara take a puff of her inhaler, and suddenly realized, save the sound of the steady roar of the fire two ridges over, how it had gotten quieter—the drone of the equipment no longer present.

Monty came back over, being careful of the markers we'd set up to designate the entry and exit point to the site.

"Gretchen," he said.

I stayed kneeling, bent over the grave, but turned my head to look up at him.

"Wilcox just said that the airport reading says the wind's beginning to shift and Ole has reached Trigger Point A. That's the signal for us to vacate. He's called his men back. Wants us to wrap it up and get back to the vehicles."

"How much more time?"

"Ten minutes," Monty said from behind his face mask. "More like eight now."

"Eight?" I looked up at him in shock. That was hardly enough time to wrap up any crime scene, much less an anthropologic dig. He was still holding his radio. I stood up to face him. "No way."

"No choice," he said. He hooked the receiver back on his tool belt, turned away, and quickly began to pack up the chisels and picks. He ordered Tara and Ray to get the rest of the bones that were already laid out on the tarp into the bags.

"Wait, we haven't even—"

"Doesn't matter," Monty said. "Get the rest of the bones in the bags."

My heart began to hammer in my chest. "But we haven't even gotten the ribs free yet—"

"Get them however you can. Wilcox says we need to clear out. We can't chance it."

I turned back to what was left of the skeleton before me. The ribs were the hardest, the lower side of the cage surrounded by dirt and roots from thistle, cheatgrass, and kudzu that had grown into the soil over the years. The upper side of the cage was pronounced, but the lower ribs had begun to decay a little faster, I suspected from moister, more acidic soil lower down. Thin, arched bones lay fragile in the dirt.

Tara began to hack violently again, bending at the waist. I could hear her wheezing as she tried to suck in air between coughs. She pulled out her inhaler and took another hit. "That's like your fifth hit," Monty said to her. "I'm pretty sure you're not supposed to take that much. Clearly it's not working."

Tara didn't answer him, or couldn't answer him. She plunged further into a coughing fit, wheezing loudly. She held up her finger to say something, but couldn't. She collapsed onto one knee, removing her face mask to try to take in more air. Her skin looked wan, but then again, everything surrounding us, including the air, looked sallow.

Monty went to her and helped her up, setting a hand on her back. "Ray," he said firmly, "would you please get Tara out of here now? I'll help Gretchen get the rest packed up. There should be a medic back at the rendezvous site not far down the road at the fire camp. Take her there. They'll have oxygen. We'll meet you there."

Ray looked at Monty with a mixture of curiosity and doubt, as if he wasn't sure whether to take orders from Park Police and not a county officer and didn't necessarily want to leave me out here.

"Do as he says." I nodded to Ray. I didn't bother to remind him that we were on Park Police jurisdiction as well as Flathead County's, and short of the sheriff being here, it was Monty's call. "Monty and I will get this packed up. We'll be fine."

I continued to work frantically, trying to dig the last of the dirt away from the rib cage so it could be lifted intact from the ground. Monty set two paper bags by our side after he packed up the soil samples and tools. "Put them right in the bags." He looked at me as he rolled up the tarp.

"Not yet, the ribs still aren't free. They might break, and they have to be labeled one by one."

"Just grab what you can and I'll label 'em." He held up the manila tags. "Right and left side. I'll get them on, but we don't have time to dig anymore."

I stuck my gloved hands under the set of them and pried, but they wouldn't budge. I grabbed the chisel and furiously scratched around the edges. I tried again, this time able to lift two of the ribs, but not the others. I continued to scrape.

"Gretchen." Monty grabbed my shoulder, his head tilted in earnest. "Do you know how fast a fire moves once it goes?"

I didn't answer, just kept frantically working.

"It will blow through here in seconds if the line doesn't hold. We can't chance it."

"Okay, okay," I said, frustrated. I'd been called in for this dig that should have really gone to an FA, and now I didn't have the time to do the damn thing properly. I was cursing myself for agreeing to do a job I knew I wasn't completely comfortable with. "Shit," I said. Sweat poured down my stomach and back.

Wilcox's voice came over Monty's radio. "Are you out of there?"

Monty grabbed his radio again. "Not yet. Almost."

"Get out. Now." Wilcox's voice boomed firmly through the receiver. "And I mean it."

I grabbed for the ribs again, this time pulling harder. I heard a snap. "Shit," I yelled.

"Just get them," Monty said.

I pulled again. Another snap. I wanted to cry. I was decimating the bones. Another snap. Lucy would be mortified. I was already thinking about attorneys in court having a field day with a testimony I might need to deliver at some point.

"Grab those last two," I yelled. Monty jerked the rest out and jammed them into the bag. I was still attempting to label when Monty started yelling.

"Gretchen, you heard him. Now. Throw it in the container and let's go!" He had thrown his pack over his shoulder and was holding the case of chisels, the rolled-up tarp, and small shovels. Suddenly he put down the tarp, lifted his face up, and removed the white face mask as if trying to feel the wind on his cheek like an animal checking for a scent.

I watched him as if time had slowed—as if I had the luxury to do such a thing. Because of the smoky air and the muted sunlight, the whole scene was taking on a sepia autumnal tone, as if we were locked in an old war photograph, aliens in dirty white hazmat suits glowing eerily in the gloomy light.

Monty stood right above me, his cheekbone glistening with sweat. The leaves of a birch we'd passed on the way in seemed to stir, and I thought I heard a faint, dulled chime. The angles of his face looked sharp and stunning even in the dimness, like a statue of some hero. In spite of the fire's distant roar, a strange, watchful silence hung over the scene as if we were waiting to see an image or a sign emerge from the smoke and the ash. Monty turned to me, his dark eyes stern. "It's shifting and it's definitely blowing harder."

I nodded and swallowed, my throat parched and burning. I glanced up at the dense gloom above. *Rain*, I wished again. I looked down to finish labeling the bag when I felt Monty's hand on my arm, grabbing with force. He threw the case holding the chisels, picks, and brushes on the ground, grabbed the duffel bag, yanked me up, and began rushing me out.

"Okay, okay. I get it." I shook my arm away. I was furious for reasons I couldn't explain. I know he was only trying to be safe, but this was my job. *My* job. And nobody, not even trusted Monty Harris, had the right to pull me away from it. I hated that I was being sloppy, but I also hated that I was feeling like that young Norwegian girl again—hopeless, needing to be corralled away from her own dangerous self like the forest needing to be felled of its own hazardous fuel.

Right then, I had a split-second vision of cross-country skiing with my older brother Per, of him gliding ahead of me across the fjord and me not being able to get my ski boots laced up. He was screaming at me to hurry—*skynde deg*—red-faced and angry with me for being so slow while I sat with my butt freezing in the snow, a thick coat of ice above a dark sea, cold and black.

Monty dropped his grip. "Look." He motioned behind me with one of his gloved hands—flashes of white nitrile like a dove amid the dingy smoke—as if to say, *Don't you get it?* "We've got to go."

I didn't budge, just looked over my shoulder, back at the once-clandestine grave and the box of tools flung like a metal skeleton next to the disturbed earth. I glanced beyond it up the ridge. The flames were over three hundred feet high, ominous and massive like blazing tidal waves of fire. It had become so opaque I couldn't see anything but the furious, lashing fire.

"Jesus, Gretchen. Come on," he repeated as he turned around and headed back for me.

"I'm coming." I quickly shoved the tools back into the case, grabbed it, and ran toward him. We sprinted the rest of the way to the ranger station, clumps of grass trying to trip us and the smoldering air choking us in spite of our face masks. Finally we reached the car, my lungs on fire, my heart pounding.

Wilcox waited for us in the lot, his face grimy and flushed. "Get in your car and go now. One mile west and you'll be out of range. You'll see other vehicles there, including the firemen and the medic who's treating Tara."

"Where's Ray?" I asked.

"He went with Tara."

Monty set the equipment in the back of his SUV and urged me to hurry. I crammed the rest of the gear in, shut the back hatch, and jumped in the passenger seat.

Monty hopped in and turned on the ignition. His face was intense, his hair wet and spiky with sweat. I was still panting, and tried not to think about how I'd just done an incomplete, shitty job excavating a pile of bones that at one time was a living, breathing person.

. . .

Neither of us said a word until we made it to the holding spot a mile down Highway 2, a large field that had been rented from a local rancher for the purpose of setting up the fire camp. Monty pulled up next to the van where Ray stood waiting. "Sorry for grabbing you like that," Monty said.

I nodded but was still trying to regain my composure. I opened the door and went to the back to transfer the remains and the gear. Monty looked across the lot to a trailer labeled Medic, then turned toward Ray. "They have Tara?" he asked him.

"They're on their way to the hospital."

"Hospital?" Monty asked.

"Just a precaution, I'm sure. We were making our way back and she got worse and had to sit. The captain saw us and called the medic. Thank goodness they were already on standby here."

Monty shook his head, chastising himself. "I knew she shouldn't have come. I shouldn't have let her."

"She's okay," Ray said. "They've got her on oxygen."

I didn't say anything. I was still trembling from the adrenaline rush and Monty shifted his gaze to me again. "You okay?"

"I'm fine," I said, though I was scowling.

"You sure?"

"Of course I'm sure."

"Gretchen, a fire moves fast. I couldn't chance it."

Ray stood silently listening to us.

"I know. I know." I was still trying to catch my breath. I glanced at Ray, embarrassed that I was so shaken, and he was polite enough to excuse himself.

"I'm going to find some water." He motioned to a tent that looked as if it was stocked with food and beverages about twenty yards from us across the lot.

Monty turned back to me after Ray shuffled off. "Look, I'm sorry you couldn't finish—"

"It's fine," I interrupted, crossing my arms in front of my chest.

"You don't seem fine."

"I was about to come," I said, even though I wasn't sure I actually was. There was no way he could understand that my job was how I coped—that since I left Norway, the only thing that made me feel human was when I could return someone's body to their family or help some detective better comprehend who hurt the family's loved one and why, just so that they could move a little further along in the recovery from their loss. There was no way he could fathom the desperate need to disappear when life shattered into irreparable pieces—the need to make the best of things by losing yourself in your work and performing it flawlessly. "I didn't need you to tell me how to do my job," I added.

"It had nothing to do with your job or my job. It was about a fire that is plowing through this place at jet speed."

"I'm aware of how fast a fire moves."

"It didn't seem like it out there." Monty lifted his chin to the direction of the site and to the mountains that are usually our haven this time of the year.

"Give me a break. I've worked these parts long enough. I know what the hell I'm doing. Why don't you just stick to your job and let me do mine." I knew I was being completely unreasonable, but I couldn't help it. My knees had now begun to shake and my lungs were still screaming at me.

Monty held up his palms in front of him, either in surrender or as a typical male calm-down gesture, which angered me even more.

"You're shaking. Would you like some water?" He studied me with dark, narrowed eyes.

I ignored his question. I looked around the camp and saw rows of RVs, portable toilets, and tents for sleeping. I had heard that the RVs were equipped with state-of-the-art kitchens and showers for the camp workers and the fire crews. I turned back to Monty. "I didn't get all the lower ribs," I finally said. "And the ones I did collect have been cracked. I heard snaps."

"But you got everything else? The most important parts: the skull, the pelvis, right?"

"Yes, but I shouldn't have left anything behind. If that fire doesn't cross the line, I'll need to go back."

"Fair enough," Monty agreed. I wondered if he noticed my watering eyes and the trembling that had now moved up to my arms. I was glad to be hiding behind my suit, but he was staring at me as if I were completely exposed. "Look," he finally said. "I didn't want to botch that up any more than you. It's Park Police's jurisdiction first and foremost, and I take full responsibility for the excavation. But we needed to be safe."

I glared at him, ignoring the sting in my eyes. I felt silly, and I sensed that the anger that had begun stirring in me when I'd woken up to my stacked books had been intensified by the incomplete dig. I looked up into the dense gray smoke falling around us and ran my palm over my head. "I just didn't want to mess this up," I said. "I think . . ." I shook my head and wiped the water draining from the corners of my eyes. "Never mind." I walked to the back of the van.

"You think what?" Monty followed me.

"I think it may be someone young." I turned to face him again.

"Young? How young?"

"That I can't say, but I don't think the coronal and sagittal sutures were fused yet."

"And that means younger than what age?"

"Probably younger than thirty or so."

"That's a big range."

"Yeah, yeah, I know, but still. I have a strange feeling about it, that it's younger than that."

"Because?"

"I don't know for sure." I didn't want to sound foolish by telling him that if you do this long enough, there are things you just sense. That there was something about the skull and the flimsy metal buckle that whispered younger man, but I couldn't be sure at all. "But of course the FA should be able to narrow it down much more."

Monty nodded solemnly, studied me for a second longer. I excused myself and went over to the back of the van. "I've got some rearranging to do here before we drive back to the lab." I went to work as he walked away, still quivering, still frazzled by my own anger and frustrations, but having no sense of the heavy weight that was about to descend upon me, upon us all.

4

Monty

I WANDERED TOWARD WILCOX, who was talking to some of his men across the lot. I wanted to see if there were updates on Ole. He looked busy, and I figured that meant he and his crew were gearing up for another round. I shuffled over to a boulder by the side of the field close to them and sat, waiting for a decent moment to grab his attention.

My eyes and lungs burned. I thought of what Gretchen had said: *I think it may be someone young.* Damn. I wiped the sweat from my forehead. I knew we did our best and had to get the hell out, but Gretchen had treated me like I was some unreasonable jerk who was getting in the way.

I knew that the remains would first be sent to the local morgue, where a coroner would take a look, and if available, a forensic osteology expert would weigh in as well. From there, they'd end up on the third floor of a stucco high-rise housing the University of North Texas Health Science Center for Human Identification, the only academic DNA lab in the country equipped to identify human remains.

My heart sank when I realized how long the identification process could take. At least we had saved most of the remains and had prepped a good portion of them for analysis. And if the line did hold, and we had rushed for no reason, we could return when it was safe to complete any odds and ends.

While I waited, I thought of the missing boy at Fish Creek. On a

regular, smokeless day when I could actually see the sky, I could easily tell by the color of the choppers whether they were S&R or tourist
joyrides, visitors paying to fly through the sky over the tall mountains
to get an eagle's perspective. Now, with the smoke jumpers flying all
around, the intense heat, and the fatigue from digging, I felt disoriented. Earlier, during the dig, while endlessly pouring soil through the
handheld sieves Tara and I had used to collect dirt samples, I had to
admit that my mind had continually flitted to the missing boy.

When my friend Nathan disappeared, the world tilted off its axis,
though at the time, I wouldn't have thought it was possible for things to
get any worse, given my parents' miserable states. My brother, Adam,
played a Halloween trick on us that ended in disaster: Nathan went
missing after he and his friends dumped us in a cemetery to scare us.
Adam, who never expected for Nathan to go missing, began to descend
further into drugs and alcohol after the incident, so my dad sent him to
a "therapeutic" boarding school that harmed him more than it helped.
I never got over my anger at him, though, and Nathan's disappearance,
a dark cloud that hung over most of my young adult life, haunts me to
this day.

I pulled out my cell to see if we had any service and saw that we
still didn't, so I grabbed my radio instead and called Joe Smith. IC had
flown a repeater up to the top of a nearby peak called Scalplock. I was
thankful for good old-fashioned radios.

"You back at the camp?" Joe asked as soon as he picked up.

"Affirmative. The excavation, at least for the time being, is halted.
Probably completed, if Ole blows through. You find that boy yet?"

"Negative. We have not."

"No?" I did the math in my head. We'd been out on the site for over
five and a half hours and the child had already been missing before we
left. "How long has it been now?"

"Over nine hours," he said. "We're intensifying the search. We do
not want this boy out in the woods overnight. We've called in Two Bear
for when it gets dark." Two Bear was a search and rescue service that

used thermal-imaging technology to detect a person's heat profile in the woods, but it had to get dark first. "Between the fires, this, and the evacuations, it's a shit show."

Normally, when someone goes missing, we all get on it right away. We begin sweeping down nearby trails, asking other hikers if they've seen the missing person, and questioning neighboring campers. With a teenager whose family is from out of town and claims the teen would never be gone for so long of his own volition, we sometimes dispatched the S&R choppers if the group in question was backcountry camping or hiking in the higher elevations. But Smith said the teen had gone missing near Fish Creek Campground, a heavily wooded area at the base of Howe Ridge, and choppers would not be able to spot anything until nightfall.

"I'll be right over as soon as I check in with Wilcox." I released my finger from the transmission button. Wilcox was wrapping things up and his men dispersed quickly, their faces intent as they gathered their supply packs and other gear. I stood and approached him as he was lifting his radio to his mouth. I called out to him. He stopped and turned, gave me a curt nod and lowered his radio.

"How's it looking?"

"Not good," he said. "The line held in parts, but it's broken it in others, still too close to town. We're basically just trying to save structures and livestock at this point."

I thought of the small ranches with cattle, horses, and goats and the many houses, barns, sheds, log cabins, and historical lodges in the area that the firemen would be trying to save. "Any idea if it burned the area around the grave?"

"Not yet, but my guess is that it did. I'll let you know as soon as I find out," he said as his radio came to life. "Gotta grab this, though." He turned away and started toward his men. The camp workers helped the hand and field crews, and the firefighters grabbed their supplies and were piling into trucks and buses.

I stood for a moment, rubbing the back of my neck, gritty from sweat and dirt. There was nothing to do now except let the firefighters work to save Essex. I got back into my car and watched all the workers hurrying around. Then I headed northwest—away from the grim, frantic scene of firefighters rushing to save houses and buildings, out of the smoldering canyon where I couldn't see more than twenty yards in any direction. Milky smoke dispersed evenly toward the blocked sun, which gave its heat but wouldn't shine.

. . .

When I reached Fish Creek Campground, it was eight thirty. The sun had not yet set, but it was sinking. Between that and the smoke, it felt darker than it normally would on a Montana evening in August when the sun doesn't set until around nine. The sky in the west glowed orange as an ember through the haze. I went straight to campsite 23A, the one where Joe said the family had been staying.

A Park Police vehicle belonging to one of my coworkers, Ken Greeley, sat on the shoulder of the narrow, curved road leading to the site. I couldn't decide if the anxious feeling in my gut was more about the rushed dig or the missing boy, who had been gone now for longer than I wanted to think about. I decided it was probably both.

Ken greeted me first as I stepped out of the car. He tipped his head, but his usual grin was missing.

"How're they doing?" I asked in a low voice. It was quiet, except for a soft murmur emanating from other occupied campsites. In fact, the grounds were full. All of the ones that remained open were at capacity. Even during fire season, visitation was at an all-time high, topping two million already by early August.

He shook his head as if to say, *Not good.* Ken liked to chew gum pretty much whenever he wasn't eating, and I could see his jaw moving and working on a piece now. He had a wife and a young boy, three or four now, and I knew whenever a child was involved in any dangerous situation in the park, it scared the crap out of him.

"Okay," I said. "Let's go have another chat, but maybe lose the gum. You know, out of respect."

Ken, big and burly, plucked it out of his mouth and wrapped it in a tissue. He was amicable, and usually never took offense at instruction. He let me take the lead since I was the more senior investigator.

I had stopped briefly at headquarters on my way and knew from the statements taken earlier that the missing boy's name was Jeremy. They were the Coreys. The mother, Linda; the father, Ron. They were in their midforties, visiting from Ohio. He was a musician, played guitar locally, and sometimes traveled around his state. Ken had informed me that he'd apparently had a hit single in the last year, some sort of a ballad on lost love. Linda was a fourth-grade teacher.

I could see them from where we stood. They looked like normal tourists, both in khaki shorts and T-shirts—Linda with her dark hair in a ponytail and in her hikers still, pacing by the picnic table, and Ron with wavy, longish brown hair and wearing Teva sandals. They seemed like sensible people, but one can never rely on first impressions.

I remembered another piece of information from the statement: they had spent the early morning at the campsite, eating instant oatmeal and drinking coffee with water heated on a Coleman stove. No camper, in the sites or in the backcountry, would be allowed to make a fire during fire season for fear a small glowing spark might float off and embed in a nearby larch branch, a cluster of dying witch's moss, or a dried bed of needles and end up igniting another inferno. It might sound foolish, but I couldn't help feel that saving Essex was somehow linked to finding the boy, even though I knew there was no connection. It was simply a trick of the light—of the smothering smoke, like a full moon effect that had people doing crazy things when it swelled large and round. Full moon nights were some of the busiest shifts at police stations.

We walked to the table and they both stood, their faces expectant. I tried to shoo away the hard squeeze of dread that gripped me.

"Hello," I said. "I'm Officer Harris. No news yet. I'm sorry." I wanted to get that out of the way from the get-go. Any other way would be cruel.

Both of their postures deflated with my announcement. The Coreys' two other children played with plastic figurines, perhaps Tech Decks, in the dry, dusty dirt near the trunk of a small cedar. I only knew the name of the things because my ex-wife's nephews loved them.

Ken had filled me in that Jeremy was the oldest, and that the middle brother, Garret, was nine. The youngest child, seven-year-old Cassie, kneeled next to him, tracing lines in the dirt with her fingers. Ken had said they had two tents, and I saw them now: a bright blue three-man for the parents and Cassie, and another gray and yellow-trimmed two-man set up for Jeremy and Garret.

We sat at the wooden picnic table at their campsite. Normally you'd be able to catch a glimpse of Lake McDonald and its clear blue water through the trees surrounding us, but the darkening sky and the air quality, only just beginning to clear as the wind pushed the smoke east, clouded the view. Cedar trees dangled above us. Their normally lush plumes were now dry and trimmed a yellowish brown, as if they'd been dipped in mustard.

Jeremy's parents had become panicky about the amount of time he'd been gone, the smoke, and the lowering sun. I didn't like it one bit either, and I could tell by Ken's expression that he felt the same. Linda bit her nails, looking frantic, her eyes rimmed in pink, either from crying or the smoke. She paced and seemed half crazed, her short hair escaping her ponytail and clinging to the side of her sun-freckled face.

"Please sit," Ron said, attempting a smile. He motioned to the picnic table, and the four of us sat down.

"Mr. and Mrs. Corey." I set my hands on the table, then realized they were trembling slightly, so I put them back in my lap. I still felt grimy from the dig and was starting to become irritated at how long it was taking us to find this boy. "I know Officer Greeley has been over everything with you, but I'd just like to ask you a few more questions. The more of us out there looking for your son, the better."

"Of course, of course." Ron nodded, clearly very anxious too, though he didn't show it the same way as his wife. He sat still, slumping over the picnic table as if a heavy cloak was weighing him down, a hopeful, searching look in his eyes. I thought of how when they left the campsite midmorning for their stroll around the lake, their faces were probably fresh, unlined, and rested from three peaceful days spent in the park. Even in this climate, camping in Glacier held its joy: a chance to be away from cell phones and TVs, to be among babbling streams, fluttering birds, scurrying chipmunks, and other excited and happy campers. Now both their faces looked aged, gripped by fear.

"People do go missing in Glacier frequently, and most often, we find them. There's just a lot of countryside out here"—I gestured to the mountains to my north, as if I figured that's the way he'd gone, although I had no idea—"and a wrong turn on a trail can get people turned around quite easily, especially if he tried to take a shortcut. If your son thought he was hiking back toward the campsite, but instead was heading a completely different direction, it could have led him hours away. If he's out on those trails," I said, "we intend to find him."

The Coreys nodded, taking in my every word for some new angle, some fresh bit of information that would change the status quo, but I was certain I hadn't provided it. Linda searched my eyes for any sign that she could trust me to bring her boy back to safety.

"I'm sure Officer Greeley has also informed you that we've got rangers still sweeping all the trails accessible from this area. We've pulled in extra men to take care of the questioning. We've been asking other hikers and nearby campers if they've seen Jeremy. We're searching the waterways and—"

"Oh, God." Linda slapped her hand to her mouth.

I held up mine. "We have no reason to believe he's fallen into water. Just following standard procedure, that's all." I didn't want to say it, but it was actually quite common for a tourist, especially a teenage boy, to be tempted to walk out onto the big, colorful bluish-green and red boulders to steal a peek at the water crashing down from McDonald Creek. And sometimes the boulders and cliff edges were slick. We usually had at least one drowning a year from a tourist slipping off an edge and getting swept by the stream's sheer force down the rapids, into an undertow, and beneath a tangle of logs that held the person under; someone could also smash into the boulders and be knocked unconscious, the frigid water filling their lungs. I shook the image away.

"We're also checking all of our security cameras at any entrance points to see if he's walked out or . . ." I paused, and Linda's body went rigid as she bolted upright.

"Say it," she said.

I hesitated because I didn't want to make things any worse than I already had by just mentioning the water, knowing full well the roaring, powerful streams would have come to mind. "I don't mean to alarm you any more than you already are. Again, it's just standard procedure I'm talking about here. I know you want us to cover all avenues, and one of those is to look at the footage in case, like I said, he walked out or got a ride out or, heaven forbid, was picked up unwillingly. But, let me be firm about this: that option is highly unlikely, and not what we're suspecting at all."

"Jeremy wouldn't walk out and he certainly wouldn't hitchhike somewhere with a stranger. Oh, God," she said. "Do you really think someone could have taken him?"

"Like I said, we have no reason to think so. We're following standard procedure, that's all."

She swallowed hard and tried to take my words in, but she looked confused, like she couldn't believe the day was turning to night without a ranger or policeman driving up with her smiling, hungry boy ready for some dinner. She stood up and began to pace again.

I continued. "A press release has been sent to the local media outlets, and people will be on the lookout. In fact, if there were TVs out here, you'd see it now on the news bulletins. The picture you provided from yesterday is perfect."

They both stared at me, and Ken looked down at his hands, which he'd laid flat on the smooth slats of the picnic table.

"And even though you've been through this all afternoon," I continued, "I do need to ask you some more questions." I pulled out a small

MP3 recorder and placed it on the table. "I'm going to record you now, just like Officer Greeley and the chief did earlier. Is that all right?"

"Yes," Ron said, and Linda sat back down.

"So, Mr. Corey, I understand you're a musician?"

"Yes, I play guitar and sing. I'm mostly a one-man show these days. I used to be with a group, but we broke up, and now I hire out my services to local bars, restaurants, a few larger venues around Ohio, some radio shows, that sort of thing."

"And we hear you've done pretty well lately—a hit single and all."

"Yeah, that was fortunate. One of my songs hit the charts this year. It's helped a lot. I mean, we're not rolling in money or anything. But more than enough to get by."

"Take a trip to Glacier on." I smiled.

He nodded, and Linda got up and began pacing again. The small talk was driving her crazy, and I couldn't blame her. But I had to do it, had to try to get a clear picture of these folks. Some troubles followed families, even on vacation. For example, was there debt? Was there tension between dad and son? Was there a secret gambling or addiction problem that was somehow causing conflict in the family? Was the boy angry, or did he perhaps have a drug problem himself? It all counted.

"And Jeremy, was he rebellious?"

"No, for God's sake," Linda chimed in. "We've been over this. We've already given him"—she motioned to Ken—"information about where he was born, who his doctor is, even his goddamn dentist's name." She was right. It was standard procedure to gather as much information as possible on a missing child, initially to verify that he actually exists in the first place. You'd be surprised what parents were capable of inventing for all sorts of insane reasons, and we did not take lightly the manpower and resources necessary to search for a missing child, not to mention that if we did find the child and he was unidentifiable, we needed to have dental and medical records available to try to make an identification. "He's a sweet kid," she continued. "No issues at all. Sure, he's beginning to want a little independence, sometimes gets a little tired of hanging out with his younger siblings, which is why we let him stay here for a few hours to play his 3DS. There's no service here, so he hasn't been able to use his smartphone, which he got this Christmas for pulling straight As at school, but we figured a little time on his old DS would be fine. In fact, I was glad to see it. Reminded me of the old days when that was a big deal for him, before all the ridiculous Droids and iPhones and Snapchatting . . . ."

"And the game? Is it here?"

"No, no, it's not. We can't find it, so he must have taken it with him. But, like we said earlier, his initials are on it. JRC. Jeremy Richard Corey."

I jotted that down. I liked to take my own notes in addition to the recording. I knew Ken had already gotten the Droid, which the boy had left behind since it had no service and was useless to him. We were having it searched to see if it could provide any clues, like if the boy had made or taken any calls to or from someone in Montana.

"Did Jeremy have money on him?"

"Just a little. Maybe a few dollars from before the trip. We didn't leave him money or anything because we weren't gone that long."

"And were you all getting along before you left? Any fights in the past few days, or this morning?"

"No, nothing out of the ordinary. Maybe a little whining about something one of us asked the kids to do, that kind of thing, but nothing major. Look, Mr.—or Officer Harris, is it?"

I nodded.

"There is nothing strange here on our end. Our son has somehow wandered off or disappeared and we're waiting for you to help us find him." She began to circle around the table where the three of us sat, until her husband asked her to sit down, which hit a nerve.

She snapped at him. "How can you just sit there like a bump on a log, talking about your music?"

"What am I supposed to do? Pace with you? Go out walking into the thousands of acres nearby?"

"Listen—" I interrupted before we had a marital fight on our hands. It wasn't uncommon given the level of stress. It was probably insignificant, although it was worth noting. "In not much longer, Two Bear Air, a local search and rescue service, is going to search the area with their thermal night-vision technology. I'm sure it's been explained to you that helicopters weren't dispatched until now because they wouldn't have been able to see anything. It would be like looking for needles in a haystack in the heavily wooded forests around this particular part of the park. But now as it gets darker, we'll actually be able to see more because of the thermal sensory equipment and infrared camera systems." This last update settled Linda down for a moment. She stopped, came over, and scooted into the table next to Ron.

Cassie crawled in next to her on the bench and hugged her dirt-stained knees into her chest. A gleam of hope flashed in Linda's eyes, and Ron sat up a little taller.

"So they'll be able to spot any human out there?" Ron asked.

"That's right, anything with a heat imprint. It's easy to tell humans from wildlife—deer, bear, moose, and the like. We should be able to spot him unless he's crawled under something that would obscure the view."

"Mom." Garret came over and was standing next to Linda, trying to get her attention, but she wasn't answering, just staring at me.

"Mom," he patiently said again, but she still didn't respond.

"Mom," he said a little louder.

"Yes?" She finally turned to him.

"Can I go down to the lake to skip some rocks?"

Suddenly fear lit her eyes. "No, honey, absolutely not."

"Why not? It's still light out."

For a moment, it didn't look like she knew the answer.

Ron intervened. "It's getting too late," he said.

Linda nodded ferociously in agreement. "You need to stay here with us, okay, don't go anywhere, you understand? Anywhere," she said with force. I noted her protective nature, and took it as a good sign. But the steely look of fear on her face froze Garret, froze us all, and made me anxious. I kept my eyes on them rather than letting them catch me checking my watch again to check how long it'd been. The reality of how much time had passed, combined with the sheer panic on Linda's face, suggested we had a long road ahead of us, one I knew would feel endless and desolate to these desperate parents.

5

Gretchen

Ray and I drove west toward Kalispell, where the lab is located. Back at the camp, Ray had insisted on driving, probably sensing my shakiness. The wind began to push southeast, and the valley started to clear. As we exited the mouth of the canyon and entered the open fields, I could make out a hazy silhouette of the Salish Mountains with their tree- and meadow-covered summits for the first time in days. We both let out a sigh of relief to be able to see even that much of the horizon.

"Man, you don't realize how much we take clean air for granted until you get robbed of it." Ray motioned with his chin to the skyline. It was the first thing either of us had said since we'd left the fire camp. Adrenaline's aftereffects made me feel light-headed, and the increasingly visible sky buoyed me, even though it actually meant the wind was pushing the fire southeast, right to the fuel break line, right toward Essex. I said as much to Ray and he agreed. We drove in silence for a moment before he asked, "You okay?"

"I'm fine," I said. I didn't try to find out why he was asking. "You?"

"Hungry." He smiled. "Very hungry."

"I bet." I looked at the clock on the dash. It was almost eight thirty. "I just need your help unloading, that's it. I can do the rest."

Ray nodded, and we didn't say another word as we made it down Highway 2 and cut over to Highway 93. He slowed and stopped at an intersection north of Kalispell where a host of box stores had gone up

54

in the past decade: Target, Lowe's, "Super" Walmart, Pier 1, Petco, Cabela's. Chain restaurants were sprinkled in between them. It seemed never-ending and I wondered about Norway, about Europe in general, and if it had been affected by such aggressive enterprise. I did have to admit that I missed some of the charm from home: the quaint cobblestone streets, the local restaurants and pubs, the ancient buildings and hotels, the colorful wooden houses dotting the coastlines. I used to ask myself how something so terrible could have happened to me—to my brother—in those picturesque streets with the candy and chocolate bars for sale at the local kiosks, the scent of the sea wafting in on the cool breezes and washing everything clean.

I was conflicted about Montana. On the one hand, this type of sprawl was so quintessentially American that it comforted me to know I was in a land far away from a place I didn't belong. But on the other hand, the box stores were ugly. They blocked the gorgeous views of the meadows and mountains and destroyed large fields for their parking lots, even though those fields were precisely what made the area special.

I no longer felt like a Norsk, and didn't really feel like an American or a Montanan either. But I came to this land, to the vast jutting and bruised shape of it, partly to lose myself to it and to make the best of things. I did like the Flathead Valley and the towns it held. I loved the nearby town of Whitefish on the northern end of it. I liked the way it nestled against the Whitefish Range and how the runs of the ski resort fanned down toward it like arteries giving the town sustenance. And there were things about it that reminded me of Sandefjord in a vague, distant way: the local ice cream shop and the shiny green bench on the street corner where you could sit on a pleasant summer night to eat your locally made huckleberry ice cream, watch residents walk their dogs on leashes, and see tourists laughing and smiling with their children.

I enjoyed the jewelry and art studios with colorful canvases and interesting pottery that wasn't always typical western flare, and the Snowghost Bar and Café where you could get decent lox and bagels.

I loved hearing the kids chatting and laughing when they passed my house on weekday mornings on their way to the only public elementary school in town. How the mist rose off the valley's lakes as it did in the Sandefjord Bay, and how, in even the coldest winters, the deeper parts of Flathead Lake—the largest freshwater lake west of the Mississippi— still wouldn't freeze and remained dark and mysterious like a fjord. How when the snow fell, it smelled just like home, a metallic, ozone scent, like fresh warm water pouring over cold stones.

Whether in Montana or Norway, each season ultimately suggested the same solitary, ephemeral nature of everything. There was a small amount of comfort in knowing that what I'd done would all fade away at some point, like the needles of the larch falling to the ground, so vital, but so temporary. I thought of my brother's honey-colored locks, then quickly pushed the image away.

Thoughts of my father came in its place. I recalled how when I was six or seven he took Per and me to see some of the Viking burial sites just outside Sandefjord. We stood by the side of ancient stones erected in the shape of a ship as he explained to us that they were put down in AD 400 to 600 and that objects found nearby revealed Viking settlements since the Stone and Bronze Ages. He had told us stories about the Vikings since we were tiny—about how they were fierce, strong, and fast. We learned that they were excellent explorers, afraid of nothing, not even the cold, sometimes vicious North Sea. They would set out across it to unknown lands: Iceland, Greenland, Britain, Newfoundland.

He told us about how they'd go out to take what they needed, sometimes by force, but that was common for the times. In reality, if they could make more through trading instead of raiding, they would, but not because they considered marauding shameful. It was simply about survival, and riches brought that. If a nobleman paid them well for their military skills, they served loyally and were men of honor. "Although," my father said, "there were always exceptions—always are exceptions—in any group of people."

After seeing the burial site, I later came to connect it with all the stories he'd told us over the years. Sometimes I still wonder about them because I think the history and energy of the place where you grow up never completely leave you. They continue to move through you like deep ocean undercurrents. For me, I think of how the proud, opportunistic Vikings built Sandefjord on whaling profits. I imagine how they did whatever it took, ethical or not, to survive in a stark, cold land, and I sense that Montanans did the same: they trapped for fur, mined for gold, and fought the Indians using whatever tactics they could. I can sometimes feel the desperation and grit from those ancestors and the Natives riding on the mountain winds into the valley just as I could feel the echo of the pain from my people and the whales they killed gusting off the North Sea into Sandefjord Bay.

Norwegians were a proud, independent group of people where roots ran strong, and suddenly I had become an outcast to this group. After what happened, I felt like a stranger in my hometown. It took me a long time to even find a modicum of enjoyment in anything. For three years I was numb. Everything I did felt like a lie because I felt like a mistake myself, an aberration—"an exception" to human beings in general. Every small task I performed—buying something at a store, eating a meal, or listening to a song—felt like I was only faking trying to be normal. The little things I used to take comfort in didn't appeal to me anymore: my favorite books, songs, and food. I used to collect snow globes from new places I'd visit, and I used to love to shake them and watch the white flakes fall around the buildings: the Eiffel Tower, the Leaning Tower of Pisa, the Royal Palace in Oslo. All of that stopped making sense, and at some point—maybe with the help of my therapist in Norway—I knew that if I didn't at least try to appreciate the nuances again, I'd have nothing.

Eventually, when I realized the pain was too great for me to remain in the place where it all happened, I left. People, of course, looked at me differently. The whispers never ceased, and I'd even received anonymous death threats claiming that a freak like me should not be allowed to live in public, and if the Norwegian court system wouldn't lock me up, someone needed to put an end to me. I already lived with extreme guilt, sadness, shame, and terror of what other terrible acts I might be capable of committing, but the added fear of what other people might do to me made whatever raggedy life I patched together rip a little more each day.

Call it running. Call it whatever you like. But if I couldn't be a part of Norway, I could at least remain anonymous and relatively safe, if not proud like a Norwegian.

Ray reached over and turned the air on higher, which snapped me into the present. I forced myself to focus on the road ahead, wondering why I was even entertaining such thoughts in the first place. I chalked it up to the way my lungs hurt and my head floated, my dizziness making it seem like I was hovering. I was glad Ray was driving. Since I had woken to see the stacked books, my guard had been down, and now the incomplete dig had shaken me even more, making me feel raw and exposed. I thought about the bones in the back—about the snapped ribs and the pieces left behind to be incinerated if the line hadn't held. I made a mental note to call Monty after unloading to see if he knew the status of the fire.

You're okay, I said to myself. *You're okay.* I glanced at Ray. He started blankly out the window at WingStreet, the chain restaurant that had gone up to replace a failing Sizzler, until the light changed and he pressed on the gas pedal.

"You were great today, Ray. Proficient. Thank you for your hard work. And thank you for helping Officer Reed."

"All part of the job," he said.

· · ·

After we reached the Flathead County Justice Center, where our lab and offices were located, and finished unloading, Ray left. I went to a Thai restaurant on Main Street in Kalispell and grabbed some pad thai to go, took it back to the lab where I'd gotten the bones and samples organized, and made my calls to the local coroner and to Lucy in Bozeman.

The coroner would look at what we'd gotten first thing in the morning, while Lucy said that she was studying up on the acidity of the soil in the area the bones were found.

Then I called Monty. "Gretchen," he answered my ring. "You're back at the lab?"

"Yes, all unloaded. Everything will be run by the coroner by morning and then we'll ship it all to Lucy in Bozeman. How are things in Essex?"

"I hate to tell you, but not good. The line broke. Firemen are just trying to save structures at this point. Houses, the Izaak Walton Inn, the train depot. . . ."

I slumped in my office chair, any last reserves of energy I had completely dissolving at the news. I didn't say anything, just pictured the grave, our grid, the ribs that were left incinerated, all blackened beyond recognition.

"You okay?"

"Yeah," I said, wondering why everyone kept asking me that, and hoping I hadn't seemed that frazzled. I wanted it to stop. "Let me know when it's safe to go out there. I'll want to see what's left anyway."

"I'll do that," Monty said. "And Gretchen . . ."

"Yeah?"

"Get some rest."

. . .

Eventually I wrapped things up and drove home. My house sat on an acre on the east side of Whitefish and was flanked by a field of horses on one side and a small forest of lodgepole pines on the other. A copse of birch trees towered next to the small white farmhouse. It was only a mile-and-a-half walk into town, but I felt like I had the best of both worlds: country and town living. I'd leased it when I first moved to the Flathead four years before. At some point the owners approached me about buying, so I put down seven thousand dollars and made payments to a local mortgage company, which ended up selling it numerous times to national companies that I could barely keep track of.

The place had gas heat, a view of the Mission Mountain Range, and a bright, cheery kitchen with warm sunset-colored tiles on the backsplash behind the stove and sink. It had a fireplace too, also framed with Tuscan-colored insets. I kept a cord of firewood stacked outside the back door for when the cold rolled around, but often toyed with the idea of replacing the fireplace with a gas unit. It would make life easier, but I had a hard time parting from the smell of woodsmoke that reminded me of my family's house.

I pulled into the drive, cut the engine, and went into the dark house. When I entered, I turned the outdoor and indoor lights on and looked at the fireplace perched on the side wall—cheery, but lonely looking. I thought of the books arranged neatly before it and turned away, went and took a hot shower, rinsing all the layers of sweat and grime from the dirt and smoke off me. Then I made some tea, drinking it in silence, my eyes stinging from the smoke exposure and exhaustion.

My previous doctor in Seattle, a neurologist who put me in a sleep lab and stuck electrodes all over my body to observe my slumber, told me what the doctors had already told my parents and the court in Norway fifteen years before: my disorder is caused by a deficiency of dopamine, a chemical released from the brain into the body that paralyzes you so you don't act out your dreams. "People who have this," the Seattle doctor had told me, "are commonly dreaming about running away from demons, evil killers, or wild animals or fighting someone or something harmful. People who have this have actually *killed* people while remaining in their sleep." He was a short, stocky guy with a receding hairline and a comb-over, and his eyes had been dead serious.

I remember looking down at the shiny, waxed linoleum floor when he'd said it, even though he knew nothing of my history or anything about my past. I had sought him out only because I was having trouble sleepwalking again. I had woken up to a pile of torn and crumpled magazine paper in the center of my Seattle apartment living room, the edges of one piece partially burned. And of course my apartment did not have a fireplace. I was fortunate the whole place didn't go up in flames. I also kept having dreams about freezing, being stranded in a cold place, and needing to start a fire to stay warm. I had nightmares about breaking through the iced-over fjords, dropping abruptly and sharply, like some Tower of Terror ride made of sea ice. I knew I couldn't go any longer without medication, so I googled neurologists and sleep specialists and found this doctor's name.

He prescribed Klonopin, an anti-anxiety medication, the same one I took in Norway and that I had brought over in bulk in my suitcases when I first moved to the States. "It's not a cure," he reminded me, pinning me with his round beady eyes. His breath smelled like salami, but I tried not to let it bother me. "But it can help. I also suggest you make it difficult for yourself to leave the apartment when you get into one of your somnambulistic phases."

"Difficult?" I asked.

"Yeah, try a sleeping bag and double locks on your doors, and don't forget to hide the key."

Besides those tactics, my overall strategy was to try not to think about my disorder very much. It's a catch-22: if you overthink it, it causes stress, and stress, *min venn*—my friend—is what intensifies the disorder in the first place. But sometimes it hits me in a big, paralyzing way. Usually my work preserves my sanity, gives me purpose, and the methodical nature of it keeps me calm, which is why the uncharacteristic rushing and the craziness of the dig got under my skin.

Another part of my strategy involves not just diving right into sleep after a long, troubling day. Which is why even though every muscle in my body ached and craved my mattress, I made Sleepytime tea and sat in the kitchen, listening to the crickets outside instead of turning on the news—the worst possible thing for me to watch at bedtime—before fetching my sleeping bag and mittens. Yeah, that's right. Mittens. Because even though it was hotter than hell out, I needed to bind myself up in the sleeping bag, and the mittens might stop me from opening the zipper. I set my teacup in the porcelain sink and got my sleeping bag out of the hall closet. It smelled of dust and the woody linen scent of the closet. It had been five years since I'd needed it last.

I know it all sounds crazy, almost silly, and it is. It's no way to live. I take my medication regularly; it just doesn't always do the job, which is why I woke to the stacked rows of books. But sleeping with mittens on a summer night is better than jumping through a window or hopping in my car to drive off because I think I'm being chased or, heaven forbid, hurting someone because I'm dreaming they're a demon.

I laid the bag out across my bed, climbed in, and zipped it up. Then I put on the lightweight black North Face mittens, tied the Velcro straps tight at the wrists and shoved my arms inside. I felt like a mummy, and all I could say was this: thank God I wasn't also claustrophobic.

6

Monty

BY TEN THERE was still no sign of Jeremy. Night had settled like an angry beast, the western sky glowing red before fading to a murky darkness. The air search was in full swing. The choppers cut in and out of the mountains in quadrants, slicing large beams of light through the still-smoky air onto the dense trees and making them appear bluish white. From the helicopters, I knew the pilots and their observers—even through the veils of smoke—would be looking at obscured land that went on forever and spread into a vast sea of rugged mountains. If the boy was out there—injured from a fall or huddled in the forest, lost and confused—he'd be able to hear the engines overhead, their blades beating out the sound of urgency, all directed toward him. Wherever he was, I hoped it was comforting and that he was still alive to *be* consoled.

So far the thermal imaging had come up with nothing out of the ordinary. I'd been told by the Two Bear director that it wasn't the best night for a thermal search—the heat from the fires would make the imaging screen harder to read since hot images come across less clearly when found among other masses of warmth. "If he's out there, though," he told us, "we'll find him. Hopefully we'll come across some hot spots." I held on to an image of the searchers spotting his red and yellow glimmering form, his little arm like a glowworm waving the pilots down.

Smith, Ken, and I were at headquarters while the Coreys waited at their campsite, desperately hoping their boy would walk up out of the dark any minute. But the night slowly crawled on without news. By two a.m., Two Bear had finally called back its choppers. Every passing minute felt like another heavy rock piling on my shoulders. Around two thirty, I told Ken to go get some sleep and I stayed for another hour, checking my watch over and over while I finished paperwork and kept one ear to the radios.

Eventually, around three thirty, I knew there was nothing more I could do for the time being and that I needed to finally go home for a shower and a little sleep before morning hit. I walked back to my dorm, where I'd been living for two years now since my separation—and later divorce—from Lara. She and I were together for seven years until she split because I didn't want to have children, something she knew and agreed with before we married. Somewhere along the line during our marriage, she changed her mind, and what I considered a rock-solid bond had slowly but surely crumbled.

The temperature had dropped slightly as I walked home, the night sky still hazy and no stars to be seen. The larch and pines hovered around me on either side of the road until I rounded the corner and saw the Community Building. My apartment—or, rather, my dorm—was on the small side. It was supposed to be temporary, but even after the divorce, I didn't have the desire to look for anything else because it was incredibly convenient, located down the road and around the corner from headquarters. And as far as I was concerned, I was more than content to have not only an office but a home among the serenity and splendor of Glacier. Plain and simple: on most days, the wilderness gave me peace.

But not tonight. The forests were quiet. No rustling, no owl hoots, no coyote yips, most likely because of the fires. I didn't want to think it, and Ken and Joe didn't want to voice it either: Jeremy might be dead, killed either by nature or by a perpetrator. Or even by the fire, if he'd somehow found himself that far east. Either way, the following morning would bring a busy day of searching.

When I turned the lights on in my tiny living room, I remembered Tara. I felt bad that I hadn't called to check on her, but I knew she'd understand under the circumstances. Joe had told me that she was fine, that she'd been under observation for a period of time, then released. I figured I'd see her in the morning, anyway; I doubted she could be talked into staying home to rest when a boy was missing.

After I peeled off my stiff, dirty uniform and let the shower's hot water run down my back, I considered the dig. The bones we found were still nagging at me, and even though I was utterly exhausted, a surge of anxiety darted through me. I couldn't shake the memory of that Halloween night years ago when my best friend, Nathan, didn't make it home.

I was twelve when I lost him. Nathan had disappeared in the night after my older brother, Adam, and his friends played a trick on us by leaving us alone at an old cemetery. On the way home, Nathan and I got into a fight. He was blaming me for believing my brother and getting us stuck out in the woods. He stormed off into the dark trees; I tried to catch him, but he was too quick for me. He disappeared into the forest and I never saw him again. The police never knew if he'd been attacked by a mountain lion or a bear or had simply frozen to death somewhere.

I stood for a while, the hot water streaming over my head and running in rivulets down my chest. Usually, this was all it took to wash away the day's troubles and snap me out of my worries—a signal to shut off my thoughts by the time I turned off the water—but not this time. My mind was spinning even as I grabbed a towel and stepped out.

My face looked tanned but tired, fresh stubble dotting my jawline. I headed to bed, where I continued trying to shut off my thoughts. In the dark room, I glanced over to the side window. No moonlight, no starlight. I tried not to think about the boy out in the wild.

In the early days after Nathan's disappearance, when the police were coming over for information and the whole town was searching, I couldn't sleep. My aunt told me to think of nothing but my breath—to trace it. My aunt wasn't some new-age meditating guru who imagined beams of light spiraling through her, but she was practical—even more pragmatic than my dad, who became less sensible over time by drinking too much booze—and she told me that always, in any situation, the best way to self-soothe was with your breath. She told me to imagine it going in, down my windpipe and into my lungs, even past them and into my lower back and tailbone, then trace it going back up the opposite direction and out. Usually I began to drift off somewhere on the fifth round.

It took longer this time, but eventually my ruminations subsided and blended into the stillness of the night. That is, until the first light of dawn came and I rose, frantically checking my phone, thinking I'd missed something. I hadn't; no one had called and that made me feel even worse. I quickly splashed my face with water, brushed my teeth, dressed, and went to work.

When I walked out, I saw a pale, blushing stretch of sky—a small reprieve as the wind continued to blow the fires in the opposite direction. Glacier's tall rocky peaks loomed nearby, their dominant stance impervious to the wildfires at the lower levels. Their demarcation of the park's borders usually comforted me and made me feel at home, but not this morning. A herd of deer grazed the lawn in front of the Community Building, which made it all seem like a normal glorious Glacier summer day was about to begin.

Yet today its beauty and its ruggedness felt entirely foreign and left a pit in my stomach. The air still smelled like burnt paper from the fire that dominated the eastern ridges. A boy was still fighting for his life (if we were lucky) in the woods after being lost for eighteen hours. Not to mention, a strange shallow grave had produced unidentified bones. I knew any respite we were experiencing in the west side of the park was being paid for dearly in the east. In Essex, the Ole Fire had not only plowed through the gravesite but had taken two houses, a barn, and a trailer.

At headquarters, I made some coffee, set up an incident room that we could use through the day until we found Jeremy, double-checked

that all the news sources were still posting on him, and began to organize more searches. By seven a.m., I already had ten rangers canvass-
ing the area, sweeping trails, and continuing to interview anyone who
might have seen the boy. By eight, the case began to develop legs, but
not at all in the way we would have wanted.

Of course, the day before, Ken and some of the other officers and
rangers had already asked around the campsite and the general area
about any strange vehicles they may have seen hanging around, or if
anyone had seen the boy talking to people other than family. No one
had until now. We got a call from a man, a Mr. Roger Kelly, who'd been
fishing near McDonald Creek the day before. He called in to say he'd
just seen the local seven a.m. news with the information about the
missing boy and claimed he had something pertinent to share with
us—that he'd seen the boy while fishing in the park the afternoon
before.

Ken stayed back at headquarters while I drove through the canyon
away from Glacier to Columbia Falls, a town in the northeast corner of
Flathead Valley. I can't say I was too bummed about going alone since
on this particular morning, Ken reeked of aftershave, as if he were a
teenager who didn't know how much Axe to use. I chalked it up to
exhaustion from working late hours.

The sky had mostly cleared outside the canyon as well, and was
almost back to its summer blue. I parked outside a small gray house
and got out. Roger Kelly was waiting for me and opened the door as I
walked up. He introduced me to his wife, Vera, and she offered me tea
or coffee. I declined. "As you can imagine," I said to them, getting right
to it while standing in the entryway as their black-and-white border
collie sniffed my hands, "we're all in a bit of a hurry to get on with the
search. What is it you'd like to share with us?"

"Come, come in." The man ushered me in, and we sat at a Formica
table with chrome legs in a cheery yellow kitchen smelling of bacon
and coffee. The dog sat to my side, eyeing me suspiciously.

"Any information you have at all, Mr. Kelly, I'd like to hear."

"Yes, yes," he said. "Well, I was out fishing by the creek yesterday, by the mouth of it, just coming out of Lake McDonald, when I saw a boy that I'm sure was the one on the news this morning."

I perked up, noting the use of the word "sure." Usually people were unsure, saying they couldn't be positive, but thought that *maybe* they saw someone who looked similar. "You're certain, you say?"

"Yeah, I'm sure. He looked so much like our grandson." He motioned to Vera, who was sitting quietly, her eyes wide with concern. "Anyway, he was walking down the road and I didn't think anything of it, just noticed it because he looked to be the same age as my grandson, who's about twelve."

"Thirteen now, Roger," Vera corrected him. "Parker turned thirteen two months ago."

"Which way was he walking?" I asked.

"West, toward the bridge."

"Do you recall what he looked like or what he was wearing?"

"He had wavy dark hair. A little shorter than the photo on the news. And I seem to have blue in my mind, like a blue T-shirt or shorts or something. I'm not superclear on the clothing, but I know he had wavy hair, like my grandson. I did a double take because I almost thought it was Parker."

"Light blue or dark blue shirt?"

"Light. Not navy," he said. I knew from the mother that Jeremy was wearing a light blue T-shirt. I felt relieved that the man probably *had* seen the boy, and I wasn't wasting my time. In the photo we used on the news, he was wearing a red-and-brown-striped shirt, so I knew he wasn't going off that image.

"How tall was he? Did you notice?"

"Again, like my grandson. About five-four, five-five. Hasn't hit his growth spurt yet."

He had that detail correct as well. "Is that all? You just saw him walking?"

"No, so after about another five minutes of fishing with no luck—

too warm, really, and I knew better than to try and fish on such a hot day, but I had cabin fever from staying inside so long from the smoke and wanted to get out. Anyway," he continued. "I decided to head to West Glacier's little golf course instead. I had my clubs in the back in case the fishing stunk, so I hopped in my car and headed back toward the bridge, and before crossing it, I noticed the boy talking to someone in a truck by the driver's-side window. I figured it was the boy's relative or someone he knew."

"Did you notice what type of truck it was?"

Roger slowly shook his head, rubbing the back of his neck. "I didn't. I didn't pay attention to it, really. Just the boy, because of the resemblance to Parker."

"How about the color? A license plate?"

"I want to say dark, but I couldn't really tell you whether it was black, brown, maybe maroon . . ." He squinted. "I'm sorry, I just didn't pay attention to the details. I only noticed the boy, not the type of truck, or the driver and not the license plate either. Couldn't even tell you if it was a Montana license or some other state. Like I said, I only noticed because of my grandson. I was kind of in a lazy mood, daydreaming and thinking that I'd like to get Parker out fishing with me, that it'd been a long time since I'd taken him and with him becoming a teenager and all, it wouldn't be long before he wasn't going to want to do things like that with me at all. I guess we feel the *cat's in the cradle and the silver spoon* even more from a grandparent's perspective, only from the other side. We're the ones asking them to play."

I finished jotting it all down, then for no particular reason, wrote *Cat's in the cradle* in the corner of my paper in cursive letters. Like I said, I didn't have kids. I know it seems stubborn that I didn't give in on the child thing with my ex, but my genetic tree was not a pretty one. My mother was diagnosed with schizoaffective disorder (an umbrella diagnosis that includes depression and schizophrenia). With paranoid schizophrenia's tendency to skip a generation and my father's alcoholic tendencies, it would be pure foolishness to bring a child into the world with that kind of DNA tangled in the family tree branches. "That's okay, Mr. Kelly," I said. "You've been very helpful already. Do you remember anything else?"

"Yes, so I looked in the rearview after passing and I saw the boy get in to the truck, on the other side."

A pang of dread shot through me, but I forced myself to stay still. "You're sure? You saw the boy get in?"

"Yes, I'm sure. I saw him open the passenger door but, you know, I didn't pay much attention. I figured whoever was inside it was a family member or a friend—that the kid belonged with the truck."

"Was the truck there long?"

"I couldn't say. I kept going."

"Did you have reason to be suspicious about anything?"

"No." He shook his head, thinking. "No, nothing like that. I didn't think twice until I saw the news and knew that I'd definitely noticed that boy. I'm one hundred percent positive it was that boy."

"Did you see the boy or the truck again?"

"No, I didn't. And like I said, even if I would have seen it again, I'm not sure I would have even known it was the same truck since I didn't pay that much attention to it, just to the kid." Roger stared at me, his head tilted to the side and his eyes now drooping with the realization that without information on the vehicle, the task of locating the boy would be much more difficult. I could see he felt bad for not being more observant about an adolescent who'd hopped into a truck and turned up later flashing across the nightly and morning news. "I'm sorry," he said.

"Is there any reason you didn't call last night, Mr. Kelly?"

"We didn't watch the news last night. When I got home, we went out for some barbecue at Tracy's." Roger glanced at Vera and she nodded in agreement. "I wish I had, though. Damn, I wish I had. I would have called you right away."

"Okay then, thank you, Mr. Kelly, for contacting us. I would like a little more of your time, though, if you don't mind." When I stood up, the dog got up too and sniffed my hand again. "I'd like for you to follow me back to West Glacier and point out exactly where you saw this boy and the car. I'd really appreciate your help."

"Of course." He looked around for his car keys, which were sitting on the kitchen counter, then motioned to the front door. Vera followed us, and before we stepped out, she asked, "What do you think happened to him?"

"We're not sure, but we're considering all possibilities."

"Do you think you'll find him?" She looked genuinely worried, her brow creased, her eyes sharp.

"We all hope so. He's got some very anxious parents waiting for him."

"But you do think the truck has something to do with him being gone?"

I tried to ignore the steely shiver running through me and looked into her hazel eyes. I didn't want to tell her that the story her husband just shared was taking my worry to new heights and that I really, really disliked the idea of a strange vehicle in the picture, turning this into something much more terrifying than the case of a boy who found himself on the wrong trail in the woods.

The forests were daunting enough; but a strange vehicle—that changed things, especially the time frame within which we were working. I didn't want to jump to conclusions, but a young teen—provided he didn't fall into a dangerous stream, stumble off a cliff, or get attacked by a bear or mountain lion—could survive several days out in the elements in August, when the temperatures often stayed above sixty degrees. But a child in the hands of a human predator? Statistics said we had only twenty-four hours—a deadline that was rapidly approaching—and that the first three hours are the most critical. It had already been twenty-one hours.

"There's probably a very reasonable explanation for why the boy was chatting with the driver," I said, smiling politely. "It doesn't necessarily mean anything," I fibbed, trying to curb any possible gossip before Park Police decided how we would proceed. "I'm just covering all our bases by having Roger show us where he saw the boy. It's standard procedure." I pulled my car keys out of my pocket. "I appreciate your time. Your husband will be back soon."

•   •   •

After Roger showed me the spot, I thanked him again, handed him my card, and told him to call me if anything at all—any other details, no matter how small or insignificant they seemed—came to his mind. Ken had met us along the Fish Creek Road, and after Roger left, we searched for tire tracks, but unfortunately the stretch of road had a hard shoulder of packed gravel, and other than a small amount of mud and some flattened grass, there were no obvious tread marks or any other suspicious signs. Still, I'd have forensics check out the place. It was now considered a crime scene. I took out my phone to call county forensics to put in the request and then snapped a few pictures of indentations in the grass.

I hesitated before making the call. After the craziness of the dig the day before, I wanted to leave Gretchen alone. She'd been very upset—shaken and angry. I'd never seen her that way. A part of me felt protective, but I knew better than to show her that. We had become friends from all the time spent working together, but she'd given me the vibe that she wanted nothing more, and I heard her clear as the cold water of McDonald Creek. Not that she ever said it directly—I could just tell by the precise and utilitarian way she treated me, treated everyone around her, for that matter. She had a lot of boundaries for reasons I didn't understand but ultimately accepted. I could sense something contained, something deeply buried, but I respected that. I had my own things that needed emotional burial—most people did. But damn if I wasn't curious. If there's one thing I understand about myself, it's that I like order, and part of maintaining that order involves me figuring out what makes people tick.

But I wanted to leave her be for now, so I called Sheriff Walsh instead. He could send someone here to examine the area, but my hopes weren't high without fresh mud or dirt on the side of the road for the tires to make clear imprints.

I asked Ken to search the surveillance footage for dark-colored trucks entering or leaving the park with a boy in the passenger seat. Without a make or model number, it would be like looking for a needle in a haystack. We had nearly twenty-five thousand visitors a day driving through Glacier Park's gates during its busy months.

I made sure the few details we had about the vehicle were wired to all local law enforcement agencies. Then I went back to campsite 23A to visit the Coreys and give them an update. Now that we knew about the truck, the investigation would transition to a whole new level. The FBI would need to be called in, and I would need to ask the family the difficult question of whether there was anyone in the area they knew who would possibly have offered Jeremy a ride.

7

Gretchen

I WOKE VERY EARLY, drenched in sweat but still safely fastened in my sleeping bag, with the mittens on. Relieved, I went to the kitchen, where I stood before the window while waiting for water for my herbal tea to boil. I have this recurring dream where I'm desperately trying to reach my father to plead with him to forgive me, but I can never reach him. All sorts of obstacles prevent me from reaching him—thin ice that breaks below me, stacks and stacks of furniture that keep growing wider and higher no matter how many pieces I move out of the way, fires that rage before me, flooding roads with currents that sweep me away right before I can get to him. It was the breaking-ice one last night. I remembered it. I stared out the window at the field and the horses grazing, their long necks curved to the ground. The sun barely crept up over the trees and yellow spears of light pierced the lawn. The kettle moaned, then cried loudly, and I switched the burner off. I would forgo caffeinated beverages like coffee until this episode of *Gretchen's Sleep Adventures* passed because I didn't need the caffeine making me jittery. My doctor in Norway had told me that any caffeine during the day at all could have an effect on my disorder, even if it was still early. Herbal tea and a caffeine-deprivation headache was a price worth paying for a better night of sleep.

An hour later, I parked at the county building, grabbed my carrier bag, and walked in. When I entered the fluorescent-lit corridor, my feet tapping out a quiet, hushed sound on the linoleum, I was relieved to be at work again. Here I had tasks, commitment, a life where I was in control, a reprieve from my nocturnal instability. After I dropped my bag in my office, I grabbed some more herbal tea and called Lucy in Bozeman to let her know we were sending out the remains as soon as possible.

I had just hung up when Wendy, one of our latent print examiners, gently knocked, came in, and slumped into the extra chair by my desk. She was holding a silver coffee thermos. Wendy was the only other female on the CSI team and I was happy to have her around. Sometimes it was challenging to be the leader, to make decisions for the team: Ray, Paxton, and Wendy, two of whom were older than me. But it helped to have Wendy around, especially since she never seemed to doubt my decisions.

A studious-looking woman in her mid- to late forties with wire-framed glasses and a narrow pointy nose, she was a great technician in the lab and had a motherly way with the rest of the crew and with me too, probably from practice. She had a son, Kyle, a seventeen-year-old who was in all sorts of trouble: in and out of JD court for acting out in various aggressive ways, like vandalizing local businesses and starting fights with other students. He had been arrested for stealing money and other items from people's garages that he hawked at pawnshops to support a drug habit. I knew it ripped her apart, that she felt guilty for not intervening when he was younger, although if you asked, she probably couldn't name exactly what she would have done. And if there was ever an emotion I could fully, unequivocally relate to, it was guilt. When guilt and grief combined, a wicked, potent cancer was born, one that colonized your bones and could remain forever.

"You're here early," I said to her.

"Couldn't sleep."

"You all right?" I asked. Her face looked pale, her hair a little messier than normal.

"Yeah. Nothing new, really."

"Is Kyle still acting up?"

She laughed and raked her fingers through her short brown hair, tilting her head to the side. "That's a nice way to put it: acting up."

"How should I put it then?"

"Try wreaking havoc."

"Oh, gosh, that bad? What's going on now?"

Wendy winced, then took a sip from her thermos. "The usual," she said. "Told me he's going camping with some friends, but wouldn't say where. I tried to ground him, tell him he can't go anywhere. I took his keys, but he ended up finding them and took off anyway. I have no idea where he is or when he'll get back."

I nodded and looked at her sympathetically. "That's tough. Are you really worried?"

"Par for the course. It's always worrisome, but this isn't the first time he's taken off like this." She let out a heavy sigh, then forced herself to switch gears. "So, why are you here so early?"

"I always come in early." I picked up my phone and hit a button to light up the screen. I figured it was later, but it was only seven thirty. I must have left the house before seven.

"Not this early." She looked at me, concerned. Sometimes I felt like Wendy took the time to focus on me since her own son wouldn't tolerate any doting. She was the only person in Montana—in the United States, besides Jim—with whom I'd been tempted to share what had happened in Norway, but I hadn't. I decided that no one in Montana except my doctor could know. I would no longer be respected, and being team leader of the forensics unit was challenging enough for a smallish blond female with a foreign accent. "Anyway, the buckle you found . . ." Wendy set her thermos down on my desk, pulled some gloves out of her lab coat, and walked out to her station. She came back holding an evidence bag containing the buckle. "I haven't done anything to it because I'm assuming it's going to Bozeman."

"Correct. Lucy might have a different way of studying it with the soil and determining how it has affected the surface area."

Wendy inspected it through the plastic, turning it from side to side.

"I'm guessing at one time it was shiny black: a durable nickel plating. And you know what I think it says?"

"What?"

"Well, I've been looking at it with a magnifying glass, and in this lower left corner I can make out the bottom of a red letter in that kind of curlicue writing. I can make out the same on the right side as well."

"And?"

"I could be wrong, but I think the first letter is an *A* and the last, an *H*. And here in the middle, I can make out part of an *O*."

"And that means?"

"I think it says Aerosmith. You know, the band."

I held out my hand. She passed it to me, and I studied it through the plastic. My heart sank; there was no way to be sure until Lucy soaked it and let us know exactly what it said, but it did look like maybe Wendy could be correct. Of course, even if she was, it proved nothing, but my hunch that this belonged to a young person was now stronger than ever.

"It's a rock band from the seventies all the way through to the nineties," Wendy said. "Huge in America for several decades."

I smiled. "I've heard of Aerosmith. They were world-famous. 'Janie's Got a Gun,' right?"

"Of course *that* would be the song you'd recall." Wendy smiled.

"Anything to do with ballistics," I shrugged, trying to resist the flash of memory that stung me. I would never forget the song. After my incident with Per, I ran into two boys I knew from school and they taunted me, singing, *"Gretchen's got a gun / Her whole world's come undone."* Of course, I didn't actually use a gun. Gun control laws were very strict in Norway, and my family didn't own one. It was a fire iron that I used on Figment Man. That's what I called him in order to be able to talk to my counselors about that night long ago in Norway. Figment Man was the one in my nightmare.

One time I saw a self-styled medium on TV talking about people who received visits from the dead. He said that you knew when you'd been visited by someone from the afterlife because you'd recall every detail about them, and with regular dreams or nightmares, you didn't. The figments eventually faded away. I call bullshit on that. I recall every detail about Figment Man, and as much as I wish he had, he's never faded away.

He was stocky, no more than five-nine. He wore a red face mask and a black leather jacket turned up at the collar. He slunk into my brother's room with a glinting fat knife with a serrated edge poised above his right shoulder, his beefy arm held at a rigid right angle, poised to slice Per's peaceful, still body.

I was petrified, and I froze for a moment. I yelled at Per to wake up, to get up and run, but he didn't. He just kept sleeping serenely. He'd always been a deep sleeper, the kind who could doze on the train sitting straight up and surrounded by strangers. I scurried down the dark hallway into the shadowy parlor and it felt like it took me forever—that surely the knife has already been plunged into him. I frantically grabbed a fire iron from the living room and ran as fast as I could back into the bedroom. I screamed for him to stop, my voice moving like water through my own head.

He didn't listen to me, only continued to repeatedly stab Per, who made awful grunting sounds. I went over to the invader, to his broad, hunched back. There was something demonic in the way his dark shoulders angled over Per, about the way he didn't even bother to look at me when I yelled. With all my force, I hit the man on the back of his shoulder . . . once, twice, three times, then switched to his arm and struck it again and again.

Or at least *I thought* that's what I was doing. Until I woke after my dad tackled me and began to slowly make out the room again. I was confused and asked what happened. "*Hva hendre? Hva hendre?*"

Lights flicked on and my mom's yells pierced the room. My father was holding me on the floor, restraining me. He yelled, "*Du er gal; du er gal,*" *You're crazy. You're crazy.* My mom kept shrieking for my dad to grab me—*grab henne, hindre henne*—grab her, restrain her, then she ran to Per, to the bed.

He held me tight, and I tried to wriggle away, yelling, "What happened? What happened?"

"Oh, *gud*, oh, *gud*. I need my phone. *Fonen min*," she cried frantically. "We need an ambulance." She ran to find a phone, and when she moved away, I saw Per—bloody and lying still in his bed. Too still.

Pablo Neruda, one of my favorite poets, whom I learned about in Ungdomsskole, used a line in one of his poems: *the blood of the children ran through the streets / without fuss, like children's blood.* Oh, I know he was talking about Spain's civil war, but in class (it was Herr Gunderson's class, and I was thirteen) all of my classmates had different ideas about why he'd used the image of children's blood twice: that he was maybe giving two meanings, one referring to blameless children and the other to adults, who ultimately in war can be just as innocent and helpless as kids in the face of a violent regime. During a time of war, Tor Bjørgen, one of my friends with curly gold locks like Per, said that no one has any control over what happens during invasions. They are helpless; they are like children. I remember him saying, "Just one morning in Spain during the Civil War had the power to change everything in Pablo Neruda's world."

It was like that for me. There'd been no war; there'd not even been an intruder, but just one night changed everything for me, for my family, for our friends. Only I wasn't innocent. I had caused the pain for my parents, the emotional war that would never end. One day Per was teasing me, pulled my ponytail, and helped me with my schoolwork, and the next—gone. Untouchable, unreachable. Gone.

Later, when I tried to describe to my counselors in the Bergen mental health facility how Per lay there, his head, pillow, and sheets bloodied from my own doing, I came to understand those two lines of the poem differently. There were no similes. There were no metaphors for how horrible it was . . . for how utterly horrific it remains. The blood of my brother ran onto his pillow, like, well, like the blood of my only brother. An older brother. A hero. That's why Neruda wrote it twice. There were—there are—no references for the magnitude and grimness of things like that.

"All right then." Wendy startled me back to the present by holding out her hand to grab the Baggie back. "Back to work. We'll see what Lucy comes up with."

I returned the bag to her and she left me to the quiet of my office.

. . .

An hour and half later my phone buzzed and startled me again, and I berated myself for being so jumpy. I saw it was my division leader, Ridgeway.

"Good morning, sir," I answered.

"Morning," he said. "You still at home?"

"No, I'm at the office."

"Good. I just got off the phone with the sheriff. We need you in Glacier again."

I paused, wondering if he knew that I'd screwed up, that there were parts of ribs still left in the soil and if he wanted me to go back.

"At the dig? Is the area clear already? I heard the line didn't hold, but I definitely want to go back out since we had to leave in such a hurry."

"No, not where you were yesterday. Something new. A boy's gone missing from Fish Creek Campground in West Glacier."

"A boy? How old?"

"Thirteen."

"And for how long?"

"I've been informed since yesterday around eleven."

"That long?"

"I'm afraid so, and a witness recalls the kid talking to someone in a vehicle, which suggests the possibility of an abduction. So we need you to process the area where he was last seen and also take a quick look at the campground where the family was staying. Chief Smith or the lead investigator will be waiting for you at headquarters to show you the exact spots."

"Okay, will do."

"You decide who to take. You're the lead."

I hung up and went into Wendy's office. She cocked her head to the side, her way of saying "What's up"?

"Ridgeway called again," I said.

"Another job?"

"Yes."

"Shit, these fires are like full moons or something—stirring all sorts of crazy stuff up."

"Yeah, I'm going to call Ray and load the van."

"Ray again?"

"Paxton worked the day before with the young firefighter. Someone in his family—I believe his sister—knew the man, so he was pretty sad about the whole thing. I figured I'd give him a break."

"All right, good luck." She stood up and followed me down the hall.

"I've got everything wrapped and ready to go to Bozeman," I said over my shoulder. "Can you make sure that everything makes it into the transport vehicle?"

"Will do. And the buckle?"

"The buckle too. Lucy might have some additional thoughts on it. She'll send it back to us once it's cleaned."

"Will do. Don't worry about a thing," Wendy said as she started heading back to her printing station in the lab. "And Gretchen, just so you know, I'm going to take some time off today. My dad's going to come help me look around for Kyle."

I turned to look at her. "That serious?" I asked.

Her shoulder twitched slightly. "Not necessarily, just want to rein him in before it gets out of control. We know a few of the spots he and his friends like to go."

I felt bad for her, but was glad she had her father's help. I had met him before—a kind-looking man, a pastor in a local church—and knew they were pretty close. I wondered what it would be like to still have a parent involved in your life that way, to be there for you or to simply ask how you were . . . what it would be like to look into their aging eyes and see love and pride instead of regret, mistrust, and blame. Don't get me wrong: I deserved everything I got, but I couldn't help but wonder about it anyway. "Hope you find him soon," I said.

"Thanks," she starting walking away, then looked back over her shoulder at me. "And G"—she used that nickname sometimes—"don't forget to eat today. You look tired."

"Yes, ma'am," I said as I punched in Ray's number and headed toward the lab's back exit, where the CSI van was parked. "I won't if you don't."

. . .

"I'm beginning to feel like we're in that movie where the guy relives the same day over and over again," I said to Monty and Ken Greeley, whom I'd met before on another case. They had just walked out of Glacier Park headquarters, a 1970s-looking Arizona brick structure about a half mile off the main road.

"You mean *Groundhog Day*?" Ray asked.

"That's it!" I said.

"Only it's looking like there's six more weeks of fire instead of six more weeks of winter," Monty said, glancing to the smoke billowing from the east.

"Hope not," Ray said. Monty nodded at Ray, then introduced him to Ken.

"Rested up from yesterday?" Monty asked us.

"Yep," I answered. Monty's eyes looked tired and his shoulders slumped with a new heaviness. Ken looked less tired, but he had that shocked, faraway stare that said *This kind of stuff doesn't happen in Glacier Park. Drownings, grizzly attacks, falls to death—yes, but not child abduction.* "Doesn't look much like you are, though. I'm guessing your day just got rolling after the grueling dig."

"I guess you could say that." Monty had forgotten to shave, and that alone told me just how serious the situation was. He rubbed the edge of his chin with his knuckles, making an intimate sound that embarrassed me for no good reason, as if I had been the one who'd kept him from shaving. I could see he was thinking about the boy. "It's been almost twenty-three hours now," he said.

"That's what my supervisor told me." I motioned to the vehicles next to us. "Shall we get to it, then?"

"Follow me." Monty headed to his SUV, hopped in, and pulled out of the lot. He drove to the main road, in through the park entrance, where lines of cars crowded the gates and waited to pay or show their passes. Even with the smoke looming like a thick curtain in the distance, tourists stayed intent on fulfilling their vacation plans. We bypassed them on a road for authorized vehicles and headed north toward McDonald Creek. Monty and Ken had already cordoned off the area and were not allowing traffic through unless the visitors were currently staying in the Fish Creek Campground or lived up Apgar Road.

We crossed the bridge where McDonald River flowed peacefully below, away from Lake McDonald. I could see it was lower than usual, the pebble-covered brown banks on each side wider than I'd seen in past years. Green bushes clung to the banks. Several harlequin ducks dove under the water, popped back up, flapped their wings, and shook water from white, gray, and bright red heads. I pulled off onto the shoulder of the road where Monty and Ken pointed for us to park. We both hopped out.

"Witness claims the boy was talking to someone in a dark truck right around here. Not sure if male or female. As you can see"—he pointed to the area secured with caution tape—"there's a bit of flattened grass that we were able to pinpoint with our flashlights, but no tread marks. Anything you can do with those?"

"We'll try to get what we can. We might be able to get a plaster, depending on how deeply they're indented into the grass. Sometimes they hit the lower soil, it's just hard to see."

"After, we'll need you to go ahead and check out the campsite, number 23A, just in case anything unusual shows up there. You won't need to fully process it, since we now have a third-party report that the kid got in the truck, so likely nothing happened there, but some prints would be helpful. Parents left the boy to go for a walk around the lake around ten thirty. Maybe someone visited him there, although we have no evidence to back that up. We need to be on the safe side, though."

"And the family?"

"We've moved them to a motel down the road this morning, but everything at the site is left pretty much the same. When they returned yesterday, they cooked a few meals and stayed the night waiting for their son to come back. Their other younger kids played in the dirt and around the area. FBI is on their way, so you may be reporting to them before too long."

"The local guys?" There were a total of ten satellite offices, or resident agencies, in Montana under the governance of the Salt Lake City Field Office, and one of them was in Kalispell with two agents. They sometimes got involved in the cases that occurred on park territory since it was federal, but usually they were busy with other issues: fraud, cybercrimes, corruption, criminal networks, terrorism, child pornography. . . .

"Both are trained in handling abductions. We've already contacted them to notify NCMEC." He was referring to the National Center for Missing and Exploited Children.

"I see . . ." I studied Monty's face for a second. I couldn't tell whether it bothered him to have to hand the case over to some agents who would not know the park or the area as well as he did. He was hiding his emotions well. The only sentiment I detected was concern—pure worry for the boy.

A heavy silence hung for a moment between us. "How's Essex?" I asked, changing the subject at the risk of sounding callous when a boy was missing. But I really wanted to know what was going on.

"From what I've heard, they're still fighting hard there. They saved some structures, but don't get your hopes up about our dig site. It's toast at this point."

"It's still worth going back to check. The few bones we left may have been low enough that the fire blew right over them and didn't incinerate them."

"Possible, but we can't get in until it's cleared to even find out. I haven't had time to speak to Lucy with the boy missing."

"I spoke to her this morning. Everything is on its way to her now. She should have it all soon. Anything in particular we're looking for at the campsite?"

"The usual. Footprints, signs of a struggle. We didn't see anything unusual, but you might pick up on something that we didn't. The boy had a 3DS—a Game Boy–type thing—about yay big," Monty made the frame of a six-by-four rectangle with the thumb and index finger of each hand. "They can't find it anywhere, so he must have taken it with him. Had his initials on it: JRC. Jeremy Richard Corey."

Ray and I went right to work getting plasters. We found some shallow indentations in a small area that was bare of grass or gravel. Two reporters on their way to the campsite saw us working behind the caution tape and pulled over to snap some photos. For the most part, I kept my head down to work, but when I looked up I saw Monty addressing the reporters, his face stern, motioning for them to leave.

When we finished with the roadside, we worked the Fish Creek Campground and took everything back to the lab again.

8

Monty

AFTER I RETURNED from speaking to Roger Kelly, Ken and I went back and questioned the parents for the third time. With the prospect of abduction, we approached the Coreys differently. We separated them and took extensive family histories of each: where they were born, who each of their parents were, who their siblings were, and so forth.

Afterward, we asked them to relocate to a motel so that Gretchen and Ray could inventory the campsite. Linda Corey had at first refused to leave in case Jeremy wandered back, but I was able to persuade her to go by stressing that Ken would stay behind while forensics worked and would be there to greet the boy.

Additionally, I had begun to complete the piles of paperwork associated with the missing minor. Without hard evidence, the search through the forests continued while notifications about Jeremy's disappearance spread to all of the Montana news bulletins. Having been presented with the possibility of abduction, we drastically widened the search beyond the network of rangers and Park Police searching for him across Glacier and began to venture outside the park, with traffic cops inspecting dark trucks and keeping eyes peeled for a teenage boy. Concerned citizens who heard the news were asked to stay on the lookout for any child fitting Jeremy's description. By joining forces with the county police and the Kalispell, Columbia Falls, and Whitefish forces, we were organizing a larger investigative team until the feds called in their agents.

By noon, a man and a woman in blue FBI garb arrived. Joe showed them the incident room and had me get them up to speed. I'd met both of them before, when a militiaman involved in a plot to blow up the local county building was on the run, suspected of hanging out up at the North Fork drainage on the northern border of Glacier, near Canada.

The woman, Ali Paige, looked like she had some Italian in her, with raven hair and olive skin. I recalled that she was from somewhere in New Jersey and her accent confirmed it. Her partner, Herman Marcus, was black, a big guy who wore hip burgundy-rimmed glasses, which made me wonder whether it was time to upgrade my boring wire-rimmed ones. He was from Reno, Nevada. Both looked to be in their midthirties. It was hard not to wonder if Herman ever received threats as an FBI agent in a white-bread state like Montana.

I told them everything we knew about the family and what we'd done once we figured out the case could be bigger than a lost boy in the woods. I showed them my paperwork, then took them to the Coreys' campsite to have a look around.

Gretchen and Ray were still working it. When we walked up to them, Gretchen glanced over and came to greet us. I introduced her to them and she said she'd found nothing so far, other than some possible small patches of tire treads from the side of the road where Roger had taken us.

"Okay," Ali said. "Take us to the motel where the Coreys are, then."

. . .

We had relocated the Coreys to the Lazy Fir, a humble place outside the town of Hungry Horse in the canyon that ran between Flathead Valley and Glacier Park. It was the only spot with a vacancy this time of year.

At the motel, Ron tried to keep his composure and remain the voice of reason for Linda, but I could see the anxiety straining his jaw, the fear like a large wave building higher and higher before the in-evitable crash. For now, though, he was holding it together. In both of their desperate, nervous eyes, however, I could see that leaving the campsite and staying at the motel felt like an act of surrender. I assured them again that it wasn't, that we would do—were doing—everything in our power to find Jeremy and return him safely to them.

But it was a hellish situation, just entering their bleak, cheap little pine-paneled room and seeing them pop up from those budget bedspreads patterned with pinecones and needles, their shell-shocked faces lighting up with hope when we came in, then sinking back into unfathomable despair. It ripped me into a hundred pieces. I felt like I was entering someone else's grotesque fever dream, only I could exit—even if I felt sick inside—and they couldn't.

The little girl, Cassie, was cranky and crying, her nose slick with snot as she threw her pink plastic Barbie convertible car at the wall and asked for Jeremy. Linda didn't even try to calm her. And Garret, the nine-year-old, just sat frozen and scared before the Nickelodeon channel, his eyes large.

"How long do we have to stay here?" Linda asked.

"For a while longer." I couldn't be any vaguer, but I didn't have an answer for them. Now that the campsite was being handled as a crime scene, whether it actually was a crime or not, it was unlikely they would be allowed back to it for some time.

I introduced them to the agents, and Linda drew in a sharp breath at the idea of needing FBI agents in general. "I know you've been through this so many times already," I offered in the calmest authoritative voice I could muster, "but Agents Marcus and Paige are going to ask you a few questions. The FBI has extensive resources, and we collaborate closely with them." I could have rattled off some of the acronyms for some of the FBI's programs or other resources—ECAP for Endangered Child Alert Program, or the one I'd already mentioned to Gretchen, NCMEC—but decided it might scare them rather than offer them solace.

Ron reached out to touch Linda's arm but stopped shy, as if he thought she might slap it away. His hand stayed in limbo, divided by the shards of sunlight filtering around the window frame, not pulling back, but not touching her. The sun caught one long fingernail on his index finger, grown out longer than the others, I presumed, for the purpose of guitar picking. I thought that if we did not find Jeremy, the rest of their lives might be suspended in midair like that. Deferred. Unable to fully commit to anything again because such loss made people numb, incapable of enthusiastic love, and confined them to a purgatory of uncertainty and unanswered questions.

Agent Herman Marcus took charge first, asking Linda Corey to come with us for yet one more interview with the FBI agents to an office behind the reception area that the motel owners had agreed to let us use. Even though Ken and I had already separated them earlier, it was still standard procedure for Ali and Herman to separate the couple again. Linda followed us, her head down, holding her arms across her chest as if trying to shield her shredded heart. The attendant gawked at us as we crossed the lobby to a small rectangular office. Ali shut the door and motioned for Linda to sit.

With the four of us crammed into the small room, I felt like we were crowding Linda, but the agents wanted me there to hear her answers, specifically to verify that they hadn't changed since earlier interviews at the campsite. I leaned back against the wall as if I could fade into it and create more space. Linda immediately began to rock back and forth on the edge of her chair. Her hair was a mess, her face blotchier than the previous day, and her eyes red and swollen. Herman pulled out his notebook and took her through the facts again, nodding and encouraging her as she spoke.

He had a no-nonsense way about him, but his soothing voice made him seem compassionate, as if he could have easily been a doctor or nurse instead of an FBI agent. Clearly, Ali knew he was a pro and automatically backed toward the wall as I had, to let him do his thing. I sensed she was relieved.

Herman asked question after question. In reference to the gaming device, he asked: "Would he have taken it with him? How often did he play it? Did he prefer to play alone or with others? Please describe it again." Linda snapped, jumping out of her seat and shoving her hands into her hair. She yanked on it as if she might actually pull clumps out. "How many times do we have to go over this? We've told you this so many times already. Find our son. Just find my son. Find that truck."

Herman sat stone still.

Ali pursed her lips for a moment and took a big, impatient breath in through her nose. She pushed off from the wall and took a step toward Linda as if she felt she needed to get the show on the road. I couldn't have agreed more, but Ali had a brusqueness about her that could set the family even more on edge than they already were. "That's exactly what we're aiming to do, Mrs. Corey. Now please, sit back down. Just a few more questions. Is there anyone in this area who knew you were here that your boy could have known?"

"No, no. No one that Jeremy would know." She slumped back into the chair, putting her face into her palms. Ali and Herman let her sit quietly. Then suddenly she peeked her eyes out from her hands and looked at them. "Unless, the only other thing I can think of," she said in a confused voice, "is that I've got an estranged uncle that came out to Montana years ago. He's kind of weird and he's never met the kids."

My ears perked up. I was surprised she hadn't mentioned him earlier.

"Weird how?" Ali asked.

"Like, wants to live off the grid. Hates the government, that kind of thing. Paranoid. In fact, I've only met him a handful of times. But, yeah, come to think of it, he did call a few weeks before we came out here. I guess he heard about Ron hitting it big with his single. Wanted to borrow some money, but I said no. We didn't really get into an argument or anything, but it wasn't exactly a pleasant conversation. I was shocked that he'd called out of the blue like that and was put off that he was asking for money, of all things. I got off the phone quickly, and I guess I was kind of short with him."

"Did you tell him you were coming out here?"

"I . . . I don't remember." She scrubbed at her cheeks with her palms. "Maybe, maybe at the beginning of the call, making polite conversation. Yeah, I do think I mentioned it, that we'd be out in his neck of the woods, visiting Glacier, but, but, I can't see how . . ."

"What is your uncle's name?"

"Minsky. Alfred Minsky. He moved out here years ago. Decades ago. My family barely mentions him. He's an embarrassment. Was tied up with some strange groups for a while. Some group called the Identity Believers, racists. He's come home back to Ohio maybe twice, but I always kept him away from the kids because, like I said, he's pretty strange."

My ears perked up. The ATF had a list of people they paid attention to—mostly conspiracy extremists, guys interested in the disintegration of the social order and in stockpiling weapons for the purpose of fending off the ever-intrusive, poison-breathing feds. Since Glacier shared the Canadian border where many of them liked to hang out, we kept an eye on the list as well.

"Alfred Minsky," Ali said, writing the name down.

"I think he lived in someplace called the Yap."

"The Yaak?" Ali asked.

"I guess, yeah, Yaak, not Yap."

"Why didn't you tell the officers"—she motioned with her pen to me—"that you have an uncle living in Montana?" She said it accusingly, and I noticed Herman cringe at Ali's insensitive tone.

"I didn't think of it. He only asked about my mom and dad, my siblings . . . but why does it matter?"

"It might not, but it's interesting that he called you asking for money."

Linda snapped her head back like a turtle. "What are you saying? That my own uncle would steal my child?"

"I'm not saying anything, but we certainly need to check out all possibilities. You said yourself that he's not a typical uncle, that you've even kept him away from the kids."

"Yeah, because he's a racist, not some, you know, pervert." Linda shook her head back and forth in a daze. "I don't understand this. It makes no sense. The Yaak? What is that?"

"It's an unincorporated community in Lincoln County, in the Kootenai National Forest. It's in the far northwest corner of Montana, north of a town called Libby, near the Idaho and Canadian borders. It's about an hour from here."

"What kind of people live there?"

"All types. Just like here, but because it's fairly remote and close to the border, it's a draw for people that want to live off the grid or are antigovernment."

"And you think it's possible that my uncle has Jeremy and that he might have taken him to this place?'

"We don't know that, but at this point, we're investigating all possibilities, including your uncle."

After we finished with Linda, we escorted her back to the room with the kids, fetched Ron, and went through the same drill. Eventually, Herman brought up the uncle and asked him some questions. He knew of Minsky, but not about him calling. When we finished and took Ron back to join his family, Ron immediately turned to Linda and addressed her with a bite of irritation: "How come you didn't tell me that your uncle called asking for money?"

"Because it didn't matter. I wasn't going to give it to him anyway." She pushed her hair behind her ear and I could see her hand was shaking. "There was no reason for me to think anything could go wrong." She paused, her brow crinkled. "I don't get it . . . what would my estranged uncle want with Jeremy?"

Everyone looked over at Ali. "We're not sure," she said. "We're just speculating at this point, covering all bases. We'll look into it and let you know what we find."

"But, but if he's with him, that's a good thing," Linda said, hope flooding her eyes. "I mean, not great, but better than some. . . . Oh, God." She put both hands over her face and started to sob. She seemed to be hanging on by a thread, upset that she'd forgotten to mention the uncle, but still confused as to why we were even discussing one of her family members as a possibility.

Suddenly the little boy, Garret, pointed the TV remote straight at Ali, Herman, and me. "Go away," he yelled at us, as if the gadget would make us dissolve, make the entire situation fade, return his family to happy normal. "Go away," he said again, this time in a softer voice.

I nodded. "We'll do that, son. We'll do that. Come on." I motioned to the door, hinting to Ali and Herman that the Coreys needed some space.

• • •

We left the room and walked toward our vehicles, leaving the fractured family in the room looking like ghosts, their eyes glassy with shock, confusion, fear, and too many unknowns. While we were there, I could tell our presence didn't really help, that they wanted us out searching, not interrogating them. But on another level, leaving them alone frightened them more. They appeared as if some alternate universe witnessed only by the severely wounded and the nearly dead might swallow them alive. I'd seen the look before in Nathan's parents' eyes when I was a teenager. It's one you never forget.

Ali and Herman slowed and started talking in hushed voices, motioning for me to continue on. It irritated me, but there was nothing I could do. A part of me was relieved to have their help and expertise, and another part of me felt like a useless appendage now, unable to do much to help Jeremy or his parents.

But I also knew that the idea of the FBI coming in and usurping cases was a myth—maybe true in the fifties and sixties, but times had changed and the Bureau had worked hard to change that image. But still, I couldn't shake the feeling that I was an outsider on my own turf. When they finished talking, they came over to my car.

"Thank you, Officer Harris. You've done a good job with the situation, with this family." Herman motioned to the room we'd just left.

Then Ali piped up. "Agent Marcus and I are going to track down this Alfred Minsky up in the Yaak, run a check on him, see if he has a record. We'd like you to stay here with the family."

I nodded. Of course, babysitting duty. I didn't mind entirely. It was obvious they were hurting and someone needed to be with them, but it seemed like a job for a victim's specialist and not the lead investigative officer of Park Police. If the feds were sidelining me, I didn't like it one bit. But for now I could deal with it, because I had other things to look into, like a pile of bones in a shallow grave near Essex. "Look," I said, "if you don't need me, that's perfectly fine. But I've got another case to work. I can stay with them for a bit, but you'll need to call in a chaplain or a victim's specialist for this. I'll give you an hour. I'll get them started on making some flyers and posters to place around the valley."

"Good idea." Agent Marcus smiled. "That will help them feel a tiny bit less helpless."

"But if you want to find Minsky," I told them, "you'll need a little help."

"How's that?"

"Last I heard, he wasn't in the Yaak."

"You know him?"

"I don't know him, but I know where he's been living. Or at least *was* living in June, but I've heard he's still there."

"How do you know this?" Ali asked.

"About two months ago, in early June, I'd been sent to the area to visit a guy who owns property up at the North Fork Road with access to the park. There had been some complaints that the man, a Mr. Chiles, had been riding an ATV on Glacier's land." Using ATVs and snowmobiles on any part of Glacier Park is strictly prohibited because they destroy vegetation, harass wildlife, cause erosion, and ruin the peaceful experience of the park for others. Landowners who share the park's boundary hate these restrictions with a passion. "I'd been asked to go remind the guy of the rules," I told them.

"I bet that went over well," Herman said.

"Not as bad as you think. He kind of looked at me like I was only a harmless ranger, not Park Police, and he didn't really seem to associate me with the feds, the real right hand of the devil, even though we actually are," I said. "Feds, I mean, not the devil. Treated me like an annoying fly buzzing by. Didn't really care or listen to what I had to tell him."

"And?" Herman asked.

"I had a look around while I waited for Chiles because he wasn't there when I arrived. I wanted to see how much of his property bordered the park, so I hiked around a bit from the park side and noticed a yurt through my binoculars near the back end on Chiles's land. You know what that is? It's a Turkish or Icelandic tepeelike structure, only there's no—"

"Of course we know what a yurt is." Ali cut me off and shook her head with annoyance.

"Just asking." I shrugged. "Not everyone does." I remembered the tan octagonal structure with a collapsible frame set back in a grove of buckskin tamaracks. "One was set up on the border of his property. When Chiles finally returned, I mentioned it to him, and he waved a hand in the air and casually explained that he'd been letting some guy shack up on his lawn as a favor. When I asked for his name, he told me: Alfred Minsky. I got the feeling Chiles didn't care for Minsky all that much and that's why he gave up his identity so easily. I took note, and when I checked on the name back in the office, I saw that he'd been listed on the AFT watch list."

"You talk to Minsky?"

"No, never saw him. Just Chiles. I warned him about the kind of fines he was looking at if they broke the rules on federal land and that he ought to keep an eye on his new guest."

"So it's Chiles's land we need to look at," Ali said.

"He's tough to track down."

"No shit. That's what off-the-grid means." She crossed her arms before her chest. "No address, no phone, no electricity bills."

"So how well you know the North Fork? Because last I heard, Minsky was still up there, hadn't been back to the Yaak."

They looked at each other, then excused themselves again to shuffle to the side and whisper a few things. When they came back over, their black boots scuffing on the gravel parking lot of the run-down motel, Ali lifted her chin to me and said, "Forget the posters. You're coming with me to find this Minsky. Hollywood here"—she motioned to Herman, and I assumed she called him that because of the fancy glasses—"he'll stay at headquarters and run the search."

I knew there was a lot to do back at headquarters: organize a press conference for the parents to speak later in the day, schedule volunteers to comb the widened grid, continue to track down known sex offenders in the West Glacier, Columbia Falls, and Essex areas, take AMBER Alert calls, and keep an eye on searches still sweeping through the wilderness by foot and by helicopter. Joe Smith would be there making sure Park Police did their jobs well and interfaced with the Incident Commander, since the case, like the fires, fell under the umbrella of the IC. As long as the fires continued to create a state of emergency, the command structure would stay in place.

Herman nodded and she turned back to me. "Before we go, can you please go back in and let the family know that someone will be coming soon?"

For a moment, her eyes looked pained.

So, I thought, she had a heart after all. "Yeah, I'll do that." I called Tara and asked if she could swing by and sit with the Coreys for a bit until we could get a victim's specialist or a chaplain to come. She agreed. I looked up at the brilliant sky, which I hadn't seen in days—at the cerulean oasis above me like a mirage, like a fake movie set; then I sighed, gathered my nerve, and headed back to the Coreys' room.

· · ·

Ali and I drove in silence, taking the Camas Creek Cutoff Road, also known simply as Camas Road, toward the North Fork of Flathead River, which courses through British Columbia, Canada, and south into Montana to form part of Glacier Park's western border. The road was built in the 1960s in the Mission 66 program—a long-abandoned effort to beef up infrastructure in the park to handle growing throngs of visitors. Most national parks were established before national highway systems were built and were not equipped to handle the post–World War II boom that had put so many cars on highways across America and brought even more tourists.

On our left, tall peaks jutted toward the sky, including Huckleberry Mountain, and on our right, we passed sprawling meadows, including McGee Meadow, where white-tailed deer and elk often grazed. Ali had a file open before her and was studying it. Finally she said, "Guy like Minsky, living like that for over thirty years. Moving from place to place in a damned yurt. Who lives like that?"

"Different sorts of people, but from what I've read, Minsky is the sort who doesn't trust the system."

"And what exactly have you read?"

"That he's been watched for buying and selling sawed-off double barrels. That he was mixed up with the Christian Identity Believers for some time after he moved out here years ago and is now hooked up with some other antigovernment types. But ironically, the more you try to wipe yourself clean of the system, the more attention you bring yourself from that very system."

"You sound like you're sticking up for the guy."

"Absolutely not sticking up for him, just know how it goes." I thought of my brother, Adam. He had been a handful his entire life and often did things outside the norm, probably outside the law. He was currently trying to run an iron-welding business in Columbia Falls. But most of the time, he had his own system of reasoning. I spent a good part of my life hating him for it, though I'd actually recently been forced to collaborate with my brother on a case I had worked. I had learned to be more tolerant of him, perhaps more understanding of his way of living.

"And how does it *go* for your average Identity Believer or neo-Nazi?" Ali asked.

I slowed down to point out a black bear on the side of the road that was nibbling some shriveled berries off some huckleberry bushes. There were hardly any to be had because of the drought, and the bear looked skinny. Ali wasn't having it. She glanced, nodded slightly, but didn't speak. I can't say I blamed her under the circumstances, although I did have to wonder if that would be her reaction even without a missing child in the picture. "Regardless of religious thoughts, of how despicable some of their beliefs are," I answered, "a lot of these folks, well, they try to live outside the financial system, try to barter, stock up on gold and whatnot. It just ends up making it harder for them to survive. So ironically, they need to take illegal jobs like trading and selling firearms, growing and selling weed . . . to make money to get by in the very system they're trying to avoid. I'm not condoning it, just explaining it."

"Not just avoid. *Destroy*. You left that out. His file said he was detained for some half-assed plot to knock over the Wells Fargo branch in Kalispell. Then they set their sights on an elaborate plan to take down the city government building. I personally know a judge in Kalispell who wore a bulletproof vest to work every day for two years—he was on their hit list for sentencing a member of their group who was picked up in the early nineties for carrying a box of pipe bombs in his trunk. One of Minsky's fellow group members. You defending that?"

"No, I told you, I'm most definitely *not* defending that." I figured I should keep my mouth shut. Although it was worth trying, tracking Minsky down seemed like a long shot. "Do you really think this guy fits the profile of a child abductor?"

"I think he fits the profile of someone who's off his rocker. Plus, you said it yourself, some of these guys end up needing money, not just to live, but to carry out their crazy antigovernment plots. With Jeremy's dad making the news for hitting it big with a few of his songs, maybe he thinks he can make a little ransom money, calling Linda out of the blue like that. Don't you agree that that was strange?"

"I do," I said.

"I'm well aware it's outside the norm, that it doesn't fit the profile of an abductor, but don't you think it's a weird coincidence? The mother of a boy who happens to be vacationing in Montana has an estranged uncle who happened to call for money several weeks before, after her husband gets a hit single playing on the radio. And now we know he's not just in the northwest part of the same state, that according to you he's closer, in the vicinity of the very park they're visiting?"

"It's strange," I agreed. "But have there been any complaints about him over the years, any incidents of lewd behavior or crimes against children?"

"No, but that doesn't mean they don't exist. Plus, like I said, the motive doesn't have to be sexual. He could have been looking for money, or thinking that he might take some sort of revenge. Years of estrangement can mess with your mind. Who knows, maybe he figured Jeremy was the ripe recruiting age for his cause. Maybe he knew he'd never get to know him unless he just took him. Maybe he's getting too old to set up and take down his yurt," she said flippantly, "and he needs a young man around to mold into a separatist, a sympathizer."

The asphalt road came to an end, and I turned north on the gravel road leading to the tiny town of Polebridge. I knew she was just speculating, but I wanted to say, *Don't you think you're making some huge assumptions without any evidence?* I decided I better not piss her off. She seemed to be just barely tolerating me in the first place, and a huge part of me hoped she was correct—that this case was as simple as an abduction by a family member. Not that it was ideal by any stretch, but, as Linda said, perhaps it was better than a stranger.

I stayed quiet as we drove toward Chiles's property. He owned a large piece of land that spread away from the North Fork River, his cabin squatting back about two hundred yards in a forest of skinny lodgepole pines and tamarack trees. The cabin looked out at a field filled with drying red Indian paintbrush and fireweed with a view of the Livingston Range. Its peaks reared up to the sky and made an impressive thirty-six-mile majestic chain from the United States to

Canada. No smoke hung over the range and light clouds laced the mountains as the wind still held the fires' dry precipitate of ash and smoke to the east.

"This is it," I said.

"A slice of heaven," Ali said. "Guess you gotta be willin' to live far away from all the conveniences if you want something this pretty."

"Pretty much," I agreed. "It's not for everyone."

"Funny"—she chuckled—"how the wacky ones are the ones willing to live out here—around all this beauty and fresh air. Too bad it doesn't breathe some sense into them."

Our plan was to ask Chiles for permission to visit Minsky's yurt, which wasn't on Glacier's access land, so we wouldn't be trespassing.

Not all of the people living in the Yaak near the northwestern Montana border were there for political reasons. And even though many were downright anarchists, some just wanted to be left alone. It was a way of life. The year-round residents lived there because they felt far away from the government, even from the post office. They plowed their own roads, hunted and fished whenever they wanted, and avoided authority. But those up in the North Fork, well, they knew they were near the park, close to federal land. They knew they might need to put up with a ranger or Park Police once in a while, even if they didn't like it.

We both stood still for a moment and took in the cabin. It was fairly crude, with thin spaces between the logs, a bitch to heat in the winter. Something about the place told me this was no summer cabin and that old man Chiles took residence in it year-round, unlike many others in the area. Clotheslines hung between two lodgepoles on the side of the house, and long stacks of freshly cut wood lined the side of the cabin. Old rusty wind chimes dangled from one corner and an old empty hummingbird feeder from the other. They framed a slanted porch that looked like it was falling apart.

We walked slowly toward the cabin, guessing we were being watched by Chiles, maybe even Minsky. Before we knocked on his dilapidated gray door, Chiles swung it open. "What'd'ya here for?" he asked me, but instantly took in Ali and her blue FBI uniform. His eyes reminded me of a rodent's, sharp and twitchy. He wore a black flannel shirt and saggy old jeans. A stringy gray-and-black beard that resembled Spanish moss dangled from his chin.

"Sir, we'd like a word with you, just a moment, if you don't mind."

"Hell yeah, I mind. What makes you think I have a moment?" he said, and slammed the door in our faces.

"Guess he doesn't really want us to answer that," I said.

Ali glared at Chiles's door and held up her fist to knock again. I could see her jaw tense with anger. I reached over and gently pushed her arm down. "I've met him before. Let me handle this, okay?"

Something told me she did not like taking direction from anyone, least of all Park Police, but I could see her turn it over in her head for a second. She dropped her arm and gave a curt nod.

"Chiles," I yelled without knocking. "We're only here to ask you a few questions about your neighbor. Nothing to do with you, nothing at all."

"Ain't got no neighbor," he called back.

"I'm talking about Minsky. Just a few questions, that's all."

"He in trouble?"

"No, no, he's not."

"I don't believe shit coming from the likes of you. I ain't stupid. What the hell you bringing the feds to my place for?"

"It's not what you think. Really. We're simply looking for a missing boy. You've heard helicopters flying around?"

"A few. 'Cause of the fires."

"Yes, but also for a missing boy."

"What does that have to do with Minsky?"

"Open up and we'll fill you in."

Ali and I waited by the door as Chiles considered what I'd said. We had been standing there a good half minute when Ali shifted impatiently in her stance, lifted her chin, and was about to say something, but stopped when the door clicked. She took a step back as it swung open. Chiles stood in the dim light of the cabin.

"Can we come in, Mr. Chiles?" Ali said sweetly, in a tone I'd not yet heard.

He looked down at her, his chin lifted in distrust. He didn't answer.

"Just a few words," I added. Dealing with suspicious mountain men was nothing new to me, and I sensed it wasn't new to Ali either, but I could tell her patience was running thin. She wanted to find this boy, we all did, and the urgency was building with each passing moment.

Chiles finally backed up and let us enter. I looked around and saw the log walls lined with deer, elk, and moose heads with dull, dead eyes. Dioramas of game birds—grouse and pheasant sprouting long, dusty tail feathers—sat on two wooden side tables. The cabin smelled pungent, like smoke, bitter coffee, and old clothes that had been drenched in sweat one too many times.

"What do you want?" He motioned for us to sit at a small table near the rustic kitchen. A big, colorful bird—some kind of parrot, alive and watchful—perched on one of the backs of the four chairs, its exotic orange, blue, and yellow tail swooping away from the table. Ali eyed it as she took a seat. I sat down too. "Nice parrot," I said, noting the irony of the beautiful bird held up in a dingy cabin full of mounted wild game. "Is it a particular type?"

"Nah, just a parrot," he said.

"Pretty," Ali said.

"Want to let 'em perch on your shoulder?"

"No thanks," she said. "Where does that thing poop?"

"Around." Chiles waved, then grabbed a round, daisy-colored container of disinfecting wipes—the cheeriest and most colorful item in the entire cabin—off his counter and brought it over to the table. "These come in handy."

Ali nodded. "I see."

"If you're lying to me and this is about ATVing or something"—

Chiles pulled out the fourth chair and took a seat—"I haven't done any of that, so you can turn around and leave."

"It's definitely not about that," I said.

"Like he said, it's about a missing boy," Ali offered. "One we believe is related to Alfred Minsky."

"Gunner?"

"Yeah, I guess. That what you call him?"

Chiles nodded. "Name he got in Vietnam. It stuck."

"We thought he might be able to help. We understand he's been staying on your land."

"Wonder where you heard that." Chiles turned his head and glared at me almost comically.

"We just want to ask him a few questions, that's all." Ali set her hand on the table, and as soon as it settled, the bird dove over and pecked—or rather, jabbed—her wrist. "Bitch." She pulled it back quickly, cradled it in the other, and slid them both under the table while the bird strutted back to his perch.

"It's a he, not a she, and he don't like strangers," Chiles said, one corner of his mouth slanting up into a wry smile, obviously enjoying the show.

"Thanks for the warning," she said, pulling her hand back out from under the table and shaking it. "So, what about Minsky?"

"He's gone."

I glanced at Ali, then back to Chiles. "Gone? When?"

"Left a few days ago."

"Where'd he go?"

"Couldn't tell ya. Have no clue."

"He have anyone with him?"

"Not that I saw."

"Can you tell us why he was here in the first place?" I asked.

"Said he needed a place to stay for a while."

"And why did you feel the need to oblige?" Ali asked. "You two good friends?"

"I wouldn't call us that. Like I said, we were in Vietnam together, and let's just say I've owed him a favor or two for some time and it wasn't until recently that he's come calling for one."

"What kind of favor?"

"Hell if I know what kind. The usual kind—guy gets down and out and needs a place to stay. Glad it was only that and not much more. Old man like me doesn't need any trouble."

"What makes you think he's trouble?"

"I don't," he said, but I could see in the shift of his eyes—how he looked away to the window—that he did. "Anything out of the routine at my age can be trouble." He grinned, showing rotten tea-colored teeth. I sensed we weren't going to get a whole lot out of the guy.

"You notice anything strange about his comings and goings while he's been living here?"

"Can't say that I do. I hardly noticed him much at all. He kept to himself, way on the back end of my property. It's not like he came over for evening cocktails." The bird cawed loudly, and both Ali and I flinched. Chiles laughed, reached into his pocket, pulled out a peanut, and held it in his slightly quivering palm before the parrot's yellow beak. "There you go, Crook," he crooned.

"Crook?" Ali lifted an eyebrow.

"'Cause of his beak. It's curved, crooked."

"How long did Minsky say he was going to stay?" she asked.

"Didn't really. Just said awhile. Turns out he was here about two months."

"And you don't know why he left? Because it's important, Mr. Chiles."

"I told you, I don't. One minute he was here, the next he was gone. Didn't even say good-bye or thank you."

"That's kind of odd," I said. "Why wouldn't he thank you?"

Chiles pulled out another peanut for Crook, who was spilling bits of shells all over the wooden floor from the first one, then sighed dramatically. "You guys really don't get it, do you?"

"Get what?"

"That guys like Minsky just want to be left alone. It don't mean they've done something wrong. They just don't want to be bothered, especially by the likes of you. He probably left because he simply thought it was time. Hell, maybe he knew you came by." Chiles lifted his chin to point to me. "Maybe you spooked him. That'd be enough to drive a guy like Minsky off."

"What's there to be spooked about?" Ali asked, absentmindedly placing her hands back on the table. Crook dove over and got her other hand, and she let out a few more choice epithets. Chiles simply shrugged and smiled wryly.

"Mr. Chiles." I repeated her question. "Agent Paige asked you what there is to be scared about?"

"The hell I know." Chiles shrugged.

"You mind if we take a look at where he set up?" I asked.

"Help yourself."

. . .

We left Chiles to his cabin and his exotic bird and drove the access road as far as it would take us. Chiles's property stretched back into the woods for at least a mile and a half, and we were able to drive about two-thirds of the way before having to stop and walk the rest.

"That bitch went after me twice," Ali said after she shut the car door.

"It's a male," I reminded her.

"Whatever," she said. "It didn't need to do that."

"No, it did not," I agreed.

"And Mr. Handi Wipes enjoyed it."

I was beginning to gather that she liked to give people nicknames, even if she was the only one who used them. We walked, taking in the forest—the chipmunks scurrying in the brush off to the side of the path, the sky beginning to turn from blue to milky white, since the high smoke from the east had begun to spread back over just during the short time we were in the cabin.

When we got to the general area I remembered spotting the yurt, it didn't take long to find it. Dead yellowed grass suffocated under the round Turkish structure, which lay flattened on the forest floor. A fire pit was nearby, encircled by medium-size tan rocks that reminded me of the skull we'd found the day before. *The day before.* It felt like a week had passed.

"Gone, all right. Didn't leave much here." I said. "What now?"

"I think it's strange that he's gone. Don't you?"

"Guys like him, could be any number of reasons for leaving. Two months might just be his limit anywhere."

"Might be," Ali said. "But I don't like it. How did he get this thing back here? It's definitely bigger than a tent."

I pointed to the ground off to our side. "Looks like he just did a little off-road driving. Looks like something big, maybe a truck with a flatbed. Mr. Kelly said he saw some sort of dark-colored truck. Should we get some plasters?"

Ali considered that for a moment. "Yeah," she said. "We should definitely do that."

9

Gretchen

Wᴇɴ ʀᴀʏ ᴀɴᴅ I were back at the lab, Ray went straight to his station to finish treating the scraps of tire impressions we had managed to pull while I put a call in to Lucy in Bozeman to see how things were going with the bones. If the trip went smoothly, she should have had the packages by noon and had the rest of the afternoon to examine the evidence. I knew Monty would be calling her as well, but I wanted to get the information myself. Monty would be tied up with efforts to find the boy, and the excavation had gotten under my skin. I wouldn't be able to settle my nerves without hearing Lucy's conclusions.

"The skull," she told me. "The sagittal suture and coronal suture are not fused, which means this was a young person."

"I noticed that. I was hoping I was incorrect."

"Unfortunately, you were correct. It belongs to a sub-adult."

I'd met Lucy once before, when I attended a lecture she gave at MSU on forensic anthropology. Ray, Paxton, and I went, leaving Wendy in case anything came up locally. Ray had teased Lucy about being like the gal on the TV show called *Bones*, although Lucy was on the large side with short, curly hair and looked somewhat matronly. She had cracked up at Ray's suggestion and commented that the *only* difference between her and the TV star was that the star made a lot more money and could afford a better hairstylist and a penthouse in LA.

"Do you have a range?" I asked now.

"I do," Lucy said. "Judging by the skull sutures, which are slightly fused, this skull belongs to an older adolescent or younger teen. The development and union of the separate bone parts is not complete. For example, the tibia and fibula have partially fused growth plates. All of these things plus a few others, like the size of the clavicle, tell me this is an adolescent anywhere from ten to fifteen years old. Skull shape and pelvis tell me it's a male. White."

"And you can tell this because . . . ?"

"Orthognathous shape, the way the teeth and the jaws don't slope or angle outward. White faces are flatter than black. What, it surprises you? A white person in Montana?"

"Ha," I said. "Just making sure. This part of my training was a long time ago."

"Here's the catch, though," Lucy said more seriously. "I'm sure you noticed the caved-in gap, almost a cleave, on the left side of the temporal bone above the left ear opening—a large enough chunk that makes me think this youngster didn't meet a very cheerful ending."

"What could have caused it?"

"Something substantial, firm, sharp. Something able to cause a cleaved separation: possibly something like a crowbar, but more likely, I hate to say, an axe. Falling on a rock or something of that nature would have crushed the skull differently. And a baseball bat, a fist, or the butt of a rifle or a hammer all would have left a more rounded depression and wouldn't have caused such a cleave." An image of a fire iron slamming into Per's skull flashed through my head and a shudder went through me. I refocused on what Lucy was saying. "It's the left temporal region that has been affected and that's a pretty easy place to fatally injure someone anyway, but whatever crushed through this skull was sharp and hard enough to not only create blunt-force trauma but cleave the skull and break through the frontal bone, the temporal bone, the sphenoid, and even part of the parietal bone."

I paused before going on, taking it in. Lucy waited. I could hear a tapping sound and wondered if she was rapping her pen on her desk. "Okay," I said. "What about the time frame, the year?"

"Harder to say," Lucy sighed. "I'm going to need some more time to run the soil samples to try to figure out how long these bones have been buried. I can tell you from a glance and experience that it's been longer than five years." She paused before continuing. "I have to say, you're very interested in this one. Usually I just hear from the investigator, since you guys are busy with processing other stuff."

"Yeah, the dig was hard. The ribs and all. I felt awful having to rush it, and I'm no expert like you. I just feel a bit responsible."

"You don't need to worry. The ribs, in this case, weren't so vital. You got the skull and pelvis; if you'd gotten the ribs over those, I'd be fuming. So don't worry, you did great under the circumstances. I have all I need here and you saved me a trip to the Flathead."

"When do you think you'll have some ideas about the soil?"

"Soon. Maybe by the end of the day or tomorrow."

"Then what?"

"Then the bones will go to Texas. There they'll see if they can extract physical as well as mitochondrial DNA, but the center prioritizes easy identifications, remains that are relatively fresh or a family connection is already suspected. As you probably know, Gretchen, colder cases with no leads do not take precedence. If you go back even twenty years, there are literally hundreds of thousands of families who have loved ones that are missing. They'll give these remains a profile number after identifying the DNA. Then they'll check it against the database of samples that have been sent in."

I knew that in 2005, the U.S. Attorney General's office formed a Missing Persons Task Force to create the National Missing and Unidentified Persons System, or NamUs, and launched a searchable database in 2007. In 2009, the cross-searchable database system that would automatically match the missing with the dead if the missing had been entered in the first place was formed. All of us in forensics followed these sort of breakthroughs. I thanked Lucy for the information, hung up, then headed to Wendy's office to see if she'd downloaded all the photos from the gravesite yet. Wendy's father was coming out of her office, jangling his keys in his hand.

"Oh, hello, Mr. Combs. Good to see you."

"Nice to see you too, Gretchen. How've you been?"

"Been good. And you? Any word?" I asked, referring to their hunt for his grandson.

"No, we haven't found him." He looked down with disappointment. "But I need to get back to Hungry Horse. I have a community fellowship group to lead." I knew Mr. Combs was a pastor at a small church in Hungry Horse and he'd just returned from a meeting in Great Falls. Wendy was proud of her father, of the work he'd done to bring goodwill and faith to rural communities in northwest Montana. Her mother had died from cancer when she was an adolescent and she was an only child. "Wish I could help her continue to look, but it will have to wait a few hours. It's not like he's never pulled this before. He's probably just holed up at some new friend's house." He gave me a faint smile and we said good-bye.

Wendy sat at her desk with her head in her hands, pressing the bottoms of her palms into her eye sockets. I gently tapped on the door. "Need some coffee? Tea?" I offered.

She looked up, dropped her hands, her eyes tired and a little red from rubbing them. "Oh, hi," she said. "No, thanks."

"No luck, huh?" I wondered where they'd gone to look. Wendy had shared with me several months ago that Kyle had begun shooting up. She'd found needle tracks on the inside of his arms, and he'd recently gotten tattoos up and down them, she figured, to disguise the marks.

"No. We looked in all the usual places, went to several of his friends' houses, their garages, down by their hangout near the river, near the old bridge. There's one place though, we didn't go. I . . ." She paused and looked to down to her side at the floor by her desk and bit her top lip. "I don't know, I just couldn't take my dad there. Couldn't bear the thought of finding Kyle at such a place while he was with me. I'm going to have to go there myself."

"For goodness' sake, where?" I asked.

"You know the abandoned, boarded-up hotel on the south end of town, the Ridgeline?"

I knew exactly where she was talking about. It was known for housing druggies and runaways. There'd been a drug bust there two months before. Several youngsters had taken over one of the filthy rooms and almost burned the place down trying to cook some meth. Anyone looking for drugs could probably go there and pick up some nasty concoction.

"I'll go with you," I said.

Wendy looked at me. "No, no, I know you have work."

"It's okay," I said. "I'll go with you." I remembered the photos of the place. There was no way I could let her go there alone.

• • •

Wendy and I drove to the south of town, where the streets had a lazier feel and the houses turned from gentrified to ramshackle, some of them clearly abandoned. I felt a twinge of unease as we parked in front of the dilapidated, empty hotel. It's not that I hadn't seen a fair share of shitholes in my line of work, because I had: rodent-infested sheds, slime- and trash-filled ditches, scuzzy basement meth labs in shabby houses and garages, derelict apartments, drained swampy sloughs, run-down warehouses, musty crawl spaces, and dusty attics. It's that this time, it felt entirely different. We weren't going in with our hazmat suits and the police backing us. We were simply going as two concerned women looking for a screwed-up teenager. Still, there was something else edging up my spine, some vague notion that I couldn't quite identify.

The heat from the pavement radiated to the soles of my shoes the second we stepped out. Wendy and I quietly shut our car doors and looked at each other. "Are you sure you want to come in with me?" she said.

"Come on," I said. "We're already here. This is nothing compared to some of the creepy places I've worked. You're just not used to it—always tucked away in your clean lab studying prints," I teased her, trying to get her to smile. She gave me a faint one, but I could tell she was worried about finding her son inside.

Weeds reached up through the cracks in the parking lot, and dirty dried leaves, cigarette butts, used flattened paper cups, candy wrappers, and other trash littered the area. Some of the doors remained boarded up, though and one leading to the main part of the hotel had been pried off, the planks dangling loosely to its side. It looked like you could enter through it if you wanted.

"Should we knock?" Wendy whispered.

"I don't think so," I said. "I think we just go in." The lock on the door had been broken, so I pushed it open and took a step through, partly wishing we'd brought our gear so we wouldn't be exposed to any chemicals. I knew that the cops periodically came, cleared the place out, and reboarded it up. But they couldn't monitor it on a daily basis, and the homeless and the drug-addicted simply moved back into different parts of the huge, sprawling complex, which spanned an entire block.

We gingerly entered a dark cavelike hallway. The ceiling was high and the hallway wide, but I felt claustrophobic anyway as we were met with a mixture of musty, stale, and rancid smells, presumably piss, pot, and other chemicals. As my eyes adjusted, I made out broken brass lamp fixtures hanging from the hallway walls. In some areas, the ceiling was caved in and drywall and plaster hung down like spilled guts. I hoped it held and didn't come crashing down upon us at any minute. Trash littered the hallway and the dirty carpet squished under our feet as we slowly walked.

When we got to the first few rooms, the doors gaped open and we peeked in. Thin cracks of bright afternoon light sliced in through the boarded-up windows and dust floated in the beams, exposing old, broken mattresses and piles of trash swept into the corners. "Nobody in this one either," I said to Wendy, her face looking ghostly in the dark gloom.

We continued down the hall and eventually rounded a corner, went down another long hall, pushed open cracked doors, and peered into more empty rooms. One had several blankets scattered around like it had been used the night before to sleep in, but no one was there.

We kept checking rooms and finally, at the end of the hall, we came to what must have been the lobby at one time. Several shopping carts full of blankets and other junk stood in the corners and some couches and ripped-up armchairs crowded the side walls. Bottles of liquor and cans of beer were scattered on the floor, and a sweaty, musty smell permeated the room. On the couches were several dark shapes—bodies, I thought. People.

I heard Wendy take a sharp breath. She pressed her hand on her breastbone as if she was stopping herself from going forward.

"Come on," I whispered. "It's okay. If he's here, we just take him home. If he's not, well, then we keep looking." We slowly stepped over something sticky, crunched broken glass, when suddenly we heard a mumble from the corner. "Hey," the voice said, slurring. "Whaz fuckin' up?"

He sounded young, like a teenager, and I felt a sadness course through me. We didn't answer. I thought about leaving, grabbing Wendy and leading her straight out as fast as I could. Every part of me wanted to run. This was crazy, we shouldn't have come to this hellhole. But I knew I couldn't leave. I had to be strong for her, and a part of me didn't want to go, like a motorist who can't look away from an accident. Still, that unidentifiable something else squirmed inside me. I briefly wondered if it was fear, but I'd seen far worse, so it couldn't be. This was different, I thought. These bodies were not dead; they seemed dead, but they were moving, breathing and drugged up, and I certainly wasn't used to that. As morbid as it may sound, I was used to the dead: people burned up in meth lab explosions, women and sometimes children beaten to death by raging spouses or parents, people shot in drug deals gone wrong.

We poked our way through the dim light using the flashlights on our phones. I shone mine on the couch where two bodies—a couple—lay tangled up with each other, and the girl put her hand before her eyes and said, "Hey," when the light hit her young face. She looked no more than sixteen. I moved the beam so I could see the other person's face, an acne-scarred, greasy-haired male who looked like he was in his midtwenties.

"Not him," I said to Wendy. I knew what Kyle looked like because I'd met him before at the office and at her house one time when she had me over for dinner.

"Not here either," Wendy said after flashing her light on a boy slouched in one of the old easy chairs.

We heard a low moan from the next room and the girl who had said "hey" yelled like an angry older sister for the guy to shut up. He began to moan even louder. I looked at Wendy. "Does it sound like Kyle?"

"Honestly, no, but I don't know." She sounded scared to death.

"Let's check it out." I walked toward the moan, to the next room, an even bigger area with a high ceiling. Boards hung across the large front windows, but streaks of light carved up the dark floor. Several more bodies in sleeping bags stretched across the floor and others were lying on old run-down, bug-infested furniture. The moaning boy sat crouched in the corner on the floor and Wendy shone her light on him.

It wasn't Kyle. Kyle had dark hair and this boy had wavy blond hair. Like Per. Something turned in my stomach. The boy had a fat split lower lip and swollen eyes. He was holding his stomach and rocking back and forth. There was a puddle of slime on the floor next to him as if he'd recently thrown up.

After Wendy shone the light in his face, he began to wail and moan louder, a low and achy sound that reminded me of shifting, groaning ice. And then it hit me what was bothering me. My life could have turned out exactly like these troubled teens. After I left Norway, there were times when I swung from extremes, going from studying, doing everything to march steadily forward with purpose—classes, exams, an internship, and eventually a job—to nearly tossing it all away, to fantasies of self-destructing in some suicidal act. I'd never taken to heavy drinking or gotten into drugs, but in my darkest moments, I'd seriously considered jumping off the Aurora Bridge in Seattle and had driven out to it a number of times to sit in my car and gather the courage, but I could never shut my mind completely down. Always, my mind kept turning. I'm not a religious person. For me, there wasn't anything better on the other side, unless I considered complete blankness better, and trust me, sometimes I did. But for me, tiny, microscopic pieces of hope always resided in the here and now, and even if I had to find them like pieces of lint on a broad, fraying piece of fabric, that's what I somehow always came to do.

"Come on, Wendy," I said. "He's not here. Let's go. Let's get out of here."

"Okay," she said, and followed me out.

When we exited the complex, I shielded my eyes and squinted. It was like coming out of a movie theater in the middle of the afternoon—a horror movie. We got into the hot car and sighed.

"That sucked," Wendy said, wiping the sweat off her forehead with her hand.

"Yeah, it did. I'm glad he wasn't one of them."

"I can't believe, I just can't believe it's come to this. I'm looking for my child in . . ." She choked up and couldn't finish, just lifted her chin to the door we exited, her eyes tearing up.

"I know. I know. But, if it's any consolation, he wasn't in there."

"But where is he then?"

I didn't know what to say.

"That boy, in Glacier? Could, could Kyle also . . . ?"

"No," I said firmly. "That boy is younger. Kyle's just with some friend somewhere. He'll turn up. But if you feel this time is different from what he's done before, then you should report him missing."

"No, it's not really different. He's been gone this long before." Wendy continued to search my eyes, though, wanting for me to say something more.

"I'm sure he'll turn up," I said.

She nodded and started the car. We had to get back to the lab. I saw that I'd already missed several calls, one of them from my boss. Before I called back, I tried to settle my own nerves. I felt shaken too, and the sensation that there existed in me something more than just empathy for Wendy and her situation still clung.

No, it wasn't fear—what I felt was more akin to embarrassment or shame. I was shaken with a familiar twisting, acidic sensation in the pit of my stomach and a pinching at the base of my lungs. It made me feel as if I was somehow betraying someone or something. Because, I thought, on some distorted level, I felt guilty for not being them. Whatever those young kids had done might or might not compare to my past. Whatever troubles drove them to drugs and misery and dark places probably weren't any worse than the darkness I experienced, continue to experience daily; yet I never did—and continue to try not to—succumb to it. My father used to say I was bullheaded and stubborn—that when I wanted something, I couldn't let go of it. He wasn't entirely correct. When I wanted death, I couldn't do it. Even though I woke up daily as Prometheus chained to my own rock of guilt, I still refused to completely let it crush me, to prevent me from carrying on.

But I wasn't sure I deserved *not* to succumb to it, to carry on like I did and do—to live like a regular working professional in America. I couldn't help but feel on some level that I should have been one of those wrecked people in there. I should have self-destructed long ago. In some way, seeing such misery—such self-obliteration—made me feel like I hadn't done enough penance myself. I didn't deserve to end it all, but I didn't deserve the pockets of resolve I had scraped together to keep going, to make a life as a forensic scientist.

I looked out the window for a second, at the bright, blinding day, and closed my eyes to shake it all away. Coronas of red worms bloomed and squirmed behind my eyelids. Then I held up my phone and said to Wendy, "Excuse me. I've got to call the boss."

. . .

Fifteen years earlier, two days before it happened, Per and I had gone cross-country skiing with our dad. We were out of school for Christmas and Pappa had taken some time off from work at Nordea Bank, where he managed investor relations. Mamma had taken the train to Oslo for the day to visit our aunt, Tanta Britta, and Pappa suggested we gather our gear and ski the bay, since it was so unusual to be able to ski where we lived and was possible only because we were experiencing one of the coldest winters in a long time. A recent snowfall had covered the fjord and all the local lakes in several feet of snow.

The night before, Pappa had told us that he was going to wake us while it was still dark out, which isn't hard to do in the south of Norway in December, since the sun doesn't spread over the land until after nine a.m. Sure enough, it was still dark when he got us up, and we ate breakfast while he examined the map. We drove to the bay, passing the Park Hotel and Knut Steen's huge lit-up Hvalfangstmonumentet, a statue of a great whale with a Viking ship riding onto it. The whalers row the boat, while the one in front rises tall and proud, holding his spear to demonstrate victory and power. We parked by a huge boatyard and watched as the pearly hue of dawn spread across the bay. It was silent in early morning over the holidays with the formation of ice over the water.

Huge icicles hung from the large rocks on the coastline, and behind us, the town looked cozy draped in fresh snow and Christmas decorations. Narrow rectangular windows glowed yellow from inside lamps, and while a part of me simply wanted to be back in our warm house with the fire on, another part of me thrilled to be included in something my father and brother were doing. Often the two of them went out fishing and said I couldn't come, that I should stay home and keep Mamma company, that fishing was a "guy thing."

We put on our gear outside the car, and Pappa started to explain a few things to us. "You'll both stay behind me. If I fall through, which

I won't—the chances are slim—you will throw the rope you've got in your rucksack." Pappa was addressing Per, pointing to my brother's chest, where he wore a daypack with an abundance of straps that doubled as a life jacket in case we went through. I wore one too, but Pappa wanted to make sure Per understood because he was the older, bigger, stronger one and would be able to pull him out. On our packs, we also had two screwdriver-like tools attached to the pack's shoulder straps.

"What are these for?" I asked.

"If you fall in, you just pull yourself out with those, change your clothes and head on home," he said as if plummeting through the ice and hauling ourselves out with ice picks was no big deal. Just carry on like penguins or seals.

I must have looked frightened because Pappa smiled and said, "It's just a precaution. Nothing is going to happen. Just stay behind me. I've been reading sea ice for a long time. Sea ice is different from freshwater, like at the ice hall. It's flexible, so you'll be able to feel it move. You know, the movement of the sea."

"Cool," Per said.

"Yes, sea ice is interesting. Denser water sinks beneath the colder water, which has formed the ice, and when that happens, it expels the salt, forming a layer of really salty water below the ice, which then sinks and makes powerful currents. The Arctic thermohaline circulation. You've learned about such currents in school, yes?"

I shook my head while Per said, "Of course."

"Good, 'cause these powerful currents help drive ocean currents across the globe. They circulate warm and cold water around all the oceans and have a major impact on the earth's climate and weather patterns. This is why shrinking polar ice caps will cause huge disruptions."

"How thick is it?" I asked.

"About fifteen to twenty centimeters."

Again, he read my shocked expression. I had been picturing meters of solid ice beneath where we planned to go.

"Ah, Gretch, fifteen to twenty is good," he said. "Enough to drive a car over."

Per looked at me like I was only five and shouldn't even be out with them if I was going to keep asking such stupid questions. I tried to assume a braver, more nonchalant air, lifting my chin to make myself taller.

"We'll be okay," Pappa reminded me, grinning and excited to get going. He patted my shoulder. "We'll be just fine."

. . .

We were just fine that day skiing with our father, and that evening snug in our house with Mom home from Oslo. We went to bed exhausted but happy. I took a warm bath in the bathroom, then brushed my teeth before the mirror. Per pounded on the door for me to hurry. "What?" I opened the door.

"I want to brush my teeth and you're taking forever."

"Just come in, but shut the door," I told him, wanting to keep the tropical feel of the warm, humid air around as long as possible.

He closed it, grabbed his toothbrush, and looked at me. "Want to go again tomorrow?"

"Go where?"

"On the ice?"

"Dad has to work tomorrow. *Det er Mandag.*" It's Monday.

"*Uten han,*" Per spoke through the suds and around the toothbrush in his mouth. Without him.

I stared at him in the mirror, watched him work his teeth, his mouth set in a growl so he could reach his gums, a wave of blond falling across his forehead. If I said no, he'd bug me, and I didn't want to seem weak. I considered that if he was asking me to go instead of one of his buddies, I must have done well enough to impress him. My tired thighs reminded me of how I took extra-long strides to keep up with them, my poles hitting the hard floor of ice beneath the powder, my breath fast and steady in the cold air.

"Sure," I said. "Where would we go?"

"Same place. It's just a little longer walk down there."

"Walk? Mom could drive us."

"No, she can't know."

"Why not?"

"She'd say no. So would Pappa. There's no way they'd let us go on the ice alone."

"Then why do you want to do it?"

"Just because . . ." He spit toothpaste into the sink and turned the water on to wash it away, then placed his toothbrush back in the holder, wiped his mouth with a hand towel, and smiled. "Just because it will be fun. And it's Christmas break. Who wants to sit around here doing nothing? Besides, didn't you hear Pappa? He said that if you keep going farther, you can sometimes reach the ice edge and sometimes it's a straight cut and you can go right to the edge. That sounds so cool, and I want to see that, don't you?"

I shrugged.

"What? You afraid?"

"No," I said. It was like this with him. I wanted a better, wiser, quicker comeback, but they never came when I needed them. Always after, when it was too late. He was the quick-witted one, not me. "But what do we tell Mamma?"

"That we're going skiing around the school fields. She doesn't need to know it's in the bay."

"Okay then," I said, not really sure if I had any desire to go or not, but I knew the last thing I wanted was to disappoint my older brother.

• • •

The dirt road to Alfred Minsky's yurt site ended at the edge of a creek where the bedrock shone in pastel and terra-cotta colors, and the shallow stream caught splinters of sunlight dappling through the spindly lodgepole pines. On the other side stretched a game trail—mostly elk, which I could tell by the scallop-shaped scat and the size of the hoofprints—that led to a clearing where the yurt had stood. Monty led Ray and me there; otherwise, it would have been difficult to find.

When I had called Ridgeway back after leaving the derelict hotel with Wendy, he asked me to head to the North Fork immediately for another possible lead on the missing boy. As soon as Wendy and I returned, Ray and I packed up and drove north. When we arrived at the spot, I saw that Monty had hung some tape around the perimeter when he'd been working with Agent Paige earlier.

"If you can, let's make this quick." Monty said.

I sensed he was cranky. He paced around the edge of the site and looked at his watch repeatedly as if he'd had too much coffee. He had mentioned that he and the agent drove back to headquarters; then she had insisted he drive back out to Polebridge to meet us at the only store in the area, Polebridge Mercantile, to lead us to the spot. She stayed back with her partner to keep working on the case. Monty was clearly irritated at having to drive up again and babysit us in an area with limited cell service while time slipped away.

It was quiet out in the woods, the silence a stark contrast to the dig we had worked the day before, with the fire raging in the distance and the backhoe clearing trees. The fires still burned on the other side of the park, but the wind blew the dense smoke eastward, away from where we were in the North Fork area. Ray and I got right to work, measuring tracks, getting fiber samples, and lifting shoe prints from the soil. Monty supervised us for about ten minutes, then announced he was heading out, back to headquarters where he could be of more use. "Let me know what you find," he said to me. "You know your way back to the van?"

"Yeah, no problem."

"Okay then," Monty turned and started to hike back to his car. I thought for a second. I didn't want to keep bringing up the grave when a child was the number one priority, but our jobs remained our jobs. "Monty," I called. "Just a second."

Monty stopped, turned, and waited for me.

"I know you're in a hurry to get back, but I just wanted to ask if you've spoken to Lucy yet?"

Monty shook his head. "Not yet. That's one of the reasons I want to get back. No cell service out here is making it hard to work. The radios aren't good for calls to Bozeman."

"I spoke to her this afternoon."

"And?"

"I was right. The skeleton belongs to a sub-adult. Probably from ten to fifteen years old. White male."

Monty glanced into the trees to our side. They created a collage of shadows. A breeze was beginning to collect, and the tops of the trees rustled like soft ocean waves. Then he looked back at me, rubbing the back of his neck like a farmer, and I wondered if that's what he did when he got anxious. "What else did she say?"

"That there was blunt-force trauma to the head. The left temporal lobe has a large cleave in it."

"Does she have any idea from what?"

"Don't know that yet, but something sharp and hefty, like an axe or a hatchet. She's going to send the bones to Texas. To the center there."

I could see the disappointment in Monty's face as he realized that it was going to take some time to get an ID, if we could get it at all.

"As you probably know, the center puts together a DNA-collection kit with swabs and appropriate storage packaging for family members of the missing, which it sends out free of charge to the police and sheriff's departments across the country. Of the missing around here, it would be good to see who's submitted. That way, if a match doesn't come up, we can perhaps see if some of the families that haven't yet submitted would be willing to."

"I agree. I'll call Lucy as soon as I get within range."

"Sounds good."

Monty considered what I'd told him. He stood in the dappled shade of some pine trees beaten by mountain pine beetle infestations wors-

ened by drought and mild winters. The tall pines stood like a large congregation of skinny spires worshipping the sky. Shadows from the trees
darkened half his body, and broken spears of sunlight illuminated the
other side, giving the impression that he was comprised of separate
people. Monty had always been the calm one, always in control. And
it wasn't that he wasn't now; it was just that he seemed slightly off his
game, like a dark brew was being stirred in him along with the gentle
sway of the trees.

I knew that he had a reason to care more than most about the
bones of a sub-adult found in the ground from years before, and also
reason to worry more than most about a missing teen in the park. He'd
never told me about his childhood friend, but I'd heard it through the
law enforcement grapevine. Those sorts of things got around, which is
why I'd never breathed a word to anyone about my hideous past. I don't
see why I should; it would lead only to endless gossip, fearmonger-
ing and finger-pointing. I would become marginalized once again and
might even lose my position. I'd become trapped once again by what I'd
done. I'd worked too hard to break free from those chains, and had no
intention of putting them back on.

"I'm going to have more time to work the case now that the FBI are
on board for the boy," he said, looking less than relieved, then checked
his watch again. "I better fly."

"Yeah," I agreed. "Me too."

. . .

Afterward, in the great shifting of the ice—in the exquisite sorrowful
moan of it—I came to believe that I was being warned. That if I'd just
listened more closely, it would have held secrets, instructions for me
for that night to somehow avoid what was to come, and Per would have
been saved. My family would have been saved.

The next morning, by the time we reached the edge of the bay near
the silent boatyard, my mouth was already dry. Per began to put on his
boots and skis while I drank from my water bottle.

"Save some of that. We're going to ski farther than we did with Pappa."

I looked at him in the flat light. The sheet of ice covered by white snow stretched out for miles and was broken only by small islands dotted with pine trees. Per finished putting on his gear and was impatiently waiting for me. "Hurry, Gretch, we don't know how long this will take. We may need most of the day and it's getting dark around three thirty now."

My cold fingers fumbled with the laces on my ski boots. He was right, of course. The sun rose late and set early, around three p.m., making the days very short. We were lucky in the southern part of Norway, but many towns got only about an hour of light in December, depending on how far north they were.

Finally I stood and was ready to go. My legs felt a little shaky at first from the day before. Per plunged ahead right from the get-go as if he were in an Olympic race. "Try to keep up," he yelled over his shoulder.

I took off too, at first a little clumsy, then found my rhythm. We passed some of the islands with frozen silver waterfalls halted in their drop to the sea. They looked like opalescent columns, and I felt like I was in some other silent world, like I'd entered some great Norse myth about Valhalla. The farther we skied, the islands fell behind us and there was nothing ahead except a long thin line that marked the horizon. The sky was the color of chrome, and Per was already beginning to look like a speck in the cold gray distance. "Per, wait!" I yelled out.

I felt small and flimsy, but heavy too, like it would require a lot of energy to keep moving for as many kilometers as Per said he wanted us to cover—twenty kilometers, more than we had with Pappa. "*Faen.*" I swore out loud without caring. There was no one to hear me. I stopped in spite of knowing that we shouldn't be so far apart from each other. And I knew I should keep trying to catch him, but my mouth and throat were dry again and I wanted more water.

The floor of ice stretched underneath me. I wondered how thick it was. The previous evening, Pappa had said after we'd returned, after

dinner, that there could be unexpected thinning of the ice—that sometimes pancake ice formed, layers with air between them that will suddenly crack and drop you down to a lower strata. He said he didn't
tell us earlier, before we went, because he didn't want to frighten me.
The thought scared me now, and I pushed it away and took a sip of
water. The cold air bit my cheeks. In the distance, Per looked like he
had stopped to wait.

"Good. Asshole," I swore out loud again. *Rævhøl*. I screwed the lid
back on my water bottle, put it back in my pack, and started to ski
again. Eventually, in the rhythm and the quiet of it all, with nothing but
a dark-colored thread of a line for the horizon among the uniform gray,
I thought of how simple everything seemed and how lucky I was to be
out in the fresh air, no homework to do and the vague scent of salt and
ozone filling my nose. Other than the ski tracks from my brother leading away in a straight line, only fresh prints from otters and fox dotted
the thin layer of fresh snow nearby. I kept skiing until I reached Per.

The snow had grown thinner, and the ice was visible beneath us.
We were actually skiing across the floor with only a microscopic film
of snow, and each glide made a strident, fricative sound. "I think we're
close to the edge," he said in a whisper when I got to him, and I almost
wanted to say, *Why are you whispering? There's no one out here.* I didn't,
though. It was like that too. I held things back because so often I'd said
something only to have Per tell me how stupid I was. *Mom's going to be
angry if she finds out. / No shit, stupid.*

"I think skiing across the ice like this is ruining our skis. We should
be on skates out here. Mamma and Pappa are going to be angry. We
should go back. It's not safe."

"Yes, it is safe, and they won't even know."

"How do you know it's safe?"

"Because I can see the ice." He pointed with his pole. "I'll be able to
see it when it gets thinner because it will have a different hue."

I shook my head. "We should go back. It's getting late, and if you
fall through—"

"Don't be silly. I'm not going to fall through. Just a few more meters. You follow me."

"No." I could tell my bottom lip puffed out with stubbornness and anger. I was certain this was a bad idea. "We should go back." I could feel the ice move below us, the sense of the ocean that Pappa had mentioned, and it scared me more. Something about it reminded me of the feeling I had when I woke up and I found out that I'd walked in my sleep and rearranged something. Unstable, like I couldn't count on the solidity of sleep or the very ground I was on. Suddenly a low, soft moan cut free from the slightly flexing and shifting ice, like the ocean was speaking to us, whispering to us. The moan was terrifying and beautiful all at once, like the song of a great whale.

Per ignored it. "Suit yourself," he said. "I'm not going back." He started to ski off. "I came all the way out here to see the edge, and that's what I'm going to do."

"Per," I yelled. "Don't be stupid. You don't know if it's safe. If something happens . . ."

"I'll be fine," he called back to me. "I can see the thickness, and you can too. You just won't use your head."

I stood for a second. My anger running deep and far as the North Sea. It was him that wasn't using his head. Why was he always such a jerk? I shook it off, and followed after him. I had no choice. If he went through, he'd need me with the rope on my pack. I prayed the ice would stay the same thickness.

Luckily, he wasn't skiing too fast, and within minutes, I saw him stop and quickly reached him. Per held out his arm for me. "This is the limit." We stood a good six or seven meters from the edge. "*Faen.*" He spit onto the ice. "I wanted it to be a straight cut. To ski right to the edge and look at the sea, but we can't. It's thinning too much to continue."

He knew exactly where to stop because he could see it. I could see the change in the color of the ice as well, and once again, he was right. But still, uneasiness settled upon me. "Please, Per," I pleaded. "I'm cold. Can we go back now? Mamma's going to get worried?"

Per looked at me, gold tendrils waving out from under his red hat and his bluish-green eyes intense. His vibrant, radiant face contrasted jarringly with the grim light. He looked like a mythical god out of Valhalla too, put into the steely afternoon just for the day to play with us mere mortals.

"*Ja*, sure, Gretch, we can go back."

10

Monty

I PICKED UP A sandwich and some coffee on my way back to head-quarters from the North Fork. When I got back, I found Agents Paige and Marcus immersed in meetings, interviews, and phone calls. I went down the hall to my office, dropping my carrier bag and sandwich on my desk. Then I headed to the incident room for an update from Agent Marcus.

They'd brought Mr. Kelly in and showed him some video footage of dark-colored trucks to see if one out of the hundreds they had taped might ring a bell. He kept shaking his head, rubbing his eyes, saying that he didn't pay enough attention to the vehicle, only the boy. He wished he had, he whispered. He very much wished he had.

I asked the agents if there was anything they wanted me to do, and when I didn't get any clear answers and only a few grumblings, I went back to my office and began working on the Essex bones, telling them both that if they needed me, that's where I'd be. I also went up front to Emily's desk and asked her if she'd put together the file that I'd called about after talking to Lucy when I got back within cell range. She winked, swung her chair around, and reached for a folder already thick with papers. "Files from NamUs and NCIC."

I went back to my desk and unwrapped my sandwich, staring at the National Missing and Unidentified Persons System file on top, try-ing to shake my head clear of the search for Jeremy and recalibrate on the case of the bones. I glanced at the local paper on the corner of my desk to see the front-page headline: "Human Remains Uncovered by Fire Crew."

I quickly skimmed it and read a quote from Joe Smith: "We know very little at this point, only that the bones had been buried near Essex. We'll release more information as it comes to us."

Calls were already pouring in—people wondering about lost and long gone relatives: men who'd gone fishing or hunting and never returned, women who'd left for some reason or another and not come home. Now we had a little more information—that the bones belonged to a white male between ten and fifteen years old and that he'd suffered a head injury. First and foremost, I needed to identify the victim. Without this knowledge, there was no way to proceed locally, and soon I would just have to put it aside and hope for the best in Texas with NamUs.

Without identification of the victim and without knowing the circumstances surrounding the death, we couldn't begin to understand who was responsible for the blunt-force trauma to the skull that Gretchen and Lucy mentioned and for the burial of the bones. Without an ID of the victim, the chances of finding the perpetrator would be nearly impossible.

I took a bite of my sandwich and opened the file, where I saw a pile of NamUs reports. NamUs contained around 23,000 cases, about 12,000 of them still open.

I felt relieved that the town of Essex and the surrounding area were not high population centers. In Montana, there were sixty-five cases still open. Thirty-nine were closed. If we could assume that the bones came from someone local, and not someone like Jeremy, who was visiting from out of state as one of millions that Glacier Park drew each summer, then the numbers of the missing should be manageable. Including Glacier's missing was not a formidable task either. Since Glacier Park's inception, we have kept solid records on who drowned, who fell, who was crushed by falling rock, who was attacked by a grizzly, who froze to death, and who disappeared with no answers.

In the last twenty-five years, for the Flathead and Glacier counties, a total of four males between the ages of ten and sixteen went missing and were still unaccounted for. I knew Nathan's file would be included. He vanished in 1991, when we were twelve. I held off on looking through our own files to find his. I told myself that I would not be swayed by his, which seemed to whisper to me to open it first—that I would maintain my order and proceed methodically so as not to jump to unwarranted or biased conclusions.

I grabbed a highlighter from my desk and began marking the names. Most were assumed to be runaways. Fourteen-year-old Zachary Newton vanished after a fight with his parents seven years ago. Thirteen years ago, sixteen-year-old Tyler Alsworth never came home after going to work washing dishes at a restaurant in Kalispell. He showed up for his shift, left, but never returned to his house. In 1999, thirteen-year-old Shane Wallace from Columbia Falls went missing from a campsite at a place outside the park called Lake Five while his family camped there. If it hadn't been so many years ago, it would have raised a red flag in terms of what had now happened to Jeremy. I made a note that I needed to check if the family had submitted a saliva sample in case the bones we found were his. I made a note to check with the Alsworths as well, even though he was outside the age determination Lucy had given.

Then Nathan. October 31, 1991. Twelve-year-old Nathan Faraway—soon to be thirteen, on November 7—never returned after going with a friend—me, one Monty Harris, and his brother, Adam Harris, and two friends of Adam—to a local cemetery for a Halloween prank.

Even though I could hear a low mumble from those working in the incident room down the hall, all went quiet then except the hum of my computer's hard drive and the sound of the air-conditioning coming through old vents. Usually we didn't use the air, just let Glacier's breeze slide in through open windows, but with the fire season, we'd cranked the old unit up to cool the place down so we didn't invite all the dust and smoke in. I stared at the file. I didn't need to read the details. I found a picture of Nathan and looked at it, at his unkempt dark hair falling below his brow, freckles on his cheeks, his cockeyed, shit-eating grin, his intelligent eyes. He was one of the smartest in class and other kids teased him for it. Not me. He was my best friend, my only real friend growing up.

It was another lifetime ago—a time of extreme uncertainty for me. My mother was mentally ill, suffering from paranoid schizophrenia, and Adam was angry, rebelling and bullying me incessantly. My father worked hard at his construction company and drank even harder when he wasn't working. Nathan was the one person I trusted, and he had trusted me. And I . . . I had unwittingly led him into a snare that my brother and his friends had set. Inadvertently, I had played a part in his vanishing.

Looking at the photo brought back raw, sentimental feelings, plus a fresh shot of pure guilt. From an adult, intellectual perspective, I knew that the disappearance of Nathan Faraway was not my fault. I was a child. We'd been lured into going along with my brother and his friends, and there was no way I could predict that Nathan would leave me in the dark woods in a fit of anger at me for trusting my brother. Nathan's last words to me were: *You should've known.*

It wasn't the anger in the words that got to me the most; it was the disappointment, and when the memory of them hits me, I always feel like I'm suddenly coated with a thin film of something dirty. I'd never fully forgiven myself because, on some level, I knew that Nathan was right. I should have been smarter than to trust my malicious brother and his friends. I knew how he treated me on a regular basis; why did I think it would be different that time? I've always been a realist, and the cold hard truth was that he was always up to no good. It's just that I simply had believed for once that it would be different, and that I'd be accepted by him and his friends. I had been very naïve, and swore I'd never be that way again.

I thought of Nathan's family. His mother, his father . . . and he had an older sister, Molly. She was the reason my brother and his friends said we needed to join them that night. Molly, with her curvy teenage body, her pink lips, and the bossy way she'd stand with one hand on a hip, was supposed to watch Nathan later in the evening, after we finished hanging out after school. Their parents were at a Halloween party, and they wanted Nathan to be with her when the trick-or-treating went into full swing. Adam had told me that his friend Perry had a crush on her and that they simply wanted our help. The plan was for all of us to go pick up Molly from her friend's house and give her a ride home to babysit, which would also give Perry a little time with her in the car. It was all a lie.

I refocused on the file. I didn't know what Nathan's parents did now. I knew they eventually divorced, as many couples do after the loss of a child. I thought they both still lived in Columbia Falls, but I wasn't sure. I did know that Molly lived in Kalispell—that she'd had a few children and was also divorced. I had a strong sense that saliva had not been collected from Nathan's mother, father, or sister. Back when Nathan disappeared, no process existed. I looked through his paperwork, and sure enough, no sample had been submitted.

"Okay," I said out loud to myself. "Parents." I straightened in my chair and looked for information on where the parents of all the missing currently lived. After jotting as many down as I could find that still lived in the area, a total of six parents, I grabbed my bag and headed for the door, telling Emily I was off to go visit a few families.

• • •

When I pulled up to the Faraway house, it hit me what I was about to do. I'd decided to get Peter Faraway's over with first—a kind of get-back-on-the-horse line of thinking—and suddenly I felt like a chicken, and that I shouldn't be the one to do this at all. Maybe I should have sent Ken, I considered.

Yet here I was. Mr. Faraway still lived in the same house. Apparently, it was Mrs. Faraway, Alice, who had been the one to move out first. I remembered Alice clutching Peter's arm in the early days while the search ensued, as if she'd never let him go, as if she couldn't stand up on her own without his help. Sadly, that grasp loosened over time and broke. I thought of the Coreys, of Ron's hand reaching out to Linda, but not making it.

The road and the house looked narrower and more cluttered than I recalled, but then again, everyone said that about childhood places—some function of space appearing different through the eyes of a child. The lawns looked cramped and brown, rather than lush and expansive like I remembered when Nathan and I ran around playing hide-and-seek.

The color of the house had been changed, but not for a long time. I recalled that it had been a happy yellow with cream trim, but now it was a faded and chipped green. Tall, unwieldy lilac bushes grew against the side fence in the back, those actually much bigger than I recalled. Perhaps Mr. Faraway didn't spend much time trimming back bushes around his lawn anymore, even though I had memories of him pruning roses and other foliage and calling out to us to stay off his gardens and suggesting that we go inside, where Mrs. Faraway would make us some lemonade.

Peter answered the door. He had been a tall, handsome man, and in a distant way, I could still see a sliver of his old looks in his stiff posture and his rustic, weathered skin. But his cheeks had hollowed drastically, his hair had thinned and receded, and his dark eyes looked large and buggy. I introduced myself, and saw him flinch and pull back slightly at the mention of my name. I couldn't tell if the gesture was brought about because I was now a cop in uniform and it brought back an old spark of fear mixed with hope; or quite the opposite, that the sight of me, uniform or not, disgusted him—the boy whose brother lured his son into the woods to never be seen again.

I brought up the newspaper article about uncovering the skeleton. Surely, if he'd seen the news, he'd have wondered.

"Yes, of course I saw it," he said grimly. "Come in, Monty." He held the door wider. Hearing him say my name like that hit me full on. It echoed all the times I'd come to visit Nathan. *Hi, Monty, come in. Na-*

than's upstairs. Then off I'd run, light as a feather, taking two stairs at a time to blast through Nathan's bedroom door, where I'd tell him whatever I had to tell him that day. For me, visiting Nathan's house, with its cheerfulness, sunny light, home-baked cookies and lemonade, offered a reprieve from a house where my mother insisted on closed curtains for fear that bad people might be watching us.

Peter brought me into the sitting room, which no longer held the sunny, happy quality I remembered, although I had to admit, from the looks of the outside, I had expected worse. There were still some throws over the sofa and some knickknacks around. Sunlight slanted between eyelet curtains in the front windows. Several school pictures of Nathan and Molly stood on the mantelpiece, and they seemed dust-free. I wondered if Peter had taken up with another woman at some point. Although the look of the place was dated, there still seemed to be a female touch to it.

"So, have you found him? Is that why you're here?"

"We're not sure yet, but I'd like to talk to you about that." I was surprised at how even my voice sounded; it's not the way I felt inside, but after years of working as a game warden and now a park officer, I was comfortable with visiting people, asking questions, and taking statements from strangers and even those from my past. No matter how emotional I felt, my voice rarely failed me.

He stared at me, inspecting me, his eyes narrowed, and I felt ashamed on too many levels to count—that I was the one who came home that night and not Nathan, that I was currently the one standing before him talking about the possibility that his son's corpse may have been taken and buried near Essex. Peter's kitchen windows were open, and I could hear the faint high shrieks of children playing somewhere in the neighborhood, each cry of glee sounding more like a cry for help as I stood before Nathan's father. A dog also yipped in the distance, high-pitched and frenzied. "He didn't disappear in Essex," Peter said gruffly.

I felt my shoulders tense as I realized there might be some denial going on. That on some level, he did not want to know about the buried bones almost more than he did want to know.

"Can we sit, Mr. Faraway?"

He waved me to one of the chairs, and I took a seat. He slumped into the couch across from me, leaning forward, and placing his elbows on his knees. The dog had quieted down, and so had the children. The house went still, except for the hum of a fan in the kitchen.

"Mr. Faraway, I don't mean to sound intrusive, but I'm going to need to ask you a few questions."

He watched me with narrowed eyes, then said, "Like what?"

"Basics. Like, have you remarried?"

"No, I haven't."

"Oh," I said.

"Has Ms. Faraway?"

"No, she hasn't either."

"Do you still see her?"

"I do. We're friends. She checks on me still. Sometimes she comes and cleans or tries to make the place a little cheerier. She tries to get me to garden again, and sometimes I start, but I never can get very far." He looked out the window wistfully, then back down at his hands. He massaged one thumb knuckle with his other thumb, and I couldn't tell if he always did that or was doing it only from nervousness now.

"Is she up to things like that—gardening and all?"

"She claims she is, but I don't know. I guess she tries. Goes to church still, knits these blankets"—he pointed with his chin to the beige knitted throw hanging over the back of the couch beside him—"that kind of thing." He gave a deliberate shrug like he wasn't convinced of anything ever, not even the simple activities of his ex-wife, who still visited him. That was one of the many things that the loss of a child could do to you, I thought—take away your sense of purpose, of direction.

"What about you, Monty?" he asked. "I heard you got married. Do you have children?"

"No, no, I don't. We . . . we didn't make it. I'm divorced."

Peter didn't say anything, didn't even nod, just looked at me with a hard stare like he already knew that was the case, that he could have predicted it, and there was absolutely nothing more to add to it.

"And Molly?" I shifted the conversation back. "I hear she's in Kalispell?"

"Yeah, got married to some guy named Tom Sands, had kids. Now she's divorced too. She runs a water delivery business. You know, supplying bottled water all over the valley for people who don't trust their faucets. As if it's fresher in plastic containers than out of the wells and city systems around here."

"She still go by Sands?"

He nodded, and I pulled out my pad and wrote the name down. "Mr. Faraway, we don't know if it's . . ." I paused, finding it difficult to suddenly say his name. Not only had I not said it in a long time myself, saying it to his father compounded my unease.

"Nathan," he said, slightly annoyed.

"I know. I'm sorry. Mr. Faraway, several agencies are already involved in the process of identification. The police may ask you to go in to the local police station to take a DNA sample. It's just a quick swab inside your mouth. They simply need a close relative—a parent is best—in case they can make a match."

Peter stared at me without saying a word, as if he could see right through me and had already catalogued the sweetest and darkest moments in my life. I fidgeted, cleared my throat, and continued on. "It doesn't mean it's him—"

"Nathan," he said.

"That's right. It doesn't mean it's him," I repeated.

"No," he said abruptly. "I know what you mean. I wasn't getting clarification. I was telling you what his damn name is. Nathan. You can say his name. It's not taboo to say it within these walls."

I swallowed hard, could feel the tension in my chest and neck, like water to the overflow line. "Of course not," I nodded. "Of course it isn't."

"What happened to this Essex kid? How did he die?"

"We don't know yet."

He looked down at his hands again, one thumb still working the lower knuckle of the other.

"Mr. Faraway?"

He looked up, his lower jaw canted to the side, as if he purposefully had it cocked that way to prevent himself from saying anything more to me because whatever he'd say wasn't going to be nice. It made his face appear crooked. Seven years after the disappearance, when I was at college, Peter had gotten my number somehow and called me to grill me for information. Eventually he broke down sobbing. I wanted to help, but I didn't know anything more than how we got separated—just that Nathan had stormed off into the woods by the cemetery to start walking home.

I had followed, calling out to him, watching him walk into shadowy trees in the pale moonlight. I had stumbled on a fallen tree, my foot catching the soft, rotted-out piece in its center and my heel catching underneath the log. I had to take a second to pry it out, and by the time I stood back up, I couldn't see him. I continued to call for him, but he didn't answer. I kept walking, searching for him, but never found him, never saw him again.

"Would you be willing to give a saliva sample if it increases the chances of us identifying this boy?"

Mr. Faraway leaned back in the couch and studied me. "I don't think so."

"Why not? Don't you want to know if it's him?" I shuddered at the thought of the skeleton remaining nameless when there was even a small possibility of it being Nathan.

Peter stood and walked to the door. "You can leave now. How dare you come in here and ask me that? You have no right to ask me anything. To ask anything of us."

"I know that, sir. I know that, but I just thought for you, for Alice, for Molly, that you might want to know."

"Then you don't know everything, do you?"

I didn't answer him, just put my notepad back in my pocket and walked quietly past him and out his front door as requested.

. . .

When I got to the car, I felt like hell, the full viscosity of Peter's angry stare and his words sifting through me, burrowing into every weak spot inside me. *You have no right to ask me anything. To ask anything of us.*

The last thing I wanted to do was make Peter Faraway angry or make the family relive old wounds. I started the car and drove off, thinking more deeply about the implications of identifying the bones for not just the Faraways, but for any family. I wasn't wrong; most people did want to know. Desperately wanted to know. But perhaps not everyone. Perhaps for many, the worst part was knowing for sure that your child was dead, that even though the uncertainty eats away at you, at least you're left with a thread of hope to constantly grab onto.

For most of my life, I thought the worst part of Nathan's disappearance was the not knowing. The uncertainty of what had happened to him that night plagued my mind constantly. Had he been stalked by a mountain lion, the stealth hunters of the woods? Had he fallen in the river and drowned? Had he been attacked by a hungry bear that hadn't yet gone to the high-elevation northern slopes for hibernation? Had he been abducted? Had my brother and his friends circled back to him, caught up with him? Had something gone entirely wrong that they all were sneaky enough to cover up?

There had been rumors, of course, around town. That he'd committed suicide or was taken by phantoms—it was October 31, after all—that his spirit swept through the canyon and across the fields and into town every Halloween at nightfall.

I thought about what it meant if the grave was Nathan's. He had disappeared right outside Columbia Falls, past the river and past an area referred to as Columbia Heights, the name implying wealth and gentrification. The area was anything but that, home to an A&W Root

Beer chain store, a gas station or two, a few homes, a run-down, abandoned old western hotel, and a tavern. The area led into the canyon going to Glacier Park, and the Flathead River ran nearby as it wound its way out of the canyon.

Nathan would have had to walk through the woods, to the heights, and down Highway 2 for a bit to get into his neighborhood in Columbia Falls. Had he made it to the highway and been hit by a car? Had a reckless driver decided to dispose of the body himself rather than face the consequences? Had he taken him to Essex to bury?

Or, had Nathan hitchhiked with the wrong person—some sociopath? Nathan was too smart for that. He would have known better than any kid to hop in a car with a stranger, but maybe he threw caution to the wind. I remembered that walk home in the cold: the long, eerie shadows from the trees, the silver slashes of moonlight cutting through them, my legs tired and my fingers numb and frozen. Perhaps he decided a ride was better than the biting wind. And if so, what had he thought when the car turned around and went away from the canyon toward Essex?

It's not like these thoughts hadn't crossed my mind before, but I had always thought it was more likely—or perhaps I'd preferred to believe—that he'd died in a more natural way. As awful and frightening as it sounds, being attacked by a hungry mountain lion and dragged somewhere no one could find him in the searches through the woods seemed somehow more understandable—because it was part of the cycle of nature—than thinking he might have been abducted by someone cruel and twisted enough to crush his skull and put him in a shallow grave.

When I turned onto Highway 2 to head back to the park, my phone started ringing. It was Lucy.

"Monty, is this a good time?"

"Good as ever," I said. "I've got you on speaker while I drive, but I'll pull over as soon as I see a turnout."

"Want to call me back?"

"No, go ahead. There's one coming up," I told her.

"There are a few more things to report. First, I've got a better idea of how old the bones are based on further inspection and the analysis of the soil. I'm thinking they're at least twenty to thirty years old."

"So sometime from 1986 to 1996?"

"Yes, give or take a few years on each end. There's no way to be exact, I'm afraid."

"Okay," I said, thinking that the time frame didn't rule out that the remains belonged to Nathan. "What else?"

"The buckle has been completely cleaned. It looks like something from the late eighties or early nineties, but that alone doesn't mean much; especially if someone has kept a buckle around for a long time. I've sent it back to the lab, to Gretchen, so she can show you. She'll probably get it by tomorrow or the next day."

"And the bones, is it possible that a hit-and-run caused the break in the temporal region?" I asked.

Lucy didn't answer immediately, and I could tell she was mulling it over for a second. Then she said, "No, not likely at all. All the other bones show no trauma and a car would not be able to hit only one spot on the skull—it would affect more of the skull and other body parts that would show as breaks in the skeleton.

"There are usually three kinds of bone injury, and I'll save you the lecture, but this one is perimortem, meaning it occurred at or close to the time of death. We know this because there is none of the bone remodeling that happens when an injury occurs when the victim is alive long enough for healing to occur. Also, there is no sign that the injury occurred postmortem, or after death. When an injury is perimortem, the edges of the affected area remain relatively sharp and crisp, which tells me the contusion occurred shortly before death. Most likely, it caused the death, but we don't know that for sure."

"Could they have been made by an animal?"

"That's unlikely as well. There are no signs of tooth marks. Although it's possible a bear knocked him over and he hit his head on some very strange and sharp-shaped rock or object. But then again, why would he end up buried in a grave?"

"So"—I sighed—"we don't know for sure what the cause of death was?"

"I'm afraid not, but I'd be willing to bet it has something to do with the severe fracture of the skull. To make a depressed, cleaved skull fracture like this, this child had to have been specifically hit with a sharp, hard object in the frontal and temporal region along the transverse access. The dead always have a story to tell, Monty," Lucy said. "And I'm afraid this person's is not a very nice one."

I thanked her for the call and continued to drive back to headquarters, going a little too fast on the highway. I made myself slow down, drive the speed limit, and ease my grip on the steering wheel while her words *This person's is not a very nice one* rang in my head.

11

Gretchen

EVENING BEGAN TO settle when Ray and I left the yurt site on the North Fork, and a glowing orange orb sunk below the mountains by the time we reached Glacier's headquarters in West Glacier in order to update the FBI agents. When we pulled into the parking lot, Monty arrived too. We walked with him toward the building in the soft light of the lingering dusk.

"How'd it go?" he asked.

"Okay, we found three sets of footprints."

"Three?"

"That surprise you?"

"Only in that I took Minsky for a loner, figured there'd only be Chiles's and Minsky's prints there."

"One set belongs to Minsky, of course. We can tell because of the sheer number of them. It's definitely the dominant print. Several belong to Chiles, which we checked on the way out by stopping by his cabin and comparing it to the dominant print there. Thought the ol' coot was going to shoot us, but I managed to talk him into letting us be while we did our work."

"And the third?" Monty asked.

"We aren't sure about it. It came from a smaller shoe, a running shoe, and could belong to a younger person, a woman or a smaller man, but it didn't match any of the prints from the Coreys' campsite at Fish Creek."

"How long has he been missing now?" Ray asked Monty.

142

"Too long. Around thirty-three hours," Monty growled.

I wanted to say, *It's not looking good, is it?* but I resisted. I'd found it best to never be openly negative around anyone when working a case. Just give the findings.

"Agent Paige will be all over the fact that a third shoe print was at the yurt site," Monty added.

"Not you?"

"I'm happy to have any lead, but I'm not feeling this is the direction to go. Doesn't fit the profile of a child abductor. Other than the fact that the family's got money and the guy called them out of the blue before they left, and I'll admit that is a little strange, I can't really see how it plays. Did you get any sense of how long it's been since someone besides us was actually at the site?"

"That's hard to say for sure. As you know, the fire didn't look fresh, but that doesn't say a whole lot. It's been warm and there are fire restrictions across the entire state. If he was up to something bad, the last thing you'd do is start a campfire and call attention to yourself."

We walked up the stone steps to the front door and Monty paused before he opened it, as if he could read my mind and knew I wanted to ask about the bones. I could hear crickets piping up in the woods off to the sides of the building. Soft summer birdcalls and bustling sounds filled the evening, and a bat swept by us, chasing insects against the darkening sky.

"Did you call Lucy?" I asked.

"I did and she filled me in. In between all the craziness, I've been checking missing person reports for ten to sixteen years old for the entire Flathead County. I also just made a visit to a family to see if I could talk them into giving a saliva sample for DNA."

I stayed silent while Monty kept his hand on the door without opening it. I knew there was a good chance that Monty's friend from years back would be one of those names, and possibly even the family he visited. I almost wanted to ask, but didn't. On some level, it seemed private, especially in front of Ray.

"I've also expanded the search to Canada, to Waterton and surrounding areas," Monty continued as he finally opened the door for us. Glacier Park spans two counties, Flathead and Glacier, and continues into Canada, into the provinces of Alberta and British Columbia. "I plan to visit the rest of the families who haven't submitted a saliva sample to see if I can get them to do so. Hopefully it increases the chance of a match at the center."

Monty showed us the incident room where Ali, Herman, Ken, Tara, and other officers, rangers, and volunteers gathered. The room buzzed with concentration, intensity, and chatter. Karen Forstenson, one of their best rangers, efficiently manned the volunteer table, where she kept track of at least forty volunteers in groups of four performing searches in well-documented grids so that no one overlapped. Ali clicked away at her computer, Herman made marks on a map on the wall, Tara sat with Mr. Kelly in a corner going over surveillance tapes, Ken took phone calls, and Emily used the photocopy machine in another corner by a big ficus plant. On top of busy, everyone looked cranky, as if they were all fighting off migraines. Or maybe I was simply projecting my own caffeine headaches onto them all.

When Ali spotted me and Ray, she announced that we should move to the smaller conference room next door for a quick briefing. Monty, Ray, Ken, and I filed in behind Herman and Ali and took seats around the table.

"Everyone comfortable?" Ali closed the door with her foot, shutting out the rest of headquarters and the busy din of volunteer workers checking in at the main table with the results of their searches.

"Gretchen Larson." I held out my hand to Ali, then introduced Ray to her. I hadn't met either of the agents yet, and took them in. Herman stood by the counter along the wall, his arms folded in front of his chest. He was just a tad shorter than Ken, which wasn't saying much. Ken was tall, at least six-two, and built like a professional football player. Herman was right in there with him—at least six foot. His thighs were massive in his navy blue FBI uniform pants and he had his sleeves rolled up casually, displaying well-muscled forearms and an expensive-looking shiny silver watch. He also wore glasses, designer frames on his eyeglasses.

Ali motioned for Herman to take a seat, and he pulled out a chair and sat, keeping his legs firmly planted apart in front of him. Ali stood behind him, more disheveled. Curly, almost frizzy dark hair shot out in tentacles. She had olive skin, not so different from Monty's, and was in her midthirties. She spoke with some kind of an accent—East Coast, I thought by the way she said, or rather didn't say, her *rs*: *comf-tible*. No matter how long I'd been in America, it was harder for me than it was for natives to pick up on specific regional or state accents. I mixed up New Jersey, New York, Boston, and Maine. I also couldn't hear the difference between southern states, and those from Texas sounded exactly the same to me as those from Georgia.

Ali had no watch, no earrings, no rings, no makeup. She seemed the type to charge right ahead, no matter the obstacles. She also seemed like the type who wanted to be the center of everything and to do things her way. That was okay by me, but I couldn't decide if I liked her or not. I liked that her channel was set on "go," that she seemed the type, like me, to roll her eyes when someone who knew very little about you told you to smile when your face looked serious and long. Because, obviously, whoever tells you that has no clue about the kinds of things Ali Paige probably has seen in her line of work, or the kinds of things I'd done in my life from the ripe old age of fifteen. But, still, she reminded me of a spoiled mean girl in some ways. Perhaps it was her sideways glare that seemed to come straight from the devil.

"Gretchen, Ray"—Ali swung a chair out from the table and straddled it, elbows on its back—"what have you got?"

I filled them in about the yurt site, the tire tracks and traces of fabric that we'd need some time to process, and then about the three sets of prints, including the one smaller unidentified set.

"Smaller." She tapped her foot nervously on the floor. "That's interesting."

"But we've already compared it to all of the available prints at the Coreys' campground site and there's no match. Jeremy's shoe print is from some kind of a jogger, his mom confirms a Nike shoe. The one at Minsky's site is also a jogger, even possibly a Nike, but it's not a match. Although we don't know how long ago the print was made. Seeing as how we haven't had rain in over a month, we don't know how long it's been there."

"Shoes can be changed," Ali said.

"What about the tire tracks?" Herman asked.

"Some kind of large truck with a trailer, I'm guessing a flatbed trailer if he's hauling a yurt around. They fold up, but it would still be pretty big to haul around."

Monty sat still, his face set and unreadable. Clearly he somehow annoyed Agent Paige because she looked at him, held out a palm, and said, "What?"

"I didn't say anything," Monty said.

She looked like a pissed-off big sister. "You didn't need to. Do you have a problem with us figuring out this Minsky situation?"

"Ali," Herman chimed in. "He didn't say anything."

Ali shot him her signature glance, and he rolled his eyes ever so slightly.

"I think it needs to be checked out," Monty stated. "But I still think it's a long shot. It doesn't fit."

"We've recently learned that Minsky has hit up more than just his niece for extra money in the last six months. We have reports from AFT that he'd sold some gold he's been hanging on to for a while at a local pawnshop, but it must not have been enough because he also tried to sell off some of his firearms. We have no idea what he needed the money for, but maybe he's also planning on getting some ransom money from the parents. Guy finds out his niece has married some musician that's hit it big. Maybe it's too tempting, especially with a family that's shunned you, disowned you."

"Why wouldn't they get a ransom call then, a note, something?" Monty asked.

"Maybe he's keeping the kid for a few days to make the whole damn family squirm. Payback."

Monty slowly nodded as if he was considering it. Then he said, "What about the tracks near Fish Creek? They don't match."

"Vehicles can be borrowed, loaned, taken . . . ," Ali said. "Minsky's part of a network, an antigovernment, anti-law-enforcement network. He's not completely a loner. Word has it that they've been helping a leader of a paramilitary group who's been hiding out in a compound we have yet to find."

"That's all very interesting, but don't you think it's an entirely different law enforcement matter?" Monty pressed. Ali glared at him for questioning her in front of everyone, but she had brought it on herself by questioning Monty when he hadn't said a word.

"Tracks found outside Fish Creek where the boy was last seen are consistent with tires that come on a Chevy or Ford truck," I inserted, drawing her attention away from Monty. "Tracks found at the yurt site don't match that brand. They're a generic brand, Cooper, probably fitted to an old Toyota pickup.

Ali stood up and went to the large whiteboard at the front of the room. She wrote Minsky's name on it with "uncle" beneath his name. Next to it, she jotted down Mr. Kelly's name and the word "vehicle" with a question mark by it and the words "dark-colored, possibly black, navy, dark gray" underneath. Next to that, she scribbled the details I'd just given about the extra shoe prints at the site and the type of vehicle tracks that were there, possibly from a trailer or flatbed truck.

Monty took some notes and Ken sat nodding, chewing a piece of gum vigorously, his eyes sharp and energized.

"Have you looked at other missing boys in the area?" I asked.

Ali turned, holding her chalk an inch away from the board. "We *haaave*." She drew out the word as if she was addressing a child, clearly insulted that I'd asked something so simple. "First thing."

"Okay, of course, I just wondered if there were any similarities."

"No, there aren't," she said more professionally. "There haven't been any abductions like this in many years. There are missing children, but most are older, assumed runaways."

"But does that matter? The number of years?"

"Typically"—Ali gave me an impatient glance, but not her signature full-on glare, which I was thankful for—"a serial abductor can't wait for too long before they strike again, because whatever twisted thing that makes them do it can't be suppressed for too many years in a row. Plus, once they begin, activity usually intensifies or increases."

"Studies show," Herman piped in, "that your average male serial killers average six to eleven victims over a nine-year period. And females, like health-care workers, about seven to nine victims over the same time frame."

"That's correct," Ali said.

I nodded, reminding myself that just because we found a sub-adult's male bones the day before did not mean there was any relation. The bones we found were much older by at least ten to twenty years, and I wasn't the detective here, nowhere near a detective. I was only trained in forensics, and quite glad to stay that way.

Ali turned back to the board and continued to jot bits of information on it when the door opened and Tara walked in. She had her hair pulled back in a tight bun and looked serious, but her color was back from yesterday. I was glad to see it.

"Excuse me," Tara said, "Mr. Kelly thinks he's recognized one of the trucks leaving the gates of the park at twelve thirty p.m."

I sat forward, and I saw Monty do the same.

Ali dropped her chalk. "I'll be right back. Everyone stay." She pointed at us all as she and Herman left the room, following Tara out.

Ken looked at me and whispered, "I guess we don't move a muscle. The boss has spoken."

"I guess not," Monty said, then glanced at Ray, then me. He studied me for a moment, and I looked down at my hands on the table, my fingers laced together.

"It was a good question," Monty said.

I looked up at him and gave a one-shoulder shrug. "It was just a thought."

We all sat and continued to wait for a few more minutes. Monty checked his watch a number of times, and I could tell he was impatient with having to wait. Finally Ali and Herman came back in.

"He's a bit fuzzy about it," Ali announced. "But when he saw it, the look and age of it rang a bell . . . an older truck, some kind of Chevy with back cab windows. Tara's working on identifying it as we speak, but we can't see the license plate on it. There's no plate on the front, which is the side the cameras are trained on for exiting vehicles, so the driver potentially had that thought on his mind. We've caught a sticker on the front bumper, though, that seems to be an old parking sticker for the old CFAC aluminum plant. So, good news, we think it's local. That might help run down a registration, if we can stick to this county."

"Did you get images of the driver or passengers?"

"No, there's a lot of glare and too shadowy inside. Looks like it could be a male wearing a cap, but we can't make out any facial details. There's no one in the passenger seat, and we can't see the backseat."

"What about coming in?" I asked, referring to the possibility of the cameras catching a better glimpse of the man when it entered as well as him needing to stop to either pay or show a prepaid pass to enter. If he'd stopped, one of the on-duty attendants manning the entrance booths would have had to have dealt with the driver.

"We don't have it coming in. Not yet anyway, so it's possible he came in through the Camas Road entrance, which doesn't have cameras. We're repulling in that station attendant as we speak to see if she can recall anything. We're looking back further. It's possible he came in the day or even days before and has been camping out in the park."

Tara came back in. "Okay, so we've identified it as a late eighties or early nineties Chevy Z71 1500."

"Thank you." Ali said, looking at the clock on the wall. "It's late. Shit. Nothing's easy." Montana Department of Motor Vehicles was several hours past closed. "Herman," she said, "get the attorney general on the phone ASAP. We need to get someone back into the records office to run a printout for us."

"I'm on it," Herman said, walking out.

It was hopeful news. If Mr. Kelly was correct, it was a lead. If we could find the person registered to the truck, we might make some progress. Since we had tire tread prints from the Camas Road near the bridge where Mr. Kelly saw the vehicle, not far from the campground, we might be able to match the tread to the registered vehicle if we could find it. Ali told Monty, Ken, and Tara to wait around for the printout and that she expected them to help track down the Chevy truck registrants on the list.

"Divide and conquer," Monty said, agreeing with her. He stood tall, shoulders back—galvanized, I thought—to finally have a lead better than the Minsky one.

· · ·

Ray and I headed back to the lab, not saying much after leaving headquarters. Monty had walked us to the door, always the gentleman, I had thought, even among all the chaos, and I thanked him. He had shrugged and said, "For what?"

"For seeing us out. You've got your hands full." I tossed my head toward the incident room.

"You mean with both the cases or with the agents?"

"All of the above," I said.

"You've got yours full too," he said, and I laughed because that was indeed true. It felt like a week had gone by since we'd found the bones in Essex. We said good-bye, and as we headed out of the canyon, it was beginning to feel like another endless day.

By the time we reached the valley, the brilliant yellow canola fields shone like neon in the dark. More and more farmers were turning to that crop in the last five to ten years, since the demand for canola oil had gone up and farmers found it to be a useful rotation crop.

Often at sunset, after a long day, I ran along these types of roads—

paved and gravel ones that traversed farmland, often for miles past fields bathed in coppery light and pastures with cows and grain silos. I passed farmhouses with old, peeling red barns and grazing horses. I ran until my legs ached and sweat covered me, in the heat or the cold. It was one of the tricks I used to calm my anxieties and achieve a healthier night of sleep.

The doctors told me long ago that exercise would help. But for me, it had become more than a doctor's prescription. Over the years, it had become a way to quell my thoughts and apprehensions, and it was the best tool I had to try to keep the self-hate and awful memories at bay. Right now, as spent as I felt from working several separate crime scenes in the park for two days in a row, I craved one of those runs because too many thoughts were streaking through my head. I wondered about the boy. Where had he gone? Had he really been abducted, and if so, at what point did Jeremy realize that things were changing for him irrevocably?

And the bones in the grave, they kept pushing into my mind as well, and now I couldn't quit thinking about our visit to the old hotel. Even though Kyle hadn't been there, what the hell was wrong with him? He had a loving family, and he was choosing to ignore them, reject them. Many kids who got mixed up in drugs were born into ugly, dysfunctional situations from the start. Not Kyle. Other than watching his mom and dad divorce, he had a pretty cushy life from what I could gather. What I wouldn't have given to stay in the loving cocoon of mine before it all went horribly wrong—in the days when we skied, sledded, and skated together, then found refuge before our fireplace in the blue wood-paneled house with slate roofing. In the days when we picnicked, picked berries, boated, and fished, the summer sky staying light nearly all night so that I could see the rust-colored church spire peaking over bushy summer trees from my bedroom window until well past two a.m.

But that was then, and this was my life now. Sometimes it felt so strange to think of how I had been responsible for shattering my family. When I was younger, I could never have guessed that life was so fragile, and that a strong family could crumble—a broken string of beads falling to the floor and scattering everywhere. My mother swung from bouts of depression with vacant stares and silent periods after the death of my brother, when she couldn't bring herself to utter a single word to me, to great bouts of anger. She screamed at me, glared at me as if I was an enemy within the gates. If I left anything messy in the sink, she'd yell at me, "Can you not clean up after yourself at the very least? Can you not quit making messes everywhere?"

Messes. Such a euphemism. But I needed to stop obsessing and screw my head back on straight again. When we returned to the lab and unloaded, Ray left to get some food and rest. The crime lab was quiet except for the steady hum of refrigerators and the equipment.

I was starting to get another headache, since I'd been abstaining from caffeine and sticking to herbal tea. I craved coffee, but went to the small break room to make myself some more tea. I patiently waited for the water to boil, clicked the kettle off, and poured the steaming water into my coffee mug. I walked down the empty hall back to my office and sat at my desk. I tried to keep my office as cheery as possible. Pictures of golden Tuscan settings hung on the walls, and a citrus-scented orange candle, a few nice pieces of pottery, and a potted plant lined the top of a bookcase on one wall. I liked my office and was happy to linger a little longer before going home. Besides, I still had work to do.

I pulled out the file on the Essex site and took out all the pictures. As is true with every crime-scene photo shoot, there were loads of them from every possible angle. I found the ones of the skull to study. I looked at the coronal sutures again and at the deep gash above the left ear. Something about it rang a bell, so I pulled up the NamUs database to look into all incidents of unidentified and unclaimed remains in the area as well as all missing persons.

I started my search with the early 1970s. Three early teenage girls had gone missing in the late seventies and in the early eighties, all three on the north end of the valley, none of them ever found or heard from again. Then there was a long break with some older missing teens—sixteen-, seventeen-, and eighteen-year-olds who were presumed runaways—during the late eighties and early nineties. Then, in 1991, Nathan Faraway was reported missing on Halloween night after not showing up at his sister's friend's house as he was supposed to. His friend, Monty Harris, and Monty's brother, Adam Harris, and Adam's friends Todd Wright and Perry Milliken were the last to see him and underwent intensive interrogation.

I thought of Monty. I had known about his childhood incident, but I had not thought through all the implications—about the guilt he must have felt, maybe still feels. Perhaps we had more in common than I'd ever considered.

I pulled a notepad from my drawer and began to take notes. I wrote down the names of the missing girls and boys, which ones returned safely, which ones were still missing, which ones were suspected runaways, which ones weren't. I also looked up all unidentified remains.

In the early nineties, several older teens went missing. Then, in 1999, a boy by the name of Shane Wallace vanished from a campground at a place called Lake Five, located just outside Glacier Park. The boy was never found, but his bicycle was left on the side of the road. Apparently, the family had been camping and brought the boy's bicycle along so he could ride around when he became bored.

I sat back in my chair and stared up at the ceiling, my thoughts scrolling through cases I'd worked over the years since I'd come to the valley. I thought of an incident I had not worked but had heard about after I first came from Seattle to work for the CSI unit.

There'd been some talk about this case, which had shaken the community to the core. A boy's remains had been found on the northeast side of the valley near the foothills of the Columbia Mountain Range after he'd been missing for a number of days. It had happened several years before I came, and Ray had told me about the case when a birthday ad was placed in the paper for the boy, saying something like *In loving memory of our beautiful boy.* It had a picture of him and his name. It also said something about his tragic end having no bearing on the wonderful afterlife he would receive.

Ray and I were having coffee in the break room, and I had asked him about it. He had told me that the boy was found buried by some bird dogs hunting grouse in the foothills. The hunter followed his dogs and found them digging at the shallow grave. It was fresh enough that authorities were able to ID the boy immediately.

I found the case easily and studied it. Samuel Erickson had gone missing on July 7, 2007, and was found six days later, on the thirteenth. Definitely a cold case now. Because they found the body so early—I considered the irony in the statement, since clearly it was not early enough. But then again, perhaps after such an abduction, some would consider the boy was better off dead and buried. The autopsy report indicated that Samuel's time of death was some time on the twelfth, that he'd died between six to twelve hours before he was buried.

I opened files with photos of the remains. The report was written by an ME named Marcus Prior, who claimed that the cause of death was a severe head wound. Then I clicked on a file that had an ID number and the words "head wound" next to it. I opened it and inspected it. I clicked on another image showing a different angle and leaned in closer. There was a messy, bloody major injury on the left side under the left ear, around the jawbone and spreading to the back of the head, completely disfiguring the side of the boy's face and head. I read Prior's report again. Documented clearly, he wrote, *The mandible and occipital bones on the left side have been cleaved in two by a sharp object. The victim has undergone blunt-force trauma with a very sharp object, most likely an axe or hatchet.*

My heartbeat quickened at the mention of a cleave, of an axe or a hatchet, and I sat back in my chair, feeling it pound in my chest. My mother always said I had a healthy, blood-pumping heart. When I was little and I'd feel it hammering against my chest after running or when I was told scary stories about the female *vette*, Mare, or the ugly trolls in the mountains, I'd make her put her hand on my heart to feel it pounding away. *Ja da, Gretchen, hjertet ditt er sunt,* she'd say. Yes, Gretchen, you do have one healthy heart. Now I could feel my blood racing through my veins—the pulse and rush of being in deep concentration, like a balloon being steadily expanded and tightened with the fill of air. A sense of dread accompanied the feeling. I took more notes.

The report also indicated that it had, very unfortunately, rained heavily and that trace evidence around the site had been wiped out. I looked up the lead investigator's name, Carson Belson. He was a detective with the county sheriff's office who was no longer on the force. I'd met him before, but he'd retired shortly after I came in 2010. He must have been devastated that it had rained so heavily and destroyed evidence, as if the gods were on the killer's side.

I wrote his name down, deciding I'd give him a call in the morning to ask him some more questions about the case. I wondered if Monty recalled the case as well. If Lucy was correct and the bones were a minimum of twenty years old, it was a long shot that the cases were related, but worth exploring anyway. I looked at the clock. It was already one a.m. I needed to get home. Still slightly light-headed, my thoughts whirling, I put the files away, turned off my computer, gathered my things, and headed home to get some sleep.

12

Monty

KEN AND I stayed at the office. We were waiting for the attorney general to get some law enforcement to bang on doors, do whatever they had to do to get someone into the DMV after hours so we could get that printout. For a while after the briefing with Ali and Herman, I spent some time going over the surveillance tapes to catch the image of the older dark blue Chevy truck edging out the entry gates. It was frustrating to not be able to make out the driver through the windshield and I kept trying to, even though I could see nothing but a wash of reflection from the glass.

After I got a good look at the truck, I went back to my office. Ali found me in there, going over past abductions. What Gretchen had said only reminded me of something I'd already been thinking and wanting to check out, but I hadn't had time to look at anything other than the missing persons reports Emily rounded up for me. I hadn't looked at actual cases where bodies had been found, identified or not. But I knew I had to be careful not to mix the Essex case in with the current situation with absolutely no proof of their relationship.

"You," Ali said.

I looked up from my desk at her standing in my doorway. "It's Monty," I reminded her. I knew she hadn't forgotten my name, and probably hadn't decided on a nickname for me yet, and she certainly didn't have time for me to correct her, but I didn't care what she thought of me. I knew she was just trying to get the job done, but she didn't need to be impolite about it.

"Excuse me. Monty. There are thirteen registrations for a Chevy Z71 1500 between the years of 1988 and 1993 registered in Flathead County. We need to visit each address associated with each registration. I want you to check out these vehicles even if it means waking people up in the middle of the night."

"Of course." I stood up from my desk and reached to take the printout from her, but she simply tossed it onto my desk. I looked her in the eye for a second, wanting to ask, *Why are you so angry?* We were all scared for the boy, and certainly angry and disturbed that we lived in a world where such things even occurred, but I didn't understand the need to be so gruff. Still, I kept my mouth shut—I'd had a lot of practice in my life doing that with both my brother and father—and simply picked the printout up from my desktop instead. "Will do." I tipped my head.

"Out of the thirteen, two have expired, and the rest are current. Divide them up between you and Ken, and Tara and Herman. That gives you and Ken about six or seven places to visit depending on how you divvy it up."

I wanted to say, *I can do the math*, then chastised myself for being pissy and ridiculous when a boy was missing. She was just doing her job, and she just had a different style than I did. I wondered if it irked her that she'd put so much stock in the Minsky lead when the new evidence was leading away from him, since the tire tracks at the yurt site didn't match the ones Gretchen and Ray pulled near the bridge. Although, if we didn't come up with anything by morning, I could imagine her saying, *Vehicles can be borrowed or he could own more than one and we should still locate Minsky.*

Which was true; we should, but in the meantime, I was happy to be checking out the registrants of a Chevy Z71. I refocused on the printout. We needed to visit each address associated with the registrants regardless of the status—current, revoked, expired. Herman, Tara, Ken,

and I divided the names according to region. One of our thirteen registrants had died and his offspring had never sold the truck, transferred
the title, or renewed the registration, which was why it was expired,
but we still planned to visit the offspring. The other expiration was due
to the truck getting totaled when the owner rolled it on a washboard
country road. It now sat in a junkyard south of Kalispell.

That left us twelve. Most people would be shocked to get a call from
law enforcement at ten at night, but it didn't matter. Time was of the
essence. Herman, Ken, Tara, and I headed out. We split the list evenly,
so Ken and I had six people on our end.

· · ·

The son of the guy who died showed Ken and me the truck behind his
house. He had it jacked up, parts stripped from it, the tires gone, the
wheel wells gaping like wounds. We could easily see that it had been
that way for some time, with rust on its fenders and debris and dust
from surrounding trees covering it. "Boy, sorry I can't help ya out, but
we retired this thing when the engine broke down after 220,000," the
guy said.

The next registrant wasn't home and several days' worth of news-
papers cluttered the sidewalk and entryway. We took some extra time
to check with the neighbors, who all confirmed that the retired couple
liked to take their RV to different parts of Montana for a week or two
in August. Everyone said that they'd been gone for at least four days
and no one had noticed anything suspicious or unusual. One neighbor
said he was in charge of taking in their papers and mail and felt embarrassed that he hadn't done that yet before we stopped by, adding that
he'd pick up the stray papers first thing in the morning. He had a key
and planned to water their plants for them as well.

The next three registrants on the list were in Kalispell, and all
were normal, average families and altogether unsuspicious: older, retired couples, moms who owned minivans while the fathers drove the
trucks, as they claimed, to make dump runs, haul firewood, move fur-

niture, or transport their snowmobiles or motorboats. All showed us their trucks without ado, and none had a front license plate missing or a CFAC Aluminum plant parking sticker on the front bumper.

The last address on our list was out toward the Swan Mountain Range, or as the locals liked to call it, the Columbia Range, which framed the eastern border of the valley. The dark mountains loomed like monsters in the distance, and we kept our windows down to get some cool air on our faces, to keep us as fresh as we could manage at the hour. The blowing air provided a reprieve from Ken's aftershave, which still surprisingly clung to him after nearly eighteen hours. Axe, I thought.

We drove a long county road called Church Road for some time until we eventually found a smaller gravel one that led to the driveway of the Tuckmans. We turned east onto a tree-lined drive and went at least three-quarters of a mile, passing several dirt roads sprouting off the main driveway, but figured staying on the main drive was our best bet. Eventually, we pulled up to a large white farmhouse at the end of it. Our headlights flashed across a bright red-and-white-trimmed storybook barn towering off to the side of their home in a wheat field before we turned onto their paved circular driveway.

"Hmm," Ken had said. "Big barn. Always interesting."

"Seeing as this is a farm and knowing how many of those are around the valley, I'd hardly call that unusual, but yeah, never hurts to be curious."

We pulled up, quickly peeked in the garage windows using our flashlights, and spotted a shiny red pickup and white Subaru parked inside. Dogs began barking ferociously from inside, jumping up and down and snarling. "Doing their job," I said to Ken.

Lights from inside began turning on, first upstairs, then down the stairway leading to the foyer. Someone in a dark robe peeked through the side windows, turned on the outside light, and looked out. I saw it was the man of the house. I held up my badge for him to see, and said loudly so he could hear my voice over the barking, "Sorry to disturb you so late. Urgent matter. Could we please have a moment with you?"

"Quiet, quiet," he commanded the dogs, which I could now see were two chocolate Labs with bright orange collars. One was plump and stocky, the other sleek and athletic.

The front door clicked and he swung it open, holding both dogs by the collars. They strained toward us, sniffing, trying to get a sense of us. "They bite?" Ken asked.

The man considered the question for a moment, then decided we weren't pulling any fast ones, and said, "Nah, they're all bark. But what's this about?"

"Walt," a woman's voice came from behind him. "What's going on?"

"It's two officers. I'm not sure."

He turned back to us with a questioning look, the dazed hint of sleep still in his gaze.

"Are you Richard Tuckman?"

"No, that's my father. What do you need with him at this hour?"

"Is he here?"

"No, he lives in an assisted living facility in Kalispell. We had to put him in it just about three months ago after he had a stroke and he needed more care than we could handle here."

Walt's wife came closer, trying to peer around his arm, which was on the doorframe. When he saw her, he dropped it, and she quietly regarded us in her pink robe and messy strawberry-blond hair. "What do you want with him?"

"We're here about a truck that was registered in his name. It's routine but important. Otherwise we wouldn't bother you at this hour. We're looking at all trucks in the valley that fit the description."

"What on earth for?"

"Sir, can we ask what your name is then?"

"I'm Walt. Walter Tuckman, and this is my wife, Anna."

"We're checking all Chevy trucks from the late eighties and early nineties in the valley, and your father happens to be an owner of one of them. Do you know where he keeps it? I'm assuming not at the facility."

"God, no. No one there can drive at all, but sure, of course I know where it is. It's here on the farm. We've got all sorts of old vehicles out here. You tell me the name of a farmer that doesn't have a collection of old trucks, and I'll tell you he isn't a Montana farmer."

"I believe you. You mind showing it to us, then? Like I said, routine check."

"Sure, just give me a minute. I need to get some clothes on."

"That's fine. We'll wait out here."

He shut the door and we heard his footsteps as he ran upstairs, his wife following him and asking questions as he went, the dogs still by the door making sniffing sounds. After a few minutes, he appeared, jiggling his keys and wearing faded jeans, steel-toed cowboy boots, and a flannel shirt hanging loosely over a T-shirt that was once white but now was the color of a manila folder.

"Thank you," I said. "We appreciate it. What kind of a farm you have here?"

"Potato." He punched numbers into a keypad by the garage doors, hit Enter, and one of the garage doors started to slide up.

"Potato?" Ken said. "I thought that was Idaho that did the potato thing."

"Potatoes from Montana are better. You can follow me." Walt pointed to a relatively new shiny red truck in the garage.

"Follow you?" I asked. "The Chevy's not here on your farm?"

"It is, but it's too long of a walk in the dark. We've got over five hundred acres here, with numerous buildings and sheds scattered around."

"How many outbuildings including your barn?" I asked.

"Five. Two old barns, two sheds, and a Quonset hut for additional equipment storage. Two of our trucks are kept out by the strawberry barn. It's got a side carport on it to park the trucks under."

"Strawberry?" Ken asked.

He chuckled. "We don't have strawberries, other than wild ones around. Just potatoes. We just call it that 'cause if you go upstairs in the barn, there's a nice view of Strawberry Mountain. All right, so I'll pull out and you can follow me. That good?" He opened the truck door and both Labs happily jumped in, looking like the Grinch's dog excited to go for a sleigh ride. Their tails thumped back and forth.

Ken and I caught each other's eye, thinking of the possibility of him driving off, trying to run, but he—like all the other registrants so far—looked wholly unsuspicious, and with two joyful retrievers jumping in next to him, he was unlikely to be going anywhere. "We'll be right behind you," I said.

"It's just the second left off the main driveway."

• • •

When we reached the strawberry barn, I could see in our headlights that it was less stately than the one by the house—rust-colored with chipped paint. About twenty yards off to the side, the carport Walt mentioned stood alone. I could see the outlines of two trucks under it. An old Airstream trailer stood beside the carport.

Ken and I got out, turning on our flashlights, and a neighing sound drifted over the fields toward us. "You have horses?"

"Two. I like to ride and so did my daughter before she went off to college. This way," he said.

Ken and I followed him a short distance from the parking area before the barn down a short drive, with dry, tangled grass on either side and in its center, toward the carport. The dogs frolicked back and forth for a bit, excited to go for a walk even though we weren't walking far.

The moonless night blanketed us. The sky was clear with the curtain of smoke from the forest fires drawn to the side, at least for now. Stars filled the infinite dome above—brilliant and ubiquitous. Without the heat of the sun, a legion of scents surrounded us. I could smell the complexities of the farmland soil and dried grain from the barn for the horses. The scent of tubers growing ready for fall harvest surrounded us, as if the soil claimed the air for a ceremony to celebrate the coming release of its vegetation.

When we reached the carport, Ken and I lifted our lights like protective swords, sweeping them over both vehicles. Red taillights glinted in our beams. The one closer to us was an old green Ford, and the other, on the outer side, was a dark Chevy.

"There she is," Walt said.

"If you could stay put with your dogs here, that would be great."

"Okay then," he said, calling them—Cocoa and Guinness—by his side. "Stay. Sit," he said firmly and they obeyed, whining slightly as if they knew something was up.

I didn't say anything. Neither did Ken. We just walked to the Chevy, continuing to slide our cones of light over it as we went closer. It fit the color description, but most of them we'd checked so far had. That's why we were honing in on them in the first place: the color, the time frame, and the make. Ken and I parted as we came up to it, each taking a side until we met in the front and illuminated the bumper. I steadied my beam in the right-hand corner, held it there as I kneeled down and looked more closely at the sticker. CFAC #127/Permit.

I could feel the blood rush to every part of my body. I looked at Ken for a second, kneeling beside me, his broad nose catching the glow from the flashlight, his aftershave still present, then looked back at the bumper. Every sound out in the night made me tremble and spooled me into a tight knot. An owl who-who'd in the distance and I could hear the Labradors leave Walt's side and scurry around out in the field beside us.

"Jackpot," Ken said softly, almost like a breath, and I felt a shiver go up my spine.

"Jackpot," I whispered back. "Let's call this in." I stood up and continued to inspect the truck without touching it. "You comfortable inspecting that barn if he agrees while I ask him some more questions?"

"I am," Ken said.

"When you get inside, go ahead and call Ali. We can't be sure if it's the actual truck that took the boy since the witness wasn't one hundred percent positive in the first place, but it's a huge lead. If he allows us to search, we're going to need all hands on deck—the county, KPD." I was referring to the Kalispell Police Department. "We're going to need to comb every inch of this place, and we're also going to need forensics here ASAP to look at this truck," I whispered.

Ken nodded vigorously. "And if he hears me make the calls?"

"It's okay. I'll be with him. He's not going anywhere." Walt Tuckman wasn't setting off any alarm bells with me, but that didn't mean I wasn't going to watch him like a hawk until the others arrived.

We backed away, trying to not create any more shoe prints than we already had and made a large arc back to where Walt stood.

"Mr. Tuckman," I said, "I hope you don't mind if my partner here looks around your barn while I ask you a few more questions."

"My barn? But what on earth for? What are you looking for?"

"Is that a yes or a no?" I pressed.

"Yes. Definitely. I don't mind. I just don't understand, is all."

I gave Ken a firm nod to go ahead, and he headed straight for the dark looming structure, with less apprehension than I thought he might display, his light brushing back and forth over the road and the dry grass as he walked. Each step crunching on the gravel sounded precise and loud in the quiet, still night.

"Mr. Tuckman, when was the last time you drove the Chevy?"

"It's been a long time. As you can see, I've got my own." He waved at his. The dogs followed Ken to the barn entrance, and Walt whistled for them to come back. "I don't need it much. Just when I haul something messy and don't want to dirty my own truck bed."

"How long?"

"Let me think. Two and a half months ago, in early June. I had to haul some gravel for a friend."

"Anyone else have access to this truck?"

"Sure. That's the point. That's why we keep it around and keep it registered. My farmhands all have access to the keys for all our vehicles. They use them as they need. I trust them and they always put the key back, keep 'em filled with gas."

"And where are the keys kept?"

"In the barn."

"And how many farmhands do you have?"

"Two."

"Okay, Mr. Tuckman. We're going to need to get those names from you. Additionally, we're going to need your permission to search your truck, and maybe your place. Will you give us that?"

"Search my place? What do you mean?"

"For starters, your Chevy truck and your barn. We need to dust your truck for prints. We may need to move it to a forensics garage to check it out under different lighting and to run some more tests."

Walt's forehead stayed wrinkled in confusion as he listened to me.

"We need to understand if your father's truck was, indeed, involved in the crime we're working on. We may need to search more, your other buildings and your house. We may need to see your whole farm—all the buildings, the entire property. Is that going to be a problem, sir?"

Walt didn't answer me at first. I could see he was trying to wrap his head around it all.

"Because if you say no, we'll more than likely do it anyway, but with a search warrant."

"No, no, of course, we want to help. Have at it. Anna and I have nothing to hide, and I highly doubt that truck is the one you're thinking it is, whatever you think it may have been involved in."

"We'll see, Mr. Tuckman, and we'll let you know, but in the meantime, we need you to stay put."

• • •

When the others began to arrive at—or, I should say, descend upon—the place, a pale light had started to fan over the mountains. I say "descend" because of the sheer numbers pulling up the drive: Flathead County, Park Police, Kalispell Police Department vehicles. I figured Ali wanted to cover every inch of the place, and excitement reared up in me when I thought of the possibility of finding Jeremy.

Ali and Herman pulled up in their discreet, dark SUVs—Tara still with Herman from working on their list of registrants. I showed the agents the barn and the truck; Ken showed some of the county guys the main house. Ken had not seen anything unusual or suspicious in the strawberry barn. Walt cooperated on everything, drawing us a map of the entire farm, indicating where all the outbuildings were located. Morning light was quickly spreading as well as a blanket of dark clouds. I lifted my nose to the air and caught the sweet, pungent scent of ozone, signaling that a storm might be on its way, its downdrafts pushing the sharp smells from higher altitudes toward us. After such a long dry spell, the odors were stronger than ever.

"What have you got so far?" Ali asked.

"Six people, including Walt, his wife, his two twentysomething kids, and two farmhands. The owner, Richard Tuckman, is ruled out because he had a stroke several months ago and is in a home. The son says he can't walk, drive, or even talk."

"You know I'm going to want verification on that."

"Yep. Will do." I had already made a note in my pad to do so.

"Where are the kids? They live here?"

"No, off to college. Both of them stayed for jobs and summer school."

"Where's that?"

"The son, Mitch, is in Bozeman at MSU and is working at a hotel this summer. The daughter, Hunter, is out at a university in Portland. She's taking summer classes. Neither have been home in a month. I think we can rule them out for now."

"Hunter?" Ali rolled her eyes. "Why can't people pick names anymore that don't confuse everyone about what gender they are?"

I shrugged. "I don't see why Hunter can't be a girl's name."

Ali waved her hand between us to brush the thought away like an annoying fly. "Okay, so that leaves four people. The Tuckmans and the two farmhands. You have names and info?"

"I do," I said, already handing her the sheet of paper. She held my eyes for a second, then took it and studied it. "Good work, you two. Good work finding this truck."

"All just part of the job," I said, "but thank you." I was surprised at her sudden kindness. I recalled when she'd worried about the Coreys inside the motel and wanted me to stay with them until a victim's specialist or a chaplain arrived. It occurred to me that her brusqueness was only a wall, an armor for obvious reasons: to live or work without a shield in this world, especially in this business, was like being an open, exposed wound. To live without protection meant you had to absorb the world as it really was, and for some, that was too difficult. But Ali Paige had a sweetness under it all that trickled up and out every now and again like a spring seep.

"So here's how we're going to work this," she said. "Herman and I are going to question Walt again while the farm gets searched and that truck gets processed. Since your man has given us permission to search, we can move quickly, which is a huge relief. It moves him down the suspect list a tiny bit, but still, Herman and I are going to make sure no stone is left unturned, no candy box left unopened. So, what I need from you and Ken now," she continued, "is to find the farmhands as quickly as you can. Find out if they have alibis for the morning and afternoon Jeremy went missing." She looked to the eastern mountains and frowned. "And for shit's sake, if it decides to rain today of all days when it hasn't rained in months, I'm going to lose it."

• • •

"She already *is* pissed all the time, so it doesn't really matter," Ken said as we hopped in the car.

"But this time, I have to agree with her. As badly as we need the rain, we don't need it on this farm on this day."

We hit a convenience store off the highway to get coffee and whatever we could find for breakfast. Ken grabbed a plastic-wrapped cinnamon muffin, some beef jerky, a purple-colored Gatorade, and a fresh pack of chewing gum. I plucked a banana from a basket sitting near the cash register, some OJ, a granola bar, and some microwavable egg sandwich wrapped in plastic that looked entirely indigestible.

We went back to the car, the sky turning steelier and large clouds still knotting above the eastern mountains. The wind had begun to pick up, and in spite of having stayed up all night, a part of me felt giddy and excited—like a frisky horse that senses a weather change—for the huge downpour we'd been awaiting to help extinguish the fires. But a bigger part of me wanted it to stay dry to preserve any evidence the teams might discover at the farm. One more day, I thought, or at least a few more hours if it helped us find Jeremy.

"I hate to miss my morning routine," Ken said, twisting the plastic top off his bottle.

I knew he was referring to the one hundred push-ups and the two hundred sit-ups he did each morning before coming to work. Ken looked down and flexed one of his biceps, which reminded me of Popeye. "How can you even think about that after pulling an all-nighter?"

"Have to," he said. "Keeps me sane."

I pulled out the list of names. The farmhands both lived on this end of the valley: one in Columbia Falls and one near the minuscule town of Creston with its tree farm, auction center, and post office. We visited the Creston guy first—a Paul Stewart—since he was closer. He lived in a nondescript beige one-story house not far off the highway. He was a potbellied, brown-haired guy of about forty who wore muddy boots and old faded jeans. When we told him we needed to ask him a few questions, he told us he'd be happy to help but had to get off to work to get there by eight. When we told him work could wait and that the questions involved where he works, he invited us in and led us to the kitchen table. We took seats and he offered us some coffee.

"It's okay," I said. "We're fine." He looked like he lived alone with the kitchen bare of decorations or any color. No curtains or shades dressed the windows, and they weren't picture windows, just average run-of-the-mill rectangular windows with dirty screens.

"You sure? I always make extra and I only just turned it off, so it's still hot. I try to make enough only for one cup, but it always tastes like crap that way. I find it tastes best when I brew at least four cups worth, and I never have that much, so I just end up wasting it."

"You've talked me into it," I said. Ken said he'd have a little too, commenting that it did smell way better than the stale, watery cup we'd just picked up at the convenience store.

He set the mugs of coffee in front of us and took a seat himself.

"You live alone?"

"Yeah, it's better that way. Used to have a girlfriend, but she moved out about six months ago. Just didn't work out."

I nodded that I understood. "Here's the deal, Mr. Stewart. We need to ask you a few questions specifically about your whereabouts two days ago, on August 16—this Tuesday—from around ten a.m. and through the rest of the afternoon."

"My whereabouts?"

"That's right."

"What's this about?"

"Please just answer for us."

"Two days ago"—he tilted his head to think for a second—"I was golfing. At Northern Pines with the guys. We had a ten thirty a.m. tee time."

"The guys? Can you give us their names and can they confirm that you were playing with them?"

"Of course I can. What's this about?"

"How long did you play?"

"Four to five hours, eighteen holes, like usual. Then we had some drinks in the club bar."

I tried to picture the guy in front of me playing a sport like golf because he certainly didn't look like the type with his grubby clothes and muddy boots, but I knew that in Montana, golf was no New York or San Francisco country club sport. The valley was the perfect spot for sprawling gorgeous fairways, and all types of people loved to get out in their jeans, Carhartts, and coveralls to play among the mountains that encased the valley on all sides.

He gave us the names of his golfing buddies, and I wrote them all down, handed the list to Ken, and nodded for him to go check it out. He excused himself and went out to the car.

"How long have you worked for the Tuckmans?"

"Few years now. Almost four."

"And you're full-time?"

"About thirty to over forty hours a week depending on the season. During spring, summer, and fall, I work a lot more, over full-time. On the off-season, not as much and I scrape other jobs together, but I still do maintenance for Walt in the winter too. Help feed and care for the horses, mend fence, plow snow, that kind of stuff."

"And do you have another job you're working now?"

"No, just at Walt's. It's pretty busy this time of the year."

"So, how do you have time to take the day off to golf?"

"There's two of us. The other guy, Brady, he works a lot less than I do, and sometimes both of us have it off if it's a Saturday or Sunday. Sometimes I get a weekday off if Brady is working, and sometimes we both work. It just depends on what's going on and how much Walt needs us."

"And when did you work last?"

"Yesterday."

"And did you drive Walt's trucks—the ones stored under the car-port near the barn?"

"No. I helped out in the field all day. Didn't need the trucks. Haven't needed them in a while. Why? Did someone steal one of them?"

I didn't answer him, just kept asking questions. "How long's a while?"

"A week or so."

"So, you haven't used either truck in a week?"

"No, I haven't. Just the tractor and test-drove the potato harvester to make sure all is okay for the coming harvest. Oh, wait—" He looked out his kitchen window. There was a scraping noise from a bushy tree limb blowing in the wind and hitting the side of the house. "Yes, I did. I used the Ford to move sprinklers the time before. We've been finishing up irrigation, getting the storages ready. We've got our last inspection by the university staff coming up later this month. So that was like three days ago."

"And you didn't use the Chevy?"

"No, I like the Ford better. Newer. I hardly ever use the Chevy unless Brady's using the Ford and I have to haul something messy, like dirt or gravel, and that's not all that often anymore because the Ford's been broken in enough now that we've been using that to haul just about anything anyway."

"And when was the last time you did that?"

"Few weeks ago, like I said. Went to the dump. I only used the Chevy because Brady was using the Ford for something, can't remember what for."

"And where do you get the keys for these trucks?"

"Walt keeps them in the barn, on an iron hook. We just grab them as we need them. We have a rule that we keep them filled up at least halfway, no less, so no one gets stuck with an empty tank when they go to use it."

"You use your own money for this?"

"No, we have a gas card for the Cenex in Kalispell near the feed and farm place, so it works great for us when we need to go for supplies."

"Okay," I said, jotting the information down, and then looked back at him. "Mr. Stewart, I want you to think really carefully about this: do you recall anything different or strange at all around the Tuckman farm lately, say in the past few days?"

He looked perplexed, his brow deeply furrowed, as if he'd be shocked to find out that there was any connection to anything suspicious at all going on at the Tuckman farm. "I don't get it," he said. "I don't get why you're here, but no, I don't. I really don't. Has someone stolen the Chevy?"

"No, it's still at the farm, but have you noticed anyone strange around it?"

"No."

"Do you know when Brady drove it last?"

"I don't, but I think it's been a while for him too. He prefers the Ford like I do, but I can't say for sure." He stood and pulled out a pack of cigarettes from a kitchen drawer. "You mind if I smoke?"

"Actually, I do," I said. "We're close to finishing. If you could just hold off for a bit, that would be great."

He shrugged, threw the pack across the counter, and came and sat back down. I continued to question him, but he had nothing more to offer that Mr. Tuckman hadn't already given us.

Ken came back in and said, "All clear," meaning that the alibi checked out. He told me later that he called some of the men in the golfing group as well as the Northern Pines Golf Club, where a guy named Shelby who worked in the starter booth remembered Paul Stewart checking in to play. Just the same, we told Stewart we might need to talk to him again, and when he asked about going to work, we told him he might want to check in with his boss first. We left him finally lighting up at the doorway as we hopped into the car.

. . .

The second man—a Brady Lewis—had already left for work and was heading to the Tuckmans for the day. His girlfriend had answered the door and let us know. She was a tall brunette with rosy round cheeks and a cute smile, but when she saw our badges, she looked frightened and seemed to move the door an inch closer toward us. I couldn't be sure, but I detected a slight whiff of pot when she'd first opened it.

"And you're Mrs. Lewis?"

"No, I'm Samantha Armstrong."

"But, you live here, correct?"

"Yes, I'm Brady's girlfriend. Have been for over five years. We came out to Montana together from Massachusetts."

"I see. Well, Samantha, we need to ask you a few questions. Do you recall where Brady was on Tuesday, the sixteenth?"

She thought about it for a second. "That was his day off from both places."

"Both places?"

"Yeah, he works at the Tuckmans and he also works part-time at an agriculture supply store."

"The one in Kalispell?"

She nodded. "Yeah, the one on Idaho Street, but he wasn't there that day. Like I said, he had it off, and when he has some time, well, he goes fishing." She said it in a resigned singsong manner like she didn't like it but that there was not a thing she could do about it.

"Any idea when he left to go fishing?"

"Early, like seven a.m."

"And when did he return?"

"Past dinnertime, because I remember wondering if I should make enough for him, but I know better. Once he goes fishing, he's always staying out as long as he can," she grumbled. "Doesn't matter how many things we need to do around this place, like clean the garage or do some lawn work, he's always just gotta blow outta here on his days off and go fishing, leaving it all to me."

We thanked her, left, and called the agriculture supply store. Brady's boss, a British-sounding woman, confirmed that he had the day off and wasn't at work. "Probably fly-fishing," she said, echoing the girlfriend's sentiments. "He loves to do that on his days off." We phoned it in to Ali and Herman to let them know to have their guys on the entrance roads keep an eye out for him when he drove up, and to check the amount of gas in the Chevy. If it wasn't below half a tank, there was a good chance it had been either filled recently or not used at all.

Before we went back to Kalispell to the nursing home to check on old Mr. Tuckman, and then head back to the Tuckmans' farm to see if Ali and Herman were making progress, I wanted to make a stop while we were in Columbia Falls. So I turned to Ken and said, "You mind if we make a quick stop while we're here?"

"Nah, I don't mind. Who needs sleep anyway?"

"My sentiments exactly."

"What for?" he asked.

"There's a woman I want to visit. Has to do with those bones Tara and I found the other day. It shouldn't take more than a minute."

"Fine with me," Ken said, unwrapping the new pack of chewing gum he'd bought at the convenience store. "Who is she?"

"Just the mother of a boy who disappeared without explanation a long time ago. The father refused to submit a saliva sample to the center in Texas, so I'm hoping she'll be game."

"You think the bones you found might belong to that boy? We *are* talking about your friend from years back? Right?"

Ken knew bits and pieces of the Nathan Faraway story, but I didn't know if he'd remember much at all, and to be honest, I'd have been perfectly fine if he didn't. Apparently I'd underestimated him. "Yeah, that's right. The time frame fits, but who knows."

"So, this is, Mrs., Mrs. . . ." He squinted, trying to recall the name.

"Faraway," I mumbled, not really wanting to talk much about it. I just knew she lived nearby, on Nucleus Avenue where it dead-ended close to the Flathead River. We were coming up on the road any second and I needed to fill Ken in if I was going to drag him along, even if I did plan to go in alone and let Ken wait in the car. "She and Mr. Faraway are no longer together," I added. "But she's kept the name."

"Makes sense," Ken said. "You'd never change your name from that of your missing boy's. Ever."

I pictured Ken going home and hugging his boy just a little harder and longer now that Jeremy had gone missing. "No," I agreed. "You wouldn't."

• • •

Alice Faraway answered the door. She was still much like I recalled—slight and child-size with chestnut hair and a wide smile. I had remembered her as beautiful, and her prettiness had faded some, her face sagging with age and her large eyes even more prominent on her delicate face. She still held a certain beauty, though, like a washed-up model that the industry had spit out, but in her case, it was no industry; it was the cold dark underbelly of a parent's worst nightmare. When I introduced myself, she didn't flinch as I'd expected or show a spark of hope, or fear, at the sight of an officer. Then I understood why.

"I knew you'd come," she said. "Peter warned me." She stood in the doorway in a floral shirt, baggy jeans, and a pair of dirty tennis shoes. She didn't invite me in.

"Mrs. Faraway—"

She stopped me. "It's *Ms.* Faraway now. Peter probably told you we got a divorce."

"He did," I said. "I was—am—very sorry to hear that."

"Why? Why does it matter to you?"

I didn't answer. What should I say? That I cared about them as a family when I was little and that I still did? That not a week in my life went by without Nathan entering my mind in some way? "Listen—"

"I don't care, Monty"—she shot up her hand to stop me again—"I don't care what you have to say. We're not going to give saliva."

I asked her the same thing I had Peter. "But don't you want to know if it's him?"

I thought I caught a small, soft wave of hope, a sort of plea in her eyes that said, *Yes, dear God, yes, I want to know what happened to my baby*, then watched it fade as she took a deep inhale and gathered her wits. "It's not him, Monty. Those bones, they're not my boy's."

"I'm not saying they are, just that they could be. The time frame is the same, Mrs. . . . I mean, Ms. Faraway. The bones are being sent to Texas for analysis. If it's Nathan and they can get DNA from the tissue inside, then they can put this to rest. You can put this—"

"To rest?" She gave me a piercing and incredulous look, as if I'd assaulted her senses.

"I didn't mean it that way. I meant, maybe have a service. Say a sort of good-bye."

"How would you know what we'd do, Monty? Say good-bye? There's no good-bye when you lose a child." Her blue eyes sliced me like small razors. "Our family was broken and always will be, service or no service."

I stood before her, my entire body wilting like a flower without water, like she'd cut my stem. Exhaustion and a whole new level of sadness ensnared me. "I . . . I just thought that it might help, that's all."

"It doesn't. We both said no, so please just leave." I could see straight through to her pain like I was looking into a pool of stream water and noticing a complex palette of rocks and stones. I hadn't seen such intense pain in even my own mother's troubled stares.

But still I had a sense that she was of two minds about the whole thing, wanting to do as Peter had told her, but also wanting, perhaps needing, to help identify the bones. "Ms. Faraway, if it's not Nathan, then wouldn't it be good to eliminate his name so that maybe other families have a chance to find their missing? Wouldn't you like to do that?"

"You'll find that out anyway by getting their DNA samples. You don't need ours." She stared at me, her eyes hollowed in her skull.

"It's just a simple saliva test. All you have to do is go to the station, or I can even have an officer swing by."

"Monty, please leave. Just"—she began to close the door—"please just go away."

I forced myself to stand tall and brave while the scuffed white door shut in my face. I could feel Ken's eyes on me from the window of the car, but the night of no sleep and the agony in Ms. Faraway's eyes—still so many years later—made my legs begin to tremble. Several robins plucked worms at the far end of her lawn near a chain-link fence. I turned back to the car, strode back, and hopped in.

"You get what you needed?" Ken asked.

"Just what I deserved," I said.

"How's that?"

"Doesn't matter. Let's go visit the senior Mr. Tuckman."

• • •

We pulled into the parking lot of Mission Mountain Manor, Richard Tuckman's assisted-living facility. Russian olive trees draped over the side of the two-story building, and the breeze rattled their delicate leaves. One porch light hung above the entryway to the facility, leading to a brightly lit lobby. A dog barked in the distance, and a visitor—a middle-aged woman talking on her cell phone—walked out to her car.

Stale antiseptic air hit us immediately as we stepped in. The receptionist, a middle-aged woman with short, spiky hair, stood up behind the long counter and asked us if she could help. I showed her my badge.

"We didn't call for any assistance. What's this about?"

"Our apologies for disturbing you. We've been working on locating the owner of a vehicle. We understand from his son that he now resides here and we'd like to speak to him."

"Owner of a vehicle? That's all? Goodness, you scared me." She placed her palm over her chest. "Seeing your badge and all. I thought something had happened to one of our residents without me knowing."

"No, nothing like that."

"Who are you looking for, then?" She chuckled. "Our residents certainly aren't driving."

"We figured that, but we still need to check in with him. His name is Mr. Richard Tuckman."

"Mr. Tuckman? Let me get his nurse," She excused herself and went into a back room and came back out after a few seconds with a narrow-faced woman with deeply set eyes that were close together, giving her a slight simian appearance.

"You'd like to see Mr. Tuckman?" she asked.

"Yes, we would if that's possible."

"Well, he's not doing so well. You probably wouldn't get much out of him. He's had a stroke and has lost most of his speech faculties."

"Can he talk at all?"

"Very little. He has good days and bad days. He's taking his midmorning nap now, and if I wake him, he'll be completely disoriented, and that won't help at all." The nurse pursed her lips in a tight, thin line. I got the feeling she made that expression to deal with family members and to cope with the cold reality of some of the patients in the place.

"We understand. His son, Walt, filled us in." I looked for a name tag on her robin's-egg blue uniform. She wore a cream-colored sweater over the top, but you could still see her name tag peeking out. "Ms. Learner, we'd appreciate your help on this. Unfortunately, this is a situation where we don't have that kind of time. Can you please go wake him and bring him out? We'd also be happy to go to his room if that's easier."

She searched my eyes, then Ken's and said, "Well . . ." She squinted, mulling it over. She seemed wary. I could tell she was protective of her residents—a good thing, I considered. "If it's urgent like you say, then it's probably best you come to his room. If I bring him out, it will take some time. You do understand that most people are here because they cannot care for themselves? They suffer from strokes, dementia, Alzheimer's, Parkinson's, or some other debilitating conditions."

"We understand. Does the senior Mr. Tuckman have a wife?"

"Used to. I heard she passed away and that it wasn't long after that he had his stroke. Very debilitating. Give me a minute to wake him, give him something to drink, and then I'll show you in."

"Thank you, Ms. Learner," I said. "We appreciate your help."

Ken tipped his head to ditto my sentiment as she walked down the hall.

• • •

Ten minutes later, Ms. Learner showed me down a hallway with a border of flowery pastel wallpaper to Richard Tuckman's private room. Ken stayed back in the waiting room to make some calls to headquarters. We'd decided with the nurse that it would be best if just one of us went in so that we didn't overwhelm or confuse him with two strange faces.

"Richard," Ms. Learner said loudly and with cheer, "as I told you, you have a visitor today."

The old man's eyes fluttered open. She had said she'd already woken him, but that he might doze in and out. Mr. Tuckman's glassy eyes looked like small round marbles the color of pewter. His frame was gaunt and small, and I could see bony knees protruding under his blanket.

"Hello, Mr. Tuckman," I said.

He turned his head slightly toward me and simply blinked. He lay in a recliner in the corner of the room next to a round side table that had several pictures on it. I studied the pictures while Ms. Learner straightened his blanket and gave him a sip of water from a blue plastic cup with a crooked straw. A black-and-white wedding photo of a younger couple smiling before church doors angled toward his recliner. I could see it was Richard and his wife. The dark-haired bride wore a lacy wedding dress, held white roses, and smiled with pearly teeth. The younger Richard stood tall and proud, his chest broad and his chin high.

I looked at the man now before me. This man certainly was not what he once was. I felt a familiar bittersweet pang in response to witnessing the transient nature of life. Most of the time we simply looked away from it, ignored it, but there were certain times when it hit so strongly that it felt like a deep ache. I suppose the case was magnifying my emotions in spite of my training.

Ms. Learner said she was going to leave us to it, showed me a button on a remote control to buzz her with, and said not to hesitate if we needed anything. I told her we'd be fine, then shuffled closer to the recliner.

I introduced myself again and slowly, but loudly explained why I was visiting him—that his son, Walt, had directed us here to get some assistance on a very important matter. That neither he nor his son were in trouble, but that we'd been looking at his old truck and that we needed to know who had access to it when he still ran the farm. I heard my own voice as I looked into his confused eyes and realized that I probably wasn't going to get anywhere with this old man. He just stared at me, and a tiny dribble of drool even escaped his mouth and trickled down the right side of his chin. I wasn't sure whether to grab a tissue and wipe it for him or not. I didn't want to upset him by invading his space in the wrong way.

"Do you think you can help with that, Mr. Tuckman? Can you remember the individuals who had access to your farm trucks?"

Mr. Tuckman nodded slightly, but didn't say anything.

"You do remember?"

He gave a very slight nod again.

"Can you tell me?"

A slight mumble came from him, but faded as soon as it began, like a trickle of water drying up.

I continued trying to get him to talk for a few more minutes, but it was useless. Eventually his eyes closed. I grabbed a tissue and wiped the drool from his chin, but his eyes stayed shut. I threw the tissue in a small wastebasket in the corner of the room and looked at his wedding picture again. I thought of my own wedding picture. Since Lara kept the house, she had all our old pictures. She asked me if I wanted any, but I didn't know what I'd do with them, so I said no. It was one of those confusing things about divorces—what you did with pictures. Displaying them or even keeping them in a box somewhere meant you were hanging on to something that had not survived. But throwing them away felt equivalent to tossing years away—time sewn together with the merging of each other's existences.

I looked at the other pictures on the table. One was of Richard, his wife, and the three kids on vacation at what appeared to be the Grand Canyon, based on the layers of terra-cotta landscape behind them. I could tell the third picture was from the farm because I could see tall green stalks of potato plants in the background. A large group sat around a picnic table on the back patio. I recognized Richard, his wife, and the kids. About five other men and women sat around the table as well. I thought it was some kind of extended family gathering, perhaps

THE WEIGHT OF NIGHT 181

aunts, uncles, and cousins. One man had dark, close-cropped hair, the other had shaggy red wavy hair and a scraggly goatee. I shook Richard's shoulder to wake him and held up the framed photo. He opened his eyes and looked at me as if he didn't know who I was. "Mr. Tuckman. Richard. Can I call you that?"

He didn't move.

"Can you tell me who these men in the photo are?"

Again, no response. I rang Ms. Learner, and she came in and I asked her if she knew who the people in the photo were. "Oh yeah," she said. "Family members. Brothers or cousins or something, I think."

I set the picture back down and made a note to ask Walt about his extended family and if any had access to the truck. I took one last glance at Richard, now sleeping peacefully, his breathing ragged and loud, and followed the nurse out. Verification is what we needed, so at the very least, we had that—Richard Tuckman was definitely not out and about cruising around and abducting children.

13

Gretchen

I OPENED MY EYES slowly the next morning to see a blurry brown flower that slowly came into focus as the stilled fan in the center of the ceiling. I turned over and looked out the window beside my bed—another gray day taking shape, the skies filled with smoke and ash again. The wind must have shifted, I thought, blowing the smolder from the fires in the park back into the valley, just like the day before last, when we worked the dig.

The dig. Two days ago. And two days since Jeremy vanished, I considered. Then I looked again. The gray skies weren't laden with ash; they were blanketed in gunmetal clouds. Rain, I thought. It might finally rain.

Excitement for something so simple shot through me and I sat up quickly to peer out my window, but suddenly I noticed my head ached fiercely in my temple, a different spot than usual. Instead of the pinpricks of shooting pain that started above my left ear, my temple felt thick and tender on the right side, almost as if I'd been hit. I hopped out of bed and ran into the bathroom to look in the mirror.

Near my right eyebrow, I had a thick scratch and a patch of swelling skin. Several thin lines of blood spidered down the side of my face. "Shit," I said, bringing my hand to it. I scolded myself for not getting out my sleeping bag and mittens the night before. I had gotten home late after looking at files in the office, and that was after visiting the park twice in one day. Completely exhausted, I had practically fallen

182

into bed and not only didn't grab my bag or mittens but didn't even turn on the fan.

Terror shot through me, my fears rising up in me like flames snaking up a dry tree. What had I done? I ran into the living room to look, but nothing was altered. I checked my front and back doors to find them still both locked. I ran to my closet, fetched the footstool, and took stock of my bedroom and closet. Everything was as I usually kept it. I hurried back out, went through the dining room and into the kitchen, bringing the footstool with me. No furniture was moved around in the dining room or kitchen either. I placed the stool before the fridge and climbed up to check for my key. I was relieved to find it in the usual spot in the jar.

I climbed down, took my stool back to the closet, and went to look in the mirror. I studied the wound, touching my temple with two fingers and wondering how I had hurt it. I could have run into the corner of my dresser or opened a kitchen cabinet into my face. I ran some warm water, grabbed a washcloth, and gently dabbed at the dried blood. I rinsed it, watching the red trickles separate and run down the side of the sink, knowing that any potential for my own recollection of what happened was as lost as the blood spiraling down the drain.

In the kitchen, I put some ice in another washcloth and held it to my temple. Sometimes I could remember every detail of a dream, even ones that I walked in, like with Figment Man. And other times, my sleep and my dreamscape became a black hole. I decided I would make an appointment with my doctor first thing and promised myself I'd definitely sleep with my bag and mittens tonight. No laziness, I thought as I leaned against my kitchen counter.

. . .

At work, I called Detective Carson Belson from the county sheriff's office and asked if I could swing by for a visit. He was retired and living in Bigfork, a small town on the northeast corner of Flathead Lake. On the phone, his voice was low and had a smoky quality to it that reminded

me of my father's. I briefly wondered if my dad was taking on the same
ruddy look I recalled Detective Belson having. My dad would be sixty-
two now and I missed him the most of all of my family members. He
was always my hero, intelligent, strong, witty, and he wore all of the
parts of his personality gracefully—they intermingled like the finely
tuned strings of an instrument. He had an intense interest in a variety
of subjects—science, music, art, history, architecture—and he had an
appetite for life in general. He always pointed out the beautiful systems
of things: how the currents of the ocean worked, how the universe expanded, how the trees in the forests were connected through their root
systems, how one person could make a difference.

I always thought of him as a strong person—a Viking—but what
I'd done would break anyone, even a Viking, and in the end, even he
couldn't sew up the deep gash I'd sliced through our family. They divorced by the time I turned eighteen, both of them forever changed.
He was right; one person could make a difference. One person could
destroy everything.

It was still early in the morning when I arrived, and Belson offered
me coffee, but I declined, so he took me for a walk around his property instead. Other than looking a little older—I figure he was at least
seventy now—he was exactly as I remembered. He still had the same
quintessential mountain-man look. He was proud of the tree farm
he was managing since he'd retired, but upset that it had been so dry
for the past years. "Growing full spruce for Christmas trees isn't easy
under these conditions," he said.

"I can imagine," I said. Squirrels scurried here and there and other
small birds darted from tree to tree. "Well, looks like we might finally
have a storm brewing."

Belson looked to the sky. "Much needed."

Several ravens flew around us and perched in a few trees above,
squawking sharply. "Don't mind them. They're my buddies. They're
just saying hello. Smart buggers, they are. Other day, I saw them playing hide-and-seek with each other. I'm not kidding. One would fly off

and hide a twig behind a tree under some dirt and the other would go and find it and bring it back to him and then they'd cackle. You just have to take the time to watch 'em, observe 'em, something most people don't do."

"And I'm sure you have more time to do that now that you're not doing detective work."

"Absolutely," he said.

"You miss it?"

"Nah," he said. "It sucks the life out of you. Like the case you're here wanting to know about, the Erickson boy." He shook his head and scuffed the ground with the toe of one of his boot-clad feet. "I'm happier now not being faced with such tragedy all the time. Ignorance is bliss, especially in small communities like this. I used to go get soup in a few local cafés around and invariably, there'd be someone I knew who'd done something awful—some guy who'd just beaten his wife or kids two days before, but kept his wife too scared to press charges, or some great community member who you know has been embezzling money, but you can't prove it, and too many other things to repeat. Tends to make you bitter," he said.

"Mr. Belson, do you remember much from the Erickson case?"

"Of course, every detail. Still have nightmares about the damn thing once in a while because we should have made some connection, gotten some lead, but we had nothing to go on." We walked down the rows of trees and back to the porch in front of his house and took seats in two lawn chairs. "As usual, at first we thought he had just run away—was coming into some rebellious years, but still, we took it seriously, since the parents insisted he wouldn't do that. The search," he said, "was huge, like the one you've probably got going on now with that boy in the park. We had helicopters, policeman, county deputies, divers, dogs, and volunteer searchers combing the neighborhoods, the woods, the river, and the surrounding fields in all directions. We weren't sure exactly where he was taken, but we figured he was picked up from a neighborhood a little south of

Columbia Falls when he was walking home from a friend's house in the evening. It was July."

"So, no leads at all?"

"No, none. Nobody saw anything, no vehicle, nothing strange. We canvassed the area, banged on doors, questioned everyone. Nobody knew anything. We figured unknown assailant, possibly a summer tourist who lured him into their car to look for a lost dog or something, then just drove off with him."

"But you found the body."

"We did. We got lucky, if you can call it that," he said in a low voice. "A guy out hunting grouse with his dogs by the foothills." He pointed up the mountain range marching toward Glacier Park. "North past the gas station near the cutoff to Kalispell, toward Columbia Falls and off Highway 206. Anyway, the dogs sniffed the shallow grave out, dug it up, kind of made a mess of it. To make matters worse, by the time we were called and got to it, it had rained, and not just a sprinkle. It had poured buckets—big summertime drops that pelted the windshield and gave everything a good soaking. The kind of storm that looks like it might build up today." He turned his head to the clouds covering and spreading out from the mountains with their white and silver tops and purple undersides.

"What did forensics find?"

"Fortunately, that was the one break. They were able to narrow down TOD based on insects and body temperature. The boy hadn't been dead for more than twenty-four hours."

"And the boy disappeared on July seventh?"

"That's right. The monster kept him for five days, and that definitely made us think it was no random tourist—that the assailant was local. He or she spent some time with the kid, kept him around for his pleasure for that long, then killed him, or desperately tried to keep him, but something went wrong, maybe the kid tried to escape."

"Why do you think he wanted to keep him?"

"He or she, I said. It happens more than you know. It's one of the prevailing profiles we're taught to look for: middle-aged females who've lost a child somehow and who want to replace that kid, women who suffer many miscarriages and can't have their own. Twelve was a little old for that scenario, but it's happened before. It's rare, but we have had cases where a husband has been talked into bringing a child home for the wife. But that was a stretch for this case because of the boy's age. Usually if the assailant is male and he's going for a young teen, he's a pedophile."

The detective grew silent for a moment, letting what we all had already imagined anyway settle on us like a heavy, dirty net. "Hey, are you sure you don't want some coffee or tea or something?"

"No, no, I'm good," I said, my stomach feeling a little topsy-turvy. I wasn't usually the one asking questions, and it made me feel strange. I should be in the lab or on some crime scene, I thought, not digging around in cold cases. My forehead began to throb and itch in the hot morning sun. I put my fingers to the new bump and scratched, but quickly stopped because of the tenderness.

"How'd you get that cut?"

"It's nothing. Just bumped into my dresser. It doesn't pay to be short."

He smiled, inspecting me with narrowed eyes, perhaps wondering if I had addiction issues or an abusive husband.

"So, the rain destroyed most of the trace evidence?" I asked.

"That's right. I mean, the report said the usual. Tox screen was negative, so he wasn't drugged or drunk. He was covered in mud and other outdoor usual stuff: dirt, pollen. Hell, I don't need to tell you." He smiled and lackadaisically swatted at a bee that swarmed around us.

"Do you remember if the dirt and mud was consistent with the soil composition around the foothills?"

"Yes, obviously the dirt in the burial was. Again, the trace was washed clean with the rain, so forensics couldn't get a good read of the samples."

"Yeah, that fits with what I read in the file. No footprints?"

"A few blurry ones that were run over by the dogs, nothing distinctive. A handful matched the hunter's, and he definitely had an alibi. The dogs tracked through most of the mud. The site was a damn mess by the time we got to it. There were obviously hairs and saliva from the canines, and I think we found a stray hair or two on the inside of the kid's clothes that matched the mother's. We figured she did the laundry."

"No DNA, no fingerprints or anything?"

Belson shook his head. "All the blood matched the kid."

"No semen or saliva?" I could feel my brow furrow.

"No. I know, I know." He held up a callused, weathered hand, which had a slight tremor, probably caused by age. I was glad for his retirement and his tree farm. He seemed content. "The swabs came up clean—no sperm. That's one of the reasons we considered abduction for the replacement of a child. It was odd not to find semen on the kid if the assailant was a pedophile, but it's possible he made the kid bathe before he killed him."

"What about the boy's clothes? Anything on the underside that wasn't exposed to the rain?"

"No, your department taped them for possible debris, but like I said, mostly the local soil stuff came up. But even the underside was a muddy mess. I'm telling you, it rained hard and for hours that day."

"Lucky bastard," I said. "And the head injury?"

He took a deep breath as if he was hoping I wouldn't ask, then said, "Yeah, that was the worst part." He pointed to the left side of his head, and made a line with his finger from below his ear all the way to the back of his skull. "Split right open. It was awful, especially when with the parents wanting to see him. The pathologist did the best he could to cover that part of the head, and luckily the front of his face wasn't completely disfigured from it like the side of his head. We figured the boy turned to the side to avoid being struck and got it in that part of his head. Tell me, why exactly are you here? Do you think this nine-year-old case has something to do with the missing boy in Glacier?"

"Not necessarily. It would be a long shot, but there's something else." I told him about the shallow grave in Essex, about the trauma to the victim's skull, up higher near the temporal region, but still a cleaved separation. I told him the boy was about the same age of the Erickson boy and about the time frame Lucy had given us.

"But that's, well, that's a long time before 2007. At least ten years."

"I know, but I'm wondering, Mr. Belson, what you thought about a trauma like that on the skull?"

"Coroner deemed it the cause of death."

"Yeah, I know. I just think it's odd. It's such a similar skull wound." The bee had come back over and buzzed in my face, near my forehead, sniffing out the trace of blood. I shooed it away, more aggressively than Belson had.

Belson studied me. "Yeah, odd. I wish I could tell you more, but I can't. I wish we'd found whoever killed that poor boy. I can't even think about what it did to his family without getting depressed. I'm haunted by the gash in the poor child's head."

I didn't say anything, just sat still, feeling a new warm breeze brushing against my face when my phone buzzed and startled me. I pulled it out of my pocket. It was Ridgeway. "Excuse me, sir, I'll need to grab this."

"You go right ahead," he said.

I stood up and took a few steps away. "Sir," I answered.

"Another job, Gretchen."

"Where?" I asked. We hadn't been this busy in a long time.

"We need you out at a farm east of Kalispell, toward the foothills. They think they've located the truck that the witness suggests might have picked up the boy."

"I'm out that way now. I'll get Ray to bring the van and meet me."

"You got a pen for the address or should I text it to you?"

"Text would be great."

We wrapped up the call, and I went back to Belson to thank him for his time.

"Happy to chat," he said. "If you have any more questions for me, feel free to call. Anytime."

I said I'd do that and walked to my car, the bee finding me again and following me, swirling and diving around my head as I walked. I turned back to wave and saw Belson watching me.

"Hope that cut heals soon," he called, smiling empathetically, as if he knew I had something much more aberrant and mysterious going on than a casual run-in with the corner of my armoire.

• • •

I called Ray first to make sure he got everything we needed and told him I'd meet him out at the site. Then I called Wendy, who was at home, to see if Kyle had made it home yet. He hadn't and she'd been up all night, but said she still wanted to work—if she didn't have something to do, she'd go crazy. "Are you sure?" I asked her.

"I'm sure," she said. "He'll come home when he's ready. The waiting is the worst."

She said she'd go straight to the lab, and wait to hear from me. We were going to need to get every fingerprint and trace possible from the truck.

When I arrived, a crush of officers swarmed around the farm. I moved through them, many familiar since they worked for the county. I waited outside the tape cordoning off the carport for the county's white CSI van. I wondered if Monty was around, but I didn't see him.

Ali came over when she spotted me and asked why I was alone without the van. I told her about already being on this end of the valley and needing to wait for Ray with the supplies, that he'd be along any minute. She didn't look at all happy that I wasn't ready to dive in, but without suiting up and having my equipment, I could do nothing until he arrived.

I felt comforted to be back at my job after visiting Detective Belson, though. I knew that as soon as the van pulled up, I had direction, tasks to complete, and I understood that I would focus on what needed to be done. My job gave me boundaries. It led me to the underbelly of society, right where I belonged. In law enforcement, I saw the darkest side of the human existence—what people were capable of doing, how they inflicted harm on one another. It could be brutal, but it was precisely, in my opinion, where someone who had already done the tragically unthinkable belonged.

Once Ali filled me in, I told her that it would be best to get the truck to our lab garage where we could look at it under our ultrabright lights and UV lamps, and could also make it dark so that we could use the solution called Luminol, which would fluoresce in the presence of blood. She agreed and I told her that we'd at least get all our photos and footprint plasters before towing the truck.

Luckily, while Ali and I were still talking, the van rolled up the Tuckmans' long drive, dust pluming behind it and blowing to one side with the wind. Ray pulled up, lowered his window, and asked where he should park. Ali pointed to a clearing close by and he drove to it, hopped out, and grabbed our suits. We slid them on, along with our gloves, and grabbed the cameras and the carrying case with our plaster kits.

"We're going to need to photograph everything around the truck first, mark all footprints, and get plasters. We'll need to hold off on all trace and the dusting until we get it to the garage," I said to Ray. "I want this under bright lights."

We went over and started taking pictures from all angles, making sure to photograph all visible footprints around it. Ray began to ready the plaster kits. When we finished grabbing tire prints, I looked inside the truck. The first thing that caught my attention was that it was clean. The driver's seat had a rip on its fabric seam closest to the door where drivers had scooted in and out over the past decade and a half. I opened the door and ran a finger in one corner of the dash. No dust. "That's strange," I mumbled to myself.

"What?" Ray asked.

"No dust, old farm truck like this in one of the driest, dustiest summers ever?" I wiped the inside panel of the door with my latex-clad forefinger to find the same. "Shit," I said. "We may not find many for Wendy to lift," I said. "Smell," I held open the door for him to peek in.

"Lemony. Bleach?" Ray asked. "Some kind of antiseptic spray?"

"That's what I'm thinking. Let's hope it's not the kind they use in hospitals to kill infectious matter. If it is, all trace might be destroyed too." I knew that sprays like this not only killed bacteria but also destroyed skin, hair, and sweat. "If this is the truck, and it's looking mighty suspicious, this person knows what they're doing." A cold finger of dread traced up my spine.

We got to it quickly, continually glancing up at the gathering gray clouds. We were glad there was a carport over us, but if it began to pour and the wind continued this strongly, it would blow the rain sideways right onto us.

Monty showed up while we were processing the site, and I could see him talking to Ali and Herman, nodding and writing things down. I went to them, removing my gloves. All three turned to me. Ali squinted in the grayish glow of the day and Herman bowed his head in his stylish sunglasses. Monty looked exhausted, and I was sure he'd been up all night. Herman had told me that it had been he and Ken who'd found the truck.

"Hey," Monty said, giving me a faint smile, and I saw Ali notice. In contrast, she held her face stern. Herman looked neutral even behind his glasses as he often did, with an enigmatic air and a softness about him in spite of his size. He looked like he'd freely give you a hug if you needed it, no matter who you were, but still wouldn't tell you any of his secrets.

"How's it looking?" Ali asked.

"Not entirely sure yet, we'll dust when we get it into the lab. Thankfully we have Jeremy's already entered from the Ohio Child Find program they partook in when he was little, so if we get some and there's a match, we'll know soon. But chances are the ones we get from the exterior are from the farmhands, although we won't know until we get

THE WEIGHT OF NIGHT   193

comparison prints from them, if they're willing to give them. But you should know that there might not be much to grab from the inside."

"Why not?" Monty asked.

"I'm not seeing any dust."

"Son of a bitch," Ali jammed her foot into the ground. "There are multiple drivers of this truck. There should be some damn prints. He's wiped it down. Is that right?" she asked. "Has it been wiped?"

I nodded. "We think it's been sprayed and wiped down with an antibacterial cleaner, but we're not sure yet. Just smells like it could be bleach."

"Shit. This guy knows what he's doing. Hollywood, find out if Walt or any of the hands has cleaned the truck lately. Recheck Walt's and the golfer's alibi, for God's sake, and the other guy, Brady. Where is he?" she looked around. "He should be here by now. If he's not here yet, we may need to put out an APB on him. Fishing, my ass. And"—she continued to address Herman, whom I figured she called Hollywood— "see if Walt, the wife, and the one guy we have agree to giving their prints. And Mr. Steady-Eddy," she barked. "You look like shit." She was directing that one at Monty.

"Thank you," Monty said.

I halfway smiled. I couldn't tell if she disliked him or had some kind of schoolgirl crush on him and felt the urge to badger him. Because I largely missed out on interacting with males from the age of fifteen until eighteen, when I moved to Seattle, I didn't have the best radar for this stuff—flirting, attraction. I looked at Herman, but couldn't read his expression through the sunglasses, though I wasn't sure what they were shading his eyes from, since the clouds blocked the sun.

"Go get an hour of sleep. Muscles too, wherever he is." She briefly scanned the property, I assumed looking for Ken. "I don't care if it's in your car, but get an hour so you're fresh again soon."

"I'm fine, Agent Paige," Monty said. "If the truck's been wiped, chances are it's the one. We could be close. I won't be able to sleep anyway. You need someone to go get Mr. Stewart—"

"No, you're going to get an hour's sleep so you're worth a damn. Herman, you grab Stewart. You and Ken . . . you're both off now, for a little while. You've been up for too long. You'll start making mistakes and I don't want mistakes. I'll call you if anything comes up as the search progresses." She motioned to all the men swarming around the place.

Monty looked at her incredulously. "We've already met Paul Stewart. Been to his house. Had coffee. It's easier for us to go grab him."

"Monty," Ali said. Apparently, she didn't use a nickname every time she addressed someone. "I don't need officers falling asleep at the wheel. Go. Sleep. Just a little while—half an hour. I'll call you when we find the other hand. I want to take Walt, Anna, and the two hands all into the county building where they can sit in real interrogation rooms. Plus, forensics is moving the truck to the lab anyway to check for blood, hairs, and fibers. If there was blood, the son of a bitch can't wipe it clean when Luminol's around; I don't care what he used."

Ali trod off back toward the barn while Herman pulled out his keys.

"This is crazy," Monty said. "I know exactly where Stewart lives and Ken and I have already broken the ice with him."

"Yeah, I know," Herman offered. "But she's probably right. Usually is. Don't let her get to you. Underneath the hard shell, she's got a heart of gold." Herman smiled.

"I guess," Monty said. He told Herman how to get there and the fed strode away. I turned to Monty. "Sleep, huh? Mr. Steady-Eddy?"

"I knew it would happen eventually. I guess I should feel relieved that it's not something worse. And she's got a point about keeping her staff fresh, but it's going to be hard to make that happen." He snapped his fingers. "Turn it all off, just like that. The other hand needs to be found. How am I supposed to sleep?"

"Where's Ken, anyway?"

"You mean Muscles?"

I smiled. "Yeah, him."

"In the car," he said.

"Sleeping?"

"He started to doze off on the way here."

"At least one of you knows how to stay on her good side," I said.

He let loose a laugh. It was strained, but I recognized the need for a flash of levity. I joined him for a moment, then let it fade. "Monty," I said. "I want to talk to you."

"About what?"

"Some past cases I've been looking into."

He regarded me seriously and nodded. "Shoot."

"No, I need to wrap things up here first, and then I'll find you," I dug into my pocket for my keys. "In the meantime, go to my car. It's over there." I pointed to it in the distance, near the pine trees to the side of the drive. I shoved my keys into his hand. "Go somewhere where you can sleep for an hour. We won't be done for a bit anyway. Ray's still getting plasters and we're searching for trace around the carport. And you obviously don't want to be in your car with Ken." I grinned. "He probably snores. If anything comes up here, I promise I'll come wake you if she doesn't."

Monty studied me, looking like he might just give in, when a county officer I knew, a deputy named Luke Brander, came up and put a hand on his shoulder. Neither of us saw him approach from the side and Monty jerked away quickly, startled. I registered that he really was spent—or the jumpiness was a remnant from his earlier life, from being on guard around his older brother. I'd met Monty's brother during a case we'd worked, and knew he'd been hard on him growing up, a bona fide bully, as Monty had called him.

"Sorry, Harris," Brander said. "Didn't mean to catch you off guard."

"No worries," Monty said. "What's up?"

"Looking for Agent Paige. We've got the other farmhand, Brady Lewis. Just showed up for work much later than expected. Looking clueless, if you asked me."

"She's over there." We both pointed toward the barn.

"Where've you got him?" Monty asked.

"Over by the main house. I've got a deputy with him now."

Brander left to go inform Ali, and I looked at Monty. "You're not going to take me up on that offer, are you?"

"No, I'm not," he said. He motioned toward Ali. "I'm guessing she'll be busy with the farmhands and she's going to need someone around who's already questioned one of them and the owner of this place."

"Don't be so sure," I said, swiping the hair out of my eyes.

Monty tilted his head and I could tell he was looking more closely at my forehead again. "How'd you get that?"

"It's nothing. Just ran into something." I covered it with the tips of four of my fingers, embarrassed. He studied me curiously as the elderly detective had.

"Just ran into something?"

"Yep," I started to back away. "I did. I know, goofy."

"And I'm the one people think needs sleep?" He gave me a cock-eyed smile.

"Yeah. Look, sorry, I need to get this truck off before it pours on us." I turned and hurried back toward Ray, but Monty called out my name. I turned to see him holding my keys up. I held out my hands and he tossed them. I caught them, the weight of them crashing into my palms and for some reason making the ever-present emptiness slide through my being like cold heavy raindrops on glass. "Thanks," I said, shoving them into my pocket and turning back to the Chevy truck sitting safely under the carport.

· · ·

Afterward. After the insanity. There shouldn't have been an *after* for me at all. I should have somehow taken my life right then and there, but I was confused and I wouldn't have known how, and I didn't have the courage anyway. So there ended up being an afterward and it went like this.

After the ambulance took Per to the hospital, I was taken with cuffed wrists to a police car in front of our house and put in the backseat, still in the white T-shirt and pink pajama bottoms that I'd worn to bed. I looked down and saw blood splattered across them. The car was on to provide heat, the muffler breathing into the cold air like a dragon. Red lights from the strobes flashed across the snow-covered lawn while at least eight or nine neighbors gathered and stood off to the side, gawking nervously. Behind them stood their houses, some of them adorned with strings of white Christmas lights around the entry-ways. Near the car where I sat, two police officers talked to my parents, who were also still in their pajamas. My mom had a down coat on and my dad wore only his ratty, blue robe, but they both had snow boots on their feet. In a way, it looked like a normal, winter's night, as if neighbors were only out and about strolling or caroling. Except the flashing lights from the police car strobing across shocked expressions jarred me into reality.

"I don't know," my mother was saying in a high-pitched, frantic voice that I could hear through the closed window of the car. "I don't know what happened. She was like a zombie. We yelled at her, but she just"—she shook her head side to side—"she just kept hurting him."

"It's as if she didn't hear us at all," my father added. His voice was fraught with anxiousness and confusion too. I'd never heard him sound like that before—as if he was on the verge of crying or shouting. "Like she looks when she sleepwalks," he added.

"She sleepwalks?"

"Yes, ever since she was little. She gets up and does weird things. She's even made herself sandwiches in the middle of the night and re-arranged furniture without realizing it."

"Okay, Mr. Larson, thank you." One of the policemen who had been taking notes put his notepad back in his coat pocket. "I know you're anxious to get to the hospital."

I saw my mom look at me from the lawn. She took a step toward me like she was instinctively going to come and comfort me, but then she stopped, her face confused and racked with pain as if she was ask-ing me, *Gretchen, what have you done? What is wrong with you?* I put my cuffed hands on the cold glass, to wave, to reach toward her, to beg for forgiveness . . . but she didn't move any closer. The second officer looked at her looking at me, frozen in her step. He put his hand on her shoulder and said, "Mrs. Larson, I know you want to get to the hospital, so if you can just get us a coat for your daughter to take with her, we can let you go for now."

"Of course," my mom mumbled, looking away from me and hurrying into the house to grab me a jacket. I could hear the faint, muffled sound of some neighbors talking in hushed tones from the side of the street. When she came back, she didn't even glance at me. She went over and gave it to the police officer. He thanked her, and she went back inside.

My dad walked over and the other officer, who'd hopped into the driver's seat, rolled the window partially down for me to speak to him. I looked at him, not knowing what to say. "Pappa" was all that fell from my lips.

"Gretchen"—he looked at my white T-shirt, saw the blood, and winced—"we'll bring you some clean clothes soon."

"But," I said, "where are they taking me?"

"For now, to the police station. We'll be there soon. Right now, though, we need to go to the hospital to check on your brother."

"Is he okay? I want to come there."

My dad's Adam's apple moved up, then down as he swallowed hard, his eyes tearing up. He looked away from me to the house.

"Pappa, is Per okay?"

"I don't know, Gretchen. I don't know that yet."

"Is Mamma mad at me?"

"No, no, not mad. She's in shock." He took a deep breath, then said, "I have to go now. We need to get to the hospital. We will see you soon."

I watched him leave, his shoulders slumped. The window was still partially open. I listened to his boots scratching the ice as he walked away, a lonely and forsaken sound. It receded farther and farther away into the cold night until the policeman whose name I didn't even know rolled the window up from his control pad, put the car in gear, and drove me away from my home.

. . .

Recalling the early days after it happened is very difficult. They were jammed with emotion: agony, despair, ruin, fear. I hardly slept at all at the psychiatric hospital in Bergen for the first few days after it occurred. But when I did, I underwent a series of sleep EEGs where they hooked colorful wires with electrodes to my forehead, the crown of my head, the base of my skull, and my chin to measure my electrical impulses while I slept. A small device was hooked beneath my nose to monitor my breathing patterns. The test results would be used to decide if the case would go to the Norwegian court system or not—in essence, if I should actually be charged with manslaughter or murder. One morning, the neurologist and sleep specialist administering the exams looked at me over the top of his glasses while unhooking the electrodes. I wrapped my arms around my chest and was shaking slightly.

"You poor thing," he said, pulling up the blanket for me. I wasn't cold; that's not the reason I shook, but I took it anyway. "You're a mess, aren't you?"

I didn't answer for fear of breaking down in front of him, but I knew I looked pale, scared, and thin. The evening before had been miserable. I pulled my hair, dug my fingernails into my scalp until I drew blood, and ended up feeling so sick I threw up. Oatmeal-colored vomit splattered across the white floor, and I sat there wishing I had thrown up whatever was in my soul along with it—the hurt was too great to bear. I had rocked back and forth in my hospital room, groaning like a wounded animal, praying to rewind time to before I went to bed that night, but each time I closed my eyes, I only saw Per still and bloody in his bed. I wanted to die, but even that would change nothing . . . make nothing better for my parents and certainly not bring Per back. I'd barely been able to eat either, and when I did throw up again, I could only dry heave. I kept seeing Per in a stretcher being placed in the ambulance, bright blue and red lights flashing across the white snow, still in a confused state, not understanding that it was the last time I would ever see my brother again.

"You need to eat, Gretchen. You need some strength."

I nodded to show I understood, but I had no plans to eat. There was such deep anger and every other awful emotion in my parents' eyes. Of course there was. How could there not be? One child had taken the other.

"I'll talk to the kitchen and see if they can get you something a little tastier, something you can't resist. You like pizza, don't you?"

I nodded again.

"You don't want to talk?"

I shrugged. A part of me did, but a part of me had become too scared to speak. What could I say—that I was a crazy freak? a monster? that in the course of just one night I suddenly despised myself and I knew my parents did too? that when they came the day before to see me, my father couldn't even look me in the eye and my mother cried the whole time? Neither one could say more than a few words to me: *Are they treating you well here?* They both looked like ghosts. I'd never seen them look so broken in my life. Two sturdy, active people reduced to sagging, broken puppets.

No, talking implied normalcy—and I didn't deserve normal—but it came out in spite of me. "What can I do? How can I go on? They think I'm a monster." It all came out more as a series of whimpers. "And I am."

"Look, Gretchen, you're going to get more counseling, and I'm not a therapist, but I'm going to tell you that you should expect these feelings, and your parents' response is normal under the circumstances. But you should know that they're working through their bereavement and it's going to take some time. It's going to take time for you too—to forgive yourself."

"I'll never forgive myself." I looked at him like he was insane for suggesting it. But I was the insane one. "I want to plead guilty and for them to find me guilty." I was referring to the court that would hear the case.

"Your tests already show that you routinely go through hypnagogic states in your sleep where you are part awake and part in REM sleep. Basically, you're dreaming, and when most people dream, their motor skills shut down, but yours don't. And you won't be the only person to have done this in their sleep."

"You mean other people have done this?" I couldn't even say the word "killed."

"There are cases. I've read about them. In Canada, in the U.S., even in Sweden."

I was curious, but suddenly Per's face came into my mind again and none of it mattered. Nothing could make any of it better, ever. "The explanations don't matter."

"They will," he said. "Trust me. They will."

I looked at the floor.

"Gretchen, listen," he said, "These events are unusual, but they happen—instances where one child can be blamed for the loss of the other. Car accidents where a family member drives drunk and kills the other. Babysitting mishaps where an older sibling gets distracted and the younger drowns."

"But . . ." I felt tears streaming down my face, and I was surprised to feel them. How does a zombie—someone capable of maiming and killing while sleepwalking with glassy, open eyes—feel delicate tears on her cheeks? "Those examples are all accidents," I said. "No one actually took a weapon and murdered anyone like I've done."

Dr. Haugen pursed his lips and agreed that not all of these cases were identical, but then said, "It was still an accident—just one caused by your sleep disorder. Eventually you'll have to come to terms with it." He gave me a faint smile and his eyes were gentle and well meaning.

I didn't know how to explain the things I was feeling. I didn't understand everything spinning through my mind, every acidic sensation pooling in my stomach. I felt like a beast with no control—like some cold-blooded predator straight out of *National Geographic*. I felt like I was on the verge of being sucked into an infinite black hole with no discernible boundaries.

I didn't know to tell him that no matter what he said to help me see my way through this warped trauma, the overwhelming feeling of guilt and emptiness that was drowning me—that would continue to drown me in the years to follow—was unlikely to go away, ever. It was more than guilt and grief. It was a knife of self-loathing that sliced into the very fibers of how I—how my parents—saw me. I knew I would forever loathe myself, but what I didn't expect was that their silences, their anguished looks, would cut so deeply that I would feel like I could no longer live another day because the ache was too great. "How long can someone live like this?" I asked him.

He looked at me with a deep sorrow and kindness, which in retrospect was really intense pity. "I don't know," he said. "I don't know. But you'll find out because you have no choice. And it doesn't have to be right now, but as time goes on, you'll find ways to keep going."

I stared at him and my eyes must have held both doubt and hope because he answered me as if I'd pressed him for certainty.

"Yes, Gretchen, yes. I do think you'll find a way. Find some resolve. Others have."

I still think about those early conversations with Dr. Haugen. I hang on to them because just when it seemed I couldn't bear one more moment of my self, of my life, along came his kindness—a certain sweetness—that changed nothing really at all, but somehow gave me a thin rope to grab onto during my free fall into that black hole and allowed me to go on another minute, another hour, another day.

14

Monty

I<small>T STILL HADN'T</small> rained by the time we left the farm to take the Tuckmans and Brady Lewis to the county headquarters in Kalispell for more questioning. The sky stayed angry and shone like silver, but refused to rain, as if the storm was only teasing, cruelly stewing up dust in the fields and stirring the fires in the deep woods. We used both of the interrogation rooms—Walt in one, Brady in the other—and put Anna in the general waiting room. We went over all their alibis again, including Paul Stewart's, whom Herman had brought in. Apparently, Stewart had done as he was asked, and stayed close to home.

His alibi became even stronger the more we checked it out. Just in case, we reconfirmed that he truly had spent the entire afternoon golfing. It turned out that in addition to Paul Stewart's golf buddies and the guy at the starter booth, the bartender remembered everyone buying Stewart a beer because he'd hit an eagle on the thirteenth hole. The bartender said that probably five other patrons could attest to the fact that they were celebrating the eagle because they were being chatty and very loud about the whole thing, holding their beers high and hooting about it. It didn't take long after he arrived for us to cross him off our list and send him on his way.

The Tuckmans were almost as straightforward, but married couples are always a bit tricky because they tend to protect each other and will say and sometimes do anything to help one another.

They questioned Anna first, and neither agent sensed that she was covering for Walt or lying about his whereabouts on the day Jeremy was taken. Walt and Anna had been together that day. They'd been visiting a carpet and tile store in Kalispell because they were remodeling their master bathroom. She had dragged Walt along because she didn't want to pick the color scheme and then have him complain about it later. They had left around nine a.m., gotten some breakfast at a local pancake shop, then visited three different stores in the valley, checking out tile and granite selections. They didn't return home until two p.m., when Walt went into his office to catch up on work.

"I already told you"—Walt had held out his hands to Ali when she questioned him after Anna—"the university is coming to make their annual checks and do their testing on our tubers—make sure they're disease free—and there's still a lot to do to finish up the irrigation." I watched her interview him through the one-way mirror. "I didn't even want to go to town, but if I didn't, I knew Anna would be angry with me for the rest of the day, so I went. As soon as I got back, though, I headed straight to the office."

"But, you were out working on the irrigation too?"

"Yeah, we have to change some lines—the wheel lines—twice a day. The others are automatic and just need to be monitored."

Ali nodded like she cared about the irrigation process, and continued to pin down his whereabouts that day while Herman went and checked details with Anna. She confirmed that he was, indeed, in his office working from 2:00 to 5:30 p.m. To our dismay, we also found out when Ali asked to see Mr. Tuckman Senior's records of all workers in the past (wondering who else might have known about the truck) that Anna had gotten rid of all his old files because they were taking up too much space and she assumed they were no longer needed. "I figured if we ever get audited," she had said, "they'd never need records that many years back."

We were in the process of calling some of the tile stores to verify their visit, but it didn't take long before all our focus shifted to Brady

Lewis. Both his girlfriend and his boss at the agriculture store had said he'd probably gone fishing, which wasn't much of an alibi.

We made him wait a while in the interrogation room with the one-way while Ali and Herman discussed how they wanted to proceed. Ali had forgotten about sending me to get some sleep and seemed glad to have Ken and me at the station making all of the confirmation calls. We spoke to a woman at one of the stores who remembered helping the couple and even recalled which kind of tile they looked at—some kind of Franciscan slate tile.

"Harris, Greeley." Ali waved us both into the small observation room to discuss a game plan after we had taken the Tuckmans' statements and sent them home. "How should we do this?" Ali asked us all once we were gathered in the room. Through the glass, Brady sat annoyed in his metal chair, one hand tapping on the bolted-down table before him and occasionally running his fingers through his hair.

"I think you should start," Herman said to Ali. It seemed to me that Herman always deferred to Ali, but this time I disagreed with that approach. I stayed quiet and watched them continue.

"Okay," she said. "I go in, act all sweet and girl-like and see if I can't set him at ease."

"Then I can come in later and pour on the mean big guy act if we need it," Herman added.

"Hmm," I said.

Ali and Herman both looked at me. "What?" Ali said.

"I don't know, let's think about this."

"That's exactly what we're doing."

I wondered why she wanted Ken and me in the room with them in the first place if she didn't want to hear what we had to offer.

"Okay," I said. I'd walked on eggshells nearly my entire life when I was around my family, and quite frankly, I was good at it, a Master Tiptoer, in fact. But a boy was missing and I was too tired on this particular afternoon to try to tread around her irascible ways. "Look," I said, "you asked us in here. I could be wrong, but this Brady guy"—I looked down at my notes—"he's lived here for about five years, right? That's what Samantha, the girlfriend, said when we went there."

"Walt said the same," Ali said. "That they both moved here from Massachusetts and that he's worked for him since he got to town."

"Exactly," I said.

"What's your point then, Harris?" Herman chimed in.

"My point is that he's been with his girlfriend for probably more than five years, hasn't bothered to marry her, fishes on his days off instead of doing something as a couple. My guess is he hates commitment, hates the idea of compromising for a woman. When we spoke to her, she seemed irritated about the whole fishing thing, like fishing was the other woman." I looked at him through the glass again. He leaned back in his chair and folded his arms, his head positioned in a dogged tilt to the side, like he was bracing himself, fortified with a teenage stubbornness. "Look"—I motioned to the glass—"obstinacy is his go-to stance. Guys like that . . . a woman makes them feel like they're sacrificing, being controlled. So I'm just suggesting that Herman goes in first. He might relate to the guy better than to a strong-willed female agent. Ali might make him clam up, you know, like his mother is busting him in front of the cookie jar."

"Jesus, Harris, you've got an overactive imagination and what, you think you're a psychiatrist now, too?" Ali crossed her arms, leaned against the cinder-block wall, and glared at me. "All that just by looking at him through a one-way?"

"Just telling you my gut instinct on this. Take it or leave it."

Ali and Herman looked at each other. Herman gave a twitch of a shoulder, turned, and studied the guy through the mirror. Through the glass, Brady continued to look sullen, more annoyed than scared.

Finally, Herman said, "I think Monty might have something here. Let me go in first, see what I can get. He might relate better to *one of the guys*." He curled his fingers into quotation marks. Then, if we need a hardass, we bring you in to scare the little boy in him."

Ali rubbed her face, making her cheeks pink. She thought for a moment, then agreed. "Okay, we'll stay in here and keep a close eye on his reactions."

. . .

Herman started out nice and cordial, apologizing for keeping him waiting, asking Brady how he was and if he needed anything, but then grew a bit more serious. "Brady, we're really sorry to bother you, and we wouldn't even have you in here if we didn't have a very serious situation on hand—a missing boy."

Brady looked confused as to why he'd be brought in for something like that, and Ali, Ken, and I looked at one another, wondering whether he was just putting on a good act.

"How does this have anything to do with me?" Brady asked.

"For starters, the Chevy truck that all of you farmhands have access to has been identified as the truck involved in the abduction," Herman said, stretching the truth. We had not yet verified that the boy had gotten into that truck. "We're not accusing you, but the other farmhand, Mr. Stewart, has an alibi, and so do Mr. and Mrs. Tuckman. We need to see if you have any information for us. That's why you're here."

I was impressed with Herman's ability to dance around any accusations in an attempt to keep Brady unguarded. He didn't even bring up the fact that fishing could be construed as a sketchy, unverifiable alibi.

"This is the first I've even heard about any abduction," Brady said.

Herman nodded calmly. "Okay, well, can you tell us what you were doing on the morning and afternoon of the sixteenth, two days ago?"

"I think you know that. I already told one of the officers when I arrived that I was fishing."

Herman took him through it all again, asking where he went, all the parts of the river, what time he left, when he returned, what stops he made. His answers matched up with Samantha's. He'd been fishing up the North Fork of the Flathead River, by Glacier Rim, and no, he didn't make any stops. He returned home around nine in the evening.

"Mr. Lewis," Herman said, "did anyone go fishing with you?"

"No," he said. "I usually go alone because most of my friends can't hang as long as I do. They start bitching and getting bored and want to go home before the evening bugs even come out."

"Mr. Lewis," Herman said. "Is there anyone who can verify that you were fishing?"

"Samantha already did."

"No, I mean, is there anyone who actually saw you while you were fishing?"

"No, I told you, I went alone."

"You didn't see anyone you know up there—anyone else out on the river who might remember you?"

"No, just a few rafters going by, a few other fishermen that I stayed far away from, but no one I knew personally."

Herman laced his fingers together and leaned casually and attentively on the table toward Brady. "Okay, well, would you be willing to run some prints, just for elimination purposes?"

"Prints? What the hell for?"

I glanced at Ali to see if she caught it, too. In that instant, the defenses I sensed in Brady from the minute he came in cropped up. We could hear it in the tone of his voice, sharp and peevish.

"I just said, for elimination purposes. We're dusting the truck as we speak. If we come up with a number of prints and we identify yours, the Tuckmans', and Stewart's, then that's useful information."

Brady leaned back, folded his arms in front of him again, his eyes hooded as he looked to the side and considered it. "Makes no sense to me. You know my prints are in it, since I've driven the truck many times, so why do you need them?"

"We need them to eliminate them, that's all—so that we can figure out which ones might be the foreign ones if something shows up."

"I'm sorry if it takes you a little more time, but I got no desire to give the government any more information on me than they already have. Why the hell do you think I moved to Montana?"

"Jesus Christ," Ali whispered. "How many of these nutwings are there in this state?"

"I don't know, Mr. Lewis," Herman's voice grew sharp. We all turned back to the one-way. Herman indulged Brady: "Why don't you tell me?"

"To get the hell away from having the government breathing down my neck—always coughing up some state tax at every fucking store I went to back east, always paying at tollbooths to drive on the high-ways that should belong to us in the first place, never having access to streams, the price of fishing licenses going through the roof. . . . I just want to work, fish, and be left alone."

I rolled my eyes, knowing that it was the state government that allowed him access to all lakes, rivers, and streams in Montana. That we had a law that allows the public to use rivers and streams for recre-ational purposes up to the standard high-water mark. It doesn't allow people to enter through posted land or to cross private lands to gain access, but if you access it somewhere legitimately, you can continue to follow the body of water as long as you are within the high-water mark. When I was a game warden, I ran into this type all the time—entitled enough to fish anywhere and take any game they damn well pleased, but not interested in paying the state taxes or appreciating the very laws that gave them access to all the places they wanted to use.

"And how exactly are they breathing down your neck?"

"You know how. Don't tell me you're not creeped out when each time you get on your computer and you see some ad telling you where you've already been shopping and looking at something. I've had enough of Uncle Sam."

"That's businesses, the Internet, Google. That's not the government," Herman said. I was surprised he was even bothering to comment.

"Ha," Brady said with a wry grin. "All the same."

"Maybe you're right, but with all due respect, Mr. Lewis, there's a boy missing and I don't give a rat's ass what your politics are." Herman glared at him.

"I'm sorry about the missing boy, but I'm not giving my fingerprints so I can permanently be on some record of yours." Brady stiffened, folding his arms tighter and clamping his mouth in a thin, straight line.

"This isn't working," Ali said. "I'm going in. Red flags are going way up if he won't agree to prints, and Herman's no longer playing it smooth. As long as he's going bitchy, we might as well switch to me."

I took her point, but still, I was skeptical. She started for the door.

"I don't think that's a good idea. Just leave him. He'll swing back. He's fine. Brady's just going to clam up more if you go in."

"But the bastard's guilty. Look at him." She threw her hand at the mirror. "Sitting there all smug, refusing to give prints, probably already knowing that he's wiped the damn truck down and that we won't find prints anyway."

"We don't know if he's guilty," I said. "It's suspicious that he won't help, but I thought I got a whiff of pot when his girlfriend opened the door. Probably just wants to be left alone to string a few jobs together to pay bills while he grows a little stinkweed and fishes. He might just be nervous about losing that."

"Harris, why the fuck are you defending all these nutjobs?"

"I'm not defending them, Agent Paige." I looked coolly into her electric eyes. They brimmed with anger. "I just think it's wise to stay controlled."

"Controlled? We've got a boy missing for three days now."

"Exactly, and jumping to conclusions and allowing anger to get the best of us isn't going to help."

"I'm sorry I asked you in here." She paced around the room. "Maybe you should go back to the park where you're appreciated."

A smile crept onto my face at the rudeness of her statement—at the nerve it took to say something like that to someone you worked with. I was intensely aware that she didn't *appreciate* me, but I wanted to laugh and nearly did, my mouth twitching slightly at the corners. I could see that irritated her even more, but I held up my hand to

smooth the waters. I'm good at that. I've got a lifetime's worth of practice at staying calm amid erratic behavior, especially within my family.
My ex-wife was the only one that wasn't irrational and unpredictable,
and eventually even she surprised me and uprooted our relationship
by changing her mind midstream. "Here's what I think," I said evenly,
trying to draw Ali back in, but she didn't fall for it.

"I don't give a shit what you think. You weren't correct about this
one. The guy's not going to be helpful either way."

"Perhaps not, but I think once we have confirmation that the truck
is the correct one, we should try to get an order from a judge to force
his prints as soon as possible. Even if the truck is wiped clean, we
might need them later, and he shouldn't have the right to withhold
them under these circumstances, as a driver of that particular truck
without an alibi on the day the boy went missing."

She took in what I said, then left.

I watched her make a dramatic entrance into the room, her hair
like Medusa and her face flushed with energy and impatience. She
didn't bother to address Agent Herman and I was surprised. Most part-
ners always did a bit of a hunting dance—a circling of sorts around
the suspect, no matter the circumstances. She skipped that, went right
to Brady and got in his face. "You're being an idiot by not giving your
prints. Any idea how much our suspicion meter goes up if you won't
help us when a child is missing?"

Brady looked at her curiously. "As I explained, I'm sorry about that,
but I have my limits when it comes to Big Brother."

"And if something happened to one of your own children, you'd
come begging for our help then, right? Big Brother or not, right?"

Brady sat stone-still, as if Paige really were Medusa and had used
her powers to freeze him. I was right—he had a "naughty little boy"
face the minute she got in the mix. He clearly didn't have children, so I
didn't expect him to identify with what she said, but I thought at least a
speck of compassion would flicker across his face. It didn't.

"I'd like to speak to an attorney now," he said.

"I don't think you understand the gravity of what is happening. There is a life at stake, and if you are uncooperative, you don't understand the hot water you'll be in."

"I'm sorry," he said again. "You've got my Social Security and you've got satellites all over the place. Is that not enough?"

"Look." Ali sat up on the table and leaned toward him, and I saw him stiffen even more, his face going blank as he looked away from her. "We're not interested in your damn Mary Jane, got it? We just want to find a missing boy. Are you telling us you wouldn't help our investigation by giving us some lousy prints?"

Brady fumed, his leg bouncing up and down in anxiety and his face reddening. He had full-on entered the stubborn mode and refused to talk. He sat silently before her, his arms folded tightly across his chest.

"You're an idiot." Ali shook her head, then looked at Herman. "Come on, he can sit and think about it while we get a judge to order him to give not just prints, but a saliva sample for DNA analysis while we're at it."

"I'd like to speak to an attorney now about my rights," Brady said as they opened the door.

Ali turned back and sneered at him, then whispered something to Herman that sounded like *Rights, my ass.*

"I have civil liberties," Brady called out, looking indignantly at Ken and me through the glass even though he couldn't see us.

• • •

Ali didn't return to the observation room, and I suspected she went straight to the judge. I was surprised she actually took my advice. It was an unusual request, and I wasn't sure she'd get a warrant, given that the prints wouldn't necessarily prove anything. I was certain she wouldn't get an order for a swab, since we had no DNA evidence yet, but I figured she knew that and was simply bluffing. But I did as she said and went back to the park, where I was *appreciated.*

It was late in the afternoon, the sky still brewing with anger, the wind whipping branches and swirling leaves. Horses bucked in the fields and thunder had begun to grumble in the distance. I caught a faint smell of rain riding along the bitter smoky air, making it feel sticky and heavy even with the wind.

I had stopped at two more houses of families with missing kids before heading back to park headquarters. To my relief, the father of the first one had already sent samples to pass on to the center in Texas several years before, and the mother at the other house agreed readily. Then I stopped by to see Molly Sands, Nathan's sister.

She lived on the west side of Kalispell, near the railroad. The trail system Rails to Trails, where people walked, biked, and skated, ran directly behind her apartment complex. Molly was surprised to see me at the door, putting her hand up to her mouth when I explained who I was and why I was there. She invited me in. She looked disheveled, her hair messy and holding several toys in her arms—she'd probably been cleaning up when I rang.

I thought of how she used to look: fresh-faced and ready to tackle the world. She used to talk to Nathan and me about how she couldn't wait for college and spoke of getting out of Montana because she wanted to live in a bunch of cities where she could wear nice clothes and meet interesting people. Now she barely resembled that sexy, sparkly-eyed teenager. She looked haggard and stressed. She wore jean shorts that were too small for her, a T-shirt, and flip-flops. The curvy body that drove all of the guys crazy in high school had given way to rolls across her belly and thighs.

"Molly," I said. "I'm so sorry to bother you like this."

"It's okay. I know why you're here. My mom filled me in." She led me to a couch and we sat.

"Then you understand the situation."

"Kind of."

"We've found some bones. They'll be sent to a center in Texas for identification, but if DNA hasn't been submitted by a family member, then there's a possibility that they won't be able to pull a match. I'd like for one of your parents to submit so that we can rule out Nathan."

Molly thought about it, biting a nail. "They don't want to do that."

"I realize that, but what about you? It's not as good as a parent, but a sibling's DNA would still help. Would you be willing?"

I could hear her breathing through her nose while she thought about it. Clearly, I was putting her in an uncomfortable position. "I don't know, Monty. I just don't know. My parents are fragile enough. Do you really want me going behind their backs to do something they would prefer we stayed away from?"

"I understand. I completely understand, but your mom seems to be going along with it only because of your dad."

"Possibly, but right now she's not saying that to me."

"Would you at least speak to her? See if she'd be okay with you doing it, or even better, is if you could talk her into doing it?"

Molly stared at me, her hazel eyes watery. "Sure, I can do that."

"I appreciate it. It's important to get a sample from a parent. A sibling helps, but a parent is more conclusive."

She nodded.

"Like I said, I'm sorry to pop in on you like this." I wanted to leave. Seeing her was no easier than seeing her parents. I thought it would be, but I was wrong. Still, I sensed from the way she looked at me with wide, curious eyes that she wanted to talk more, so I stayed seated. "Have you been well?"

"Yeah, I've been pretty good. Got out of a bad marriage, and other than the hassles of being a single parent, I'm hanging in there."

"That's good to hear," I said.

"And you?" she asked. "You good?"

"Yeah, I'm good. Went through a divorce myself, so I know how that goes, but all in all, I'm doing well."

We looked at each other for a second, deciding if there was any more to say. There was so much that could be discussed—all the years that had passed, old times before Nathan went missing, why she never followed her dreams and moved to a big city (I could guess that she didn't feel right leaving her parents after they'd already lost one child), the many apologies I could throw out for the part I played in getting Nathan into that situation in the first place. . . . But we both sensed there was no use in going into any of it. Sometimes moving forward is the only chance you have of not drowning in the pain. I slapped my knees, thanked her for her time again, and stood.

"Monty," she said, following me to the door. "You remember, the plan was for Nathan to go home with you after school, then walk to my friend Susan's house to meet me there, right?"

"Right."

"Only once you guys got home, your brother, Perry, and Todd told you and Nathan that they'd give him a ride to Susan's so he didn't need to walk."

"Correct," I said.

"But you all never came to Susan's."

"No." I shook my head sadly. "We didn't. They took a detour to the cemetery, for that prank." She knew this. We all did, by heart. It had been gone over and over and over at the time.

"Did you know they were going to do that?"

She knew I didn't, but maybe time had made her forget. "No," I said, "I did not. I only knew that they wanted to drive you back from Susan's because Perry liked you and he wanted to spend time with you, and they wanted to use Nathan so they could do that. That's what Adam had told me, anyway, to get me to go along for the ride with them."

"And you weren't skeptical?"

I shrugged. "I guess a part of me was because it was my brother and he was always up to something, but it's hard to say when you're in the moment. I guess I wanted to believe that the older boys really needed our help for a change."

She nodded, as if some of this somehow made a difference. I couldn't imagine how.

"Why do you ask?"

"I don't know," she said. "You know time. It's weird—plays tricks on your mind. I just wanted to make sure I remembered things correctly. Anyway, I'll speak to Mom," she continued. "We're due a visit. I'll take the kids over this weekend and talk to her then. If she won't budge because of Dad, I'll talk to him as well."

I started to walk to the car when I heard her call me again. I turned to see her standing on the front stoop. "I'm just wondering." She pushed her hair behind her ears. "Did Perry even really have a crush on me, or was that just part of the prank?"

It seemed to me to be such an odd question. I wondered why it mattered. I honestly couldn't say, but the look in Molly's eyes told me it was somehow important to her all these years later. Not because she was interested in Perry back then or now, but because perhaps it was some validation—small consolation in the whole awful ordeal. I tried not to look perplexed, kept a poker face, and said, "I think he did, Molly. I think there were a lot more boys than just him who had a crush on you."

She didn't smile; she just gave me a small wave. She seemed to be weighed down by something, and as I drove off, a poem by Langston Hughes that I'd read in high school popped into my tired mind—the one about having a dream and what happens to it when it's not realized, how it can shrivel up, like a raisin, or fester, or eventually explode. Or, the speaker suggests: "Maybe it just sags / like a heavy load."

With Molly, I figured it did just that.

• • •

By the time I reached headquarters, it was early evening and my windshield was speckled with black gnats. I went in, feeling numb and robotic, and made sure the search was still proceeding smoothly. I called Herman—happily bypassing Ali—who said that the Tuckman farm had been turned upside down and they'd found nothing of interest. The place was completely kosher at this point, but they were still trawling through the surrounding farmland and woods with dogs trained on Jeremy's scent. Within fifteen minutes, I hit a wall and felt like I could no longer function, I took Ali's advice. I would at least get an hour of sleep, wash my face, and brush my teeth.

When I pulled into my driveway outside my dorm, I saw that several tree branches had been ripped off and blown into the small lawn out front. I'd pick them up later, after the storm passed.

The front had been forming and threatening the valley since morning. It seemed like it would never end, like a counterpart to the fire that still continued to rage in certain areas. It would continue to taunt, but never leave, gathering above us as the fires consumed acre after acre. It felt as if they were both somehow linked to the abductor—inexplicable forces weaving through the trees, surrounding us and watching us.

I thought of Jeremy and wondered how afraid he was, if he was still alive. Another day was passing and soon it would be night again. I picked up a pine branch that had blown onto my porch step and tossed it out farther onto the lawn with the others. The aspen trees by the side of the Community Building near my dorm shimmered with quivering silver leaves. The air still felt heavy with smoke and moisture.

I went inside. It was stuffy and warm, so I cracked a window, then took off my gear belt. I looked at my kitchen, thought about making something—tea, a bite to eat, or even just a glass of water—but instead slumped onto my couch. My whole body ached. I felt useless, unable to offer much, unable to formulate some sort of plan, and thoughts of Jeremy kept pinging through my mind. "Damn," I said into the quiet room. I leaned back against the cushion, closed my eyes for a moment, and listened to the building storm until my anger was absorbed into the sounds of the breeze and the distant thunder.

15

Gretchen

IT TOOK ALL afternoon to do the initial processing of the van, and there would still be much more to do in the morning. When we finished for the day, I called the station and spoke to Ali, giving her the details. She had thanked me for our work and told me to call if anything else came up. I grabbed the printouts I'd made on some of the old cases I'd been looking at, headed to my car, and drove to Glacier's headquarters. When I arrived, I found Tara crashed on one of the easy chairs along the side wall in the incident room and Karen Forstenson, one of the rangers, still running the volunteer shifts. She told me Monty had been by and went to his dorm to get a bite to eat and freshen up before returning for some work later in the night.

I knew exactly where Monty lived because I'd been to his place one time after he'd been beaten up in a bar during an investigation and I'd helped him home, fetched him some ice and Advil, and we'd chatted. It was the only time I'd really gotten to know him personally. It was then that I learned about his brother, his family, and, not long after that, about Nathan Faraway.

I knocked, but he didn't answer. I was almost about to turn and leave when I heard the latch and Monty opened the door. He was still wearing his uniform from the morning—a pair of dark pants and a short-sleeved navy button-up that was untucked and wrinkled. He looked disheveled, like he'd been sleeping, not getting ready to go back to the office as Karen had mentioned.

"I'm sorry," I said. "I shouldn't have woken you. Karen told me you were getting a bite and—"

"It's okay. What time is it?" He ran his hand through his close-cropped hair.

"Around ten thirty."

"Damn," he said. "I didn't mean to sleep that long. Come in."

"Monty, you've hardly slept at all."

He didn't answer, just swung the door open farther so I could enter. Inside, the small apartment was cool. One window was cracked about an inch and the wind moaned through it. He went over and closed it, then gestured to his tiny living room and I took a seat on the couch. I felt that the cushion was warm and figured he'd fallen asleep on it.

"I just sat down for a minute . . . ," he said incredulously, motioning to the sofa and shaking his head to drive the sleep away. He grabbed his phone to check it. "Three hours." He seemed surprised. "Have you heard anything new?"

"No, not really. I've filled Ali in with the early results of the truck. So far, the prints on one of the seat-belt clasps match the boy's prints. As far as I know, there are no new developments, but I can wait while you call in to check."

He thanked me, excused himself, and went into a bedroom off to the side, shutting the door behind him. I could hear him talking for a bit followed by water running and figured he had a bathroom attached to the bedroom. When he came out, he was in jeans and a T-shirt. The light in the room was pale—still twilight—and I figured Monty had forgotten to turn the lights on, like when you're driving at dusk and your eyes adjust accordingly so you forget your headlights. His hair was wet on the sides from washing his face. A bead of water slowly slid down his temple toward his cheekbone, and I felt a strong desire to reach over and gently wipe it away. I looked away from his intense eyes, over to the window, where tall pines were visible swaying against the fading deep indigo.

"Sorry to make you wait. I had to get out of that uniform before my skin started to become one with it."

"I know the feeling." I smiled. "Only, if my skin becomes one with a hazmat, I'll look like a ghost for the rest of my life."

"You'd still look good." Monty said, then set his gaze on me. He ran a hand down one side of his face, wiping the drop away. I could hear the scratch of stubble under his palm.

"Doubtful." I smiled and set my gaze at the green trim of the neckline of his T-shirt, hoping my face wasn't turning pink even though I felt it heating up. I was thankful for the dim light, but suddenly I realized I shouldn't have come to his home. It felt too intimate, seeing Monty in jeans and a soft, weathered T-shirt. "These have been such long days. You haven't slept since the dig?"

He shrugged like it wasn't important. "I did just now. Can I get you something?"

"No." I held up my hand. "I'm fine. I came, like I said, because I wanted to talk about some old cases. I know it might sound silly, but I just think it's worth a shot going over this stuff. There are a few things that I found interesting."

"Sure," Monty turned on a small table lamp and sunk down next to me. He had a rip in his jeans right above his left knee, and when he sat, it parted so I could see his skin, the dark hairs on his thigh.

"So shoot," he said. "What do you have here?"

I spread the files across the coffee table in front of us. "Well, don't get your hopes up. I don't have anything definitive, just ideas. But look at this list. I've written down all the kids who've gone missing during the time frame Lucy gave me for the bones. It starts with your friend Nathan Faraway. There have been some kids that have returned, some still missing, but suspected runaways, and some missing who were not suspected runaways. Additionally, I've looked for all unidentified remains that have been found, and there are none besides the ones we dug out."

"Hmm. I've been studying the missing myself, as you know. Asking their families to give saliva samples for the center."

"Yeah, I knew that, but I figured you weren't looking into the remains that were discovered *and* identified. It's only happened once.

In 2007. You might recall the case. I flagged it here. I also flagged your friend Nathan and a teen who went missing in 1999 at Lake Five Campground. Shane Wallace."

"Huh. I actually just visited his parents today. His father has already submitted a sample, so if the bones we found are his, they should get a hit. I haven't been able to get the Faraways to submit yet." Something unsettled swam across Monty's eyes and he looked down at my list to check the names and dates of the teens I'd starred. "And you flagged all these boys because they're male and close in age?"

"Yes, and I put a star by the Lake Five boy because he went missing nearby." Lake Five was a recreational lake with a popular campground just down the highway from West Glacier. "All that was left was his bike on the side of the road. Police figured he didn't run away or he'd wouldn't have left his bike." I let that sink in, then I said, "Notice anything else?"

Monty studied my list for a bit longer. "No, not really, just what you mentioned: gender and age, and that the Lake Five incident occurred from a campground, just like Jeremy's case. But Nathan and the Lake Five boy disappeared years apart. I don't see how they could be connected. And the Erickson boy was also some time ago, in 2007."

"I thought the same thing at first, but look." I grabbed a pen from my bag and a notepad and rewrote the names:

1991—*Nathan Faraway, Columbia Falls*
1999—*Shane Wallace, Lake Five Campground, West Glacier*
2007—*Samuel Erickson, Columbia Falls, body found six days later*
(he had been dead for twenty to twenty-four hours)
2016—*Jeremy Corey, Fish Creek Campground, GNP*

"Now do you see it?"

Monty looked at the list, then up at me. "A lapse of about eight to nine years between each boy."

"Exactly. I think that's strange, don't you?"

"Sure, it seems like a pattern, but it's too long in between for it to be the same person. Plus, *if* we have a serial abductor on our hands, they'd be doing it much more frequently than every eight or nine years. Like Ali said, pedophiles and serial killers intensify their killing over time; they can't resist."

"What if this one can? What if he's different? What if this one is trying to stay controlled, to keep it under wraps for a period of time, then can't stand it any longer and snaps?"

Monty thought about it. "I suppose it's a possibility, but there's zero evidence. It's still an enormously huge assumption to make. A boy could go missing every single year, and we wouldn't necessarily link them all together. The mind loves to look for patterns, connections, Gretchen. That doesn't mean there are any."

"I know it's a leap, but there's more." I pointed to the boy found in 2007 by the hunter and his dogs. "Samuel Erickson. Severe head trauma on the left side of his skull—lower on the mandible, under the ear—but cleaved, just like on the boy we found and on the same side. When I studied the pathologist's notes, he said it could only have been done by a very sharp and hard object, like an axe or hatchet. Lucy said the same thing about the skull we found. You saw it, the whole frontal and temporal lobes were cracked in."

"That's interesting," Monty agreed. I shuffled through my files and handed him the pictures of Erickson's gruesome remains. Monty studied them one at a time.

"And here's the thing. If it's the same guy and he sticks to the same pattern at all, we know how many days he kept Erickson alive. If he does it the same way, or even close, then we can guess that, if he has Jeremy, that Jeremy is still alive. That we have approximately two days left to find this boy before he kills him by hitting him in the head with some kind of hard object." I turned to face Monty.

"Gretchen, you know that it's a myth that serial killers have some precise schedule that they stick to. Like I said, if anything, their killings become more random and accelerated. It's an issue of convenience for them."

"I realize that, and I'm not necessarily saying that this guy is acting according to a schedule. It could be a year off, or there could be ones we don't know about interspersed all along. I'm just saying that for these particular cases"—I pointed to the sheet—"there seems to be some common threads: the head injuries, the locations of the abductions, all on the north end of the valley or in Badrock Canyon."

"Okay," Monty said, still looking at the images he'd pulled out of the file. "Tell me more about Erickson."

I told him everything I'd learned from Detective Belson, about the pouring rain and how it destroyed much of the evidence. About the entomology report. "Should we take this to Ali?" I asked.

"No, it's too circumstantial. I know it makes sense to you, and I think there's a very small possibility that you might be onto something, but it's just a theory—a theory that won't change things either way. Ali, Herman, and Park Police are going to continue pouring every effort into looking for Jeremy regardless of this information and any possible timeline. I suggest you keep it to yourself for now."

I looked at the files as Monty replaced the gruesome images of Erickson. I was still lost in thought about the missing boys, about Jeremy possibly still being alive, when a clap of thunder sounded nearby, breaking my ruminations, breaching the silence. "I should go now," I announced. "It's getting late and I should get home before this gets worse." I waved to the outside. "I've got to be at the lab early again."

Monty looked to the front window. "It's getting nasty out there," he said. "Are you sure you want to drive in it?"

I didn't say anything. I felt torn. A part of me wanted him to encourage me to stay and wait and another part of me wanted to get out as soon as I could. I began to shuffle the files together, and Monty didn't say anything, just watched my hands as I gathered the information.

"I actually don't think you should drive in it just yet," he said. "You know, I could make us something to eat—some sandwiches or something."

I shook my head. "No, thank you, I'm fine." Then, as if on cue, lightning flashed and turned the room silver blue, followed by an enormous clap of thunder. I could feel my shoulders go straight to my ears.

"Too close," he said.

"Yeah, makes me jumpy." I told myself to relax, stood up, and peeked out the window to the bruised blackness outside. I could see my reflection with the help of the yellow lamplight—my hair framing my face. I stood for a moment until another violent crack split the darkened sky into luminescent veins above the massive black peaks. I quickly backed away. "Why doesn't it rain?"

"It feels like it will. This isn't just from the heat. The air feels even heavier now." Monty sat still on the sofa, leaning forward and looking at me, his tanned arms propped on his knees.

"Do you think he's out there in this?"

"I don't know," he said. "I wish I did." A branch flew and hit the window and I flinched.

"Come back here." He twitched his head to motion for me to sit. "Just wait it out. If you don't want anything to eat, you at least need to hang until it passes. If you want, you could crash here tonight. I don't mind the couch."

"No, once it passes, I'll be fine." I went over and sat back down, this time in a chair and not right next to him. He caught it and a smile played across his lips. I could tell he wanted to say something like *I'm not going to bite*, but was too much of a gentleman. I narrowed my eyes at him, studying him. It felt like he could read me and was just toying with me, and I couldn't tell if that made me angry or happy.

He studied me back. "What happened to your face?" he asked again.

"I already told you."

"That the truth?" His head cocked, his brown eyes clearer now that he'd logged a little sleep. He was handsome, all right, but I pushed the thought away and looked at my fingernails.

"Yeah, why wouldn't it be?"

"I don't know," he said. "Just sometimes it feels like you're hiding."

"Hiding? I'm not hiding anything."

"That's not what I said. Not that you're hiding something, just that you yourself are hiding."

I shrugged. Now I was positive it was anger rising in me. How dare he sit there and assess me that way. "Monty, come on, why are you analyzing me?"

"Because . . . ," he said, but his voice faded, and he didn't offer anymore.

"Look, I'm short. I got up to go to the bathroom and it was dark and I ran into the corner of my dresser. You think I'd make something like that up?"

"I don't," Monty said, sighing. "I don't know. I just worry about you sometimes, that's all."

"Worry? Why?"

"I'm not really sure why." He smiled.

"Well, you don't need to and you really don't even have a right to worry about me."

"I don't?"

"No." I know I sounded mean and childish, but I needed boundaries to form quickly in this small space with the storm thrashing around us, and Monty studying me more closely than ever before.

"Why not? Aren't we friends? You've worried about me in the past. . . ."

I knew he was referring to the last case we worked and how I'd come running whenever he needed help. "Yeah, well, yeah, we're friends," I said. "And friends let friends be."

Monty closed his lips into a straight line and nodded like he understood. "Okay, fair enough. I'll let you be." He stood and went to the kitchen. "I'm making some tea for you. Herbal or caffeine?"

"Herbal," I said. "Please."

While Monty clanked around in the kitchen, drops the size of marbles began to pelt the roof and the window. I went over and opened the door to see the falling rain. I caught the unmistakable scent of dampening pavement from the drive and the earthy aroma of wet soil, which

I hadn't smelled all summer. It was long overdue and the relief I felt surprised me. The intense, palpable aromas seemed profound.

"You were right," I called out as I shut the door. "It's finally raining." I sank back in the chair and let my limbs relax. I had made myself clear with Monty and now, rain. Sweet rain. The rush of it got louder and pounded the roof, buckets of it. I thought of it coming down hard on the fires. A sigh escaped my lips. That's one break we'd gotten and I was glad we got the truck and the shed processed before it happened.

"Finally, she relaxes," I heard Monty say softly. I opened my eyes and saw him standing above me with some tea. He placed it on the coffee table before me. "Let it sit," he said. "It's really hot. Just stay where you are and relax. I don't think I'm the only one here who hasn't gotten much sleep lately."

16

Monty

As the storm passed, I watched Gretchen for a moment. She had fallen asleep with her tea cooling in front of her on the coffee table. She was wearing cropped, fitted jeans, a sand-colored sweater, and white Converse sneakers. She was beautiful with her glistening, dewy skin, her honey blond hair fanning out on the back of the easy chair. A certain sweetness under all her self-protections shone through in spite of her intentions and her matter-of-fact ways. Asleep, without her defenses, she looked like an angel with rose petal lips, childlike.

I rose, went into my bedroom, shut the door so I wouldn't wake her, and called headquarters to see if any new information had turned up. There was nothing new, which meant there was nothing for me to do, and with the weather the way it was, I told Karen I wasn't coming in after all and to call me if anything came up. I went back out and looked through the files Gretchen had brought over, then when I realized she wasn't stirring from the noise, I decided to take a shower.

I left her sleeping, but after I got dressed and came back out, she wasn't there. I figured she woke, heard me in the shower, and left. Disappointment darted through me. A part of me kicked myself for leaving her alone like that. I would have liked to see her before she left. I went to the window. The rain had completely ceased, stopped as quickly as it began. I could see my own reflection. Then beyond it I noticed a tan car still in my drive out in the dark. I switched on the porch light to make sure and saw that it was definitely Gretchen's Honda.

I turned around. Her files still lay scattered on the table and her bag sat by the couch on the floor. I went into the bedroom, thinking she took me up on my offer and claimed my bed, but the room was empty and I would have noticed her when I came out of the shower. I called to her as I went into the kitchen. "Gretchen, you still here?"

She didn't answer. I called her cell phone and heard it buzzing in her bag beside the couch. Confused, I went and opened the front door. The car was empty and she wasn't sitting in it. Even though the rain had stopped, rainwater still streamed out from the gutters onto the lawn.

I grabbed my flashlight and my raincoat and went outside, shining the light down the street and into the woods. It didn't make sense. She'd never be out here like this. I considered that someone came by and picked her up, that maybe her car wasn't starting and she'd called someone for a ride. But still, that didn't make sense either. She would have just asked me for a ride. And why hadn't she taken her purse, her phone, or her files? I continued to search, shining my light down the road and into the dark woods.

The wet boughs of the pines glistened in my beam. The sound of the water running from the gutters filled my ears, and I glanced back at the house. When I turned back to the woods, I suddenly thought I caught a glimpse of something pale or light-colored, something or someone moving through the trees like an apparition. I wondered if it was a deer. I moved closer, walking east toward the Middle Fork River, which cuts through West Glacier not far from my dorm. Sure enough, weaving among the trees, Gretchen was heading toward the river.

"Hey," I called, but she didn't hear me. "Gretchen," I yelled louder, but she kept going deeper into the thin stretch of forest beside the river. "What the hell?" I said to myself. I began to run to catch her, dodging tall, skinny pines dripping with rainwater. I reached her just as she began wading into the river. She stumbled on some slippery river rocks, almost fell, but kept going. She seemed clumsy to me, as if she'd been drinking.

"Gretchen," I yelled firmly. "What are you doing?" She still didn't turn, and something about her movements made me understand that she was sleepwalking. I ran into the water after her. I knew there was a sudden drop in the river. Rapids formed ahead and white water rippled like fluttering ribbons. If she was sleepwalking, she could drown. I caught up with her and grabbed her arm, but she threw my hand off, mumbling something.

"Gretchen, stop," I said firmly. She did not look right. Her eyes were glassy, her face expressionless, but she fought me anyway. I pulled her in toward me and wrapped my arms around her to restrain her. Her arms flailed and she struck me across my chin. I tried dragging her back to the riverbank, but she continued to struggle. She jerked her arm and broke free, splashing down into the water. It was still shallow and she sank down on her butt to her waist.

I kneeled down and grabbed her shoulders. She felt chilled, and I could see the frigid river water begin to wake her, an ounce of recognition filtering back into her eyes. She blinked several times and looked around in the dark, then flinched when she realized she was in water and stood up quickly, almost falling again. "Gretchen," I said. "It's me, Monty."

She looked at me, confused. "Where am I?" she asked groggily.

"In the Middle Fork. You fell asleep. I think you were sleepwalking."

She stared at me, her skin ghostly in the starlight, then burrowed her face in her hands. "Oh, God," she said.

"It's okay, come on, let's get you dried off."

Gretchen began to shake her head back and forth, "No, no, Monty. I'm so sorry." She took off, stumbling over the rocks back to shore, and began to run, her wet jeans swishing and her shoes slapping the ground. I yelled for her again. "It's okay," I said and took off after her. When I reached her, I grabbed her arm. "Gretchen, just stop, will you?"

She looked terrified, panic-stricken.

"Just calm down. It's okay. You were just sleepwalking."

Her face looked strained with more layers of pain than I'd ever seen in her—than I'd ever seen in anyone, even my tormented mother. I knew in that moment my suspicions were correct: something haunted Gretchen Larson deeply. "I have to go. I have to go now."

"Okay," I said. "But—"

"Just please." She stared at me, her shoulders trembling. Her expression pleaded for me to say nothing more, so I didn't. A profound sadness revealed itself in her eyes and hit me like a spear. I moved back a step. Then she ran into my place, grabbed her things, threw them in her car, and drove away soaking into the wet night.

After her taillights disappeared around the bend, I looked up. Stars pocked the sky between sinister charcoal-colored clouds that continued to shift. I'd somehow glimpsed something that Gretchen clearly didn't want me to see. The agony in her eyes and the fear roiling beneath the surface told me that much at least. I continued to watch the remaining rain clouds move like ghosts, exposing new pieces of the brilliant sky and hiding others. "Gretchen," I whispered into the fresh air that the storm had left behind. "What's this all about?"

17

Gretchen

I RECALLED WHAT I had dreamed when I fell asleep at Monty's. I don't often remember them when I've had a parasomniac event, but every once in a while I do. Per had been ahead of me skiing, his strides long and graceful—ethereal—his skis barely even touching the ice, as if he were hovering. I was watching him, studying him, trying to follow him and be as smooth as he was—free and untethered—but I wasn't nimble at all. I was having trouble, my edges catching on watery, sticky ice chunks that clung to the smooth undersides of the long, narrow skis. I wished I had put wax on them and cursed that I couldn't catch him. He continued to ski—or fly, really—under an azure sky, until it abruptly shifted and became washed out. The ice began to crack, loud and fierce like thunder with fissures spreading out into expanding spidery veins. I tried to ski faster and faster, but I couldn't make headway. Per went crashing down, falling to a strata below, screaming, "No, Gretchen, no, stop."

I strained against the slushy muck, trying desperately to catch him, to reach him with the rope I had in my pack, but I couldn't get any closer. The nearer I thought I came, the farther out he seemed, his cries growing fainter and fainter, the sense of his person shape-shifting from Per to Wendy's son, Kyle, to Jeremy and back to Per again.

I took off my skis and tried to run, but I felt like I was walking through mud, my feet heavy like lead. I trudged on though; I had to reach him, but he was yelling at me not to, to leave him alone. And someone else was calling my name from behind. I didn't dare turn and look because I had to save my brother. It was my turn to save my brother. Then I fell myself, my butt freezing on the slushy ice, and each layer split around me, swallowing me in piercing cracks.

When I finally came to, I was horrified to see I was outside in the night, that I'd fallen in the river and was soaked from the waist down and that Monty was trying to restrain me from going in deeper.

When I come out of one of these events, I'm like a toddler for a moment, unable to make my limbs move the way I instruct them, as if I need someone to hold me up. I feel dizzy. In a few moments, though, it comes back, and when it did with Monty, I ran. I drove straight home, shaking and blasting the heat in my car. The dusty scent of it, since it hasn't been used since winter, hit me like an admonishment, as if the fusty, stale air pushed out stored-away memories that shouldn't be exposed.

I drove, my headlights exposing the debris from the storm: snapped branches and smaller, torn green-leafed stems tossed about. When I reached my house and let myself in, I peeled off my pants, took a hot shower, and changed into a robe. I sat in my kitchen with some tea. The storm had completely passed, the electricity in the air gone, and it was dead quiet—no crickets, no wind rustling the trees, no sirens or car honks from town.

I still trembled, mostly from my frazzled nerves and not from the cold, as I sipped chamomile tea and cursed myself for letting my guard down at Monty's. I had been more tired than I thought. Of course I had, how could I not have considered that I might fall asleep if I let myself sink into a comfortable armchair and close my eyes for a moment while listening to the wind and the rain? Stupid, so stupid, I thought.

When I had first come to Seattle, I stumbled through my days numbly, like a zombie, but sometimes I'd get so homesick and lonely that I'd regularly take the ferries around Puget Sound just to remind myself of the ones that traversed the fjords and the North Sea. During the summer, my family and I sometimes used to drive to a town called Larvik just to catch the boat to Frederikshavn in Denmark, a busy port where we'd go for the weekend to visit friends of my parents who also had kids around the same age as Per and me.

One time, in Seattle, on the way back from Vashon Island, I saw a young couple who had taken their bikes over for the afternoon and were also heading back to the city. It was a beautiful summer day, the breeze blowing through the open windows on the boat and the smell of salt water filling my nose. The woman, maybe in her late twenties, was beautiful, like a princess. She had pale skin, almond eyes, and shoulder-length cinnamon-colored hair that blew across her face in the wind. She wore a casual pastel dress and rested her slim hands on her bicycle handles. Her mate was equally handsome—her prince, as the fantasy goes—with thick dark hair swept to the side and a nice, twinkling smile. She said something in his ear that made him laugh. He leaned over and kissed her on the cheek and she sighed in contentment.

The image of them together has always stayed with me—a snapshot in time in my mind—not because I'm the kind of female who's fallen for the Prince Charming fairy tales. If anything, fairy tales never impressed me, and it was always someone's mind that enthralled me more than their looks. If I let the cynical side of me play it out, I would guess that the pair didn't even end up together, that they broke up or divorced somewhere along the line, but the sweet moment struck me so poignantly on the boat ride because it was one of the first times I realized I would never have that kind of intimacy. I couldn't be trusted to have that kind of connection. My sleep disorder and my history would always be the sharp needles pricking and bursting any blooming bond. I'd always be watching other couples from the outside: people getting engaged, marrying, buying houses, creating homes, and starting families. People going on outings and vacations together and sharing dreams. Of course, later I had my brief marriage to Jim, but he was only a friend, and we never even lived together. I was relieved when it ended, even though I continued to value his friendship.

I took another sip of tea and thought of my fate, how I had resigned myself to it, made peace with it—a life of solitude after what I'd done to Per. There was no choice but to accept it. But sometimes I wondered how I could continue to walk the tightrope of wanting so many things and knowing I couldn't have them, knowing that deep down I didn't really want a companion, that I was capable of harming the very person I wanted to protect.

No, just because I liked Monty and just because he made me feel things I hadn't felt in a very long time—made me tingle with emotions I didn't even understand when I least expected it—didn't mean things would change. I would never let myself harm anyone again. I couldn't bear it. I sat in my peaceful kitchen, finished my tea, and went to bed, making sure I was secure in my sleeping bag and mittens.

I always felt like I was one step away from being found out—that people sensed the secret hidden in me. Now Monty had not only sensed something, he'd witnessed it. In the morning, I knew that I needed to scrape some courage together in case Monty decided to tell someone or bring it up again.

· · ·

When I arrived at the lab the next morning, I went straight to the police garage to see what else, if anything, had been discovered. Ray was still working with dust, Superglue, and fluorescent light. He had pulled trace the entire day before using tape strips and a vacuum for the floorboards and carpeting. Taping is a wearisome task, as is processing latent prints, but Wendy had also worked late into the day yesterday, finishing the pulling of prints and creating the print cards to scan into the system. She was currently back at the office still trying to find hits on the few additional unidentified ones she'd obtained, besides the boy's whose she'd found the evening before. I left Ray to his work and went to the office.

"G," Wendy said when she saw me walk in.

"Hi," I said back. "Get any more hits besides the boy's?"

"Yes. To Stewart, one of the farmhands." I knew that our database had over 200,000 sets of 10-prints, prints rolled—or nowadays, scanned—when a person was arrested. Wendy's job consisted of comparing unknown prints to the identified ones in the system as well as to any elimination sets we'd taken, such as Stewart's and hopefully Brady's. "I should tie things up here by the end of the workday. I'll let you know if I'm able to make any additional matches besides these two sets. Since the truck was wiped down, I've only got a few—one from the rearview mirror, and two from the side windows for a total of three clear prints. The gearshift and the radio were wiped down too thoroughly to get anything else."

"Right, like we figured."

I left Wendy to her work and went back to my office to study the photographs and other data we'd gotten on the truck so far, when Wendy came in a few hours later, smiling.

"Guess what?" she asked.

"You've matched the prints."

"Actually, yes, the county scanned Brady for the agents and sent them to us. I've got a match from the mirror to his set."

"Okay, good work. At least there's only one unidentified print left. I'll let them know."

"Okay, but guess what again?"

"You've found something else?"

"No, I'm sorry, but it's still great news." Wendy's face lit up. "My dad just called. He said he's spoken to Kyle and he's on his way to my office."

"Oh. Wendy. I'm so glad." I stood, walked around my desk, grabbed her arm, and squeezed.

"Yeah, it's a relief."

"Where's he been?"

"Camping with his friends. Just as I figured. I'm so relieved and angry at him at the same time. I'm sure they've been on one big bender. When he comes, I plan to take his keys, take him straight home."

"Yeah, sure," I said. "Anything you need. Just make sure you finish checking that last unknown and get me the data before you leave for the day."

"I can't believe it's already close to four. I'm exhausted."

"You worked late last night. Go get your boy home. I'm so glad he's safe," I said.

"Me too. Thank you for everything."

"There's nothing to thank me for. Just make sure you've finished running the comparisons to that last unknown before you leave."

"Yes, mother," she smiled, seeming lighter on her feet than she had all week.

Mother. *Mor.* I thought of the word. I hadn't used it in so long, I no longer recognized how it felt in my mouth. For the first year after I came to the States, we tried to stay in touch, but the overseas phone calls were expensive and awkward and eventually they petered out.

For no particular reason, I thought of a time almost three months after it happened, at the end of March, when the days were still cold, and the light dull and pointless. I sat at the kitchen table trying to do a math problem—one of those puzzles about a train leaving a station and going a certain speed. I couldn't think through the static in my mind and the problem seemed to circle around in my head.

My father had not returned from work yet. It had become like that. Instead of staying to have coffee and breakfast, he'd leave early and come home past dinnertime. The three of us had been walking around the house like ghosts for three weeks after the hospital—after two months of testing and treatment—released me with specific instructions for how to handle my disorder. I had been assigned a social worker to help me stay on track with schoolwork while I went to see a therapist and other sleep specialists twice a week. In the meantime, I was to stay home, which was fine. I had no desire to go to school or do anything else ever again.

An outside lock had been placed on my bedroom door and only my parents had a key. Sometimes my mother wouldn't get out of bed in the morning and would forget to open it. I was afraid to call out and bug her. I didn't feel I had the right to, so if I had to go to the bathroom, I'd just hold it until she'd remember to come open my door.

That particular March day, while I was working on math, my mother came into the kitchen. I watched her open the refrigerator and stare into it. She just stood before it, not grabbing anything. The automatic light from inside shone on her ratty sweater, which she hadn't changed in weeks. There wasn't much food in the fridge. I could see why she didn't take anything. The endless meals from neighbors and friends that came in the beginning—when we had no appetites anyway—had dwindled or been tossed out, uneaten by my father. She finally shut the door without taking anything.

"Do you want me to make you something?" I asked, clutching my pencil tightly.

She flinched, surprised I'd spoken. When she turned to me, I caught a flash of disgust. Her hair wilted around her face and dark circles draped under her eyes. She shook her head no.

"I could go to the store if you need me to," I offered.

"No, it's fine," she said, her voice hoarse from disuse. "If you're hungry, I can give you some money if you want to get something for yourself."

"No," I said. "I'm fine."

She looked out the window. The snow had turned to slush, then refroze. I watched her stare blankly at the driveway. I grabbed my coat and went out the front door. I found the snow shovel and began to try to clear the frozen slush, but it wouldn't budge. I kept digging the blade of the shovel into the frozen ridges, chipping chunky pieces of ice and scattering it in all directions. I was trying to help, to do something useful. I looked back into the kitchen window, but it was empty. She had left, perhaps gone back to her room or maybe even Per's. Sometimes she would fall asleep in his room for hours, and I'd find her on his bed, tangled in his duvet. I stared at the empty window. The glass looked like a black sheet of ice, not a window to a warm home. What could I say to her or ever do that could possibly help?

I stood, holding the shovel. Stupid, I said to myself, realizing that if she'd seen me jabbing at the ice, she'd have thought about only one thing: my strong arms swinging the fire iron.

· · ·

Forty-five minutes later, I still needed to know if Wendy had come up with a match on the unknown set of prints she'd lifted, and I wasn't sure if Kyle had made it in yet. I walked down the hall, past the humming computers and the microscopes. Wendy's door was open, so I went right in, saying, "Knock knock."

Wendy waved me in from her desk, and Kyle sat in one of the two office chairs. "Excuse me. Sorry to bother you. I wanted to catch you before you left."

"That's okay. You remember Kyle?"

"Of course. Hey, Kyle. Good to see you again." It had been a while, and Kyle looked older and taller, more like a young man, but still a teen, brooding and lanky. He wore a black T-shirt and a thin yellow-checked flannel shirt over it, rolled up at the sleeves. He looked like he hadn't had a good meal in a while or a decent night of sleep. He had dark circles under his eyes and tattoos of vines and bloodred flowers ran down both his pale arms and onto his hands. The tattoos probably disguised the needle tracks Wendy had told me about. I wondered where he'd been this time.

Kyle glanced up at me and barely nodded, then shoved one hand in his back pocket and pulled out an electronic game, leaning over, his elbows propped on both knees, his thumbs beginning to work the controls.

Wendy looked at me with a torn look that said, *I'm relieved he's back, but here we go again.* "Kyle," Wendy snapped at him, "Gretchen asked you how you're doing. Can you please answer?"

He stared blankly at me again, showing zero emotion, then

looked back to his device and started mindlessly pressing away once more.

"That's okay," I said. "I just need to know if you've got any hits before you leave."

Wendy walked over and stood next to him. "Give me that." She held out her hand for the game.

"It's okay," I said again. "I just—"

"No, it's not okay. Kyle"—Wendy held out her palm—"Gretchen is being polite to you and you're being rude. Give me that or I will keep your car keys and your phone even longer than I already plan to." It seemed like an inadequate and lame attempt to rein him in, in light of the fact that he'd just disappeared for several days of his own volition, a finger in the dyke.

Kyle lifted the game and slowly placed it in his mother's hand, his eyelids heavy with boredom and disdain. That look reminded me of Per. Kyle in no way resembled Per. Per had wavy, dirty blond hair and the clean-shaven looks of Adonis. Kyle had dark hair and translucent skin. But both of them shared otherworldly luminescent bluish-green eyes and a good dose of petulance. Perhaps all seventeen-year-old boys, no matter where they came from, had that petulant look.

But Kyle *really* did it justice. His jeans were several sizes too large, and even seated I could see he wore them low enough to expose his boxers underneath. His hair looked like it hadn't seen a bottle of shampoo or a comb in weeks. His whole appearance was designed to give the finger to society and all its rules.

"Thank you," Wendy said, but I could see a deep strain in her frown, her jaw flexed with anxiety. "Where did you get this anyway?" She placed it on her desk, her brow furrowed.

Kyle shoved his hands back in his jean pockets and stared vacantly at the wall of her office without answering. Wendy gave a loud exhale and turned to me. "Sorry about that, G. What can I do for you?"

"I just need the completed file on the truck. Any hits on the other print?"

"No, other than the boy's, Stewart's, and Brady's, nothing in the system matches the other set. I've been comparing all afternoon, but I can't find anything conclusive."

Wendy went behind her desk, picked up a folder, and handed it to me. I walked back to my office, feeling sorry for Wendy again. Kyle was showing no signs of snapping out of this phase of teenage dysfunction and immaturity.

But as I rounded the corner to my office, it hit me: the game. Monty had mentioned a game. A current raced through me, but only for a second. It struck me as odd that a seventeen-year-old would be playing with one of those Nintendo devices, but Wendy had said she'd taken away his phone, so perhaps a game was the next best thing. On instinct, I turned and went back to the office, gave a small rap on the door and went back in.

Kyle had stood from his chair, and Wendy was grabbing her purse. "We're going to head out now." Wendy twitched her head in the direction of Kyle and gave me a sad, knowing, and apologetic look.

"No problem. Ray and I have got it handled." My gaze went to her desk to see if she or Kyle had grabbed the game. It was still there, but as soon as I noticed, Wendy grabbed it and threw it in her desk. "I'll call you in a bit." Wendy sighed again and looked at Kyle. "Let's go."

Kyle followed her out, his shoulders slouching with the tedium of being with his mother and his gaze on his own boot-clad feet.

I walked with them down the hall toward my office, said goodbye, then went back to my desk, telling myself I was being completely paranoid and silly.

· · ·

I had just finished talking to Ray about how much longer he'd need with some trace that he'd found—particles or materials that could have been transferred into the truck from the abductor—when Monty called and insisted that he needed to see me. "I can't," I told him. "I'm busy."

"I've got a file you left last night. I guess it fell on the floor. Anyway, I'm going to stop by and drop it off before you leave for the day."

"No," I said too quickly. I didn't want him anywhere near my place of work, even if the workday was practically over and Wendy was headed home. Ray was still working and I didn't need Monty asking me questions about the night before within earshot. "I'll meet you somewhere."

"Good," he said. "Where?"

We agreed that he'd text me when he got into Kalispell and we'd meet in the park next to my building. When his message popped up on my screen, I sighed, grabbed my bag, and left.

The storm had washed the air clean in the valley, and I hadn't seen the sky so bright all summer—almost Smurf blue—but I'd heard on the radio that the lightning had struck up more fires, including one on Desert Mountain close to West Glacier and the canyon. Luckily, the wind stayed light, and for now the fires were being contained on the east side of the park and on the eastern edge of the canyon.

I found Monty sitting on a bench staring straight at the grass ahead with his legs planted firmly apart and his arms crossed—as if even waiting in a city park on a glorious day under a sky that stretched into oblivion and birds chirping all around comprised some sort of a mission. He turned when he heard me approach and stood up.

"No, sit." I motioned with my hand, but he didn't. He waited for me to take a seat as well, but I didn't either. I avoided his eyes, still embarrassed and still anxious about the can of worms I'd opened up by falling asleep at his place.

"Sit," he said.

"No, it's okay. I'm in a hurry. Tons of work to do still. You've got a file of mine?"

"Yeah." He nodded, but I didn't see a file in his hands or on the bench and he didn't have his carrier bag with him.

"So, where is it?" Impatience rose in me.

"In the car. I can get it in a sec. Can't you sit for one minute?"

The six o'clock sunshine, still bright, felt like a hot iron on my upper back, and I could feel my skin prickle with a new, light layer of perspiration. I looked over my shoulder back to the county justice building where the cool air-conditioning and the solitude of my office beckoned my return.

This time, he actually said, "I won't bite," and motioned to the bench again. It was in the shade of a huge pine tree that appeared to be home to about fifty different birds and squirrels.

I glanced back again to my building, hesitating, still avoiding his gaze.

"I just want to chat for a second," he said.

I resigned only because the shade was inviting, and slumped onto the bench. "Why didn't you bring the file? I thought that was the point of this."

"It is, and I'll grab it, but I just wanted to chat."

"What about?"

"About you. About last night."

I crossed my arms and shook my head, letting him know that this was off-limits.

"What? I find you sleepwalking into a river, endangering yourself, and you don't want to talk about it. Do you sleepwalk a lot?"

"No, no, I don't." I lied. "It was just a freak thing. I don't know what happened." I fibbed again. I could feel his dark eyes on me, but I didn't dare look at him for fear my expression would expose my fraudulence. "I guess I haven't gotten much sleep either, and these cases have been disturbing. I suppose it's affected me too."

Monty sat quietly, not saying anything. I glanced at him out of the corner of my eyes, and I could tell he was thinking by the way his eyes narrowed in concentration.

"So, let me get this straight, you've never sleepwalked before last night?"

"I didn't say that. I said, not often. When I was little, I'd walk around the house a bit, but that was a long time ago."

"Is that what happened to your face?"

I didn't answer him for a long moment. Finally, I said, "Why do you care?"

"Why do you keep asking me that? Isn't it obvious? Friends care about friends." He sat forward with his elbows on his knees like he'd done on his couch. He rested the side of his forehead in one hand and turned his face to look at me. I stayed put with my arms folded at my chest and my legs crossed. If my body language didn't say "stay away," I don't know what else would.

"Okay, fair enough, but we have work to do. A boy's missing, and we just dug up bones of an adolescent. Have you forgotten?"

He gave me a deep frown, and I could tell I'd insulted him. He stood up from the bench and turned to me. "I'm not even going to answer that. If you don't want to talk, fine. It's not my business."

I sat still, not moving a muscle, but finally raised my eyes to look at him. I felt like a stubborn child, and suddenly I was fifteen again, racked by guilt. As anxiety climbed higher in my chest, I stood up too, but looked back at the ground.

"I'll grab your file," he said, striding toward his car. I followed him, hustling to catch him. I thought of rushing to catch Per.

When he handed the file to me, I thanked him, then took a breath, held it, and considered whether to bring up the game. It seemed silly now that we had the print on the seat belt of the Tuckman farm truck, not to mention that I'd already dumped my other theories on him, which he thought were stretches. I knew there could not possibly be a connection between Wendy's son and that Chevy truck . . . a connection between Kyle and some missing young teenage boy in Glacier Park. What are the chances? I asked myself. Monty tipped his head to me, pivoted, and bent to get into his car. I let out my breath after realizing I was holding it. "And, Monty . . ."

He stopped, holding his door open, and stood back up. I couldn't live with myself if I didn't at least ask about it. "That game you mentioned. The one the boy had?"

"Yeah?"

"What color was it?"

Monty stared at me. "Black. Why?"

"I feel silly saying anything. I mean, how many 3DS's are out there in the world?"

"A lot."

"Well, that's just it. I'm sure it's absolutely nothing, but . . ." I paused, thinking that by bringing it up, I was betraying Wendy and her son this way. She had enough trouble with him on her hands, and I was somehow introducing more.

"But what?" Monty prodded.

But still—the game really struck me, coincidental or not. And I'd already started, so now I needed to finish. "You know Wendy, my print examiner?"

Monty nodded, his brow creased.

"She has a son. He's, well, he's pretty much in and out of trouble all the time. You know the type. . . ." I knew Monty's brother, Adam, had spent his teenage years mixed up in drugs and alcohol and was sent to a therapeutic school for teens not too far from Glacier.

"I do," Monty said with a knowing chuckle, and I was relieved to hear it, relieved to think he wasn't too frustrated with me.

"Anyway, she said he'd been missing for the past few nights—something of a frequent occurrence—and he just returned today. Anyway, he was in the office with her and was playing a game—one of those 3DSs."

Monty ran his hand behind his neck. "And what makes you think it's the kid's?"

"Nothing really. I don't know, it just seemed weird and out of place—a kid his age and a delinquent to boot. The game seemed like a younger kid's thing. But you're right, I don't have any good reason to believe it's related. I shouldn't have even brought it up."

"Did you see initials?"

"No. Like I said. Nothing." My cheeks heated suddenly, and I felt foolish for broaching the subject. I detested the idea that I would waste anyone's time with irrational ideas, but I also knew that I still felt un-easy. I knew from experience in this job that ignoring a gut feeling could bite you hard later if you didn't at least bother to check up on it. And the last thing I needed was remorse for leaving a stone unturned. "There's no reason to think its Jeremy's," I said. "It just surprised me since I knew he had one, and Wendy had never seen it either. She con-fiscated it from him."

"Gretchen, we can't exactly get a search warrant on every teenager out there who's got a 3DS."

"I know. I know. Like I said. It's nothing. Sorry to waste your time."

"You haven't. Thanks for telling me. Every detail is important." He turned back to get in his car, then paused. "What color was it?"

"Black."

Monty didn't move for a moment and didn't speak either, just looked at me. I saw exhaustion and sadness in his face. I could tell he just wanted to help me, and I felt like I'd disappointed him by not answering his questions.

Guilt shot through me. An image of Monty's concerned look under the dark sky by the river flashed into my mind. I also recalled how he had looked out at the yurt site, like something stirred below the sur-face. A part of me hated to be the witch further stirring the pot, adding to the concern. I hated to put him in a position where he thought he needed to figure me out or help me in some way, but there was no way to avoid it. I was certain that if I told him about my past, he'd feel like he'd need to help me, and no one could ever do that.

I knew Monty was too perceptive, too driven, not to dig when he suspected a mystery, that my silence would forever insert something heavy and awkward between us. A truck honked as it rounded the road circling the courthouse, and I flinched nervously. A raven flew out of the nearby giant pine, its dark shadow passing over us both. Monty watched me. Get a grip, I ordered myself, and shook off the sirens of self-loathing whispering to me from my own depths. "Okay then," I said. "I've got to get back to work."

"Gretchen, it probably wouldn't be a bad idea to see if there were some initials on the game. If, that is, it'll help you sleep better." He winked and I suppressed a smile.

I didn't say anything.

"But you're right—probably a long shot," he added. "Just in case they're JRC."

. . .

I went back into the county building, finally letting a faint smile sneak onto my lips when I thought of Monty's knack for diffusing tension. It was impossible to stay angry with him, even under the burden of my fear of being discovered.

I sat before my microscope, studying the two hairs—one dark-colored, one light, almost silvery gray—through the ocular lens. Ray had lifted them from the backseat of the truck. They were definitely human hairs, and we were lucky to have found them, given the antiseptic spray that was used, but not lucky enough to have the roots still attached on both, only to one. Apparently, the person who sprayed had missed several spots on the backseat. The hairs could belong to anyone who'd ridden in the truck over the years, so it was a long shot, but we'd still submit the one with the root attached to the lab in Missoula for DNA analysis.

Ray emerged from his office, came over, and settled the side of his bony hip on the edge of my workstation, a bag of bite-size Dove chocolate bars in one hand. He held it out to me. "No, thanks," I said.

"What? You? No chocolate?"

"Trying to cut back on caffeine."

"I hardly think a bite-size Dove is going make much of a difference in your caffeine consumption."

"Okay." I stuck my hand in the bag, grabbing three.

"Three?" Ray mocked. "On second thought, three might."

"Shut up," I said. "I shouldn't have said anything to you. Aren't you going home soon?" I looked at the clock on the wall to see it was nearing six thirty.

"I'm turning into a workaholic like you," Ray smiled, then nodded to my microscope. "You looking at those hairs now?"

"Yeah. This truck situation is a mess."

"Tell me about it. Three drivers. Not much trace and only a few prints. Even if we match the print to one of the farmhands, it doesn't tell us anything other than that they drove it for their job. And with the key just hanging in the barn like that, out of view of the main house, practically anyone could have borrowed it."

"Or," I said, "it was one of the farmhands who took the boy."

"Do they both have alibis?" he asked.

"I heard that one of them didn't. Said he was fishing, but no one can verify it."

"Well now, that sounds mighty fishy to me. . . ." He gave me a closed-lip grin.

"Plus, he's not offering up his prints."

"No shit? Who wouldn't want to help find a missing child?"

"Someone hiding something, I suppose."

Ray nodded. "We should be able to get some DNA from the one strand, but I don't love the fact that it came from the backseat. The driver likely wasn't ever back there, and if it belongs to the boy, then we're only verifying what we already know from the print—that he was definitely in or around that vehicle. Hopefully the other strand leads us somewhere."

"The one without the root has some gray on it, so either the person's prematurely gray, or is at least middle-aged."

"Does the fisherman have gray hair?"

"I haven't seen him, but I'll ask Ali and Herman. They'll know."

"Anything from the floorboards or the carpeting?" I asked.

"As a matter of fact, yes, but I don't know if it's significant or not, given that the truck was used for going to the dump and moving gravel and whatnot. There's the usual stuff you'd expect would be transferred from a person's work boots: cotton, pollen, dirt, horse manure, broken glass, hay, powdery residue from gravel, a dead ant, other insect remains, cat hair, dog hair."

"What kind of dog hair?"

"Lab, like the ones at the Tuckmans."

I nodded.

"What's interesting, though, is that there were some asbestos fibers and some flakes that resemble a metal. Aluminum, I think. And the chemical analysis shows there's some lead, some fluoride, and even some crystallized cyanide."

"Cyanide?" I said. "That's weird. Is asbestos or cyanide normally found at a dump?"

"Not usually," Ray said. "You'd need a permit to remove asbestos from a building, and cyanide, well, you can't just dump a toxic chemical like that at the dump, although people don't follow the rules all the time."

"Hmm, well, given the CFAC sticker on the bumper, the aluminum might be significant."

"Might be." Ray popped another chocolate in his mouth. "But I doubt it. That place has been closed for a while now. I'm going to prepare for more slides. I'll have them on your desk as soon as I'm finished."

"Sounds good," I said.

An hour later, he called to me that he was leaving and yelled good-bye. I yelled back, shutting down my workstation, when I wondered about the Nintendo game again. I knew Wendy was up for the weekend shift, and I had planned to talk to her in the morning because it seemed wrong to snoop around her office. It was a long shot, but *if* it belonged to the boy, waiting until morning was a mistake. I walked to Wendy's office and turned the knob to see if she'd locked it. Since the entire lab was under tight security, cleaners weren't allowed in to vacuum or mop, which meant we rotated the cleaning shift among ourselves. Not exactly glamorous, and definitely not something you'd see on *CSI*. Since it was only us doing the cleaning, most of us left our office doors open for whosever turn it was to mop and vacuum the floors. Even if it was locked, as the team leader, I had a master key.

But it was open. I stepped over to the desk with one of the print analysis computers on it and grabbed a glove—we kept boxes of nitriles around the lab like others kept boxes of tissues around their offices—and put it on, just to be on the safe side. I shook my head in disbelief at myself. The chances were so incredibly slim that this was Jeremy's game. But if I didn't check, it would eat away at me. I thought of what my mother would say—*Det er noe som gnager på deg.* Something gnaws at you. Monty was probably right: I'd sleep better if I checked.

I slunk into her office, feeling awkward and guilty. I'd been in there without her around many times to clean or to grab files. None of us ever thought twice if we walked into one another's offices. It was just my intention this time that was making me feel foolish and sneaky.

Her desk was tidy and clean, all her files put away, except for an in-box with a stack of mail. A framed picture of Wendy and Kyle when he was a young boy—maybe four or five—near a merry-go-round in a park stood in the corner. Wendy, looking much younger, wore a huge smile and Kyle wore only a partial grin, as if he'd just been crying and she had cheered him up for the photo—as if even then something troubled him. Again, I felt bad for both of them, for whatever pain had continued to blossom between them over the years.

I slowly slid open her top drawer. The shiny, scratched-up Nintendo was the first thing I saw. I grabbed it and turned it over. On the back, at the top, etched into the black coating in a chicken-scratch scrawl were three initials: JRC.

For a moment, the room seemed to turn inside out, losing all of its air, as if an explosion had sucked it all out. I couldn't breathe. I felt like I'd been dropped through ice to that lower stratum I often dreamed about. My mind whirred. Was this really Jeremy's game? Could it be? It didn't make sense, but what were the chances of another game with the same three initials?

I should have checked right when I returned from seeing Monty in the park, but I hadn't really believed it could be the same one. The overhead light streaked the black reflective coating on the device with shiny bands and when I tilted it parallel to the ceiling, it reflected the oval light brightly, perfectly. Then I breathed in, slowly and carefully. I could feel the blood rushing through my body, could feel the pulse of it in my neck and in my temple. Unsure if my suddenly trembling legs would work, I walked back to my office to call Monty.

18

Monty

I KNEW WE WERE all haunted by things done to us and things we'd done to others throughout our lives. The incident with Nathan Faraway proved I was no exception. Now I sensed the same was true for Gretchen. I had no idea what was making her so skittish, but something about her episode in the river and the desperation in her haunted eyes clung to me, and I couldn't figure out why or seem to let it go, even though I could tell that she wanted me to.

I've always confessed to a sort of tunnel vision when it came to things that pique my interest, and at times it caused issues in my marriage—how I could escape for hours into a task or investigation. It's part of what made me a good officer, if not always a great husband. I didn't really even have much time to focus on Gretchen earlier during the day because of the cases we were working on, but I couldn't seem to shake her from my mind.

I had called Ali and Herman to check in for the evening. They were making no leeway with the Tuckmans or with the farmhands even after the judge surprisingly did order a mandatory printing of Brady's fingers and palms. I guess you can't underestimate what people will do when a child's life is at stake. So now they had his prints, but even with a match to the prints from the truck, it proved very little since he's had legitimate access to it, so they'd had to let him go for the time being. We were still hoping Gretchen's gang would make an identification to the unknown other set from the truck, but it wasn't looking good. Without

251

hard evidence, they had once again turned their focus to known sex offenders within a twenty-mile radius of the farm.

While they worked on that relatively short list, I set my sights on two things: one, the files Gretchen had shown me about the pattern she thought she detected, and two, the mystery of Gretchen Larson. For the first, I called Detective Belson, and he confirmed everything Gretchen had said. I wrote all of it down and studied it. I reconsidered telling Ali and Herman about it, not because of the time frame Gretchen proposed, but because of the head injury on the left side of the skull, and her discovery that an axe or axelike instrument was probably used. I decided they should be aware of Gretchen's theory in case they had come across any suspicious instruments at the Tuckmans—although on a farm there were a lot of instruments that might qualify. On the other hand, it really was a stretch and I did not want to piss off Ali Paige any more than I already had.

So I turned to my other task—Gretchen. I had never considered it before, but I decided to do a search online. First I confirmed things I already knew, that she'd gone to the University of Washington and studied forensics. That she'd worked for the Seattle Police Department's CSI Unit. That she'd taken a job with Flathead County in 2010. There were some images of her from a piece on the CSI team in the Flathead Valley a few years back.

When I searched for her adding the term "Norway," several entries came up. It seemed Gretchen Larson was a popular name among the Norwegians. I came across some Norwegian Gretchen Larsons on Facebook, LinkedIn, and other social media sites. I saw directory listings for women in Oslo, Bergen, Trondheim, and Kristiansand. I found a marketing analyst for a makeup company, a photographer who liked to capture images of the fjords in the northern tip of Norway, a Nordic ski racer who often came to America to compete, a speech audiologist in Bergen. I clicked on their photos and none of them looked anything like Gretchen. I continued to surf, clicking on random mentions in selected biographical essays and other news articles, including one on

Norwegian musicians and their interpretations. I had almost given up when I saw another article dated from 2001 that read, "Parasomnia, a category of sleep disorders that involves often unwanted abnormal behavior, movements, emotions, perceptions, and dreams that occur while falling asleep, sleeping, between sleep stages, or during arousal from sleep." Buried behind several names and an ellipsis, it continued, "fifteen-year-old Gretchen Elin Larson from Sandefjord, Norway." Then another ellipsis next to a doctor's name, Finn Petterson.

I did not know Gretchen's middle name, but I vaguely recalled her saying that she came from a town named Sandefjord. I clicked on the link. An article from a news source called *Dag og Tid* popped up. The headline was in Norwegian: "*Søvngjengeri Tenåring Dreper Sovende Bror.*"

I didn't know what it meant. There was a photo of a young blond girl, her head turned away from the camera, being escorted into an official-looking building, and below the photo were some more Norwegian phrases with the name Gretchen Larson listed. I couldn't be sure, but thought the girl in the photo could easily pass for a younger version of the Gretchen I knew. I pulled up Google Translate and typed in *Søvngjengeri tenåring dreper sovende bror.*

My stomach took a nosedive when the translation instantly popped onto the screen: *Sleepwalking teenager kills sleeping brother.* I stared at the screen. All the evening sounds, the birdsongs and the chatty chipmunks outside my office, faded away, and I felt every muscle in my body freeze. I tried to make sense of the article, but couldn't, so I googled Gretchen E. Larson and several medical journals on sleep disorders in English came up, articles about somnambulism, automatism, and pavor nocturnus. Several articles included names of individuals over the years who had committed crimes unwittingly while sleeping—a well-respected community man who'd even gotten into his vehicle and driven five miles to a different house while still asleep and killed his mother-in-law. A devoted husband who strangled his own wife because he thought she was a demon. Another husband who killed his wife and used automatism as his defense—saying that his mind was not in control of his body—was convicted anyway because the jury remained unconvinced that he did all that he did while he sleepwalked, including putting his wife's bloody clothes in a plastic bag and hiding them in his garage. His doctors, however, still insist he was capable of doing that in a state of automatism.

I pulled up another article in a different journal written in English about Gretchen and stared at it for a moment without reading. The headline read "Sleepwalking Violence: A Disorder, a Dilemma, and a Psychological Challenge in a Norwegian Town." I was nervous about what more I'd find. I must have stopped breathing because my head felt light and my pulse raced. I went to the window and looked at the dry yellowing lawn. The headline of the Norwegian article itself pointed to something unimaginable, something very tragic, and I was nervous about reading this one. I was acutely aware that Gretchen wanted to keep her past in the past and left alone. By reading about her, I was an unwelcome witness to that history.

But I needed to know the details. I needed to know more fully what kept her at a distance. I turned from the window, went back to my desk, and began to read.

Of course, as an investigator, I had heard of cases like it before, but they were rare. As I read on, absorbed and deeply bothered, Gretchen's behavior began to make perfect sense, but knowing that this was her life felt unbearable. I was placing the pieces of the puzzle into their correct positions, but the final picture was difficult to view.

Apparently, under Norwegian penal code, acts committed while unconscious were generally not punishable. In Gretchen's case, the issue was whether she had the ability to control her behavior, including taking early precautions to avoid loss of control. Since the rest of her sleepwalking habits were fairly innocuous, she was not held accountable. She was deemed a juvenile with a disorder and was sent for evaluation and treatment to a facility in Bergen.

I sat back and rubbed my eyes, feeling overcome by sadness and compassion for her, finally understanding why she kept herself so guarded. I was still thinking about it when my cell phone rang. I found it on my desk and saw that it was her. I felt guilty, as if her radar had somehow registered what I was doing. I picked up the phone.

"Monty," she sounded breathless. "The 3DS. It's got the same initials. On the backside."

"Whoa, whoa, what?" I wasn't sure I'd heard her correctly, and shook my mind clear of all other thoughts.

"The game. I finally checked it. I went into Wendy's office and found it right where she'd left it. It's got the initials JRC on it."

I sat up straight in my chair. "You're certain?"

"Yes, certain."

"Were they on the front or the back?"

"The back," she said.

"That's where his mom said they were—right on the top, in the center on the back side."

"That's exactly where they are," she said, her voice low and serious.

I felt a jolt of excitement to have some kind of a break. I stood up, pacing back and forth in my small office. "Gretchen, this is significant."

"I know."

"Can you run prints?"

"Monty, I obtained it illegally by opening her desk drawer without permission. Doesn't that pose some kind of problem?"

I considered it, drumming my fingers on the desk, then said, "If she took it from her son as you said, she doesn't own the item. In fact, she suspected he didn't own it either. Since she had no idea where it came from, the evidence will still likely be admissible. Now that we know it potentially belongs to the victim, the suspect cannot have an expectation of privacy in the office of the mother of the kid that took it, if that makes sense."

"I guess," she said, but I could tell she was nervous.

"But, shouldn't I put it back? Call Wendy and explain that the boy had a 3DS and just ask for permission to go look at it in the first place?

Would that be a better approach? I just didn't do it that way from the start because I didn't want to insult her, and I didn't think it would end up being *the* device."

"I see what you're saying and I know you don't want anything to come back to bite us in court, but we're talking about a child's life here and we don't have much time. I'm going to check with Ali and Herman, but I'm sure they'll say the same thing—to photograph it for the parents to look at and to run the prints ASAP."

"Okay," Gretchen said. "I'll wait to hear from you, then."

"You're aware that they're going to need to pull Wendy's son in for interrogation? Kyle, right?" I wrote it down in my notepad.

"Yes, I'm aware. It's Kyle Grove. Different last name from Wendy's, which is Combs. Wendy and the father split when he was young."

I thanked her, then told her to be prepared for some visitors very soon. I was still so shaken from what I'd read before our phone call, but I tried to ignore it. It wasn't pertinent to what we were discussing.

"Monty," she called out before we hung up.

"Yes?"

"Once they question Kyle, do you think they'll give the press his name?"

"I don't think they will."

"He's seventeen," she said.

"I know. You told me."

"It's important for Wendy, for him, that this stays quiet."

"It will," I told her. "I'm sure it will."

• • •

The Coreys continued to live their nightmare in the middle of paradise. The clear mountain air, pine trees, and grand peaks stretched in all directions toward the freedom of the mountains, yet they remained trapped. Those of us who lived in the area felt the ebb and flow of the wilderness and its seasons and knew it defined our way of life—knew that the wilderness always presented its challenges and demanded respect, much like those who lived by the ocean knew to respect its tides, storms, and other dangers lurking beneath the water's surface. The Coreys weren't from here, yet suddenly they'd become hostage to an unforgiving vastness they hadn't had time to even fully appreciate. They existed in the small motel, knowing their child might be swallowed by the wilderness or worse, at the mercy of human evil.

I had spoken to the chaplain before coming. From what I gathered, Linda had insisted on buying sandwiches for the volunteers and brought them a grocery bag of snacks during each day. She reprinted posters and made sure all the volunteers had those. Ron often met with Ali or Herman, and when the agents gave the go-ahead, he would be the one to speak to the reporters. Linda did a load of laundry for the family even though the chaplain volunteered to do it. She had a small breakdown over it when Ron had suggested she stay with the kids while he went and did it instead, crying and yelling that she would do it—that *she* would do *her* damn job for her other two kids and refused to be one of those moms who sunk into worthlessness for the remaining children once something awful befell one of the others. I was not looking forward to stopping in.

Flowers and gifts left by well-wishing community members were spread before the door across the walkway under the motel patio lights. Two reporters were also still parked in the lot and the chaplain had informed me that they assaulted the Coreys every time one of them came out the motel door. I parked at the far end of the lot, fended them off, and walked up to the motel door—room 16.

The room was warm and looked even shabbier than the last time I'd been there, but at least now they could open the windows, unlike before when even cracking the windows just meant getting choked out by dense smoke. Even the cheap room looked as if it wanted them out—that it just wasn't meant to have a grieving family of four cramped into its space. The old-fashioned fat TV stood crooked on its table, the beds were lumpy and sloped, and one of the lampshades tilted up so that I could see the two bulbs underneath. The boy, Garret, sat and watched some show on Nickelodeon as if he'd not moved since the last time I came. Linda and Cassie weren't there, and I asked about them.

"They went to the store, down the road, to get some snacks," Ron said. "We didn't really have much of a dinner and the kids were getting hungry again."

"They walk?" I asked, thinking that I saw their car still in the lot, and knowing that on foot, they'd be approached by reporters, not to mention that it was already getting dark.

"The motel office manager offered to drive her. She's been very helpful. When Linda tried to walk before, the press—there were a lot more of them here earlier in the day—they mobbed her, peppering her with questions. She's still slightly medicated and can't drive herself. The chaplain had a doctor prescribe something so she could sleep."

"You as well?" I asked. He looked slightly medicated too—a bit glassy-eyed and jittery. Of course, anyone's nerves would be fried under the circumstances.

"I finally took one last night."

"Good," I said. "You need sleep."

I cleared my throat. "Ron," I continued, "I have some information to share with you." His eyes brightened, and I wasn't sure how he'd react when I showed him the picture of the handheld game. Ali had asked me to swing by and to see if they could verify that it was Jeremy's. It could make him hopeful, or he could take it as a bad sign, the game left in some teenager's hands, but no Jeremy yet. "I'll preface this by saying that we have not yet found Jeremy," I told him quickly to avoid disappointment.

"Okay," he said.

"Have a seat." I motioned to one of the chairs by the window. I heard a shuffle on the sidewalk outside and peeked out before sitting to see that it was a reporter trying to listen through the open window. "You mind?" I asked Ron, motioning to the window I intended to shut so the reporter couldn't hear us. Ron shook his head that he didn't. I closed it, took out my phone, and pulled up the photo. "I have a picture I want to show you. We may have found Jeremy's Nintendo, but we need for you to confirm that it's his." I handed my phone to him. "You can swipe to the left to see it from other angles."

He looked at the phone intently, and as he swiped to pull up the next photo, I could see a quick intake of air when he reached the one with the initials on the back. He looked at me, his eyes concentrated with hope and fear, and nodded slowly. "This is it. It's his game. Those are his initials. Where did you find this?"

I went to reach for my phone to take it back, but he wouldn't give it up, as if by holding on to my phone with the image of Jeremy's game, he was holding a piece of his boy. He turned and continued to stare down at the photo. "Tell me," he said. "Where did you find this?"

I told him about how Gretchen got ahold of it, and explained that we were dusting it for fingerprints as we spoke.

"But what does it mean?"

"We don't know yet, but we're going to do our best to find out. Are you positive, Mr. Corey, that this is Jeremy's game?"

"I'm positive," he said.

"Okay then. Please don't mention this to the reporters. This needs to stay between you and Linda and us until we find the teen who had picked up the device and bring him in for questioning." I turned to go, and Ron stood up.

"I want to come," he said. "I want to see the boy who found it."

"No, I'm sorry. Until we know more, we need you to stay here. With your family."

He recoiled like I'd said something off-color, as if telling him to stay with his family were somehow grotesque. Then he recovered and nodded blankly.

I went to the door. "Officer," he said before I walked out. I turned to face him. His face looked ghost-white, his red eyes spectral in the overhead light of the dingy room. I wished we could get them a better place to stay, but I wasn't sure it would make a difference.

"I just wanted to show my family the mountains"—he said, one palm turned upward, helplessly—"let them get to know nature a bit."

I stood quietly, but he didn't offer more. "Of course," I told him. "You're a good father. You didn't do anything wrong." His statement wasn't unusual, but it sounded odd, as if nature were a separate entity out west and not surrounding them in Ohio as well. But living and working in Glacier, I'd heard such statements before.

"We shouldn't have gone on that hike around the lake. We shouldn't have left him. Linda wondered if it was okay, and I told her to quit worrying all the time. That he was going to be a mama's boy for the rest of his life if she didn't give him a little space, a little independence." His bloodshot eyes were loaded with guilt and pain. His jaw began to quiver.

"Don't do this to yourself, Mr. Corey. Don't. We're doing everything possible to bring Jeremy safely back to you and your family."

"What if it's not enough—what you're doing?"

I didn't know how to answer. I could feel a trace of sweat break at my hairline and begin to trail down the back of my neck, and I realized that I was tenser than I thought. "I have to get going now, Mr. Corey. The quicker we move, the better."

"Yes, yes," he said, snapping out of it. "Of course, please, keep us posted."

"Absolutely, we will."

. . .

"Are you fucking kidding me? The father confirmed it?" Ali said when I gave her the update over the phone. "So a relative of someone in forensics has the boy's missing 3DS?"

"That's what I'm saying," I told her. She said to meet them in county forensics as quickly as I could. Now Gretchen, Ken, Ali, Herman, and I were crammed into Gretchen's office staring at the Nintendo in a plastic Baggie. Gretchen had dusted it and came up with a match to Jeremy's prints, and with the verification from Ron Corey, we were ready to move forward with Kyle Grove. Ali picked up the file we got on Kyle from Juvenile Detention and Youth Court Services. We'd had to get a judge to order the records released since he was a minor. He had two minors in possession, one count of vandalism, and one for shoplifting, all over the past year and a half.

"So, we're ready then. He's over sixteen; he has the right to waive his rights, and we'll be notifying his mother anyway since we know she's with him now. Nor do we need her present in the interrogation room unless he requests her. So we've got an address, and we know they're home right now. There's no reason either Wendy or Kyle would think we're coming. Correct?" Ali looked directly at Gretchen, who sat behind her desk. Ken and Herman both stood exactly the same as each other—feet planted wide, arms folded, chins slightly tucked down—as they listened. I leaned against the wall while Ali propped herself on the edge of the Gretchen's desk. I could see Gretchen was jittery. Her leg bounced up and down and her eyes looked worried. I figured she was nervous at the idea of law enforcement showing up unannounced at her friend's house—as if she was betraying her somehow. I thought of everything that I'd read online, how much deep guilt Gretchen must carry around every day. The last thing she would want to do—her biggest fear—would be to hurt or betray someone she cares about. But Gretchen also knew that she needed to put Jeremy first; otherwise she wouldn't have called me so quickly.

"Correct," Gretchen answered. "But I want to come. If I can't give Wendy a heads-up, I at least want to come. You might need me to talk to her or calm her down."

Ali looked at Herman. He gave the nod that said he thought it might not be a bad idea.

"Okay then," Ali said. "But you stay in the car until we need you. You might also set her off if she gets pissed at you for not warning her."

I could see Gretchen wince, and I gave Ali my best was-that-necessary look, but she ignored me.

"Okay, let's go, then. But remember, if this kid is involved in taking

Jeremy, then he's damn clever for his age. His mom's in forensics, so that would explain why he might have known to spray down the truck. We need to be careful, I want to be ready for the unexpected. Gretchen, you'll stay in the car until we have the kid. I'll do the knock. Herman, you'll provide backup for me. Monty and Ken, you'll cover the sides and the backs of the house to make sure the kid doesn't slip out while I speak to the mother."

Gretchen looked at me and the question on her face said, *Are you sure all of this is necessary? And are you sure Ali should be the one to speak to Wendy?* I gave her a reassuring nod. I'd met Wendy once before in a previous case, and she seemed like a reasonable person who understood how law enforcement worked. Clearly she knew her son had been in a lot of trouble. She would know that she had no choice but to respect what Ali asked—having someone bullish like Ali do the talking to a protective mother might be just what we needed.

"I'll assess the situation with the mother first. If she lets us in, we, Herman and I"—Ali motioned between the two of them—"will approach the target. If he's noncompliant, we cuff him and I'll let you know." She adjusted the radio on her belt. "Make sure your channels are all the same. And on second thought," she said. "Even if he is compliant, I'll cuff him. I want to scare the shit out of this kid."

"I don't think that's necessary," Gretchen said, but Ali was already heading out the door. Gretchen looked at me, and I held up my hands. Ali was running the show, and for the most part, we had to follow. And this time I agreed with her. I hadn't met Wendy's son, and I didn't know what to expect, but because he had the kid's Nintendo, we should be prepared for anything.

19

Gretchen

W<small>ENDY LIVED IN</small> a quaint beige and cream house on the east side of Kalispell where huge maple trees lined the sidewalks. We pulled up the block in the dark, parking a few houses down. The lights were off in most of the homes except in one on the end on the corner, the yellow glow from inside spilling out onto the bushes and making a parallelogram of light across the well-manicured lawn before the front window. I felt sick to my stomach that I was betraying Wendy, the only person in the world who had been maternal toward me in the last fifteen years.

After everyone adjusted their radios, checked their gear, and took their positions, I watched Ali stride up to the door. Herman stood behind her at an angle, poised with his hand on his weapon. Ali pressed the bell, and I knew it would take a bit of time to roust them out of bed. I watched Ali's hand move up and press it again. I counted the seconds: one one-thousand, two one-thousand, three one-thousand . . . and made it to five one-thousand before the inside lights began to go on and twelve one-thousand before the front door opened. Wendy stood in her robe, her hair messier than usual, a look of total surprise on her face.

I could see Ali's head move up and down as she spoke. She motioned with her hand for her and Herman to be let inside, and Wendy, still confused, opened the door to let them in. She looked briefly out toward the cop cars, toward me in my own car, which I insisted on driving separately, before she shut the door. I was in the dark, so I didn't think she saw me, but I felt exposed anyway.

I sat in my own car alone and looked around at the quiet neighborhood and at the agents' and Monty and Ken's cars across the street.
I couldn't help but think of the night in the police unit outside our
house in Sandefjord, how it was on that ice-cold night with the blue
lights flashing on the snow and icy divots forming across the sidewalk
where the roof had dripped a few days before during a warm spell. The
lights reflected off the divots as if to send me a signal about irrevocable
things in life, the things for which no take-backs or replays existed. I
could remember the feel of the cold glass on my palm that December
night, the whir of the heater blasting from the dashboard with all its
fancy police knobs and screens, the icicles hanging from the side roof
of our house like spears, the sound of the policeman's pencil scratching
notes on his notepad, and the unbearable look on my mother's face.

The conclusiveness of that night slammed like a steel door in my
head. Contrary to what I had grown up thinking—that all of us had
bright futures ahead, the world was my oyster—I suddenly knew that
I had done the irreversible, unknowingly delivered the final blows that
would destroy everything, and that nothing, nothing at all would ever
be the same again. I can't say with certainty that I understood all of the
implications of what I'd done while sitting in the car at that exact moment, but I felt them, sensed them as sure as I felt the cold glass under
my palms. It would take years for me to learn that only the slow daily
passage of time could help a person cope with matters of the heart,
and that in the end, it was just you and the thoughts bleeding in your
head. And bleed they did—endlessly, minute after minute, hour after
hour—into cracks of self-doubt and self-hate unless you worked hard
to not let that happen.

I wondered what kind of a blow was being dealt to Wendy and Kyle
as I sat alone in the dark before her house, this time in the heat of summer, the inside of my car warm and comfortable. I thought again about
what kind of blow had already been dealt to the Coreys, and could Kyle
have been responsible for doling it out? I prayed not. It made me shudder to even consider it.

Eventually they came out the front door with Kyle cuffed. Wendy stood on the front porch with a shocked expression, her hand over her mouth, the same way she had looked in the derelict hotel. Moths frantically darted in the cones of light behind her head. I got out of the car and went over to her. "Wendy, it's going to be okay," I said.

She looked at me with terror in her eyes. "Gretchen," she said. "What's happening? They said they want to question Kyle. What's this about?"

"I'll fill you in, but first you need to get dressed so I can take you to the station."

"No, tell me now. Why are they saying they have evidence that Kyle may be involved in the abduction of that boy?"

"The 3DS," I said.

"3DS?" She looked at me, confused.

"The Nintendo game. The one Kyle had in your office matched the one the boy had. It had his initials on it. I've dusted it and the prints match the boy's."

"*You've* dusted it? You didn't call me?"

"I couldn't. They wouldn't let me. I'm sorry, Wendy, but this is serious. A boy's missing."

Wendy's confused, shocked expression turned to pointed anger. She looked at me with sheer hate, her eyes seeming to go black as the surrounding night. "You can leave," she said. "I'll get myself to the station." She turned and shut the door in my face.

. . .

Wendy's words turned my stomach. I sat and waited for her for only a few minutes and saw her pull out of her garage. I followed her to the county headquarters, no more than six blocks away from her house, right next to our own offices in the justice center.

Inside, the attendant told me that Ali and Herman had placed Kyle in the main interrogation room, and that the agents had brought Wendy back immediately. I went and sat down in the recep-

tion area for a few minutes and was debating whether to go back or
not when Wendy came back out. She walked over without looking
at me and sat down beside me. She stared at the off-white wall, nervously biting her nails. Finally she looked at me, a deep pain welling
in her eyes.

"Kyle's over sixteen, so he's able to choose whether or not to have
me in there," she sighed. "And guess what?"

I didn't answer.

"He doesn't. They told me to wait out here while they talk to him."

"Wendy," I said. "Everything will be okay. All Kyle needs to do is
tell them how he got the game so that they can find this poor kid."

She stared at me, her brow furrowed. "How do you think he got
it?" she asked.

"I have no idea."

"Gretchen, there's no way he could have hurt some boy. I know he's
a screwed-up teenager, but I know inside he's not someone capable of
hurting . . ." Her voice caught and she began to cry. "Oh my God, how
has it come to this?"

"Don't get ahead of yourself," I said. "They're only questioning him."

"How did they find it? Did you tell them about it?"

I nodded, but didn't add anything. I wasn't ready to tell her the
details.

"Why didn't you call me? Why didn't you give me time to talk to
him myself?"

I looked at her and didn't say anything. She knew the answer already. Kyle had just taken off for a few days without her even knowing
where he was. He was certainly capable of running. "You know why,"
I finally said.

I looked at the off-white floor. I didn't know how he got ahold of the
game, and a part of me believed Wendy when she said he couldn't hurt
some boy. I hoped they were careful with his name, that it didn't get leaked
to the press. When my name was published in Norway, everything, as
awful as it already was, got even worse. Take someone who is wounded

and add ostracism to the mix, and the situation becomes unbearably, exquisitely painful—a brutal punishment akin to solitary confinement.

I thought of my classmates singing, "Gretchen's gotta gun; Gretchen's come undone." Everyone in Sandefjord came to see me as a freak show. The media—specifically a magazine called *Se og Hør*—tried to get an exclusive interview with me six months after it happened, but my therapist instructed me to decline, telling me that people love to get a glimpse of people's pain and trauma: *Skadefryd*, he said. Schadenfreude.

But there is a reason high school and college kids cold-shouldered by social media and excluded from their communities sometimes got so desperate that they commit suicide. If Kyle having the 3DS was only a coincidence, he didn't need his name smeared all over the local and national news, forever altering any future he might scrape together from his already troubled life.

"Oh, God." Wendy leaned forward and rubbed her face brusquely. "This is going to drive me crazy—sitting out here like this."

"I might be able to go in," I said. "Watch from the one-way. . . ."

"Would you?" Wendy looked at me, rocking back and forth.

"I can't promise anything," I said, standing up. "But I'll try."

• • •

It turned out it was easy to get in the small observation room. I simply knocked, and Monty opened the door and waved me right in. Ken leaned against one wall and greeted me when I entered. Monty stood in the center, watching through the one-way, shifting from one foot to the other.

I saw Kyle sitting slumped in his chair in the interrogation room, his reddened, acned face full of disdain for the entire world. Herman and Ali sat across from him, and when Ali talked to him, he stared at the wall, zoning out, ignoring her, as if he was being lectured by his parents or a teacher. I saw Monty shake his head in frustration.

"What?" I asked him.

"Nothing. I just don't think she's got the best bedside manner. How's Wendy?"

"Distraught, of course, but not as mad at me as I thought she'd be."

The three of us stood and watched. Ali continued asking Kyle questions, trying to loosen him up with easy inquiries—where were you born, have you always lived in Kalispell, where do you go to school—but he didn't budge. I knew he had a lot of practice giving his mother the silent treatment because Wendy had mentioned it to me before—that even when he was young, he'd go through periods without speaking for days. *He's been a very moody kid*, I recalled Wendy saying.

Kyle shifted his stare from the wall to the table. He began to twist the back of his long, stringy hair with his right forefinger, and I was suddenly struck by how childlike he seemed—sulking before authority and coiling his hair around his finger, not unlike a young girl or a baby rubbing a blanket. I felt a pang of sadness shoot through me, but pushed it away. I couldn't afford to feel too sorry for the kid. The Nintendo and why he had it was what mattered. The agents needed answers from this delinquent, and they needed them quickly. If he had been on drugs, who knew what he was capable of doing.

I could see Ali getting frustrated with his noncompliance, his muteness. She'd moved on to his whereabouts over the past few days, and was still getting nothing.

Kyle just kept staring down. Then she asked about the 3DS, and he still didn't say a word. She leaned back in her chair, tilted her head to the side, placed her hands on each thigh, her feet splayed wide on the floor. "Kid, you too stupid to figure out what kind of trouble you're in?"

Kyle still didn't look at her, just continued to fixate on the table, twisting his hair around his forefinger, but I could see his face turn a deeper shade of red. I wasn't sure if he was getting angry, nervous, or frightened.

Ali stood up and leaned over the table onto her knuckles like she was about to do push-ups, her face inches from his, but he still wouldn't acknowledge her. "Kid, you hear me? This is not the principal's office.

You're in burning hot water here, and if you don't start talking fast, we're going to assume you have something to hide. Your fingerprints are all over that thing." She turned to Herman. "Am I right, Agent Marcus? This is serious, we've got a boy missing, and this kid is not saying a word. Fingerprints put him right in the mix. He easily gets tried as an adult under statutory exclusion laws. He could get life. Isn't that right?"

"That's the way I understand it, Agent Paige," Herman answered.

Kyle looked at the light fixture overhead.

"Kyle." Ali snapped her fingers in his face. "Look at me."

Kyle lowered his stare to the tabletop again, ignoring her.

I glanced at Monty. He looked unimpressed with their efforts. The kid wasn't budging. He even had a slight smile playing on his lips, as if he enjoyed how frustrated Ali was becoming, how she practically trembled with anger.

"Maybe I'm wrong," Monty grumbled in our quiet observation room. Only a fan hummed from a vent on the ceiling in the corner of the room. "But I think Herman should do the talking."

"Why? You don't think a female can interrogate a witness?" I asked.

"Of course I do, but it's the same thing I told her about the farmhand, Brady—that he wasn't going to respond to a female all that well."

"Yeah, and from what I heard, she listened to you. Sent Herman in and he didn't respond to him either. He wouldn't give his prints either way, right?"

"Right, but she couldn't stand it and went in before Herman had a chance to really work it. But this kid here"—Monty motioned with his chin to the glass—"see that?"

"See what?" Ali had walked to the wall while still talking.

"Watch. Just now, when she moved away. Kyle looked at Herman for an instant."

"So?"

"He hasn't looked at either one of them the entire time while she's been sitting before him, and the second she walks to the side, he peeks at Herman. It says a lot. It says to me that he's not going to respond to her, but he's curious about Herman. He's running away from a single mom with no father figure in his life, so why does Ali think he'll respond to an authoritarian female?"

"Maybe he doesn't respect authoritarian males either, if his father isn't in the picture."

"Ali's obviously running the show. Herman's a side dish in there." Ali went back over and sat down, leaning toward Kyle, asking more questions. Monty continued, "He's used to treating his mom like shit, that comes easiest."

I winced at the thought of it—of Kyle mistreating the person who cared about him the most. I never had that as a teenager. Things went drastically wrong before I reached a rebellious stage, but I remembered Per doing it—recalled him viciously cutting down our father with harsh words for not allowing him to go to Denmark on a boat with a bunch of his friends.

"Give Herman the chance to challenge him and you might get somewhere," Monty added.

"How would *you* go about it?" Ken asked Monty.

"I don't know." He sighed. "He's one tough kid. I'd probably find a different angle."

"Like what?"

"Well, I would first find out if he's got any other interests besides drugs." He turned to me. "You recall Wendy saying anything over the years? The kid have *any* interests at all?"

I thought about it for a while. "I think he likes rap. You know some good rap?"

"I read somewhere that Obama likes Kendrick Lamar."

"Okay then," I said sarcastically. I almost laughed at the idea of any of these officers trying to discuss rap with Kyle.

"Yeah, not going to work. Anything else?" Monty asked.

"I think he used to like to draw. Wendy has pictures in her office, but they were from some time ago, quite good for his age. Pictures of wildlife—mountain lions, lynx, and whatnot."

"Might be cheesy, but could work better than their approach. The kid is obviously as rebellious as it gets and they ask him about school?"

I chuckled. "You've got a point."

When I looked back through the window, I saw Herman and Ali shuffling out of the interrogation room. "Mr. Stubborn," Ali announced when she came in. "Shit, who would have thought a teenager could be harder to deal with than a seasoned criminal. Now I know why I never wanted kids."

Ken chuckled again, in spite of the fact that he had a small boy at home and I'd heard his wife was pregnant with a second.

"So, what's the plan?" Herman asked. "He's thoroughly tuned us out. How do we get this kid's attention?"

Ali considered the question, stroking her face, thinking. "We let him sit and wait for a while, get him good and nervous, then go back in."

I looked at Monty and Ken, who said nothing, probably wisely. "Any other ideas?" she finally said to us all.

"For starters," Monty said. "It needs to be a male in there."

"Oh my God, Harris, here we go again." She threw a hand dramatically into the air. "Hello, did you not see Hollywood in the room with me?"

"He didn't do the talking."

"Look, Freud, your theory didn't work last time with Brady either. I listened to you, but Herman didn't get anywhere with him and he still wouldn't offer his prints."

Monty didn't reply. I wondered if it was going to be Freud instead of Steady-Eddy from now on. Nobody else said anything either. Monty didn't even bother with the explanations he gave me earlier, as if he didn't think there was any point. After a few more moments of silence, I finally said, "Look, I've known this kid through his mother on and off for some time now." I repeated what I told Monty about the pictures and about the rap music.

Ali took it in, then said, "Okay, I'll go back in, try your angle, but first I'm going to let him sit for some time so that he gets good and nervous and starts thinking about the situation he's in."

"I don't know," I added. "Do you think someone else ought to try, like Monty or Ken? These kids have seen so many movies with FBI agents and, no offense, but they have this idea that you're all hardasses who just come in and bark at them. Nobody has any preconceived notions about a Park Police officer."

Ali looked at me like she had zero patience for some forensics person's opinion. I thought she was going to say, *Excuse me, but why in the hell is she in here in the first place?* But then she sighed. "Okay, yeah, I agree—a different approach might be good." I sighed then, probably loud enough for everyone in the room to hear. Ali turned to Monty, then to Ken. "Both of you, go in together. Give him some fresh faces, but give it a bit of time. Like I said, I want him to stew, to get a little nervous."

Ken moved away from the wall, and Monty gave one nod. "Okay," he said. "We can do that."

"Let's see what you've got," Ali said.

I decided that she wasn't so bad, just a hardworking woman trying to make it in a male-dominated profession. I could relate.

20

Monty

KEN AND I spoke in the corridor in front of the vending machines and recapped the quick plan we'd formulated while we gave Kyle a bit of time to contemplate his situation. We went in at the same time, bringing some sodas and some bags of Lay's potato chips. He was still twirling his hair at the nape of his neck below his right ear, his face set in a deep pout, and I sensed Ali was correct. He seemed upset to be left sitting and waiting.

I introduced us both when we entered the room, and we took seats, one on either side of him at the rectangular table. The plan was to make Kyle comfortable, then try to relate to him somehow, get him to relax without being too obvious about it. If that backfired, we were going to at least try playing good cop, bad cop. As far as we could tell, Kyle considered both Herman and Ali bad cops.

"Okay, Kyle," I said, throwing him the bag and opening my soda after getting comfortable in my chair. He didn't touch the chips, just stared at them. "I know you're not all that interested in talking, and I can't say I blame you, but we do need to at least try to figure a few things out. I'm sure you get that, don't you?"

Kyle didn't answer. I took a sip of my 7Up and squinted from the fizz. "Shit, haven't had a soda in ages. Forgot how carbonated they are."

Ken laughed. "Jesus, Harris. You can't handle a little carbonation?"

"Guess not." I shrugged. "Not part of my training."

"Yeah, well, maybe you need better training." He motioned with a tilt of his head toward the one-way.

"What? Like them?" I asked. "Yeah, thanks, but no thanks." Ken was doing precisely what we planned—demoting ourselves to non-threatening Park Police, separating ourselves from Ali and Herman. I knew it was silly and a little petty, but I, quite frankly, was having fun doing it. In the observation room, they'd know we were playacting, but it felt good to insinuate something derogatory, even as a joke, while they had no choice but to watch and listen. I noticed a faint smile twitch at the corner of Kyle's mouth. We knew he was probably onto our lame shtick too, but we weren't really trying to fool him—just trying to lighten the mood, and it was working, perhaps only because there was an ounce of truth to our discussion: Ken and I *were* actually slightly enjoying dissing Ali and Herman.

"Wasn't really suggesting you should become one of those assholes," Ken mumbled.

Kyle had lifted his eyes and was tracking our conversation, glancing at each of us. I reached over and opened one of the bags of chips we'd brought and starting munching on a few. Of course, I had zero appetite for Lay's potato chips, but I was up for anything that would make the atmosphere in the room more nonchalant. I motioned to the bag I'd tossed to Kyle and told him to help himself since he still hadn't touched it, but he didn't budge. "They impress you, Kyle?" Ken asked. "Those *special* agents?'

Kyle didn't answer, just stared.

"So, Kyle," I said, crunching the greasy chips and passing the bag to Ken. "Enough of that. Let me ask you: you've been in trouble with the system before . . . in JV court a few times, that right?"

Again, no answer.

"That's okay. You don't need to answer that. I'm not trying to pry. Only bringing it up because my brother was a bit like you." I groaned dramatically and made my tone more somber. "Right, Ken? You've met my brother?"

Ken nodded. "Yeah, so? This kid couldn't care less about your brother."

I shrugged. "I know that, but he kind of reminds me of him 'cause he, well, he started getting into a lot of trouble around his junior year in high school. Hated high school. Really, *really* detested it. The jocks made him sick to his stomach, the preps the same, and he really couldn't stand the geeks either. You follow?"

Kyle didn't nod or say anything, but he watched me closely, his eyes wide. At least I had his full attention, and he wasn't blocking out what I was saying. "So where does that leave someone when they don't want to hang out with anyone at the place they're supposed to spend five days of every week for a good nine months out of the year?" I took another sip and swallowed. "Sheer hell, right?"

"Yeah, it sucked," Ken said. "I mean, high school. It sucked. I hated those days."

Kyle's gaze ping-ponged between us.

"Adam," I said. "That was my brother's name." I licked some salt off one of my fingers. "He just figured he'd skip classes a bunch. Got to know some other kids who felt the same way." I took the yellow Lay's bag in my hands and stared at it, pulling on the top corners to make the bag square again. The foil crinkled. I stopped and set it down. The room got quiet, as if we were all just bored and didn't have anything better to do but sit around and chat and munch until finally, after what seemed like a long time, Kyle said something.

"What happened to him?" he asked, almost inaudibly. It was the first thing he'd uttered since he'd been brought in, and my heart raced, thrilled that he'd taken the bait, but trying not show it.

"My brother?"

Kyle nodded, but just barely.

"Well, shit. He got into drugs. Eventually heroin. When my dad found out that Adam had started shooting up, he checked him into one of those therapeutic wilderness schools. You know, the one up by Glacier. That's where he went. Has your mom threatened to send you somewhere?"

"Yeah. She's threatened me with a lot of stuff."

"Any of it make sense to you?"

"Not really. There's no point in it. I am the way I am."

I nodded. "Yeah, I can see your point. I figured the same for my brother." I didn't bother to tell him that perhaps his frontal lobe wasn't fully developed yet, and if he took care of his brain, rather than doing meth, he might feel a little different someday.

Kyle studied me. I could tell he wanted to ask more, but wasn't sure how or what to ask, and was so used to staying silent that it was just easier to remain that way.

"But I do have to say," I added. "He kind of did change some. Last I saw him. I was surprised at how he's turned things around for himself."

Kyle looked at the wall and shrugged. I could tell he didn't want to hear about the optimistic side of things, about how life could turn around. I could see he preferred the "things never work out" line of thinking, that bleakness prevails. I knew that line of thinking well from my brother, but ironically, he'd begun to turn things around to some degree. At Kyle's age, though, if you believed that life held no meaning, it could lead to really selfish behavior over the long term. You had your out, your excuse to play victim for the rest of your life, your justification for making less than optimal choices and for succumbing to drugs. "But it took a long time," I continued. "That place he went to wasn't so great. Didn't really actually help at all, probably even made things worse."

"How?" Kyle mumbled.

"Let's just say it wasn't well run back then. I hear the place is a lot better now, though, but it's expensive, so I don't think you'll have to worry about going there, Kyle, unless your mom's got a boatload of money ready and available for that kind of a thing. Does she?" I asked curiously.

"Nah, she doesn't." Kyle seemed either relieved or resigned to the idea that no one intended to send him to any sort of rehab and that he'd at least partially succeeded in trampling anyone's expectations for him or his future. He finally reached for the bag of chips and started opening it.

"What does your mom expect of you?" I asked.

"I don't know," he said, eating some chips with his mouth partly open. A tiny piece settled on his lower lip and clung. "Not much."

"Come on," I said. "I've met your mom. Great lady. Seems to care about you a lot. I'm pretty sure she has some hopes for you."

I could see the statement struck Kyle because he quit crunching and froze. His face looked pale in the overhead light, and I thought I saw a faint quiver of his lower lip until he swiped his mouth and dislodged the fleck of chip.

"Your mom's out in the waiting area, wanting to get you home."

He nodded, looked down, and started eating again. There was pain here. I could sense it. He might be rebelling against his mom, but he also ached on some level for hurting her.

"So, Kyle, why don't you help us out a bit here so that we can get you back home again. Ease your mom's mind." I wasn't sure it was time to ask about the 3DS yet but I felt like we needed to move forward. I didn't even need to look at the glass; I could sense Ali's impatience through it like a solar flare. "Why don't you tell us how you got ahold of that 3DS?"

Kyle looked at me, then at Ken, trying to read us.

I kept talking. "Because here's what I think. I have no clue how you got it, but I have a hunch that it was something a lot less sinister than what Agent Paige or Marcus might be thinking. How did you come across it, Kyle? You didn't steal it from some kid, right?"

"No," he said after what seemed like ages. The overhead light illuminated the crown of his head, turning some of the lighter stands of his dark hair almost the color of cinnamon. If I had rushed it, pushed him too quickly, he could recede back into his black juvenile cave as quickly as a chipmunk skittishly ducking underground. "I didn't even see any kid."

"You didn't?"

"No."

"So where did you get it then?"

He looked to the side out of the corner of his eyes. He was avoiding telling us where he got it for some reason, and I guessed he didn't want to rat a friend out. I'd seen that hesitant, worried look before—one that whispered, *I'm not guilty, but I'm no rat.* "I just found it somewhere, that's all. There was nobody around. I just found it."

"Okay," I said. "I'll buy that. I get that. But where? Where did you find it?"

"Why is that so important?"

"Because, Kyle, it is." I looked at Ken and lifted my chin, my cue to him to take on the bad-cop role, and he chimed right in.

"It's extremely important, Kyle." Ken cleared his throat and placed his hands flat on the table. "It's so important that you could end up in jail for obstruction of a federal investigation if you don't give us that information." Ken leveled his gaze on him.

Kyle hardened in response to Ken's tone, becoming smug. "I could tell you anyplace I wanted. Send you on a wild goose chase. Say I found it by a Dumpster, by the river, on a road. . . . You'd never know the difference."

"Oh, you're wrong about that," Ken added. "Dead wrong. If we found out that you were lying to us, you'd be charged for obstructing a federal investigation at the very least. That's why you're not going to lie to us."

"Whoa, Officer Greeley. Let's not get too far ahead of ourselves here," I chimed in. "Let's think about this calmly. Kyle's right. He could lie and send us all over the place, but then, well, Officer Greeley does have a point, considering the seriousness of the matter," I said earnestly. "Think of it this way, Kyle: like we talked about earlier, it's kind of a relief to know that your mom doesn't have plans to send you away for rehab, right?"

Kyle didn't respond, just wiped the grease from his lips with the back of his hand again.

"And I don't blame you. Therapy did nothing for my brother. But I'm telling you, jail, that's a hundred times worse than some therapeutic facility, and avoiding that, well, that's gonna be a much bigger relief for you. Now I know you know that because you've been in juvie before. But you're seventeen now, and although I don't agree with the law, Agent Paige was right—you'll get treated as an adult and that's an entirely different ball game."

Kyle considered it for a moment, looking down at the table. He'd set the bag of chips aside and his hand went back to his neck to begin twirling his hair again—a bad sign, I thought.

"Kyle," I said. "Look at me."

He did, his eyes like pools of blue-green water.

"Put your hand down." I changed my tone, going out on a limb. "Stop messing with your hair."

Kyle set his hand on the table, letting it plop down loudly, and I was surprised he listened to me. My instincts were right. He wasn't used to a male's directives. "You need to start by telling us where you were on Tuesday of this week. And you need to do it now."

He thought for a second. "How did your brother turn things around?" he asked.

"He was always good at art. At drawing stuff. You like art?"

Kyle shrugged.

"Well, he liked it. Used to draw a lot when he was little. Now he has his own iron-casting shop. He designs cool railings, fireplace tools, that kind of thing. Anyway, you never know."

Kyle nodded. "I met some friends, and we went camping."

"Which friends?"

"Craig and Bridger. And a girl named Coral."

"Where did you go camping?"

"Up by Hungry Horse. Near the reservoir."

"At a campground?"

"Yeah, Lost Johnny Campground."

"How long were you there?"

"Three nights. We slept in the back of our cars."

"Did you do anything? Go hiking or fishing or anything? Did you leave the campground?"

"No, we hung out there the whole time."

"At the campsite the entire time?" I didn't bother to ask what kind of trouble they were up to—about drugs, booze, and loud music, which I imagined disrupted every other camper in the area.

He nodded.

"You never left, or had any visitors?"

"No, just the four of us."

"Okay, so you got there on Tuesday?"

"Yes."

"Around what time?"

"Around eleven or so. We left Kalispell early, around nine."

"So when did you leave?"

"I told you, we stayed three nights. We left later this afternoon."

"And you went home?"

He shook his head.

"Where did you go?"

"I stopped by my grandfather's place."

"And where's that?"

"Past Hungry Horse. I needed some money—for gas. My tank was low. I figured he'd loan me enough to get home."

"And did he?"

"Yes."

"So he was home when you swung by?"

"No, not home, at his church."

"Where does he go to church?"

"No, not where he goes. He's the pastor."

"I see. Where is it?"

"In Hungry Horse."

"Okay, so how long did you stay there?"

"Just for a while. I found him in his office in the back, and he gave me a little cash for gas and told me my mom was worried sick and to go right to her office."

"And that's what you did?"

"Yeah, that's what I did after I got some gas."

"Where did you stop for gas?"

"At the Cenex in Hungry Horse."

"So how did you come across the 3DS?"

Kyle didn't answer.

"Kyle," I said sternly. Suddenly I heard my own father's voice in mine and wasn't sure how that made me feel, but I didn't care to consider it then. "I'm not going to ask again."

"On the way out, I saw it."

"The DS?"

Kyle nodded.

"On your way out of where, the gas station?"

"No, the church. It was on one of the pews, near the middle. Near the edge by the center aisle. The place was empty. I figured some kid left it after a service and didn't see it. Figured it must not have been that missed, if no one had come back for it, so I grabbed it. I just put it in my pocket, you know, for the time being and left." He cocked his head to the side and pushed out his jaw in a cocky, sue-me-if-you-don't-like-it posture.

"So let me get this straight. You found the Nintendo game at your grandfather's church? Sitting on a pew?"

"Yeah, that's all. It's not like I *stole* it."

"Were your friends with you?"

"No, they went home in their truck, straight from the campground. I drove separately."

"So why did you take it?"

"Don't know."

"Okay, Kyle," I said, glancing at Ken, who in turn glanced at the observation room. We both knew what Ali and Herman were doing as we wrapped up—getting Kyle's grandfather's information and as much as possible on his church. Soon we would be swarming around it like termites on wood, searching every inch of the place like we had at the Tuckmans. Kyle had wasted time by not giving the information earlier to Herman and Ali, because he didn't want to get in trouble for stealing something that wasn't his, or because he didn't want to rat on his grandfather, but either way, Wendy's father's church was our next stop.

. . .

By the time we wrapped things up with Kyle, got the warrant, and drove out to Hungry Horse, dawn spread pale light across the eastern sky above the mountains as we went up on a long, paved drive to the church. Glacier Peace Church sat on a knoll on the northeast side of Hungry Horse. William "Bill" Combs was the pastor of the church, and we found him there, up early and watering some arrangements in the flower boxes on the side of the building. The lawn was well kept and the church was simple—a utilitarian building made out of wood, painted green and white. A wooden cross perched at the apex of the roof. In front there was a large sign that read GOD'S TEN COMMANDMENTS. At the bottom of the sign, under the commandments, was written, "And Be Baptized Every One of You in the Name of Jesus Christ for the Remission of Sins. Acts 2:38."

Mr. Combs looked completely surprised when we pulled up. He wore faded jeans, tennis shoes, and a baseball cap. He seemed vaguely familiar to me, and I figured I might have seen him before with Wendy around the county building. He came over, a confused look on his face, and asked us what was going on.

"Mr. Combs," Ali said, "we have a warrant to search this church building."

"A warrant? What on earth for?"

"We need to ask you some questions. Is there someplace we can sit and talk?"

"We can go into my office."

Ken and Herman immediately began looking around and direct-ing the men who came with us to help search the entire property. Mr. Combs led Ali and me into the church, down a well-maintained oak floor, past rows of dark wooden pews with graceful curved backs, and to a side door beside the altar that led to his work area. Ali took a seat in one of the guest chairs at his oval desk. But I stayed standing, perus-ing the office.

"You're up early, Mr. Combs," Ali began. I wasn't sure if it was a question or a remark.

Mr. Combs shut the office door behind him and took his own seat. "Yes, every day. It's one of the perks of getting older—up like a rooster as soon as day begins to break. What brings you all out here this early?"

"We understand your grandson, Kyle, stopped by here yesterday, is that correct?"

"Yes, he did. Has he done something? Is he okay? Is he in trouble for something again?"

"No, not in trouble, and yes, he's fine," Ali said. "Were you here when he stopped by?"

"Yes, I was. It was in the late afternoon. He needed some money for gas."

"When he was here, he came across something important in your church. It's vital that we understand why that item was on your prop-erty, so vital that a judge has issued a warrant for us to thoroughly search your entire place."

"What item?" he asked. "I have no idea what you're talking about."

"Mr. Combs, where were you on Tuesday of this week?"

"Tuesday?"

"Yes." Ali said curtly.

"I was out of town—in Great Falls for an RMA conference on small-town pastors."

"RMA?"

"Rural Missionary Association," he said. "It's a way to offer support to us rural, small-town churches that sometimes feel isolated and alone in our work. I left on Monday morning, even gave a talk in the late afternoon on bi-vocational work—how many pastors in small towns need to work more than one job. I checked into the Hampton Inn and stayed until Wednesday. I just returned on Wednesday afternoon."

Ali glanced at me, presumably because she wanted me to take his story down so we could verify it. I took out my notebook and jotted the name of the conference down. I stood by the window, watching her question him, but also looked at his bookshelf and peered outside. I saw the county forensics van pull up. Ray and Paxton hopped out. I refocused on the shelf. Various versions of the Bible were stacked together along with many books on religious and pastoral counsel. A plaque hung on the wall beside the bookshelf. It read "On the mountain of the Lord, it will be provided. Genesis 22:14."

"Mr. Combs," Ali said, "what happens to the church when you're away?"

"It's always open during the day, for people to come in and visit me or pray or just sit if they feel the need for some peace, for a sense of God's presence."

"So who opens it when you're away?"

"Reily."

"Who is Reily?"

"Reily Terrance. He just lives down the road."

"Is he on your payroll?"

"Yes, he helps out a fair amount, but doesn't really have any set hours. The church pays him as needed."

"Mr. Combs, I hope you're telling us everything, because the life of a child is at stake."

"A child?" he opened his eyes wide and set his palm on his heart. "What on earth was found in my church?"

We both studied him, especially Ali, her eyes narrowed in distrust. Mr. Combs sat with his mouth agape, his eyes shifting between the two of us.

"You don't know?" I asked.

"I told you—I have no clue what you're talking about. A child? A life at stake?"

"Mr. Combs, do you know the Tuckmans?"

"The Tuckmans?" He creased his brow. "They might attend services here, but I'm not sure. I don't personally know anyone by that name, but we can check the registration books."

"So you have a record of everyone who attends your church?"

"Not everyone, but lots of people. I can get the lists for you, if you'd like. Sometimes we send out emails or flyers to folks, but not everyone who attends has signed our guest logs. I can give you the names of all the regulars."

"Yes, we'll need that, and we'll need a list of all your employees—names, addresses, and phone numbers."

"I also host a soup kitchen once a month for the homeless and hungry. It's on Thursday evenings at six. I have them sign in, so I can plan how much food we need to prepare."

"Okay, we'll want that, too. And, Mr. Combs," she said sternly, "you will need to stay on the premises and not leave until we've completed our search. We'll also need access to your computer system. As far as we're concerned, this is a crime scene." We both watched his expression turn fearful before leaving his office.

21

Gretchen

Per's ghost seemed to breathe down my neck while I sat at work analyzing trace. I always felt his presence, or rather the heavy cloak of guilt that signified his presence to me. Lately, though, I felt as if he had manifested more distinctly, hovering around me and fogging my brain as if he had something to tell me that I couldn't understand. I knew it was crazy, but I couldn't shake the feeling.

After they finally got some answers out of Kyle, I went out and told Wendy that Kyle was cooperating, but didn't have the heart, nor was I allowed to tell her that the spotlight had now shifted to her very own father and his church. Kyle could tell her what he wanted once he was released. In the meantime, I told her to go home to get some rest, but she refused, saying she wasn't leaving the station without him. She was still somewhat angry at me, and I had to remind myself that what I only thought was a long shot turned out to be significant after all, and that I shouldn't feel guilty about the police interrogating Kyle or her father if it helped find the boy.

I didn't want to go home, but I knew better than to go right into the office without any sleep, so I went home to get a few hours before coming back in. By eight a.m., I found out I was officially off duty. Ridgeway said I'd worked too many hours in a row and sent Ray and Paxton to the church. He also said that I had a conflict of interest since I knew Wendy, Kyle, and her father too well. When I asked why that conflict didn't exist for Ray, who had worked the same number of shifts as I had and was also a coworker of Wendy, he replied that Ray wasn't as close to her as I was, nor was Paxton for that matter, and neither had ever met Wendy's son or father before. That part was true, but the whole thing grated on me.

He told me to stay home and get some rest, but I couldn't sit still. After making myself something to eat and some tea, I paced. I felt like a nervous wreck. The department still had not found Jeremy and now my coworker and her family were somehow linked to the case. I went back to the office, figuring I could at least continue to look at the evidence we had collected from the truck at the Tuckmans' farm. There was still some trace to analyze.

At the office, I plowed through the paperwork piled on my desk, then went over to one of our microscopes to study the trace we'd picked up from the truck again, specifically from the driver's side floor and the pedals. I slid the slides Ray had prepared using Permount and cover slips, seeing all the elements he'd said he'd found: cotton, pollen, dirt, manure, hay, gravel dust, broken glass, grass, a dead ant, other insect remains, cat hair, dog hair—all of them made sense for someone walking around a farm. Then I found the slides with the asbestos fibers and the aluminum—the trace that didn't make as much sense—and studied them under the stereomicroscope, which allowed me to see the various colors and diameters of the objects.

I sat back and pinched the bridge of my nose, wondering where to go with it. I thought of all the places that might contain asbestos: a shipping yard (clearly we didn't have those in Montana), trucking facility, or perhaps a train depot where hazardous material was broken down and disposed of.

I thought of the decal on the bumper of the truck. I had just read an article in the paper about how CFAC, the local aluminum plant that had been in operation since the 1950s, had been completely shut down for several years and had sat vacant for some time while politicians had recently begun to argue over whether to try to get it on the EPA's Superfund site list. The owners, some company out of Europe, wanted to keep it off the list, along with some local politicians who felt the stigma associated with it becoming a designated federal cleanup site would hurt the already economically depressed town of Columbia Falls, assuming people would not want to buy homes in an area that is a national cleanup project. Other politicians wanted it properly cleaned, even if putting it on the Superfund site meant more red tape and it would take longer to get the job done.

The article said that asbestos found in the plant was being moved out while they were still trying to decide what to do with the cyanide and other toxic chemicals used in the large barrel containers. Those same chemicals mentioned in the article were found on the tires of the truck.

I googled the case, and an article came up on the site of the local paper. It mentioned a structure known as the Black Tower, the paste plant used for making briquettes out of coal tar, and another large building, the biggest in Montana—a 1.75-million-square-foot structure that spread across forty acres and held 451 aluminum reduction cells that weighed sixty tons each and were filled with toxic chemicals. I wondered if it was worth a visit to the Planning and Zoning Board to see a list of all the buildings with licenses or permits to house asbestos in the area, but it was Saturday and they were closed.

I called Monty to fill him in, but he wasn't answering, so I hung up. I could have left a message, but there was no point. I still felt irrationally angry at him for reasons I knew had to do with being exposed. I knew what my psychiatrist in Norway would say, and it would probably be true: that I was simply afraid of being discovered and my fear of that was manifesting as anger as a form of self-protection, and that one day I'd need to get over that fear if I ever wanted to experience real, trusting relationships. I wouldn't be able to hide my real self— *Marerittjente*—forever.

Pictures of waking before a confused Monty in the river flashed in my mind like lightning and I wondered how much he suspected. I couldn't imagine telling him about my past. It was too difficult to swallow that someone might understand what I'd done and still receive me without judgment, without recoiling. I recalled my mother's disdainful look, the accusations in her eyes slicing me like daggers.

In spite of all that, I knew Monty was busy at the church, and I certainly had nothing substantial to report, just more hunches. It was sheer dumb luck and coincidence that my intuition about the Nintendo 3DS actually panned out. I considered that the chances of my hunch being spot-on a second time were slim.

I called Ray instead. He wasn't picking up either, and I was certain he was elbow deep in evidence while he processed the church site. It bugged the hell out of me that I wasn't there working. Part of me wanted to head to Hungry Horse and join in regardless of what my boss had ordered, but I knew I didn't need to; Ray and Paxton were more than capable of processing the site thoroughly.

The more I considered it though, the angrier I became. Damn it, I was the lead and Ray had worked just as many hours in a row as I had. Why did the higher-ups always assume it was the woman who couldn't cut it, couldn't keep up under the pressure? On the one hand, I knew there was actually some truth to it—that I shouldn't get overtired, that I needed to take care of myself to not exacerbate my condition. On the other hand, my job was my sanity, and I felt I was as competent as Ray, regardless of the fact that I was friends with Wendy. Ray was friends with her too. How could he not be? We'd all worked together for a number of years.

I felt adrenaline surge through me. I was competitive by nature. It ran in my family. My father relished a challenge and rubbed it in when Per or I lost a game of cards, checkers, or chess. And everything was always a race with Per. When he'd have friends over, he'd always propose a contest: Who could run to the flagpole the fastest? Who could jump the highest? Who could ski across the field quickest? Who could score the most goals? Who could be the first to see where the ice ended in our bay?

Because he always beat me, I didn't think I was that way myself until I got into college and realized that I was driven to get the highest grade in the class, to lift more weights, or to jog farther than any of my friends, to be the first in the class to get an internship with the Seattle Police Department. When Jim taught me to play golf, I spent hours at the driving range, determined not to let the little white ball get the best of me. It's as if the need to compete lay dormant in me until I got older and was out on my own, with Per no longer around to do the winning. And sometimes I couldn't help but consider the notion that my competitive nature had somehow subconsciously erupted in the night, making sure that Per would never beat me at anything ever again. But I knew that thinking would get me nowhere, and I needed to stop it. I could still hear my therapist's voice from all those years ago: *Don't you beat yourself up enough, Gretchen?*

I thought about Jeremy, about the picture I'd seen of him on the news. It seemed that in every young boy I'd come across lately, I was seeing pieces of Per, fitting him together like some collage made out of other boys' parts: Kyle's glacial blue-green eyes, the golden hair of the boy in the abandoned-hotel drug den, and now Jeremy. It was his smile, the way his mouth stayed straight until it curved up on each end like brackets instead of the parentheses that most people's smiles evoked. All these boys needed help, and the one who needed it the most—Jeremy—we couldn't get to. Kyle and the stranger in the hotel were choosing their fates; Jeremy hadn't chosen his any more than Per had. Jeremy had been hunted, had been taken, and God only knew what had been done to him.

I couldn't think about it anymore. If I was right about Jeremy's abduction being linked to the other boys—specifically, to the boy whose body was found by the hunting dogs in the rain and whose time of death had been determined—then Jeremy had only five days to live. And if that was the case, this was the fifth, and it was well under way. Daylight had arrived hours ago. Monty said I shouldn't mention it; that it was circumstantial and simply a theory. I knew what he was getting at. You don't need to tell a pilot to fly safely because he's got your child's life in his or her hands. In reality, he or she is going to fly safely no matter what—for his or her own life, for every life on the plane. Monty, Ali, Herman, Ken, and every other police officer were working their tails off because they intended to find Jeremy as fast as they could, regardless of how many days anyone predicted we had. If they couldn't find him, it would haunt them for the rest of their lives, just as it did Detective Belson.

I knew Monty had a point, but again my anger raced inside me like the flames licking at the forest trees. "To hell with this," I said out loud and stood up, thinking today could be the last day of Jeremy's life. I'd be damned if I was going to sit around my office all day. I was on the forensics team and that meant something—it meant there was always some evidence to collect. I left Ray a message, reminding him to make sure to look for trace of asbestos or aluminum fibers in the church and that I planned to swing by the county dump to ask some questions. Then at the last minute, I couldn't help myself—I told him I'd swing by the church a little later to check that everything was going smoothly.

22

Monty

AFTER AN HOUR, Ali and I reconvened with Ken and Herman by our cars in the church drive to formulate a plan. The county had brought scent dogs to search the property and the surrounding forest for signs of Jeremy while Ray and another CSI dusted for prints on the glossy wooden pews and looked for trace.

Ali had told Ken to call the Great Falls hotel Mr. Combs had stayed in, as well as the RMA, and she also asked me to look into Reily Terrance.

"Conference and hotel checks out," Ken said. "Hampton Inn says he checked in on Monday and stayed until Wednesday. Lady from the RMA said he registered on Monday afternoon, even gave a talk that evening."

"So he's clear. Good thing for Mr. Teen Angst and his mother. What about the helper from down the road—Reily Terrance?" She turned to me.

"Mr. Terrance came by and opened the church on Monday, Tuesday, and Wednesday mornings. Went to work after he opened it up. Swung by and locked it up each of those nights around eight p.m."

"So, basically, the damn thing just stays empty and open all day long?" she asked. "Anyone and their dog could enter."

"That seems to be the case," I said. "Neighbor says she didn't see anyone coming or going, but she didn't pay close attention. Was inside for most of the day because of the smoke."

Ali kicked the tire of my SUV, growling. "Why can't this thing get any easier?"

"You check Terrance's alibi?" Herman asked.

"Yes, he works at a property management place in town. His secretary says he was there as usual and worked through lunch."

Herman asked, "And the neighbor?"

"Working on it. The missus says he was with her inside all day, but you never know with spouses."

With the break of day, an eerie orange glow began to paint the sky over the mountains. The fires were still not under control and the smoke had pushed back into the canyon, veiling the rising sun and once again offering an omen of something painful. "There has to be a connection between this place and the Tuckmans," I said as I watched a deputy load one of the police dogs back into the van. So far, the dogs had found no scent of the boy in the surrounding areas—just in the drive, into the church, and around the pews, which is how we knew which pew Kyle found the device in.

"So what might that be?" Herman asked. He leaned against their black SUV and had his legs casually crossed in front of him, his large coffee-colored eyes calm and unwavering behind his glasses. I wondered how he could seem so cool while his partner always remained coiled like a spring, ready to launch. "Anyone have any ideas?"

"No," I said, pushing up my own glasses. "But we've got the county on it. Pavement makes it hard to get tread marks, but hopefully there's something here that links the truck and this place, some fingerprints that can be lifted from the pew the dog led us to. How far back did you go when you looked into the owners of the truck?"

"All the way. We've told you," Ali said. "Only one previous owner before the Tuckmans. A Mr. David Selkirk."

"Did he work at CFAC?"

"Ken looked, but didn't see his name. We asked Tuckman about the sticker, but he said he didn't know where it came from. Said it's always been on there. Is there a Combs or a Terrance on the CFAC list of past employees?"

"I'll check," Ken offered.

"Yes, do that," Ali said. "So if the first owner didn't put it on there, someone working at the farm might have. How far back did you go with the farmhands?"

"As far back as Tuckman remembers, but he doesn't recall that many. Only three guys before the current ones, and they've all checked out. He doesn't know who put the sticker on it. Walt's only been running the farm for the past ten years now. Before the farm, he lived in Spokane, where he went to college and met his wife. They came back here when his father had his first stroke."

"So someone needs to talk to Mr. Tuckman Senior again. There must have been more farmhands over the years—maybe someone who borrowed the truck to go to work at the plant?" Ali asked.

"We tried," I said. "Can't speak. Nurse says he just stares into space, and that's exactly what he did when we visited him. And Anna, Walt's wife, tossed out all of his old files when she remodeled the house the first time around."

"What about the list of church attendees?" she asked.

I deferred to Herman, knowing he'd just begun to go over the list Combs had recently supplied from his member mailing list. Herman planned to run checks on everyone on it, looking for any name that might seem suspicious. It was a tedious task, and each person—over a hundred people—needed to be run through our databases for priors, but even that took us only so far. The ones without prior offenses would also need to be located and tracked down for questioning by all the floaters we could manage to bring onto the job.

"What about the community feeds?" I asked.

"On that as well," Herman said. "But that's an entire logbook of names, and I'm guessing half the people are homeless and impossible to track down. Many of them only sign with a first name or a nickname."

Herman turned to watch a burgundy sedan drive up a little too fast and come to an abrupt halt behind some of the police units. Wendy threw open the door and strode toward us. "What the hell are you doing here? Tearing my father's place apart?"

"Ms. Combs," Ali said. "We need to—"

"He's been out of town. He wasn't even here when that boy went missing."

Ali held up her hands to calm her. "We realize that, Ms. Combs. You can relax, but we still need to search the premises."

"My dad said you told him he needs to stay here." Wendy's face flushed with anger. "Why does he need to do that?"

"We're not holding him anywhere against his will. But the game was found on his premises, so we need his cooperation. We've asked him to make sure he's available in case we need him."

Wendy calmed considerably, but still looked frayed and nervous after having her son missing for several days, watching him get pulled into the station, and now seeing the focus of the investigation shift to her father's church. She ran her hands through her short hair and looked around, taking in the scene of cops swarming the property.

"Where is my father now?" she asked.

"He's over there." I pointed to one of the deputies. "He's with Deputy Brander."

"Can I take him to get some something to eat at least?"

"Yes," Ali said, "but make sure he stays on his phone and doesn't get out of range. Signal around here is spotty, and I don't want to struggle to reach him if we have a question."

Wendy nodded and headed over to Deputy Brander. I turned to Ken and told him I would help him scour the lists.

. . .

Half an hour later, Ken and I sat in our office at Glacier headquarters going over the lists Herman gave us to expedite matters. Ken had the list of attendees and I had the list of all the homeless or hungry who had stopped in for a Thursday evening meal and signed the rosters. The rosters were actually logbooks—about eight of them full of names. We were mainly cross-checking them with the names we have from our sex offender list and our lists of individuals involved in incidents related to missing children, attempted abductions, peeping, or flashing. We'd already scanned for the farmhand, Brady Lewis, to see if he'd ever come to the church, but we didn't see his name, and when we'd asked Combs about him, he didn't recognize him. We were also cross-checking names against people who had called the missing hotline number. Sometimes the abductor liked to call in, just to get closer to the investigation or to give a false lead. So far we'd received over a hundred and fifty calls.

Ken and I barely said a word. Both of us worked feverishly, running down the names, taking notes on anyone who rang a bell. We'd come across two men that had priors, but our team had cleared them. It was a time-consuming process, and already, several hours had flown by.

My thoughts blurred as my finger glided down the page. I thought of Gretchen. If she had really done what I'd read about in the articles, she might be much more troubled than I imagined. But how did she hide it so well? I forced myself back to the names, telling myself to slow down, not to rush. I'd gotten to the bottom of the page, Mina Lipfield, Marshal Nailer, Gunner, Frances Trippet . . . then turned the page before my mind caught up with what I'd just read. I flipped it back and read it again: Gunner. A nickname. I had heard it before, and it only took a few minutes to recall from where.

"Ken," I said. "I've got something."

"What?" Ken looked up eagerly.

"Gunner. I've heard it before. I think it's an alias for Linda's uncle. When Ali and I visited Chiles, he called Alfred Minsky that—he called him Gunner."

23

Gretchen

I DECIDED TO HEAD to the dump to get a sample first, and when I pulled up, I asked the lady in the entrance booth if anyone was allowed to dump asbestos.

"No," she said. "That's definitely not allowed. Anyone who needs to dispose of asbestos has to call the county first to get a permit for removing it, and needs to hire a trained professional to do it." I thanked her, then asked her to direct me to the dumping grounds for appliances or anything with metal or aluminum.

After I grabbed a sample in the area filled with old ovens, refrigerators, dishwashers, microwaves, and other scrap metal, I got back in my car and headed to the church. But once I arrived in Columbia Falls, I decided that since the aluminum plant was nearby, I'd go there first. I took a left onto Nucleus Avenue, the main road through the center of town, and went over the viaduct above the railroad tracks and onto the North Fork Road. When I saw the sign for Aluminum Drive, I took a right.

Dry leaves and late summer leftover flecks of cotton from tall poplars blew across the greenish-brown fields off to the side of the road, near the railroad tracks. The rain from two nights before had greened the pastures slightly, which was nice to see, but the feathery flecks and the dropped leaves drifting on breaths of dry, hazy air reminded me of the oppressive ash from the Essex gravesite several days before. It was too early for the trees to drop their leaves, but the poplars had compensated for the lack of water by dispelling some of them early. A group of turkeys fed on the edge of one of the fields, their dark bodies like big rocks squatting in the tall grass.

A few houses stood near the North Fork Road and gave way to NO TRESPASSING and NO HUNTING signs as I drove. Eventually I could see the abandoned, boarded-up plant. A behemoth of a place, it sprawled outward from the base of Teakettle Mountain toward the Flathead River. Teakettle stood like a bare hump from some legendary fire that spread over the mountain years ago and formed the northeastern side of Bad Rock Canyon where the Flathead River enters the Flathead Valley. In fact, with its scalloped ridges of rock outcroppings and sparse trees, it was one of the least attractive mountains in the area and seemed to fit next to the plant—exposed and industrial looking itself. Dark clouds of smoke had begun humping over its top, making it even uglier. Damn smoke, I thought. I was so tired of it.

Several plant towers, including the menacing Black Tower, loomed to the northwest. I pulled into the shabby parking lot with its metal-railing dividers, probably bright red at one time, now a faded pink color that reminded me of the cotton candy Jim insisted I try when he took me to the Washington State Fair known as the Puyallup Fair. Bushy weeds sprouted from cracks webbing out and connecting worn yellow parking lines. Tall Y-shaped streetlights stood like sentries across the huge empty parking lot, as if trying to protect the grounds from whatever demolition might occur in the future.

I drove slowly closer to the plant, ignoring the NO TRESPASSING signs, and parked near a run-down redbrick building with a white roof and small rectangular windows lined across the top. An old sign on the building read, STOP HERE. SECURITY. VISITORS AND VENDORS MUST REGISTER INSIDE. TRESPASSERS ARE SUBJECT TO CRIMINAL PROSECUTION. I shut the engine off and looked around. There were no cars, no people. It was quiet, truly vacant and abandoned. Dry leaves skittered across the lot. I grabbed my sampling kit and walked over. The windows of the front building were darkly tinted, and I had to cup my hands to my forehead to peek in. I could see old metal office desks but no one inside.

I walked around the side of the building into an open area surrounded by more buildings and signs, including a large outdated white billboard that read, This Plant Has Worked _____ Days Without an LTA. Previous Record Was _____ Days Without an LTA. Days Worked Without an LTA: Potlines _____ Castings _____ and so on. I didn't know what LTA referred to but assumed it had something to do with accidents on the site. It didn't appear that anyone had written numbers in the blanks in years. A traffic light with green, yellow, and red indicators was pictured on the right-hand side to warn workers when the inside temperature was unsafe.

The place reeked of a bygone era in which a mighty industrial plant could provide blue-collar jobs and define an entire town, a whole community. Now flaking metal and rust overtook huge buildings that once supplied generations of Americans with aluminum, mostly tinfoil. I thought of Sandefjord. Unlike this western American town, Sandefjord's history was known for its rich Viking history and prosperous whaling industry, which for a long time made it the wealthiest city in Norway. Today it held the third-largest merchant fleet in Norway, after the whaling industry gradually transitioned to shipping during the 1900s.

Columbia Falls, Montana, wasn't so lucky, and other than tourism from Glacier Park and the local timber company, which had itself recently undergone layoffs, the town suffered from a lack of jobs and opportunities for its inhabitants. Many residents drove to Kalispell for work at the hospital, the largest employer in the valley, or at the box stores like Costco, Walmart, and Target.

I took in the place. The article had said the site was 960 acres, but it was completely isolated out in the country, wedged in between the river and the bare-backed mountain. So many dismal buildings surrounded me that I wasn't sure where to go to get a good sam-

ple, and I began to doubt why I'd even bothered to drive out to the
eerie place. A large garage door stood in the center of the sprawling
building directly ahead of me, and it was partially open—at least
enough for me to roll under. I figured it had been some kind of
entry or exit way for trucks when it was open. I moved toward it,
deciding I'd at least take a peek since I'd bothered to drive out here
in the first place.

I thought it might be the main building just because of its size. The
light was dim inside the high-ceilinged plant, which was filled with
rows of elaborately piped heavy machinery, old electrical wiring, and
platforms with rusty metal hooks dangling from large pulley systems.
Tracks ran alongside the machinery, I supposed for some kind of in-
ternal transportation to move the large vats or tanks filled with molten
aluminum. The vats were numbered, and several of them were surrounded by wire cages, I suspected to keep workers from getting too
close.

As my eyes adjusted, I saw heaps of irregular shaped scrap metal
from where machinery had been removed and equipment salvaged.
Graffiti ran along some of the walls and trash was spread across the
floor—some empty beer cans and foil wrappers—evidence of homeless people who had taken some shelter or kids looking for a risky place
to party.

I walked slowly through the building, around the lines of heavy
equipment, looking at the high ceiling supported by gigantic girders.
The lights were covered by steel grids, and I thought of large engine
rooms in enormous ships. An old crane languished in a dark corner.
The floor was dirty and even dustier near the lines of machinery. I
pulled out some clear packaging tape and sheets of acetate and took
some samples from the plant floor, filling the tape with visible and microscopic debris.

I placed the samples back in my bag, stood up, and brushed off
my knees. I wanted to get going. I felt alone and strange in the menacing building that was once full of life and vital to the community,

but now stood ghostly and discarded. It seemed like a malevolent skeleton of what it used to be. I was acutely aware of my own existence echoing through its deserted space. I felt like I was floating, like I could simply drift up like smoke and dissipate into the dark rafters above.

I headed back toward the exit. I was almost to the door when I heard a dull scratching noise, thin as a light trickle of water. An animal: a bird or a rat, I thought. I stood still, listening, and for a moment thinking I was confusing the faint scratching noise with the push of blood through my veins. Take it easy, I whispered to myself. I could almost hear Per's voice. *Settle down, Gretch!* I began to walk again toward the opening I'd come in through. Of course there'd be small creatures in here. If I could get in, they could. I reached the opening, the comfort of brighter light beckoning me, but the noise, consistent and steady, almost determined, tugged at me and made me pause. I listened again to see if I could hear it. Perhaps mice were scurrying around, trying to find whatever crumbs the kids or the homeless left behind. I heard it again, steady scraping. "Hello?" I yelled. "Anyone in here?"

The sound ceased, but no one answered. Some badger or raccoon digging? A scavenger that had frozen in place when I'd yelled? But an animal would sense me, smell me, and scurry off immediately. Though mice behind walls might not. "Hello?" I said again. "Anybody here?"

Quiet. *All right, you're going nuts*, I told myself. Time to get going and over to the church. I turned to go back out.

Then I heard it, a faint "Wait, wait . . ."

"Hello?" I took a step farther back inside, trying to adjust to the dimness again now that I'd been looking toward the light outside. "Hello?"

"I'm here." The voice sounded small, scratchy. Scared.

"Where?" I yelled.

"In the back. Help me, please, help me."

I made my way back into the faded light and followed what I assumed were called the potlines—from the article I read, I recalled it said they were rows of electrolytic cells used to produce aluminum. I followed the aisles up and down, trying to make my way to the voice, which echoed and bounced off the metal. It could have been coming from any direction.

"Please, please, help me."

I could make my way in the light from the small, high windows above, but I took my flashlight out to help in the dim plant anyway. I shone it back and forth, searching. Layers of debris and mangled steel lay around and I tripped several times. "Who are you?" I yelled.

"Just, please. I'm here."

"I'm coming," I called out, continuing to search the vast place. Each aisle seemed to go on forever. When I'd reached the end of one, I'd round the bend and come to another lined with machinery that seemed to go on forever. After three more, my steps loud and prominent in the empty, cavernous building that smelled of oil, chemicals, and other fusty scents I couldn't quite pinpoint, I rounded the last one, shone my light and saw a line of large vats on metal platforms blocked off by wire cages.

"Are you there?" I called out.

"I'm here," the voice said.

I went closer, my eyes opened wide, my heart pounding inside my chest. Inside one of the cages bordering a large vat stood a boy gripping the chain links, his fingers laced through the small holes, his knuckles small and yellowed. He looked tiny and frail, like he was no more than twelve, but his voice sounded a bit older. The area stunk of human waste, and I could see a dirty orange bucket in the corner. "Jeremy?" I said. "Are you Jeremy Corey?"

He didn't answer, just backed away from the cage as if he was afraid of me, as if he regretted calling me over. I wondered if I was dreaming, but usually, in my dreams, I don't wonder that. "It's okay," I said. "I'm with the county sheriff's office. I'm not going to hurt you. I'm going to help you. You're safe now," I said, remembering a course all of us forensics staff were required to take on basic law enforcement procedures. Always reassure the victim. "You're safe," I repeated. "Are you hurt?"

"You're not with him?" His voice was timid, small.

"With who?"

"With him . . ."

"No, no. Listen, Jeremy," I said, quickly assessing the cage, turning my light off, since I didn't really need it so close to the northeastern end of the plant, where windows lined the high walls. A tangled sleeping bag lay on a yellow foam mat with a dirty pillow. Besides the orange bucket, there wasn't much else other than a small wooden stool on the other end of the cage. A heavy padlock kept the gate shut. Someone was intent on keeping this child here. "Is there no way out of this thing?"

"No," Jeremy said. "He put me in here. He feeds me in here. I have to pee and, you know, go number two in here, too." I looked over to see the dirty painter's bucket again, and terror twisted inside of me.

"Okay, okay," I said, trying to think. I needed to call for help, get some bolt cutters, but knew I didn't have service. "Look, Jeremy, I need to go out and get help. My phone doesn't work in here, but we're not far from Columbia Falls. I just need to drive down the drive a little bit away from the mountain where there's service. Five minutes," I said.

"No," he said. "Don't leave me."

"Just five minutes," I said, holding up my hand, splaying my fingers widely to convince him that I wouldn't be long.

Jeremy opened his mouth to speak, then said nothing. An intense look of fear overtook his eyes like a wave hurtling onto rocks. At the same time, I heard something from my side of the gate. Or maybe I simply sensed a movement of air, a swish. Whatever it was came down hard upon the back of my head before I even had a chance to turn and look. My knees buckled and I fell to the ground. A blinding pain came over me as I hit the cement floor on my side. For a brief moment, I saw silver flecks while I watched my breath blow dust away from my face across the floor before me. I heard Jeremy's feet scuffle to the back of the cage. I struggled to get my hands back under me to push myself up, but failed. My arms went weak, and I fell back to the ground, my vision going from pinkish red to gray and then black.

24

Monty

KEN AND I pulled into the only store in Polebridge in the North Fork around two p.m., after the lunch crowd had left, although the reactivated, escalating fires had scared a lot of tourists away already. A tall red-and-white-trimmed façade mimicking the stores of the Old West formed the front of the Polebridge Mercantile. It stood practically alone with only a few other small buildings around and pretty much made up the town of Polebridge. It served as restaurant, convenience store, community meeting place, bakery, and supermarket all in one. There were picnic tables outside where people could eat, and there was a wooden porch in front with lounge chairs made out of gnarled driftwood, but all was quiet with the darkening skies looming to the north.

The door squeaked when we entered, and a petite, elegant woman with pale skin and short dark hair tucked behind her ears sat on a stool behind the counter where pastries lay under glass. The place was known for its delicious homemade cinnamon rolls and huge pastries, and I knew Ken intended to get one no matter how much of a hurry we were in. The store smelled of baked goods, rich pine wood, and tobacco, even though no one was allowed to smoke inside.

I introduced us both to the woman, who reminded me of a mouse, but not in a bad way. She had pale skin, large brown eyes, and an angular face. She was actually quite lovely. I told her who we were looking for and showed her a picture of Alfred Minsky that Ali had gotten

305

from several years back, when the feds had staked out an area where they were suspected of stockpiling weapons. The photo, taken with a telephoto lens from a distance, was of Minsky exiting a cabin.

She put on her reading glasses to study the picture. "I've seen him," she said. "Or rather, I've smelled him."

"That bad?"

"Not if you like the smell of outhouses." She shrugged. "Tall, skinny guy, right?"

"That's right."

"Kind of a crazed look in his eyes."

"When was he last in?"

"Oh, he's come in quite a bit over the past month, but let me think, I believe he was in yesterday or maybe it was the day before, but it wasn't that long ago. Wait, yes, it was yesterday," she said. "I remember because I had just finished making some huckleberry turnovers, and I usually make those only on Fridays."

"Was he by himself or with someone?"

"By himself. Why? What do you want with him?"

"We just need to ask him a few questions. Did you notice what he was driving?"

"He drives some truck with a flatbed. I think it's red. Is he a criminal?"

I ignored her question and she didn't blink, just continued to chat. "I'm not going to lie," she said. "He made me a little nervous, but not too bad. I mean, I see folks like him around here a lot."

"Folks like him?"

"Yeah, the anxious type. You know, pacing around the place, looking out the window all the time. Kind of paranoid. He liked to palm all the goods in here, nervously picking them up and turning them over to look at the price tags of stuff he never intended to buy. He'd go on about money and the corrupt federal reserve system, how it was all a conspiracy. Told me to watch some video on YouTube called Zeit-something to learn more. He tried to barter with me—ammo for gas.

I told him to forget it; I have enough ammo." She pointed to a shelf on the back wall. "We keep it around, you know, for people who want to go grouse hunting outside the park in the fall. Then he tried to pay me in gold." She chuckled. "Held up a little purple satchel with gold tassels on it, like something royalty would have."

"What did you say then?" Ken asked.

"I told him to just fill up with a quarter tank of gasoline outside, on me. That my cash register doesn't take either ammo or gold as payment. I kind of just wanted to get rid of him."

"He say where he was heading?"

"Said he needed enough gas to reach Moose Lake. Not too far from here."

"I know it," I said. Before we left, Ken and I bought two huge cinnamon rolls, a bag of beef jerky, and some waters. As I let the porch door close, I said, "You know the Trail Creek Fire has picked up considerably."

"I know. I can tell," she said. She tilted her head to the windows, to the murkiness collecting once again around us.

"If the winds pick up any more, there's word they might evacuate both West Glacier because the Sheep Fire has spread farther northwest and the North Fork because the Trail Creek Fire is blowing up."

"I've heard, but usually it's just talk. Never actually happens. They've been saying that for weeks."

I glanced out at the sky to our north, the air beginning to bruise around us. "Yeah, I know, but this time, you might need to take it seriously. Make sure you pay attention to the news in case an evacuation is ordered. Being prepared is never a bad thing."

"I'm prepared," she said, holding her pointy chin high. "Don't worry about me. I'm always prepared."

"All right then," I said.

We hopped in the SUV and quickly headed up the dusty gravel road to Red Meadows, the sky darkening over our right shoulders while Ken bit into a big fat cinnamon roll.

• • •

On the way to Moose Lake, my radio went off. It was Joe Smith asking me about our location and letting me know that the fires on the east side had indeed grown. Strong easterly winds were picking up. There was talk within IC that they might advise the sheriff to call more evacuations, and this time they'd be more extensive: from the entire North Fork, which is the area we were in, to Columbia Falls, and the canyon, from West Glacier to Columbia Falls. That included Hungry Horse, where the church was located, as well as headquarters. "Shit," I said. "That close?"

"We're waiting to see what the wind does. It's supposed to pick up even more as the day goes on, but we'll see. We're no longer letting visitors into the park, and residents have been ordered to pack their kits and be on standby. I don't want you and Ken in that area long. Trail Creek might blow up. You'll need to keep your radio tuned into IC. I know you need to find this Minsky guy, but you don't want to be caught out there if the fire hits Demers Ridge."

I was glad I mentioned something to the lady in the store. "We won't be long and we'll make sure to clear out any campgrounds we see on the way to the lake."

Joe signed off, reminding me to keep him posted. Ken and I continued up the Forest Service's gravel road toward Moose Lake, wondering what the chances were that we'd find Minsky set up there with his yurt somewhere in the campsite or around the area and, if we did find him, what the chances were that he'd have the boy. I was skeptical, and yet the fact that Minsky had attended the community feeds at Combs's church had to mean something.

Ken looked out the window and chewed his jerky while I watched the road ahead. It stretched and bent into a vast area pinned in by miles of larch trees, lodgepole pines, and rock outcroppings in the distance. In 2001, at Red Meadow Lake, not all that far from where we were going, a young man had been murdered by a couple simply so they could steal his wallet and his truck. They tried to burn his body in the campfire to get rid of him and were picked up the next day in another state, only because they were caught speeding. Luck and coincidence—it sometimes played a bigger role than you can imagine in law enforcement. Was coincidence—Wendy's son finding the Nintendo in a church that Minsky attended—going to help us find Jeremy? I hoped so. The graying sky and the memory of the Red Meadow man tainted the entire area. Ragged, beetle-infested trees, generous fuel for a fire, blurred by as we drove.

I felt a surge of anxiety that we were driving into an ambush, and I wondered if Minsky could somehow be expecting us, beyond the usual paranoia the lady at the store had described. I was glad to have Ken with me for backup with us driving somewhere so remote. If we ended up needing immediate assistance, it would have to come by helicopter. Minsky had chosen a good place to hide from society, perhaps second only to the Yaak. But I'd heard that even parts of the Yaak were being taken over by rich folks from California and Texas buying huge plots of land and building massive second homes.

We pulled into the campsite at Moose Lake. Because of the fire warnings over the past weeks, the place was empty. We drove through without seeing a single tent or camper in the camping area, then hopped out to stretch our legs and have a look around. This kind of vacancy in the middle of August was eerie, but I was relieved that there wouldn't be a lot of people to evacuate if it came to that.

"What do you think?" Ken asked.

"I think we've checked it out—that's all we can do, short of continuing on up the main road or checking out that logging road." I pointed to an unkempt road laced with timothy grass, yarrow, knapweed, and some broad-leafed thimbleberry bushes. It led up the ridge and had a rusted iron gate across it, but I noticed it could easily be opened since it was tied to its post with only a faded red and black bungee cord. We walked toward it, and I circled around the gate and went a short way up the road leading away from the campsite while Ken stayed back, leaning on the gate.

"Does it look to you like it's been driven on recently?" Ken called to me.

"I think so," I said. "Looks like some of the grass has been flattened down."

"You think we should head all the way up there to check it out?"

I glanced up the road to its first bend, where it switched back through an area that had been clear-cut, probably one or two summers before. Shoulder-high saplings and other bushes sprouted up the hillside.

"Not sure. What's your gut telling you?"

"Mine?" Ken seemed surprised that I asked him.

"Yeah, what's your intuition say?"

"I don't know. . . . It sort of feels like we're barking up the wrong tree, but I'd really like to find this guy to confirm that."

I looked up the logging road again. The wind ruffled the tops of the pines and the sky appeared even darker than when we left the store. "Yeah," I agreed. "Me too. I feel like this is wrong, all wrong, but we're all the way up here, so we might as well." I tossed him the keys. "You go grab the truck. I'm gonna take a piss and then I'll come back and open that gate for you."

Ken headed back to the truck, and I started up the road for a moment, whispering to myself, "Are you up here, Minsky?" When I went to the edge of the road, a deafening crack rang through the canyon and echoed off the ridges. Immediately, I ducked, my heart rate skyrocketing. I quickly shuffled over to a tree on the side of the narrow road. At first I wondered if it could have been lightning, but as the shot echoed off the ridges, I realized it was most definitely a gunshot. I looked back at Ken. He hadn't made it to the car yet. I watched him quickly find cover behind one of the thicker pine trees by the side of the road. I scanned the hillside. Whoever was up the ridge had a clear sight line to me below through the clear-cut, but not to Ken, who had more cover.

I motioned for Ken to stay put, and thought about what to do. I was just about to wave Ken over so we could climb to a higher vantage point when a man's voice boomed down from the dry creek right above me. "What do you want with us?"

"Stay right there," I said. I had already taken my gun out and I held it in front of my chest, my elbows cocked.

"Put your weapon down," he said.

I stood behind the tree, keeping hold of my gun. "Mr. Minsky?"

He didn't confirm it. "What do you want? You with the feds?"

"No, I'm with Glacier Park. I'm not with the FBI. But you're going to need to put your weapon down. I just need to ask you some questions."

He didn't say anything, and I tried to listen for crackling twigs or bushes in case he was making his way closer. He sounded as if he were about thirty or forty feet up the draw. I looked back down and saw Ken peeking out from behind a tree. He motioned to me that he was going to begin heading up to circle around. I gave a slight nod. "If you come down here, I can show you my badge," I yelled back. I was braced for another shot, but instead I heard more silence, no movement through the brush. I saw that Ken had moved from his spot, but couldn't hear him, which was a good thing. "I'm just up here to evacuate the place," I added.

"'Cause of them fires?"

"That's right."

"Don't know nothin' about an evacuation," he said, his voice hard and edgy.

"It hasn't been announced yet. I'm just checking the more remote areas where people aren't seeing the news. I need to make sure the area's clear. You don't want to get caught up here when that wind gets stronger. The fire up Trail Creek is blowing up."

"All right then," he said. "You've said your piece. You can leave now."

"You said 'us.' Who else is with you?"

He didn't say anything.

"Mr. Minsky," I called. "You just fired your gun at me. Why did you do that?"

"Not at you. I fired it to warn ya."

"Warn me of what?"

"To stay away."

You don't own these woods, I wanted to say, but I knew better than to provoke. "Why?" I asked simply.

Silence.

"Look. I need to know how many folks are out this way. I realize nobody is doing anything wrong by being out here," I said, cringing at my sappy, placating tone when the man had just fired a damn bullet over my head. "We just need to make sure everyone is safe. How many of you are out here?"

"None of your business," he yelled.

"All right, fair enough." I looked for Ken but couldn't see him. He should have had almost enough time to make the thirty or forty feet up. "Sir, if it would be okay with you, I'd like to step out from behind this tree so we can chat. Would that be all right with you?"

"No," he said. "Drop your weapon and go. Don't come back. And you can tell that to the feds too."

"I told you, I'm not with the FBI."

"You're law enforcement. You work for the government. All the same."

"Sir, I don't intend to use my weapon, and I don't intend to talk to the FBI anytime soon. I simply want to ask you a few more questions and to make sure everyone is safely evacuated, that's all. That's my job."

"You act all innocent. All of you, all of you law enforcement, you act like you're out to help, to protect, but you're all just part of the machine. You're all just wolves in sheep's clothing, working the devil's machinery."

Shit, I thought. I expected crazy talk from Minsky, but not without being able to see the guy's face, and not with a rifle pointed straight at me. Still, I sensed fear laced in his tone, in his breathy exclamations.

Right then, Ken yelled, "Hold it right there. Drop your gun now." I heard a commotion, a gunshot, then another shot fired back. I darted out from the tree and ran up the hill. I reached the spot, breathless, to find Ken hiding behind a large rock, looking through the woods, still pointing his gun. I took cover again too, and pulled out my binoculars.

"You see him?"

"I had a line on him, but when they ran, he yelled to someone. I didn't see who."

I scanned the area until I saw movement up the hill. Two people ran through the taller trees along the edge of the clear-cut. I watched them run. I focused on the smaller person behind. I made out straight black hair pulled back into a ponytail. Jeremy had curly hair. But still I couldn't be sure if it was him or not. The person was the right size, but not boyish at all. He or she ran ahead of Minsky, moving at a good clip, arms swinging. I watched as they swiped brush out of their way, stumbled on roots, pitching forward, regained their balance, and continued to edge up the ridge.

Eventually, the smaller person turned to say something to Minsky, and I could see she was not a boy. She looked Asian and in her thirties or forties. She gestured to him for a moment and then they made their way out of the clear area toward some trees so they couldn't be seen. I dropped my binocs and looked at Ken.

"Pursue?" he asked.

"I want it to be them, but it's not. We're barking up the wrong tree."

"He fired shots," Ken said, exasperated.

"I know, but the kid we need to find is out there somewhere, and I don't think he's with them."

•   •   •

By the time we got back to the truck, the perfectionist inside of me began to nag loudly. I could hear Ali asking for the details, wondering if the couple had the kid hidden in the yurt and if we'd checked it out. My intuition screamed that wasn't the case, but I had to admit a chance existed that this couple was playing *Raising Arizona*, that maybe this woman—whoever she was—had lost a child around Jeremy's age at some point. "I've changed my mind." I said, turning to Ken. "Let's get this gate open. We should check out the site. The flatbed and the yurt have to be somewhere close by. There won't be many large pullouts off this type of a road."

We unwrapped the bungee cord, swung the gate open, and headed up, the brush scratching the sides of the SUV. As I predicted, it wasn't hard to find Minsky's setup. The truck was pulled off onto the only opening the narrow road provided, about a mile and a half up, and the yurt was set up in a clearing near a dried-out streambed. I did about six three-point maneuvers to turn our SUV around, in case we needed a quick exit, parked, and cautiously got out. Ken stayed behind me for backup, and we walked over to the opening where they'd set up the campsite and looked around.

A circle of rocks formed a bed for a fire and, of course, even with the restrictions in place, they'd gone ahead and made one, probably to cook their food. A few tin pots were stacked beside a log they'd moved close to the fire to use as a bench. I went over to the yurt, stood to the side holding my gun, and called out to Minsky. No one answered. Ken pointed his gun at the entryway. The entire yurt was made out of canvas, and Minsky could shoot right through to either of us, but I knew they couldn't have made it back yet and they probably weren't dumb enough to head straight back once they saw us drive up the road. Ken nodded that he was ready, and I picked up the canvas door flap.

Nothing happened. There was no movement. I peeked in to see a fifteen-foot canvas floor with two sleeping bags and pillows spread across it. A cooler sat on one side and some duffel bags stuffed with clothes on the other.

I felt sad not to see Jeremy there, but at the same time I was relieved not to find him tied up inside. "Nothing," I called to Ken, still on watch outside the yurt. I searched the duffel bags for any signs of the kid and found nothing of interest, just dirty, smelly clothes. I backed out and shook my head to reiterate that I found nothing of interest. We went over and looked through the windows of Minsky's truck, seeing boxes of ammo and several more rifles and shotguns inside their cases behind the front seats.

"What now?" Ken asked.

"They're around," I said as we headed back to our car. "I bet they're watching us right now." The wind had begun to sound like a surf. I looked out and into the sea of trees, brush, and young saplings, the tops waving like water. "Hey, Minsky," I yelled as loudly as I could after Ken hopped in and I stood safely behind the cover of the vehicle. Because of the steep drop-off on the driver's side, there was no way he could have a shot at me. "If you can hear me, listen up. We're leaving, but you better leave too. I meant what I said about that fire," I hollered loudly. "It's time to clear out."

I even wrote a note saying the same thing in case they hadn't heard me, then told Ken to hop out for a sec and cover me while I walked over and set it inside the entry of the yurt. Finally we both got back in the car, and as we headed back down the mountain, I had a sinking feeling in my gut.

25

Gretchen

I THOUGHT I WOKE to the sound of a low murmur in the distance, but then again, for a brief second, I considered that I might be in one of my twisted dreamscapes. Brown and gray blurry images surrounded me and pain shot in every direction through my head. I tried to open my eyes, but quickly shut them when a sharp throb pierced my forehead. For a second, I thought something had hit me again, but then I realized all was still except the murmuring sound coming from somewhere—perhaps my own mind?

I lay unmoving, my cheek smashed into the gritty floor. My left shoulder—the side I lay on—ached deeply, and I tried to roll onto my back to relieve the pain but found that I could barely move at all. I opened my eyes again, this time readying myself for the shooting pain. My hair fanned across the side of my face, creating a blurry veil before my eyes. I brought my hand up to sweep it away and was thankful that that arm didn't hurt. Images began to sharpen before me. Yellow foam from a mat under a dark-colored sleeping bag, some kind of heavy machinery, a bucket . . . A bucket. A dirty orange bucket.

It came back to me suddenly, and I jolted upright to a sitting position, but the pain knocked me back down. Panic raced through me, and I realized that whoever captured Jeremy had me now too. Again, I wondered if maybe I was in one of my nightmares.

I looked over and saw the boy. He knelt in the corner and stared at me like a wounded, trapped creature. Wary, but with hope. His bony,

316

dirty knees jutted out and his grimy elbows wrapped around his calves. I tried again to sit up, moving slowly, and he stood, came over, and grabbed my arm to help me. "Thank you," I mouthed, then cocked my head to the side, trying to make out the murmur in the distance. It sounded like a steady stream of prayer. "Change my ways. . . . Appease you among the madness. . . . Willing to do as you ask . . . it's what you ask of me, Dear Father. . . . I don't question your reasons, for to question them is to question you, Dear Lord. . . . We are all innocent. . . . We are all called to your altar. . . . But we must prove, I must prove . . ."

"He does that a lot," Jeremy whispered. His eyes were large and his round face seemed to have already thinned since the picture we'd been shown on the news. His skin looked white, almost nacreous in the pale light coming from the narrow windows above, as if he had already adjusted to his dwelling place, like a salamander that lived under rocks and burrowed into crevices between logs. When I looked at him squarely, he shuffled shyly away, back to the side of the cage next to one of the large vats. I looked down the aisle and could see there were a series of cages—each one probably set up to protect workers from getting too close to the large boilers. All the cages had sliding doors. I looked up to see that the cage was enclosed on top as well.

"Does what a lot?" I asked.

"Prays. Lights candles."

He looked in the direction of the mumbling.

I didn't know what to say. Seeing him—the dark circles under his eyes, the frailness of his frame—and wondering what unfathomable things he's been going through, scared and alone in a place like this, made a hollow pit form in my stomach. I stared at him for a moment. He blinked long eyelashes, then turned away. I tried to push myself up to standing. My left shoulder screamed at me, but I didn't think it was broken because I could move it. I fought the dizziness, reaching out to grab the side of the cage to steady myself. How had he managed, trapped in this fetid cage? I guessed he'd had no choice.

"Willing to face it again. My well . . . not dry. . . . Capable of appeas-

ing you . . . not turning away. . . . Not being too stubborn to appease
you. . . . Dear Lord . . . I am not afraid to climb the mountain again . . ."

"How long will he do this?" I whispered.

"A long time," Jeremy said. "But sometimes he leaves and is gone
for a while too."

"Just him? Is he alone?" I looked around for my pack, but didn't
see it.

"I haven't seen anyone else. He took your pack and your phone
from your pocket before he dragged you in here."

"Has he told you his name?"

Jeremy put his finger to his lips to stop me from talking.

"Gretchen." A man spoke behind me. I turned, knowing I recognized it. "It's Wendy's father. I know this must be a shock to you, but
then again, no one really understands the depths of me, of what I'd
do to save my family. But, Gretchen"—he shook his head sadly—"why
have you come here? You shouldn't be here."

"Mr. Combs." I was speechless at first, and a little confused, still
wondering if I was in a dream. I shook my head, which hurt. I tightened my fingers around the sharp metal loops of the cage. He looked
so normal, so much like the person I'd see with Wendy at work. I was
tempted to say, *Mr. Combs, you're here, get us out, get someone to help
us,* but the realization was all too clear: he had taken Jeremy. He had
put me in this cage. "Mr. Combs," I said again. "Why are *you* here?"

"I'm here to work. Someone has to do God's work."

"What work?"

"You'll see." He walked over to a rickety wooden table across from
the cage. Six candles lined the top, five of them burned to the wick. The
only one not burned all the way down was larger and a different color,
burgundy, and its flame burned steadily. "As soon as this goes all the
way down, it will be time. But now you've put me in a bind, Gretchen.
I don't want to hurt you, but God must be telling me something. Why
did God bring you to me? Are you the lamb? I must pray," he said,
looking confused. "I must pray to understand this new development."

"What? Mr. Combs. You're not making any sense. Where's Wendy?"

"Wendy is safe, and she'll be even safer when this is all done. And Kyle too, poor disturbed Kyle. Don't you understand, Gretchen?"

"Understand what?"

"If God doesn't understand my devotion, things will just keep getting worse. Kyle will keep acting out. Balances need to be restored. I have to remain strong, resolute."

"No, no, I don't understand." I shook my head. "Resolute about what? Why do you have this boy?" I pleaded. "His parents are worried sick. You know this. Surely you've seen the news. They're searching everywhere, even your church."

His eyes looked distant, truly calm and crazed at the same time. I continued to rattle off reasons for why this boy should not be here, but suddenly it occurred to me that my rant was lost on him, that it was as if I were speaking another language. There was something menacing underneath his calmness that made me shudder. This was not a dream. It was not a joke, and I'd never experienced anything like it. I wanted to laugh it away. For the first time since I was fifteen, I *wanted* to be in a dream, to sleepwalk away from the situation. How had I not noticed this delusion in Wendy's father before? How could Wendy not know this about him? Or did she?

I looked at Jeremy, who sat still as a toad, as if at this point he was accustomed to the bizarreness as well as the setting, and that sickened me.

"What are the candles for?" I asked, trying to steady my voice. He turned toward us, and the dazed, cold look on his face chilled me to the bone. Panic jolted through me.

"To help find the answers. God has brought you to me for a reason, don't you see that? Just as He has the boy. Gretchen, look at you. At your fair skin, at your stunning blue eyes—could it finally be true? Has God finally sent me a lamb?

I stared at him, my mouth hanging open, my throat dry.

"I need to pray," he said. "Yes, I need to understand. Now, please, be quiet. Ours is a just God, Gretchen. He has asked me to do this, but in the end, it will all be all right, for all of us. When the candle burns out, it will be time."

"Time for what, Mr. Combs?"

"Don't you know?"

"No, I don't know."

"Time for me to figure out if you are an angel's gift—if finally, the lamb has been provided to spare Isaac, or if . . ." His words faded and he looked down.

"Or what, Mr. Combs?"

"Or if you've been sent by Satan. If Satan sent you, the hand of the devil is at work to interfere with God's plans, and we can't have that."

"But you can't just figure that out. Mr. Combs, how are you going to figure that out?"

He didn't answer, just held up his hand, bowed his head, and walked away.

A terrible dread coursed through me. I turned to the boy. "Jeremy, do you know what he's talking about?"

Jeremy stared down the hall for minute, but didn't answer. I could tell he was thinking about whether he should or not.

"Jeremy," I whispered, moving closer to him. "Please tell me what he's talking about."

Finally his gaze met mine and he spoke softly, "I'm not really sure. He says weird things and prays a lot. Talks about a guy named Isaac, about how his father, Abraham, took him to the mountain because that's what God wanted. I think it's something from the Bible, but he talks about it like it's not very long ago." Jeremy's eyes looked scared, but resigned.

I went all the way over to him, my head still spinning and every muscle in my body aching. I knelt before him. "Has he hurt you?"

Jeremy shook his head. He had a nasty bruise above his right elbow. When he saw me look at it, he wrapped his other arm around himself and covered it with his hand and stared at the dirty floor. I could already feel the burden of shame and confusion running through him—the deep sorrow now darkly buried within him forever. I wanted to hug him, but I didn't want to scare him.

"No?"

He shook his head again.

"He picked me up near our campground. He was wearing a uniform, like a ranger. He asked me my name and where my parents were, and when I told him that they were out hiking around the lake, he said that they were in trouble because of the fires, and that he was supposed to bring me to them at the evacuation camp."

I nodded, taking it in. So that was it? That's all it took—a man in a ranger uniform and a thirteen-year-old kid who still trusted the world around him.

"But, he didn't take me to them," he whispered. "He took me to some church—his church, I think. It was nice and he gave me lemonade. He made me sit and watch him perform some sermon, said he needed to practice before he spoke before the congregation, and that he'd take me to my parents right afterward. He lit candles there too. It seemed weird, and I got a little scared by then, but I wasn't really sure what to think. I knew something wasn't right, but I didn't know what to do. Then he said we needed to go, that he was taking me to my parents, but he didn't. He brought me here and that's where I've been ever since."

I stared at Jeremy. I didn't know what to say. I didn't want to ask anything accusatory, like *Did you try and leave the church?* Or, *What did you think when you got to this abandoned place? Did you try and run?*

Jeremy looked down at the floor again. He had a small piece of burnt wood or charcoal in his hand and was scraping on the cement as if he was drawing a picture. I realized that was the scratching noise I'd heard.

"What happened then?" I asked.

Jeremy didn't reply. He continued to look at the floor, at the charcoal marks he smeared across it. He didn't even seem to hear me—as if he'd gone into a type of protective trance. I wondered if he'd been doing that the whole time he'd been in here, passing the time, turning off his thoughts, going numb.

I decided not to push it. I watched his long dark eyelashes as he concentrated on the movement of his hand. I stood up and looked through the chain-link cage toward the next line of machinery. Combs was in between two of them, praying again. His voice, steady and trancelike, drifted toward us and almost sounded comforting. A frail light fanned across the rafters from some of the high, narrow windows on the other side of the plant. The candle continued to burn, and I could smell the wax, but I could also smell the fires from the canyon. I turned back to Jeremy, but he didn't look up. He just kept scraping his piece of charcoal on the ground, his mind hopefully someplace far away.

26

Monty

KEN AND I drove straight to headquarters against the line of cars snaking slowly through the canyon. When we were back within cell-phone range, Ken called Ali, but she didn't answer, so he left her a message and contacted Herman instead. I then called Joe, who said the wind had gotten stronger and that IC ordered an evacuation of the entire canyon. He said the winds had reached thirty to forty miles per hour and had fanned the flames from both fire complexes in several directions, but mostly down Bad Rock Canyon and the North Fork.

We avoided going down the North Fork Road and cut across the park on Camas Road to reach West Glacier, which was also being evac-uated, including headquarters. We found out that Ali had ordered Tara Reed to handle the transfer of the staff and the incident room materials to the county sheriff's headquarters in Kalispell. We also discovered that another thousand firefighters were being brought in to do damage control. Apparently Wilcox, the ops manager for the fire crews, said he'd never seen a fire burn this hot and fast before. I pictured all the desiccated trees and their needles and the dried chaparral from the drought feeding a raging dragon. I thought of the gravesite, and how we'd not even been able to get back to it to examine it. At this point, I was certain it was scorched, the earth charred and barren.

I contacted Ali again. She said Ray and Paxton were wrapping up at the church as quickly as possible. She had given the task of interview-ing neighbors and church members to several other officers when Ken

323

and I left for the North Fork, and now Ali said that the fire evacuation was interfering with the interviewing, since most people on the list were gathering pets, livestock and whatever belongings they could and heading out.

Ken and I left West Glacier and went to the church. We found Ray and Paxton loading up the back of their van. It was going on five p.m. and dark, thick smoke gripped the eastern horizon. A brazen red sun glowed in the sky and ashes fluttered around us as we stepped out of the car. Dry, hot air hit my face and settled in my throat.

I asked Ray and Paxton how it went, and they said they wouldn't know exactly what they'd discovered until they returned to the lab, but they'd picked up as much trace and collected as many prints as possible. They'd checked for blood and grabbed a half-empty water bottle left at the back of the church on a table, in case the DNA from the saliva showed anything of interest. "But it could belong to anybody," Ray explained. "It's open to the community, so DNA, prints, trace, I'm not sure how much it's going to tell us. What I am glad about is that we didn't find any blood."

I thanked him and Paxton for the information, then asked, "Agents Paige and Marcus inside?"

"I think so, just grabbing some last-minute things from the pastor's office."

I turned to go, then thought of Gretchen. "Have you heard from Gretchen?"

"Yeah, she left me a message a couple hours ago. Said she was looking into something at the county landfill and might stop by to check on how things were progressing up here, but she never did." Ray shrugged. "I'll call her on the way back to the lab."

"Maybe she's finally taking some time to herself," I said.

"Unlikely, but maybe." Ray swung the back door of the white van shut. "I'll let you know what we find."

• • •

Ali and Herman were standing by the table that held the visitor log, right inside the front door to the church. "Are we interrupting something?" I said.

"No, no," Ali said. "Harris, Greeley, come in. Welcome to the show. *Please* tell me something has broken on your end with Minsky."

"No, nothing. We did find him, though. He was with a petite woman. She looked Asian."

"Asian?" she asked.

"Yeah, we figure she accounts for the extra set of prints we found up at Chiles's place. They don't belong to the boy."

"You're positive?"

"We checked out Minsky's entire site. No sign of a boy. Unless they've got him hidden somewhere entirely different."

"Damn." Ali sighed. "And you couldn't bring them in for questioning because they ran?"

Ken had already briefed Herman on our way out of the woods, so Ali knew a few of the details.

"That's right."

"And it wasn't worth the chase?"

"I really don't think they have Jeremy. There's no evidence other than that he's a distant relative and he's been here for some free food." I looked around the church again. I could hear the wind whistling against the cross, but otherwise it was quiet, peaceful. I remembered the plaque Combs had in his office. "You grab much from Combs's office?"

"Some records to find out who else has worked here, what other connections there might be, that kind of thing. I've got one of the tech guys searching his computer now in case there's anything of note. But the guy has an alibi, so we're not expecting much."

"That plaque," I said. "The one that said something about the mountain of the Lord. . . . Either of you know the Bible well?"

"I think that comes from the Old Testament," Herman said. "Yeah, that's right"—he held his palm over his broad chest—"lots of Sunday school for this kid."

"It said it was Genesis. Does the quote mean anything to you?"

"Not without knowing specifically which part of Genesis it comes from. I could look it up, though. Why?"

"No, don't bother, it's not important. It's just something that's been stuck in my head since Ali and I were in his office. I'd never seen that quote before."

"Well, we've pretty much wrapped up here," Ali said, motioning to the church. "Evacuees are being sent just west of Columbia Falls, to that large field near where the old drive-in used to be, and the high school. We plan to continue interviewing anyone from this community at those two places. At least most of the residents will be rounded up into one spot. We could use the extra help, and we should get out of here." She lifted her head to the sound of the wind moaning against the cross and the eaves.

"We'll be there," I said, and Ken seconded me. I turned to head for the door and, beside the exit, noticed a corkboard with various pictures of church members and announcements tacked on it. "Anything interesting here?"

"No, we looked. Just announcements, some pictures of church members. We've gotten their names from Combs already."

I stared at the board. The soup kitchen schedule hung in the center. An announcement for a Christian rock concert that had already passed in late July was still tacked in the top right corner. A charity notice for donations to a family who'd lost their home in an electric fire dangled on one edge. Some pictures of smiling community members in action outside the church were scattered across the board. I studied them, but didn't recognize anyone. In the bottom left corner, there was a picture of three men, a woman, and a child, and I recognized the woman—Wendy. She wore a wide smile and draped an arm over a young boy—maybe six or seven—and I recognized him as Kyle. To Wendy's right stood a man about her age whom I didn't recognize, and to his side stood another man who looked more familiar. He had a full head of reddish hair, so I didn't immediately realize that it was Wendy's father, Combs, just younger, but something about the image grabbed me. Another ghost of a memory danced in the corner of my mind. Behind me, Ali, Herman, and Ken were discussing the evacuation and who would take which evacuee camp for questioning, but I tuned them out. No, it wasn't just that he resembled the older Mr. Combs. I'd seen that very face before. I stood listening to the wind until suddenly it dawned on me.

When we met with Combs earlier in the morning, I had just assumed that I recognized him from seeing him at the county building with Wendy, but that wasn't it. Come to think of it, I'd never seen Combs before at all, only in a photo—the one taken on Richard Tuckman's patio in the old man's room. It was just like this one, when Combs was younger and sported more hair and fewer wrinkles. "Hey, guys?" I waved the others over.

All three shuffled over to me. I pointed to the picture and told them what I'd realized.

Ali looked at me. "You're sure?"

"Positive."

"What about the alibi?" She turned to Ken.

"I called the conference organizer," Ken said. "The woman I spoke to claimed he was there for the whole thing—from Monday to Wednesday. He gave a talk on Monday. She saw the presentation."

"That was the night before it happened, though."

"Yes, but the hotel confirmed that he checked out on Wednesday."

"Did he check out in person?"

Ken stared at Ali. "I didn't ask."

"He could have left the key cards in the room. Could have left the night after the talk or even early the next day and still have made it to the park by midmorning. The hotel would still have him down for checking out when he said he would."

"Did anyone see him around after the talk, at some of the other seminars?"

Ken shook his head. "Not specifically, no."

"Ken," Ali said. "Get back on the phone now and call both the conference organizer and the hotel. Find out if anyone actually saw him after Monday evening. Get the names of other conference attendees who might have seen him and verify if he was there or not."

"Where is he now?" I asked.

"He went to meet his daughter for lunch," Herman said. "I told him to stay close by, but with the evacuations . . ." Herman's voice faded, which I took as a bad sign.

"You don't know?" Ali looked at him with surprise.

"He had an alibi, and his daughter wanted to take him for lunch, but she wanted to get back home to check on Kyle first, so they drove separately. He was going to come right back, but with the evacuations, I figured he got caught in traffic."

We all turned to Ken after he hung up with the Hampton Inn in Great Falls. "They emailed the receipt to him, which probably means he did not check out in person."

Ali looked from Ken to me to Herman. "If he was in the old man's photo, he obviously knew old Tuckman, but he denied it when I asked. His alibi could be sketchy. He had to know about the car keys in the barn. Walt said they've done it that way since he was a boy. Herman, try to get ahold of the guy and let's send someone to his house immediately."

"We'll go," I offered.

"That works, but be careful. It's east of Martin City," she pointed northeast toward the park. "Off the South Fork Road East and from what I understand, they're not letting anyone through. I'll radio IC to let them know you're headed that way. Let me know if he's not there, and do the best you can to have a look around. If we can't locate him, put out an APB immediately. We need to find this guy. And someone get ahold of Wendy, ASAP."

• • •

Combs was not answering his phone, but Wendy did immediately. She said she'd gone back to her house because she wanted to check on Kyle. He'd gone home to sleep after being released after the night of interrogations. She wanted to make sure he didn't leave again to go meet his friends after he woke. Then, apparently, Wendy and her father had lunch in a café in Hungry Horse and afterward, he said he was heading back to the church. She seemed genuinely concerned that he might have gone to his house deeper in the woods instead and not made it back—that perhaps the spreading fires played some role in preventing him from getting back to the church from his house.

Ken and I hopped in the car to head to Combs's house, but before we pulled out, I quickly searched the number for the county dump and dialed it, hoping it would still be open. It wasn't, and I figured it closed at five. "Damn," I swore.

"What?" Ken asked.

"I wanted to get hold of someone at the dump. I can't reach Gretchen, and I'd like to check on why she went there. I have a feeling it has something to do with our case."

"I know the director of public works," Ken said. "Dan Hittle. He's a friend of my wife's."

"You have his number?"

"Yeah, it's on my phone." Ken pulled up his contacts and read it to me.

Thankful for small-town connections, I called the man, told him who I was, and asked if he could find out for me who had been working the entrance station and if I could get his or her number. He told me he'd look into it and get back to me. When I said it was urgent, he said he'd hurry.

I started the car and we headed in the opposite direction of the line of white and red flashing lights muted by the impenetrable smoke. When we turned from Highway 2 into Martin City and continued to South Fork Road East, it became hard to see and disorientating, almost worse than the day of the dig, the day Jeremy went missing. Flurries of ash clogged the air, and even inside the car we could feel the smoke crawling into our lungs. I tried to drive as fast as possible and was thankful that we were on a paved county road, at least for a few miles. Eventually it turned to gravel, but we didn't have to go far before we made it to Combs's property. I slowed way down in his driveway. We could barely see his house through the smoke until we parked just yards away from the garage doors.

"This property butts up against National Forest land," Ken said.

"Yeah, I know." Tall pines that we could barely make out pressed in on us from behind the house. I thought of all the many places deep in the woods that Jeremy could be if he was still alive, and how susceptible those areas would be to the fire when it swept through. The day he was taken, the smoke was already bad. The abductor likely knew there might be evacuations of the canyon at some point. Had that not been a concern because he or she didn't intend to keep Jeremy around that long? Or because the person planned to keep Jeremy somewhere else, perhaps in the valley outside the ravaged canyon? Or had the abductor simply not cared one way or another?

"Not that many houses out this way," Ken said. "You notice how far back the last one was?"

"About three-quarters of a mile down the road."

"Yep," Ken said.

"Thanks for making me feel even more uneasy," I joked.

"You're welcome." Ken smiled.

"But you're right to bring it up. Doesn't hurt to take note, play it safe," I said. "No car in the drive. He's probably not here, unless it's in the garage. First let's see if there's a window around the side, then I'll ring the bell." I opened the car door. "You cover me?"

"Sure thing."

We hopped out and took a look around the side of the garage. We found a side door near the back, but no window. We walked around to the front again. It was a clean, well-maintained place with a nice tan-and-white paint job. An immaculate lawn only slightly browned from the heat and lack of rain spread out in front of the house. Combs either spent a lot of time watering it or he had an irrigation system in place. Pretty flower gardens lined the beds below the windows and on the sides of the front porch. Small rectangular windows embedded in thick cement squatted at the base of the house, indicating a basement—not unusual for Montana homes, but it made me uneasy.

I rang the bell and stood to the side of the door while Ken took his post behind me. If this was our guy, we didn't need him coming at us both with a weapon. But no one came. I rang it again and waited. Nothing. I rapped on the door loudly, calling out, "Mr. Combs, if you're in there, we need to speak to you," but all was silent except the strong stirring of the wind in the trees and the sound of airplane and helicopter engines carrying water and fire retardant in the not-too-far distance.

"I don't think he's here." I backed away from the door and went over to the window beside it. I could make out a tidy living room with plain furnishings. Books lined the walls on shelves on both sides of a fireplace. Neatly stacked magazines lay on the coffee table before a beige couch. Through an opening near the side of the room, I could make out the kitchen—some dated appliances and oak-colored kitchen cabinets. "Looks empty," I said to Ken.

We walked over and opened the toolshed. An old lawn mower sat in the center and shovels, spades, rakes and other tall implements leaned against the wall. Several bags of mulch and soil slumped in one of the corners. On the other side, shelves stretched across the wall held smaller gardening tools, bottles of fertilizer, and several pairs of thick gardening gloves. Next to the gardening gloves was a box of nitrile gloves—the kind we used in the lab. That alone wasn't so interesting. Many people used them for cleaning, to handle toxic solutions. But in light of the other things we'd learned about Combs, along with that fact that the truck was wiped clean, my skin prickled.

"Let's radio in to see if Combs has been located yet and if they want us to enter." I looked into the murkiness, trying to make out the forest. "If there's any chance at all that the boy's in the house, he shouldn't be left behind—trapped out here in the possible path of the fires. In fact, we shouldn't be out here much longer either. I'd say we have exigent circumstances for a warrantless search."

27

Gretchen

JEREMY CONTINUED SCRAPING the floor while I inspected the cage. I had been trying to figure a way out, but it was one of those heavy-duty, small-linked industrial wire-mesh cages with sharp ridges on every loophole. There were a series of them, and they all had sliding doors. He could have put me in any one of them, but this was the only one with a dead bolt, which I assumed he had brought himself. He wasn't expecting a second victim, although now—I had begun to realize—I wasn't simply a victim. I was either a lamb or the devil. In my mind, neither one could be good.

Panic had shot through me in waves for the first hour after I came to, and I told myself to calm down. This man was Wendy's father, a pastor. . . . How could he have taken Jeremy? How could he not be reasoned with? The thoughts whirled in my head over and over. I tried to make sense of it all, but there was none to be made. Combs had spoken nonsense. Abraham? Isaac?

I didn't know a lot about the Bible, but you didn't need to be an expert to know the story of Abraham and Isaac—how God had asked Abraham to sacrifice his son Isaac to prove his love for God, and how an angel sent a lamb to be sacrificed instead at the last minute. If any of the other boys I'd researched were related to this, I wondered about the possibility of him waiting for the sacrificial lambs to materialize to replace the other boys, and they never came, until now. Until me.

A chill went down my spine. I forced myself to take a deep breath.

Crazy. Crazy talk. Crazy thinking. What was I to say to him? I told myself that I should be careful not to push any buttons. I needed to get us out of this place.

The smell of smoke had gotten more intense and the temperature hotter. Jeremy and I were both sweating, and I wondered how Combs could continue to pray in this condition, but I realized that the fervor the fire seemed to stir was exactly what he might have expected. I heard the drone of airplanes above and the sweet sound of sirens in the distance, and for a second, my hopes soared that someone was coming to rescue us. But as the plane engines and the sirens faded, I realized the sirens were for the fires. When I'd driven out earlier, I had heard the fire crews had contained the Ole Fire, but Sheep Fire had grown stronger in its march to the northwest with the increased wind, and the one on Desert Mountain close to West Glacier had grown larger. I'd also heard a new one had erupted on Columbia Mountain just east of Columbia Falls at the northern end of the Swan Mountain Range. They had labeled it the Columbia Fire. I knew this would be the one closest to us. There had been talk of a mass evacuation of West Glacier and the entire canyon as well as the North Fork area because of the Trail Creek Fire. I wondered if they had started the process.

I paced while Jeremy colored on the floor, but when he finally stood up and stretched, I stopped and turned to him. "Jeremy," I said.

"Yes?" he answered, and I felt relieved for a response at all. It seemed like a small victory under the circumstances.

"Have you had anything to eat or drink?"

He nodded. "He brought me some things."

"Enough?"

Jeremy looked in the direction where Combs still prayed. Even though we couldn't see him, we could hear his muttering, low-pitched and surreal. I could see that he wasn't sure whether to turn on this strange man who had been his only link to survival. I could also see he had glanced up at me occasionally, trying to decide whether he could trust me.

In the course of only four days, Jeremy had come to see Combs as his caretaker on some level. On another level, he was wiser than that and old enough to understand his situation.

"Jeremy," I said again. He looked at me, his eyes large. "I'd really like to get us out of here. Is there anything you can tell me that would help me help us to do that? Anything at all? Like, do you know if he has a gun?"

Jeremy shook his head. "I haven't seen one."

"Okay, how about food? How often does he usually bring you food and water, and how does he give it to you?"

Jeremy began to explain the routine—that Combs brought him food and water usually only once a day, sometime in the morning. He told me that he usually brought it in a bag, with cups and plastic utensils.

"Has he fed you today?"

"No, he didn't come today. I don't know why." Jeremy slumped back down on his sleeping bag. He cheeks were hollowed and he had dark circles under his eyes.

I went and sat next to him. I knew why. Combs had been hung up at his church and couldn't get here. I wondered if he'd leave to go get Jeremy dinner, or if it didn't matter to him at this point. I glanced at the candle burning. There was only about two inches of it left. "Jeremy," I whispered. "I know this man. I work with his daughter. I had no idea he was like this, but I'm hoping, since I know him, that I can talk some sense into him."

Jeremy looked at me and frowned, shaking his head. "No," he said. "You won't be able to do that. He's"—he shook his head more frantically—"he's not . . . he's not right. He . . ." His voice faded.

"He what?" I said softly.

"In the parking lot when we got here, I tried to get out of the truck, but he grabbed me, tied me up. He held a knife to my neck. . . ." Jeremy's face started to crinkle and tears pooled in his brown eyes. "He said he'd hurt me and my family if I screamed, but then he kept saying how sorry he was for what he had to do. And he keeps telling me I'm special. He calls me Isaac, and says that he needs to prepare me for the big day. I'm too afraid to ask him what that means."

"You poor thing." My throat felt very dry. This boy had been separated from his family for four days now, unable to leave this cage, alone for hours at a time, perhaps every night, all night in this frightening place. I couldn't imagine how hungry and terrified he'd been, how forsaken he felt. Once the seed of abandonment sprouted inside you, its ugly flowers bloomed through your entire being. "You've been in here the whole time?"

He nodded, and my words made something he'd been bottling up erupt. He dropped his face into his hands and began to sob. A pained choke burst forth from him. I put my hand on his back, but before I knew it, Combs was at the cage, yelling at us.

"What have you done to him? What have you done? Don't touch him. Get away from him." He had a black stick like a battering ram and pounded the side of the cage with it. The loud clanking of the metal rattled throughout the vast, darkening building.

I stood up quickly and moved away from Jeremy. I could see him try to swallow his cries, his face contorted with sorrow and fear. I backed closer to the vat, my hurt arm throbbing and my head spinning. I still hadn't recovered from being hit earlier, and I felt as if I might faint.

Combs glared at me, his eyes narrowing. He pointed the black stick at me. His other hand clenched tightly into a fist. "You will not hurt him. You will not hurt Isaac. He is our son. He belongs to God. Do you understand? Are you not the lamb I thought you might be?"

I stared at him, speechless, unable to think of anything to say. I felt like I might crumble to the floor, so I reached out and steadied myself against the vat. He continued to glare icily at me, trying to read me with a confused, angry expression. I felt as if time had slowed and I were in a movie or a dream. A bead of sweat rolled down the side of his veined temple and his sinewy neck glistened. Finally he dropped his arm with the cudgel by his side and marched away.

My chest heaved. Jeremy had moved to the corner and was crouching again, his head resting on folded arms. I went over to him and slowly knelt too. After a moment, after my heart rate began to slow again, I reached out and touched his upper arm. His skin was clammy and cold. The reality that this innocent boy had no one but me to help him froze me with fear. I wondered how many times Combs had lost his temper with him over the recent days.

I glanced at the candle, slowly burning down. I didn't understand how I'd gotten to this place. My motto had always been "Do no harm," to work humbly toward the greater good, but always behind the scenes, in a laboratory or behind a white Nomex suit, and steadily, in small increments, make a difference.

Whatever I needed to do to get us out of here now would not be behind the scenes, nor would it be incremental. I had to think of something big, and I had to think of it quickly. Terror swept through me like freezing water—primitive and visceral. It felt capable of knocking me down, stealing my breath and drowning me like a wooden boat sunken in the cold, frothing sea.

I swallowed my fright. "It's going to be okay," I said to Jeremy. "I'm not sure how, but I'm going to get you out of here."

28

Monty

ONCE WE GOT the go-ahead from Ali, we found an unlocked door at the back of the house and entered through it to the kitchen. I told Ken I'd take the basement and asked him to search all the rooms upstairs.

We both put on gloves, and I went down a narrow stairwell off another kitchen door and hit the light switch at the base. A bare bulb dangled from the ceiling's center and illuminated typical storage items: boxes, plastic bins, an old file cabinet, a folding card table and chairs. A used washing machine and dryer stood on the opposite side of the room. I opened the top drawer of the file cabinet and quickly fingered through the files. Years' worth of bank statements and utility and mortgage bills clogged the manila folders. I searched for bills that might indicate whether Combs had another property besides the house, but didn't see any. The other drawers were filled with similar statements, articles on pastoral duties, and other generic forms.

I moved to the boxes and started opening them, not sure what I was looking for—just any clue at all that could lead us to Jeremy. They were full of more useless items: the stubs of old burned-down white and red candles and other knickknacks. I wondered why he didn't throw the candles out—he seemed like a fairly neat person based on what I had seen of the rest of the house, and the basement was otherwise well organized.

I reached for another box and opened it. In it I found old pictures of him with a woman I assumed was Wendy's mom. She also had brown hair and a thin nose and a broad smile like Wendy. One photo in particular caught my eye. It was Combs and his wife—she had her arms around Wendy, who must have been about five or six—and an older boy who looked to be around ten or eleven years old. I didn't think Wendy had a brother. I wondered if something had happened to the boy in the photo. He had dark hair and brown eyes like his mom and sister.

I kept searching. I opened the next box. Several folded sheets of paper were stacked in the box, and I pulled them out. They were old, poster-size colorful pictures that appeared to be renditions of biblical stories, most of them of a robed, white-bearded older man with a dark-haired boy carrying a load of sticks across his shoulders. Another was a different rendition, but the same theme—a bearded man and a young boy, only in this one, a donkey carried the sticks and the older man carried a scythe.

Suddenly it made sense to me where the quote in Combs's office came from. The third picture was a smaller photo of the bearded old man standing above the tied-up boy with the scythe poised above his right shoulder, ready to strike. Behind the man, in the corner of the photo, you could see a lamb waiting by a boulder. The old man has turned to look at the animal, his scythe still poised in the air above him. Below, the caption read, "The Binding of Isaac."

I unfolded a fourth photo, very similar to the third—a boy bound to the pile of wood on the altar, only on this one, a hallowed angel hovers above Abraham and touches his shoulder gently.

I set the box down with a sense that something extremely abnormal was at play, just as Ken called from upstairs. I took the stairs three at a time to get back up to the kitchen. "Ken?"

"In here," he said, and my hopes faded that he'd found the boy. His voice sounded too calm. "The office."

I went down the hall, passing walls adorned with framed photos of his wife, of Wendy and Kyle. I didn't see any photos of the other boy from the family photo I found in the box. I entered the office where

Ken stood by a floor-to-ceiling bookcase. Several certificates of pastoral achievement hung framed on the side wall. "Have you found something?"

Ken held up a Bible in his gloved hand. "I was flipping through this and I found these sheets of paper."

Ken handed the folded pages to me. I opened them carefully and began to read. "What are these, sermons?"

"I think they're more personal than that. They read like journal entries, but they're years apart and aren't very coherent. They're like religious ramblings."

I scanned them.

The first piece was dated 1991 and contained two pages of ramblings about Isaac. I told Ken about the artistic depictions I saw in the basement, but the date 1991 flashed like neon in my mind.

I don't understand. I've done everything you've asked in your name, Lord, in your service. Isaac did not understand. Isaac was afraid. I told him God himself will provide the burnt offering. I did it for you, because you promised that he would go to a better place and that first and foremost to make things better, I must follow you and only you. That's what I have done. I have proved my love, my great, never-ending devotion. I waited patiently for three days for the angel of the Lord and for the lamb of God. But they never came. Why did you not send them?

Oh, God, I know I should not question you. I'm sorry to question you. Dear Lord, I know you work in mysterious ways.

I read on. It continued this way, perseverating about why an angel or a lamb of God did not show. Then the date changed to 1999, and again, seeing it sent a chill down my spine as I recalled the dates Gretchen showed me from her research. That was the year Shane Wallace vanished. The ramblings went on for another two pages. I caught mention of Wendy and how she'd recently had a little boy named Kyle, and how he could not be a grandfather alone without God's help. He described how Kyle was yellow, how his liver wasn't making enough bilirubin, and he had a fever. He needed to make things better. He asked desperately over and over how he could make God understand that He came first. He asked whether he should give more time, more days for the angel to arrive. He made notes about colors of candles. I thought of the melted candles in the drawer downstairs.

There were paraphrases from the Bible: *I will surely bless you and make your descendants as numerous as the stars in the sky and as the sand on the seashore. Your descendants will take possession of the cities . . . and through your offspring all nations on earth will be blessed, because you have obeyed me.*

Two pages later, my heart sank again. The date changed to 2007, and there were still more ramblings about Isaac and lines from the Bible. I remembered that Samuel Erickson's body was found in 2007, and he had the same injury to the head as the one from the grave we found in Essex.

"This is some really weird shit, Harris," Ken said.

My mind hummed with a mixture of astonishment and horror. I looked around the room at the desk drawers Ken had searched and left ajar. "You find anything else? Any paperwork on other properties this guy might own?"

"No, nothing. Just these notes."

"Damn it." I ran a hand through my hair. Every part of me ached to find some scrap of information that would tell us where he was keeping Jeremy. "He's taken this boy to perform some weird ritual, and we don't know where they are. And if Gretchen is right, it's going to happen by the end of today."

"Gretchen?"

"Long story, she'd been looking into past abductions around the area and noticed a similarity in the head traumas of two of the boys. She saw that one of the boys was found in '07 exactly six days after he was abducted. She hypothesized that if the cases were related, based on the TOD of the '07 boy, the abductor was keeping them alive for five days."

"But we don't know where," Ken said.

"No, we don't. There's interesting stuff in the basement, but nothing pointing to any location other than the church." I told him about the Bible pictures I'd found.

"All we can do is keep looking," I said. "No computer?"

"No, I think the only computer he has is at the church in his office there, and our guys took that. I haven't even made it to the master bedroom yet."

"Okay," I said, pulling out my phone. "Check the master and I'll call Ali to see if they've found anything on the guy's computer."

29

Gretchen

I SAT AGAINST THE platform under the vat watching the light fade up in the small rectangular windows of the plant. The candle still burned, its flame flickering every so often in the draft. Combs had quit praying and I didn't know what he was up to, but I hadn't heard him leave.

Jeremy had lain down on his sleeping bag and fallen asleep. He looked exhausted, and I wondered how many of the four nights he'd lain awake petrified, listening to the scurrying rodents and the creaking sounds of the plant. I wondered if he'd finally allowed himself to let go into a deep sleep since I was here—because he finally had the company of another human being who wasn't his captor.

I noticed the rise and fall of his bony rib cage under his discolored, grimy T-shirt, which looked like it was once a nice blue color. I thought to myself that this poor boy had not had enough food. He looked too pale and thin, and he seemed weak. The anger in me began to flare, and I wanted to yell and scream at Combs, to rattle the cage and draw him back over to tell him to release us right away, that I needed to get the boy food, clean clothes, and his family.

But finally, after forcing myself to take some deep breaths so I could calm down and think, I became transfixed by the dusky rose glow spreading on the metal window frames high above. I felt like I was in an alternate reality. The light looked supernatural, and I knew the fires were raging and the lowered sun had probably turned into a huge glowing ball on the horizon. The smoke infiltrated the air and it had become so hot, even inside the plant. My shirt stuck to my back with sweat. I could tell the fires were claiming more acres and getting closer as we sat captured inside the belly of the abandoned plant.

Slowly it began to dawn on me that there could be benefits to playing Combs's game. Rationalizing with him clearly would not work, but trying to use his own crazy reasoning might. I considered that if I, who was not very religious, felt the apocalyptic sense of the fires, it must be a million times more disturbing for someone as fanatical as him.

Combs had mentioned that he thought I might be the lamb, but he also entertained the idea that the devil had sent me instead. It took every ounce of determination to try to think through the static of my rising anxiety and contemplate how to get us out of this. Somewhere along the line, as the minutes painfully ticked by, I decided I had to determine my identity before Combs chose on his own. Should I present myself as the devil or the lamb?

If he considered me a lamb, it could mean, in theory, that he'd try to sacrifice me instead of Jeremy. Which also meant that he might let the boy go. I could show Jeremy which way to run once he was out of the plant. But that seemed like a long shot. Combs was delusional, but he was clearly able to plan ahead and avoid being discovered. That must take some level of rational thought.

He'd hidden his actions from his own daughter, and possibly from his grandson—although now I wondered if Kyle's extreme behavior didn't have something to do with this madness. In my gut, I couldn't imagine Wendy knew. On the other hand, how could she not? I thought they were close, but perhaps not as close as I imagined. And you always hear those stories about people having no idea about the secret lives of their spouses and children. *You think you know a person, but you never really do*—that's what people used to say about me in Sandefjord.

I changed direction and considered trying to convince him I was the devil. Clearly Combs was not planning to bring the boy food anymore. Our time was up. I was certain that as soon as the candle died, he planned to act. He had no reason to open the cage until then; he had not let Jeremy out even once the entire time. I considered asking him to let me use the bathroom, but I was certain he'd point me to the bucket, whose stench seemed to grow stronger as the temperature rose.

Then I remembered how he had come over to the cage, screaming at me not to touch Jeremy. He thought I was making him cry, that I was somehow harming his precious Isaac—the dark-haired boy of Abraham—who was "special," so special he practically starved him and made him defecate in a bucket in a cage. The lunacy of it made my anger surge again. I tried to shove it down so I could think clearly, but it kept swelling. I felt nauseated. My head wanted to explode.

The rosy light grew wider on the metal frames, and the shapes before me took on a chiaroscuro effect in the gloaming. My arm throbbed and my head buzzed from my injury, but I felt a strange sensation, as if I was transforming, as if someone had drugged me. I felt as if the blood from that unconscious, murderous zombielike girl of fifteen years ago had been transfused back into my veins.

In spite of the pain, I stood. A primitive rage I'd suppressed for too long coursed through me—anger born not just from my empathy for Jeremy and panic from this bizarre and dangerous situation, but something innate that had been with me my whole life. I wanted to grab the footstool and swing it hard against the cage. I wanted to spit in Combs's face. I was no stranger to hating myself, but suddenly I felt enraged at my parents too, for letting me leave so easily, and at the injustice of life in general. The rage roared through me. I wanted to howl with indignation and sorrow. I wanted to fight. My hands shook and my stomach somersaulted. I paced around the cage. My do-no-harm motto had flip-flopped. I felt wild-eyed and scrappy, ready to challenge a hungry predator.

I went to the edge of the cage and looked down the dark aisle in the direction where I thought Combs had holed up. Outlines of equipment, scrap metal, and other debris became dark masses. I still couldn't hear

Combs. I wondered what in the world he was doing. I looked at Jeremy, asleep like Per. He lay in a fetal position on the old sleeping bag. How many other boys had slept on that same bag?

I could barely make out his features, but he looked so innocent and frail. It took everything I had not to wrap my fingers through the holes of the cage and shake it violently. Instead, I backed away. I knew what I needed to do. At first, even contemplating it made me think I was going crazy too, that my entire dramatic life had finally tipped the scales and I'd become unmoored, just like Combs.

But as I watched the wax drip down the sides of the candle, I realized it wouldn't be much longer now. I slowed my breath and let the idea sit with me. I needed to execute the only plan I could come up with, even if it was insane. I needed to meet craziness on its own level. I needed Jeremy to scream with fright, and I needed it to be real. It couldn't be an acting job. I couldn't count on him to try to pull off some performance. He was too confused and desperate as it was.

No, as painful and repugnant as it would be for me, Jeremy needed to see me as I saw myself—my own worst nightmare: dangerous. He needed to think I was going to hurt him, and he needed to think that so that Combs would come to see me as the devil.

30

Monty

So FAR THEY'D found nothing on Combs's computer to lead us to Jeremy, just articles about interdisciplinary pastoral studies, challenges facing pastors with multiple vocations, and a series of other random searches. When I told Ali what we found, she had directed us to go to the high school in Columbia Falls to keep checking for Combs among the residents who'd evacuated. So we set off down the canyon, keeping our eyes open for any signs of his car.

All other officers had been ordered to rake the area for Combs's vehicle as well. On our way I called Gretchen twice but her phone went straight to voicemail. That bothered me, especially since Ray had said she had planned on stopping by. It wasn't like Gretchen not to follow through.

We got stuck in traffic, a long line of evacuating cars still snaking its way out of the canyon, taillights barely shining through the biting, viscous smoke. I began to sweat, and the slow driving made me twice as anxious and jittery. I gripped, pushed, and pulled on the steering wheel as if the SUV were a horse I needed to control. I wanted to make the line speed up by sheer will. Ken glanced at me. "You okay?"

"Just this traffic." I motioned to the cars ahead. "It's getting to me. We don't have time for this. I'm thinking of hitting the lights, but there's nowhere for these cars to pull over. I could make everything worse."

"Yeah," Ken agreed. "I'd stay the course. We'll get out of this canyon soon enough. They're searching for Combs, and without knowing exactly where he is, there's not a lot we can do anyway. Besides, the road's too curvy. We go into the oncoming lane, we're likely to run into a water-supply truck."

"He could be anywhere," I said, still annoyed at our creeping pace and our failure to find any more leads at the house, but Ken was right. I just needed to hear him say it out loud.

Still, the thoughts continued to torment me. Combs knew we were onto him now that we'd been to his church. If he hadn't already hurt or killed Jeremy, I was certain he would soon. And if he had already disposed of the boy, he'd be heading out of town, trying to escape. Or worse, I thought, he'd simply skipped town and left Jeremy alive and locked up somewhere in the woods—someplace no one would ever find him. And finally, thoughts of Gretchen continued to needle me.

Eventually, cars dispersed as we reached Columbia Falls. We pulled into the high school parking lot. I looked out the window at all the people milling around, carrying bags, backpacks, suitcases, and large bottles of water. Ken got out to begin scouring the parking lot for Combs's car and I told him I'd be with him in a minute. The sense of something awful and dark continued to rush through me and made my hands shake. I pulled out my phone again to see if Gretchen had called back, but she hadn't and there were no other texts or calls. I felt helpless. I pounded a fist on the steering wheel and thought of my next move. I knew I needed to get out and do the only thing we could do— keep searching for Combs.

I opened the car door, put one foot out, then stopped when my phone rang. It was the public works director, Dan Hittle. He had the dump's employee's name and number for me. I wrote it down, thanked him, and called immediately.

A woman answered on the second ring.

I told her who I was and asked her if she recalled a woman from county forensics stopping by the landfill to ask some questions.

"Sure," she said. "Blond gal. Wanted to know about asbestos and cyanide. If they could be thrown away here."

"What did you tell her?"

"That you need a permit to dump that kind of stuff, and that she wouldn't find any here."

"This lady," I said. "She say where she was heading?"

"Nope, just thanked me and left."

I thanked the woman and hung up. On my phone, I googled "asbestos + Flathead Valley." Immediately, two government websites on waste districts came up, two on asbestos lawyers, and the fifth hit was an article on CFAC. I clicked on it and scanned it quickly. I knew the aluminum plant sat abandoned, and a strong hunch washed over me.

I was torn. I asked myself whether I should go to the plant to at least check and make sure Gretchen's car wasn't there or get busy looking for Combs, as planned. Something told me Combs wasn't here, and something worse whispered to me that Gretchen was in trouble. But this was all just based on my intuition, and finding Jeremy was the priority.

I hopped out of the car and ran to join Ken, who was searching through the parking area. We walked each row of cars, looking for a white Chevy Nova. Then we waded through hordes of people milling around outside the school. Many sat outside in lawn chairs drinking water and watching the eerie dusty red glow of the sky in the distance. Officers told people to go inside, that the air quality was too poor to sit out in it.

We went through the main entrance of the school into a reception area full of people. The entire place buzzed loudly with conversation. We made our way to the gymnasium. I recognized a couple from West Glacier—people I knew who worked at a café outside the park. They stopped me to ask about the fire, their eyes swimming with worry. Another woman came up to us. "I have goats," she said. "I couldn't bring them. They wouldn't let me bring them because they said there wasn't time for me to load them up. Will they be okay?"

I gave short reassuring answers, told them that the firemen would do their best to keep all structures and livestock safe, but the main priority right now was human lives and that was the reason she was here. She nodded, her face sagging. I continued to move through, searching for Combs.

People spread across the floor on sleeping bags and blankets. A lower rumble of voices rose to the high ceilings. Many sat on the floor, texting and making phone calls. Others stood against the side walls, drinking bottled water and looking dazed and scared. Several women wept quietly into handkerchiefs. Kids ran and played, their parents trying to get them to settle down. Their high-pitched giggles rose above the rumble.

Ken and I split up and poked our way through the gym, looking at everyone. No Combs. When we reached the other side, I motioned at him that we should start working our way back. After another twenty minutes of searching through the crowds, Ken and I met back in the parking lot.

"I don't think he's here," I said. "I think he knows we're onto him."

"Especially since we can't find his car."

I called it in to Ali, who said there were no breaks yet. Airports, train stations, and bus stops had all been notified when we left the church. Wendy had been pulled into the Kalispell police station for further questioning by Herman, but so far he figured she was clueless. "All we can do now," Ali said, "is hope someone spots the guy. IC has also notified the firemen in case they come across any suspicious structures, like locked sheds or small cabins, in the woods. We could use some help at this other evacuation site, though. We rounded up a number of people that know Combs who need to be interrogated. We're short-staffed because of these damn fires."

"On our way," I said, but the pit in my stomach grew deeper. Deep down, I sensed that the other evacuation site was not where would find answers.

31

Gretchen

I KNEW IT HAD come down to just me. Finally, all the burdens I'd carried with me for so long fell away and I felt light-headed, batlike, as if I could swoop up into the rafters and fly away, but I knew it was not that easy. I was in a cage, and there was just me, Combs, and this boy. We could sit and wait for the FBI or the police to find us, but in my bones I felt that was unlikely. I had already kicked myself enough for not telling Ray where I was headed, but at the time it hadn't seemed necessary.

Kicking myself—it was all I ever did, of course with good reason, but now something stronger replaced that instinct. I understood in the dark cage that Gretchen Larson—the girl from Norway who had killed her brother, as awful as she was—was not someone who surrendered. She was someone who coped. I had felt guilty in the abandoned hotel with Wendy because I had fought for my life, but it was my own bull-headedness, my instinct to survive, that was my lifeline, the rope that pulled me from the depths of the dark, cold ice.

Jeremy still slept. I could tell he had begun to dream: his fingers twitched and his head ticked back and forth. I waited hopefully, thinking he might have a severe enough nightmare to wake him screaming, and I would not need to scare him myself. But it didn't happen. Slowly, his limbs stopped moving, and he resumed his deep slumber.

It was time. The candle had burned to a tiny stub and the flame flickered now and again as if it might give out. Combs had come over to check on us and the candle ten minutes before, mumbling something to himself that I couldn't make out.

Now I grabbed the stool he'd given Jeremy to sit on for his meals and turned it over. I knew that it was made up of threaded legs inserted into the base of the stool. First I unscrewed the smaller wooden pieces that connected the wooden legs. Then I unscrewed the legs and kept one of them. It was about half a meter, or twenty inches long. Then I put the rest of the stool back together and propped it against the side of the cage, the missing leg in the back so that it wouldn't be noticeable.

Holding the wooden leg, I turned to Jeremy. He lay sleeping like a cherub and every muscle in my body went rigid. I couldn't look at him for long or I would lose my nerve. I took several deep breaths, readied myself. I pictured my whaling ancestors plundering, unafraid to charge, lifting their harpoons high. Then I lunged. I jumped on top of him screaming and yelling at him to get up. He woke terrified, shrieking, and frantically flailed his arms and tried to scurry away. But I had already pinned his arms, placed the wooden leg around his throat in a choke hold, and pulled him up. Jeremy started sobbing and his cries pierced the cavernous plant, echoing through it and reverberating off the rafters. Shadows from the little candlelight left danced and our shadows jerked like beasts in the cage.

Combs came running over, yelling, "What are you doing? Get away from him!"

I tried to show my teeth and snarl like some deranged creature, and part of me felt shocked to find that it wasn't that hard. Years of pent-up frustration ripped through me. "You've misjudged me," I said huskily. "I'm no fucking lamb."

Combs stared at me, his eyes wide with confusion and surprise, but then he narrowed them again, and it was as though a curtain pulled aside to reveal sheer wrath. I watched the transformation from confused pastor to psycho, but I told myself to stay the course.

Jeremy's body went rigid against mine, and he fought to get loose, yelling for help. My insides crumbled to be hurting him, and I fought the urge to whisper to him that it was an act, to be calm, that I had no intention of hurting him, but I knew the minute I did that, he'd quit screaming and fighting to break free. The more he fought, I forced myself against all instinct to ram the wooden leg against his windpipe even tighter. He kept trying to pry the chair leg free with both hands, but I remained strong.

Combs had taken the bait. He got the keys out of his pocket and went for the lock. I could see his hands shake as he opened it, and my breath quickened. I felt feral, and I saw a flash of my parents' frightened faces when I came to after beating Per. Not now, I told myself. This is not that.

But in a way it was, and I knew it. I had hurt someone—taken a life—in the past, and I was capable of doing it again. I heard the click of the lock as it fell and the rattle of the cage as he slammed it open and lunged forward.

"Back off," I screamed. "Back off, or I'll kill him."

I looked from Combs to the gate. He'd opened it only enough to come inside and he stood before the opening. I knew it was still dangerous to make a run for it with Jeremy. He could grab him if we did. I forced myself to keep talking and tried to lure him away from the opening. "You know I will. I've killed before." I snarled into the still cage and my voice echoed through the yawning darkness. Because it was true, and because it was the first time I'd said it since I was fifteen, the confession burst from me with force—propelled by fury, guilt, and a powerful, interminable will to survive. I felt Jeremy freeze, his body weakening, and I was afraid for a moment that I'd pressed too hard, that I'd choked him to death, but when I slightly loosened my grip, I could feel the back of his rib cage expand with breath against my chest.

Combs stopped and looked at me, his teeth clenched.

"This boy," I said, "is mine."

"No, no. You don't understand. I need him. If I don't do it, it will all get worse."

"What will get worse?"

"Everything. Kyle, the drugs, prison." From the glow of the dwindling candle, I could see a thick layer of sweat shining on his neck. "It will hurt Wendy," he said, almost in a whine. "The fires, the end is near. I have to stop all of this with the sacrifice. God has asked me to do that. You don't understand, everything could end. I am helping him. I am helping everyone."

"No," I screamed. "*You* don't understand. Don't you feel the heat? Don't you see the flames? The men, the firemen, are coming. Can't you hear the engines?"

He nodded blankly at me.

"It's already here. The end is already here. Where will you be going, Mr. Combs?" I said in a low voice.

He stared at me, one side of his brow drawn downward in confusion.

"Answer me! Where will you be going? To heaven or to the fires? Because it's too late for a sacrifice. Don't you see the end is already here? The devil has sent me to ask you if you want to go down to the flames or up," I lifted my eyes to the dark, shadowy ceiling, imagining the dirty, oppressive sky above. "If you want to rise, you must let this boy go."

"No, no, that doesn't make sense." He shook his head and glared at me.

I began to shuffle myself and Jeremy to the side of the cage to make our way toward the door. Combs went to close it. "Don't," I commanded, "or I'll kill him."

He stopped but didn't move out of the way. He began to breath rapidly, angrily, and I could see I'd confused him. Time seemed to slow. He looked at me with distress and hatred. I'd thrown a monkey wrench into his plans, but I could see I'd also activated him. Suddenly a deep roar erupted from him and he charged toward us. I released Jeremy, gave him a push toward the open cage door, and screamed for him to run. Combs had his sights set on me and he came slamming down on me, tripping Jeremy. My head hit the ground and I saw stars, but I forced myself to yell, "Run, Jeremy! Run!"

I tried to get up to run too, but Combs's full weight was on top of me. He tried to shift positions to reach out and grab Jeremy instead, but I kicked wildly, my legs pumping and landing random blows on clothes and sweaty flesh. "Jeremy, run!" I screamed. Combs hit me, his fist crashing into the side of my face. My head snapped to the side, but I didn't black out. Out of the corner of my eye, I saw Jeremy make it through the open gate of the cage and fade into the darkness of the hallway, his footsteps smacking the floor, hitting scraps of metal, and eventually fading in the direction of the huge door at the far end of the plant.

32

Monty

KEN AND I made our way to the other evacuation site, but I couldn't fight my concern that Gretchen not answering her phone had something to do with the case. I pulled over and texted Ali: *Any information about the aluminum plant on Combs's computer?*

She texted back: *No. Techs haven't mentioned anything, but I can double-check.*

Ken and I will quickly go check out the place, I responded. *No stone unturned.*

I turned the car around and drove in the opposite direction, through the center of Columbia Falls toward North Fork Road, without waiting for a reply. Before the bridge, there was a roadblock making sure nobody entered the North Fork area.

I showed my badge and said I needed to get through to search for a missing person. The deputy manning the roadblock let me through, just warned me to be careful. He told me that the fire was being contained on the other side of the river from the plant, but that they were afraid it might hop the river with the wind conditions. He asked if we needed assistance and I told him no, feeling silly for acting on a hunch, but Ken had agreed it would take only a few extra minutes to check it out and it was worth the peace of mind.

We drove down Aluminum Drive and pulled into the parking lot at the plant. Only traces of firelight showed through the opaque air and we couldn't see anything but the flames of the raging fire across the river on the side of Columbia Mountain. Above, the fire shone an ugly tarnished light into the sky. It had spread dangerously close to the road we'd just driven down earlier. I hoped everyone had safely cleared through.

I knew the parking lot was huge, and we couldn't see from one end to the other. "Looks empty, but hard to tell with all of this smoke," Ken said.

"Let's just drive around, make sure we scan the whole area since we've bothered to come out here." We continued toward the plant, and when we neared one of the buildings, I saw a car and pointed to it. Ken squinted in that direction and we drove up to see it more clearly.

"It's hers," I said, jamming our car into park. We both hopped out and looked in. It was empty, with nothing of note on any of the seats.

"What's our move? This place is huge."

"Call for backup. I'll go in—" I had just lifted my hand to motion toward the main entrance when I heard the sound of a faint cry and saw a flash of something moving quickly in the dim light. "You see that?"

"Yes, that her?"

"I'm not sure. It's too dark." I grabbed my flashlight, and we started to run in that direction when I heard a yell for help, and saw another shape—a flash of blond—exiting the main entrance.

"Gretchen," I called out.

"I'm here," she yelled, running toward the parking lot.

"Are you okay? What's going on?"

"Jeremy," she said, breathlessly. Her face looked injured—shocked and in pain. Her hair was wild and messy, as if she'd been in a scuffle. "Do you have him? Do you have him?"

"No, I just saw someone run that way, toward the woods. Was that Jeremy?"

"Yes. it's Combs, Monty. It's Combs." She grabbed the front of my shirt and yanked desperately on it. "We fought. I kicked him back, and he fell. He hit his head, but I'm afraid he might get up. He's in there, near the back."

"Ken, call for backup and an ambulance and go try to find the boy now. I'm going in for Combs." I said, still holding my light and reaching for my gun with my other hand.

"No," Gretchen said. "I'll find Jeremy. You two go in together. You might need backup. I'm not sure if he has a gun."

33

Gretchen

I DIDN'T WAIT FOR Ken to make the calls. I took off running in the direction Monty had pointed, along the edge of the plant and into the woods. The wind pressed the heat into the side of my face, unbearable and persistent. Lights of fire trucks shone on a back road that led to Teakettle Mountain. Firemen fanned out down by the river to fight the fire in case it hopped. Red lights strobed and I could see the movement of men working to stop this inferno from coming any closer to the toxic plant.

I yelled into the blazing night: "Jeremy, Jeremy, I'm so sorry. Jeremy, I didn't mean to hurt you. Jeremy, where are you? Jeremy, please, where are you? You're safe now. I promise."

I wondered if he could have gone to the firemen, but they were still a good distance away and it was so hot, frighteningly hot, and the air was thick with smoke. I hacked as I ran. I thought he would be too scared to approach them. I turned and went farther into a darker patch of woods to my left. Large pines loomed above me, and branches lashed against my face and arms. As I ran, I felt one whip my left cheek. It stung as if it had drawn blood. "Jeremy!" I called, and somewhere behind me, I could hear Ken yelling my name, but I didn't care. I needed to find this boy.

I ran farther, then circled back and went a different direction. My voice sounded like someone else's, and I kept calling his name until I realized hot tears streamed down my face. I tried to swallow them back. If Jeremy could hear me, I didn't want him to think I was crazy like Combs, but I couldn't help it, and it was probably too late anyway, because of what I'd done to him. "Jeremy!" I howled, "I'm so sorry."

I ran some more, frantically looking around, and when I didn't see or hear him, I tried yet another direction. The hot, oppressive woods seemed to be waging battle against me. Divots, lumpy rocks, and wild, tangled grass tripped my feet. The heat seemed to swallow me, and I felt lost, even though I could see the river in the distance, red flames reflecting on the rippling water like blood. I continued to call out, my voice drowning in the wind.

It wasn't until I realized what I was saying that I understood I needed to stop, to quit running around so desperately. I had become aware of my own frantic breathing even among the loud noises from the helicopters above. I heard my own voice, distant and tinny, calling out, "I'm sorry, Per. I'm so sorry."

I stopped yelling. The absence of my calling gave way to a great void. My heart pounded in my chest. I looked back and saw flashlight beams sweeping low and wide in various directions. "Oh, God," I said out loud and crumbled to my knees on the hot, brittle ground, holding my stomach, realizing that I'd unwittingly begun to replace Jeremy's name with my brother's. My insides felt as if they were dissolving like Combs's candle wax with the hot flames surrounding me.

I surrendered, hoping that Monty and Ken would do a better job finding Jeremy than I had. I put my hands to my face and began to sob. Waves of fury and sorrow welled up and I hit the hard ground with the sides of my fists as if I might simply crack it open, allowing it to swallow me into the molten lava deep below. I felt the force of my being pounding the unforgiving earth, and I felt small and useless. The dry dirt simply rose up with the dust as if to mock me.

I put my aching hands to my face and felt my wet cheeks against my palm. Jeremy cannot spend a night out here alone, I kept thinking over and over. I looked through the woods, tall shapes merging into a mass of something so much bigger than me, than Jeremy. I thought of how scared cats bolted into the night and would hole up for days until they felt safe enough to come out. If he went into shock and we didn't find him, he would not survive the night. I wiped my tears, smearing debris across my face and forcing myself to try to calm down, to focus.

Finally I stood up and looked around. Someone had begun to search in the distance with a flashlight and I was about to yell to them that he wasn't in this direction, that I'd already checked it out, when I spotted a lighter-colored shape at the base of a tree, not twenty feet away. At first I thought I was imagining it. My eyes were burning and strained, so I wasn't sure. I went slowly toward it. "Jeremy?" I whispered.

There was no answer.

I went closer, and as I neared, I could see I wasn't imagining it. It was him. He sat in a bundle, hugging his knees, the side of his face pressed against the trunk as if he could disappear into it. "Oh, Jeremy . . ." I reached both of my hands out toward him as if I was approaching a frightened, stray pet. "I'm so sorry, please just stay right where you are. I'm going to take you to your parents. Don't move." My heart pounded with fear that he might run from me.

He sat still, one side of his face alight with the orange glow of the fire, his cheeks wet with tears or sweat and marked with dirt. I knelt beside him. "Jeremy, I'm so, so sorry for what I did. I only did it to get him to come in. I had to make it real so he'd open the padlock."

He nodded, but he seemed catatonic, and I worried he was going into shock. "Jeremy, I'm going to yell for the others now. Don't be startled."

"No," he said, grabbing my arm. "Don't leave."

I reached back for him and he fell sobbing into my arms. I held tight, feeling the ridged bones of his spine. In spite of the heat, his skin felt cold, clammy. The orange and red flames shuddered in my vision, and my blood pulsed through me with all the energy of Jeremy's life, of my life—our ichor. "I won't leave you," I said and began to cry with him. I stroked his hair while he clutched my wet, sweaty T-shirt. "I'm so, so sorry, Jeremy. I'm so very, very sorry."

34

Monty

I'D GONE IN expecting a fight with Combs. I had walked through all the aisles with my gun and flashlight, Ken behind me for backup. When we finally reached the cage at the back of the enormous plant, I saw Combs lying on his back, motionless inside a filthy cage. I carefully approached, Ken still covering me. I gave the pastor a kick to the leg, but he didn't flinch, so I checked his pulse and realized he was still alive.

I cuffed him anyway to be safe, sent Ken out into the woods to search for the boy, and waited for the paramedics. They came quickly—within minutes—since almost all of them from the valley were on standby on the north end because of the fires.

By the time we got Combs out, more backup had arrived, and I organized a quick grid to begin searching through the woods to help Ken and Gretchen. I headed to the north of the plant near the base of Teakettle Mountain, calling out both their names. I had seen the boy for only a flash, but when he ran by, he seemed to be heading in that direction.

I ran until I got to the denser part of the forest, sweeping my flashlight through the tall pines. Ash fell around me and my beam lit it up like snowflakes. My breathing was too fast in the smoke, and it made me hack. I stumbled my way through the tangled brush and the lumpy roots of the forest floor. I felt extremely relieved to have Combs in our custody, but fear for Jeremy mushroomed inside me. That we'd found

363

his captor at all was more than I'd hoped for, but I had a sinking feeling, the irony that after all of this, we might lose him again. That he might never return from these angry woods.

I brushed the thought away and kept my beam low and wide, straining to see through the cloudy darkness. The hot wind poured out from the canyon. I went up a small knoll, and when I reached the other side, I thought I heard whimpering. I strained to block out the other sounds: the men calling out to one another, the helicopter blades slicing the sky, sirens in the distance. I was certain I heard someone weeping.

I quieted my breathing myself and listened for the direction. When I figured it out, I went there, my light skimming across the trunks of trees until finally I caught a glimpse of two bodies hunched at the base of a large pine. My first instinct was that these were two horribly wounded individuals, but I could make out Gretchen and I knew she wasn't so wounded that she couldn't run.

I called her name, but as I got closer and could see them desperately clutching each other, I walked over and gently reached out and touched both of their shoulders. Even in the heat, I could feel they both had become cold. Jeremy had begun to shake, and Gretchen's teeth clattered, which told me they might both be in shock. Her eyes looked right past me at first, but after a second, she made eye contact with me. I radioed to Ken that I had found them, then I simply tipped my head to indicate that it was time to get going, time to get out of these woods and to an ambulance.

Gretchen nodded and nudged Jeremy upward. Her legs buckled at first, and I caught her, grabbing her arm to steady her. Then I held Jeremy's other arm, helping him stand, and directed both of them toward the parking lot, where the flashing lights of emergency vehicles waited.

As we walked, I looked out at the hillside across the river. A patch of fire had jumped and blazed on a small plot of land just southwest of Teakettle Mountain. The flames snaked up the trees in a great flourish. Firemen surrounded it, hoses spitting great fans of water across the wilderness, keeping it back from the toxic plant.

Because of the fire, I instinctively wanted to rush them, but I didn't dare. They both seemed too fragile and I didn't want to frighten the boy any more than he already had been. Jeremy clutched Gretchen's shirt the entire way, and when the paramedics met us on our way back with a stretcher and led Jeremy to it, he wouldn't let go of her. She walked by his side to the parking lot, and when they loaded Jeremy up, they took Gretchen too, deciding it was best if she stayed next to him.

I wanted to ride with them, to hold their hands and tell them both that all would be okay, but I couldn't. I had statements to give to the feds about the apprehension of Combs. I would have to meet them at the hospital afterward.

I could tell Gretchen had been shaken deeply, and as for Jeremy, I didn't want to contemplate the overwhelming sadness I saw in his eyes. But I also sensed he had parents who—regardless of the strains between them—would do all that they could to make his reentry into life as gentle as possible.

35

Gretchen

At the ER, they separated Jeremy and me, and got right to the examinations. Jeremy had been too weak to protest when my hand finally left his. They took me to a private room, began checking my blood pressure, my pupils, my ears, and my heart, and took some blood. A nurse cleaned the cuts on my face, including the old one I'd gotten from sleepwalking the other night, and butterflied the newer ones. When the doctor came in, I assured her I'd only lost consciousness for a small amount of time, and that I didn't need a scan, but it didn't matter. She sent me to radiology for a CAT scan to rule out a traumatic brain injury and for X-rays of my left shoulder.

When the scan ruled out a subdural hematoma, the nurse made sure I was comfortable and gave me a painkiller. I had begun to shiver from the trauma, and she placed heated blankets on me and hooked me up to an IV because they insisted that I'd become dehydrated from shock and smoke exposure. I wondered about Jeremy— thinking that if I, who'd been in the plant for only the better part of a day, experienced dehydration, Jeremy must be much worse off. When I asked her about him, she said she'd let me know how he was doing as soon as she found out. She then brought me two packs of ice, for my shoulder and my throbbing head, and told me to get some rest.

"No," I said, "I can't." I immediately pictured myself roaming through the halls of the hospital like a zombie, but my mind and my body felt weighted with a thousand stones pulling me into sleep. "I have a sleep dis . . . ," I slurred. "I can't, I can't . . . sleep here."

"What's that, honey?" the nurse asked.

"I need someone to make sure I don't sleepwalk," I said.

"Oh, okay, honey, we'll do that, but I don't think you need to worry." She smiled kindly at me. I fell asleep, unable to move, and later when I woke to the nurse shaking my arm, I heard voices in the corridor.

I opened my eyes slowly, my head still foggy with painkillers, and turned to look at her. I could barely move my head because my neck was so sore. "How's Jeremy?" I asked.

"He's fine," she said. "But there's some folks here who need to talk to you, that's why I've woken you. Are you okay to talk?"

"Yes, yes, I'm fine."

Monty and Ali came in, both wearing close-lipped smiles. "How's our star?" Monty asked.

"Oh, please," I said.

"Gretchen," Ali said, "are you feeling up to giving us a statement?"

I tried to nod, but it hurt. "Yes. I'm fine."

The nurse raised my bed so I could face them. Monty told me to take my time, and Ali turned on a recorder. "Do you think you can take us through it? Every detail?"

"Of course," I said, my voice scratchy. I cleared my throat. "I'd been looking at samples from the gas and brake pedals in the Chevy," I began and slowly told them everything, from the moment I left the dump and arrived at the plant until I kicked Combs.

"So you kicked him and he fell? That's how he hit his head?"

"I think that's what happened." I said. "It's kind of a blur, but I was kicking him like crazy. He'd hit me in the face, and I saw him reach for the leg of the stool I'd unscrewed, but I got to it first. I tried swinging at his head, but missed. I was still on the floor and he'd gotten to a standing position, so I kicked him as hard as I could with both legs and knocked him back away from me so I could get up. He stumbled and fell back, crashing his head on the base of the vat. I saw blood, and he went limp, and that's when I ran outside and found Monty and Ken."

I told them about how I went into the woods to find Jeremy. I skipped the parts about crying and hitting the ground. It wasn't their business. I told them how I spotted Jeremy by the tree, and how when I went to call for help he grabbed me and we stayed that way until Monty found us huddled against the tree.

"Were you disoriented at that time?"

I swallowed, trying to think of how to answer the question. I knew she was trying to figure out why I just stayed with the boy and didn't get help or try to get him out of the dangerous woods. "I saw the flashlights from the men looking," I said. "Jeremy looked like he was going into shock. I didn't think it was wise to move him on my own and I knew help was coming."

Both of them stared at me as if they weren't sure they were satisfied with my answer. Then Monty said, "Well, given the trauma, the shock, the fire, it's completely understandable that you'd do exactly as the boy requested of you, which was to stay with him. And you were right, we found you quickly."

"Okay then." Ali turned off her recorder, and Monty put away his notebook.

"My turn," I said.

"Shoot," Ali said.

"How's Jeremy?"

"He's fine. Sedated. His level of shock was more severe than yours and he's dehydrated as well. He's sleeping and his parents are by his side."

"And Combs?"

"In the ICU. Pretty serious head injury. We're not sure if he'll make it yet, but that's not something you need to worry about. If he makes it, he makes it. If he doesn't, well, that's just the way it goes. We're hoping he does, though. We have questions, as you can imagine."

"Do you think he's done this before? The way he went on, when he said that he needed to prove himself *again*, it sounded like he had."

"It seems that you might not only be a hero, but a damn good detective as well," Monty said. He told me about the notes in the Bible at Combs's house and how the years matched the ones I'd pointed out to Monty that night at his place. They told me Combs's house would be searched as soon as the IC gave the go-ahead to cross the canyon. In the meantime, there was nothing we could do but hope the house didn't burn down along with all the evidence that might be in it.

"And," Monty said, "I hate to inform you, but you won't be working that scene. Ridgeway's called, told us to tell you he'll visit in the morning after you've had some rest, but he said to make sure you knew that you will be taking a few days off at least."

I frowned. "I already took a day off, and I'm fine."

"Uh-huh." Monty smiled. "Getting samples at an abandoned aluminum plant is not exactly R&R."

I sighed, but I wasn't done with my questions. "And Wendy?"

"She's up next," Ali said. "Speaking of which, we should get going." She reached out and tapped my arm twice with the ends of her fingers as if she was testing my reflexes, probably the warmest gesture I was going to get from her. "We're glad you're okay, Gretchen. And," she added, "we're really glad you found that boy."

"Thank you," I said right before the nurse knocked, saying it really was time that I got some more rest.

"Couldn't agree more." Monty followed Ali toward the door. Right before he exited, he turned to Ali. "One sec," he said to her. "I'll catch up to you."

He came over to my bed. "Gretchen," he said. Something else welled in his eyes, a look I'd never seen on his face before—a mixture of empathy, curiosity, and understanding. It stunned me momentarily because the last time I'd seen that look was on my doctor in Norway.

"What is it?" I said.

He pursed his lips, still studying me with his eyes, then shook his head as if to shake all thoughts away. "Nothing," he said. "You just take care. I'd like to get your car for you. From the plant. Your keys in here?" He went to the chair on which Ali had dropped my pack and picked it up.

"Front pocket," I said, my head still spinning from the look he'd given me.

Monty dug around in the pack, pulling out the plastic bag with the belt buckle. "What's this?"

"Oh," I said, my throat scratchy again. I took a sip of water. "That's the buckle from the dig I wanted to show you."

Monty went quiet, tilting the bag around to look at it. Then as if suddenly deflated, he slumped into the chair.

"What's wrong?"

Monty didn't speak at first, just looked at me with an anguished look, then out the window behind me. I knew there was nothing out there but a dark night accented with yellow streetlights and a parking lot full of cars. "I do remember this." He held the Baggie in his palm as if it were heavier than it was, his hand sinking from the weight. "I didn't realize it when you said it on the phone, but seeing it now, in front of me. The colors. It's, of course . . . Nathan." He sighed with affection. "Now I remember, he was so psyched when he mail-ordered this."

I tried to push off the bed and sit straight up, but my neck and shoulder screamed at me and I sunk back into the hospital bed. "Monty," I said. "Are you sure?"

"As sure as I can be. But it would never hold up in court. How many kids had these belt buckles back then?"

"I'm sure a lot, but still, with those dates on the note and given the location in relation to Combs's house, it's pretty clear, isn't it?"

"Yes, it is."

"Let's hope he lives so that we can verify all this, for the Faraways, for the Ericksons."

Monty stared at me, that wounded, beautiful look swimming back into his dark eyes. He stood up and came over to me. "Gretchen, listen to me. If this guy doesn't make it and we can't question him, you will not blame yourself. Do you understand?"

He spoke to me like I was a child, and for a moment, I felt anger, but it was very quickly replaced by relief. The words were so simple— so parental, and I'd never been spoken to that way, ever. "Understand?" he repeated. "You've carried enough of that load, already."

I froze at his words. I knew he knew, but I didn't want to ask. I wasn't ready to discuss it, not while I lay like a wounded bird in a hospital bed. If I said anything, I'd cry.

Finally, when he realized he wasn't going to get an answer from me, he reached out and softly brushed my forehead with his knuckles. "I'll tell the nurse in charge to make sure you sleep soundly," he said, holding up my keys. "I'll take care of your car, okay?"

I nodded.

"And I'll check on you later." He gave me a wink and left.

36

Monty

THE COUNTY HEADQUARTERS was quieter than I expected. It would normally be buzzing with the news at a time like this, but the station was fairly empty, with most hands still on deck for the fire. Ali was chomping at the bit for the doctors to make progress with Combs, not only because she wanted the asshole to pay, but also because she wanted to see if he'd identify and claim responsibility for the other children on Gretchen's list. I'd told her about the belt buckle, about my history with the victim. She looked at me sadly for a moment, then got back to work.

She instructed Ken and me to go to Wendy's house because she wanted us to determine if she really didn't know or have anything to do with Combs's plans. She also wanted us to make sure Wendy didn't go to the hospital on her own. We were to escort her there to avoid any kind of a scene in case she ran into the Coreys.

When we arrived at Wendy's, the cop already stationed outside asked if he could leave. We told him yes and walked to the front door as he drove off.

Wendy invited us in and we all sat in the living room. Wendy looked as though she might crawl into a hole and die. She was pale, and she held her stomach and rocked back and forth in the typical way that grief makes one do. She offered us nothing, not because she was impolite, she just was in no shape to entertain guests. I went into her kitchen to grab her a glass of water. When I brought it to her, she just stared at it as if she'd never seen water before.

372

"I just don't understand," she whispered. "I just don't understand how any of this can be true. He's always been a good, good man."

"I'm sure he's been a good father to you," I said. "I'm sure he's been a good pastor, but apparently he's ill. Very, very ill."

She turned to me and with a creased brow asked, "How could I not know this about my own father?"

"I don't know. Did you have any indication at all that something was off?"

She shook her head slowly, carefully, thinking. Her eyes welled with tears. "I've been racking my brain. The only thing I can think of is that he became very quiet for long periods of time, and was sometimes difficult to talk to or get ahold of. I assumed it was just the way he was, you know, moody. I mean . . ." She motioned upstairs, where Kyle was sleeping, "I have a son who is temperamental as well. I figured it ran in the family. I never, in my worst moments, could have dreamt that he was capable of . . ." She contorted her face in pain and put her hand to her mouth. "Excuse me," she said, and got up and ran to the bathroom down the hall. We could hear her dry heaves and figured this was not the first time she'd been driven to the toilet since she'd been informed.

We waited patiently until she came back out, her face ghostly white and thin. I could tell that this was ripping her apart in every way imaginable.

"It's not your fault," I said to her as she sat back down. "But can I ask you, do you have any idea at all why your father would have snapped this way?"

Wendy shook her head blankly.

"Wendy," I said. "when I searched your father's home, there was a photo of you, your mom, and your dad and another dark-haired boy who looked a little older than you. Do you know who that boy might have been?"

She cocked her head and thought for a moment. "My cousin?"

I continued to stare at her.

"Of course," she said, as if something was dawning on her. "My cousin. From my mom's side. He used to come and spend summers with us, and one summer, well, it was tragic, but he died under our care."

"How did that happen?"

"We were all at the river and he and my dad went out fishing in a canoe." She shook her head. "It's one of those awful memories, one of those blink-of-an-eye things, but Lance didn't want to wear a life vest, said he was too old for one. My parents argued about it, but my dad said he'd be okay, that they were just going a short stretch and that he'd bring it along in the boat for him anyway."

I thought of Ron and Linda, Ron feeling responsible for thinking Jeremy was old enough to spend some alone time at the camp.

"But once they were out there, Lance had gotten too excited when he caught a fish on the line and fell out. Dad tried to throw him the life vest, but the river was carrying him away too fast. Dad tried to row to him, but a rapid carried him in a different direction. Lance got pulled under by some deadfall, and by the time Dad and some other rafters reached him, it was too late."

Working in Glacier and living around mountain lakes and rushing rivers my whole life, I had heard this story before. "I'm sorry to hear that," I said.

"It tore my mom and dad up. My mom's sister never forgave her and . . . well, a few years later, my mom got breast cancer and died. It was all such a wave of disasters for me, for us. I was so full of grief over losing my mother that I never thought of how it might have affected him, but I know he took it really hard. He felt responsible, that he'd let my mother and her family down, that he'd even let God down somehow. I remember he'd go into his office for hours and pray and pray after that. But . . ." Tears flooded her eyes. "He's been a good father to me. A little weird at times, a little strict about the religion stuff, but he's always wanted to protect me, take care of me."

I wrote it all down as she spoke. The drowning incident seemed significant, potentially the tipping point for Combs. "Weird how?" I asked.

"Just, you know, withdrawn. Silent. He left me alone for large periods of time. I figured it was normal. You don't really question how your parents act when that's all you've ever known, do you?"

"No, I guess you don't," I said.

"Do you think Kyle has any idea about all of this?" Ken asked.

"I don't know," Wendy said. "I just don't know, but if he does, it might explain why he's changed so much. Oh, God"—she clutched her stomach tighter—"I hope he didn't help my dad abduct that poor boy."

"I don't think we should assume that," I said. "We'll speak to him." I didn't say it to Wendy, but I knew we would also want to get confirmation from the officers who'd been asked to check with Kyle's friends that he was where he said he was the day Jeremy went missing. "From what we can tell, your father hid this well. We'll find out more from Gretchen and the boy, and from your father, if he comes out of this coma."

Wendy stared at me as if she didn't know what to do or say. Her grief was palpable, and in my gut, I felt she was innocent.

• • •

We escorted Wendy and Kyle to the hospital and showed her a private room where she could wait to speak to doctors about her father's condition. I left her and Kyle alone there. We'd woken him at the house and questioned him as well. He seemed better, helpful even. As if the whole event had finally frightened him—at least temporarily—out of his own selfish rebellion.

It didn't seem like he knew about his grandfather's wacked-out plans, but he admitted to thinking his grandfather was often weird and eccentric, praying all the time and losing his temper very easily at Kyle, sometimes saying things that Kyle admitted seemed overdramatic.

Kyle said he'd sometimes preach things to him through tears, and he'd wondered about his psychological stability a few times. He'd told us that he remembered his grandfather telling him that he'd caused his wife's cancer—that if he hadn't upset God, He wouldn't have taken her from him in the first place. That if it weren't for his sins, Kyle would have then had a chance to meet his grandmother.

After I left the private waiting room, I went to find Jeremy's room, which was on another floor of the hospital.

When I arrived, a nurse informed me that Jeremy was sedated and sleeping. Another nurse had the younger children in another room where they could also sleep. Ron and Linda sat beside Jeremy's bed, their chairs scooted up close, Linda holding his hand, Ron resting a palm on Jeremy's blanketed leg. I gave them both a closed-lip smile and went over and peered at Jeremy. Before I pulled the parents aside, I wanted to see him. I wanted to look into his eyes and see that he knew he was safe now, but I'd accept peaceful sleeping for now. He appeared angelic.

Ron and Linda looked tired but relieved beyond measure to have their child back. I took them in—their disheveled selves—and tried to imagine what it must be like to be these parents and to hear some of the things I was about to tell them. I realized I couldn't fathom the level of fear they'd experienced over the past days and the overwhelming relief to have Jeremy return, to be watching their sleeping child, holding his hand.

Linda reached out and pushed a strand of his hair off his forehead, then gently passed the back of her hand over his face. I whispered softly, "Would you like to go in the hall to talk?"

Linda nodded, and they stood up, glancing back at Jeremy again before following me out. We took seats in a conference room not far down the hall and I could see the familiar fear flood back into their eyes. They were afraid to hear what I had to say—that even though they had Jeremy back, I might still be able to somehow shatter the reality that he was safe down the hall, resting. That I might have the power to send them hurtling back through time to their miserable motel room filled with nightmares and unfathomable grief. "I'm so glad to see Jeremy resting," I said.

Linda nodded, a bit of the fear leaking away to hear me speak about her son's state, the reality of his safety.

"We'd really like to get back in there, in case he wakes," Ron said. "Can we make this quick?"

"Certainly," I said and filled them in about Combs, explaining that we had him in our custody. I told them about his condition and that we wanted to keep him alive to put him through a trial, to get more answers, but for now we didn't know the prognosis. I told them everything that I knew that had happened in the plant with Gretchen, about how Jeremy ran into the woods, and about blanks we'd filled in ourselves. "We think he's done this before, but we're not positive, and we'd prefer you remain discreet until we know for certain."

Ron swallowed hard. "We will."

"I know the doctors have already shared with you the results of Jeremy's examination—that there's no sign of sexual abuse that we can detect. Of course, depending on the type of abuse, we can't always determine if it's occurred unless the child tells us. But there's nothing to suggest that Combs was driven by that. What we do understand, although our information is incomplete as of now, is that he's been psychologically unwell and hiding it successfully for some time, even from his own daughter. As I just said, it's possible Jeremy isn't the first, that he's done this before. Not necessarily in the plant, because it would have been in operation during the other time periods we're investigating. We think all the firemen and law enforcement in the area may have pushed him to find someplace different, and the abandoned plant was convenient, right outside the canyon."

"It's so crazy. All of it. We just don't understand. Why Jeremy?"

"I don't expect you to. None of us can fully understand why someone does something like this. But to try to answer your question: because Jeremy happened to be there," I said. "It's difficult to know when you're dealing with this level of psychological imbalance, but we're guessing that it was a combination of things—because Jeremy happened to be in the wrong place at the wrong time, because he resembles the nephew Combs feels responsible for killing years before. Jeremy is similar in size and his hair color is the same. What we believe—and again, these are conjectures at this point—is that perhaps after years of keeping it together after the losses, he began to buckle under the stress. To feel that God had been punishing him and was speaking to him, telling him to make a sacrifice to prove his love and put things right again."

I let that sink in and gave them a moment to respond, but they didn't. They stared at me with wide eyes, not saying a word. Linda held her hand over her chest, opened her mouth to say something, then closed it.

"We know," I continued, "with Jeremy anyway, he borrowed a truck that no one would realize he'd taken because it was an old farm truck, out of sight. He knew about the truck because he used to work the farm when he wasn't at church." I thought of his talk in Great Falls on bi-vocational work. "He was smart enough to know that he could get caught if he used his own vehicle. After borrowing the truck, we suspect he went trolling, for lack of a better word. We don't think he stalked Jeremy. We think he just came across him in the park that day—very unfortunate timing—and Combs considered it a sign from God that he came across a boy who fit the profile."

Linda's face began to contort in agony and she whispered, "We should have never left him alone like that."

"Please," I said. "This is neither of your faults. These things are totally unlikely, like an asteroid hitting the earth. I know you know this, but every parent has to begin trusting their child to become independent at some point. You should not blame yourselves."

"Honey, I know it's tough." Ron didn't bother to reach out to her as he did when I first met them, and I sensed that even though they'd gotten their son back, there were now ghosts between them, things they'd said under the strain that damaged their relationship. Either that, or they simply were saving every ounce of their affection for Jeremy and the other kids until they regained their reserves. "Let's just be glad he's back," Ron said.

"Yes," I seconded. "And unless you have any further questions, I don't want to keep you from him any longer."

I told them they could call me if they did. Then we all stood and I watched them quietly go back into their son's room.

37

Gretchen

I WOKE IN THE morning to sunlight leveling in through the hospital window blinds. I'd been woken up every hour during the night to make sure I was neurologically healthy and hadn't slipped into a coma from some undetected problem. They'd already been in before sunrise to take my blood.

I waited for a nurse for little while, staring at the walls around me, at the TV hanging in the corner. I considered turning it on to see what was being said about the whole ordeal—I was sure it had made national news and I hoped that a picture of me was not being used. I didn't think it would go international, but you never knew. The thought of people in Sandefjord potentially seeing me and recognizing me on the news all these years later made me queasy. Or perhaps it was the lack of food and the smoke I'd inhaled still churning my stomach.

I knew it was early and that the nurse would be coming in soon with breakfast, but I couldn't wait. I got up, my muscles much stiffer than I expected, and put on my filthy clothes. I realized that after I'd been knocked out, I must have been operating on sheer adrenaline the rest of the day.

The nurse, a middle-aged woman with reddish hair, came in as I zipped my pants.

"Oh, you're up," she said.

"Yes, I thought I'd get dressed."

"But your, you know, your people"—I assumed she was referring to Ali and Monty, perhaps Ridgeway—"they said they'd bring you some clean clothes. Those are filthy, and you need breakfast and to be checked out again by a physician before you leave."

Fatigue spread through my body at just the effort of standing and talking to her. Again, I felt surprised at what a tussle, a few knocks on the head, and an evening running around in smoke could do to a human body. I sat back down.

"Really." The nurse came to me. "You should lie back down. Have something to eat."

"Okay." I agreed. "But can I just sit here for now?"

"Yes," she said. "Rest, and I'll get your breakfast, but first, I want to take your blood pressure, your temperature, get a read on your oxygen levels. I'll be right back."

She left the room for a moment, then came back in, clamped a temperature gauge on my forefinger, and got out a blood pressure cuff. "The doctor will want to see you to decide if you need additional tests run."

"I won't," I said. "I'm fine."

"Yes, you probably are, but it's standard procedure." She smiled politely at me.

"Can you tell me how the boy, Jeremy, is?"

"Yes, he's doing well. We checked his vitals all night, and everything looks good. He's sleeping now. His family has been with him all night."

"Do you know which room he's in?"

"He's just two doors down from you." She pointed to our left.

• • •

After I ate some breakfast and was instructed to hang tight until the doctor came for her rounds, I left my room and walked down the hall. I found Jeremy's room easily. The door was open and I peeked in. A medium-size dark-haired woman sat slumped in a chair sleeping, and when she sensed me there, she opened her eyes, then smiled, and got up and stepped out into the corridor.

"You must be Gretchen?"

I nodded. "How is he?"

"He's good. Exhausted, fatigued, you know, it's been—" Her voice broke. "My husband and I"—she put both hands on my arm—"we can't thank you enough. We owe you . . . we owe you everything for bringing our baby to back to us." She stared at me with deep admiration, and I felt overwhelmed. I hadn't been looked at that way in so long, maybe ever. I could see in her eyes the full and complete love of a mother whose child had come so close to being ripped from her and saw that the force of that love was being shared with me right there in that hallway. It was a haunting and magnificent moment for me.

She reached out and embraced me, holding me tight, and I could feel her hand patting my back. It took my breath away, feeling a mother's hug again, feeling her overwhelming gratitude wash over me, momentarily replacing all those years of blank stares and flinches from my own mother.

She pulled away and said, "My husband went home with the kids so they could get some sleep. I stayed with Jeremy all night, and I was waiting for Ron to come this morning so I could come see you. I peeked in your room earlier, but you were sleeping. Come in, do you want to sit down?"

"No, no, I just wanted to see Jeremy. To check on him."

"Yes, by all means, please, come in. He's woken a few times already, but he dozes in and out now."

She walked me back into the dark room. The shades were pulled and Jeremy lay sleeping. I went and stood next to his bed, careful of the monitor and tubes and wires still connected to him. He looked very thin to me, especially under the blanket. Linda leaned against the wall, quiet, and the monitor chirped softly. I watched him with his eyes closed and his face still and peaceful until his eyes fluttered open. Even in the dim light, I could see his pupils were large and black. He stared at me without moving. Then his eyes filled with tears, and I was worried that the sight of me had brought back awful memories. "Hi, Jeremy," I said. "It's Gretchen, from the—"

"I know," he said before I finished. "I know." He reached out and took my hand, this time gently, not frantically like the night before.

"How are you feeling?" I asked.

"I'm okay. Just tired," he said.

"I bet. Have you eaten?"

"Yes, this morning. I was hungry."

"I'm thinking you were probably *very* hungry," I said, smiling. He nodded and smiled back. We stayed that way for a few moments, staring at each other until his eyes closed again. I reached out and swept his hair off his forehead, and he opened his eyes again for a moment. They glistened with moisture, and he whispered the words "thank you."

"No thank-yous necessary," I said, and couldn't resist. I leaned over, careful of his IV, and pressed my cheek against his frail neck. I could feel myself tremble with emotion, and I could feel a single hot, wet tear fall onto my cheek.

38

Monty

ONCE THE DOCTOR declared Jeremy fit for travel, three days after we'd found him, I saw the Coreys off at the airport. They were ready to leave the mountains, probably forever. After my last wave good-bye, I went back to Glacier, my home, my haven. Rain had finally come, and it had been coming down for eight hours straight so far. The mist hung low over the mountains, and we were thankful for the long-awaited downpour, which was helping to rapidly put an end to the fires.

I sat in our conference room at headquarters with Ali and Herman. They had stopped in to fill Ken and me in on a few things. Combs had lasted another forty-eight hours in the ICU, then passed away the evening before Jeremy left the hospital. Of course, we had nothing substantial yet to connect the other crimes directly to him. The sermons we found tucked in the Bible weren't themselves proof of anything.

"The search of his house is complete," Ali said, taking a sip of coffee from a mug that read I'd Rather Be Hiking—GNP. I told both her and Herman that they should keep their cups. "Souvenirs." I smiled.

"So what did they find?" I asked.

"Ray found some trace with Luminol in the shed. It's very old and degraded. He's sending it in for DNA analysis, says we'll be lucky if we get anything. But we're keeping our fingers crossed that we'll be able to make a match to either the DNA in the bones you found or to Samuel Erickson's family. Any luck getting the Faraways to submit?"

"No, not yet," I said. "The sister, Molly Sands, called me, said she'd tried to persuade her parents, but they're being stubborn. I'm not sure we should keep pushing them at this point. I mean, if they don't want to know, we have to respect that."

Ali frowned. "How could they not want to know?"

I thought about the Faraways' sad faces. They had all been ripped apart by Nathan's disappearance, just as the Coreys would have been if Gretchen hadn't gone to the plant.

"I don't know. I keep wondering if having answers would give them unexpected comfort, or if uncertainty truly is better for them, because it means they can still hold on to some hope."

Ali didn't respond. She thought about it, taking another sip of the bitter coffee I'd brewed an hour earlier. Her hair had frizzed and curled into ringlets from the rain.

Herman nodded. "I think you're right. We can't be the judges of that."

"That doesn't mean we shouldn't keep trying to solve this," Ali said.

"I agree. We just might not be able to do it by pestering that particular family for DNA," I said.

"What about the buckle? Are you going to show it to them?"

I'd already thought about it. I knew the Essex grave belonged to Nathan, even though I couldn't prove it yet, but I didn't feel the need to push that onto the Faraways if they weren't ready for it—especially if, after all these years, they'd come to the conclusion that it was better for them to not know. After the vanishing of a child, the web that family members build to sustain themselves is so fragile. It hangs precariously in the air on tentative structures, its thin, frail filament cast in an attempt to simply get through one day at a time. To tear that filament apart now without total certainty seemed like a cruel prospect. I thought of the ways in which I'd built my own webbing over the years—my job, my compulsions for tidiness and order, and my need to search for the truth. "Probably not," I said. "Maybe I could tell Molly, since she feels differently, but I don't know. I'd prefer it if we had more solid proof first. Let me know about the blood," I said.

Herman and Ali stood, both shook my hand, and told me they'd be talking to me soon.

"Thanks for the cup," Herman said.

"Yeah," Ali said, and held it up. "Maybe I'll actually do it one of these days."

"What's that?" I asked.

"Go hiking." She smiled and left, and I sat in my office alone. The birds outside chirped gleefully in spite of the downpour, perhaps because of it. I sighed, thinking I wasn't sure how I felt. It had all happened so fast in a whirlwind of smoke, fear, and very little sleep. And I knew that in this business, it wouldn't be long before another AMBER Alert was issued, or another child turned up hurt or dead, attacked by his or her own family or some stepdad or mother's boyfriend. But for now this one was safe and sound on his way back to Ohio. And for that, I thanked the ground, the stars, and everything in between, including, of course, the rain.

39

Gretchen

Six days after finding Jeremy in the aluminum plant, I woke up at dawn to the delicious smell of wet soil and foliage. I threw on some jeans, a T-shirt, and a fleece. The temperature had dropped considerably. Three days before, the wind had finally pushed in a large cold front. It brought heavy rain, and even snow to the higher elevations, finally snuffing out most of the fires and getting the larger ones to manageable states. Today was the first clear day.

My shoulder and neck were healing from my tussle with Combs, and I felt like a kid again, giddy to see clear, blue skies. I turned on the radio in my kitchen as I made tea and listened to the local newscaster claiming that the two main fires in and near Glacier—Sheep and Trail Creek—and the most recent, Columbia Fire, were 90 percent under control, something they weren't expecting until the fall. The scope of the cold front was unexpected but very much welcome.

A pale, tangerine-colored light spread in a thin line over the eastern sky above the mountains, and I decided to take my steaming cup outside and watch the sun rise. I unlocked my front door and went out. The air smelled of tangy, freshly cut wet hay, and one of the neighbor horses whinnied in the distance. I walked over to the split-railed fence on the edge of my yard and leaned on the smoothly warped and weathered wood to stare out over the golden fields.

The horses had their heads turned toward the eastern mountains, as if they were also watching the start of the new day. Thin clouds left behind by the storm front had stretched above like silver blankets and the rising sun began to bathe them and the mountaintops pale pink and orange. Emotions I couldn't describe ran through me at the beautiful sight, and I felt a sensation that something askew inside me had been returned to its proper alignment.

Not because I had become a hero. That's what the papers had called me, but don't think the irony wasn't lost on me. The last time I was featured in a newspaper, I was *Marerittjente*—Nightmare Girl. And deep down, of course, I did not feel like a hero. In fact, I felt fraudulent even thinking of that. I still felt terrible for attacking Jeremy, adding insult to injury, even though I know it got the job done. I suppose when you've spent fifteen years beating yourself up—carrying a bleeding albatross around your neck—it doesn't simply go away, even after such profound catharsis.

I had spent some time with Jeremy in the hospital before he left. We played cards and watched a little TV, just sitting quietly together. We've agreed to stay in touch and exchanged email addresses. I think he'll be happy to be home in Ohio, and to see his buddies again, but I'm not sure how that will all go. He fell silent when I asked him about his friends, and I could sense he was nervous about how he might be perceived.

Linda said she also wants to stay in touch and has promised to keep me posted on Jeremy. She, Ron, and Jeremy had already spoken extensively with a psychiatrist during the first few days while Jeremy recuperated. They've been advised to watch him carefully, to avoid overloading him with schoolwork or simply assuming that everything should just return immediately back to normal. Linda said the doctor also warned her that Jeremy would probably exhibit erratic behavior for some time, as well as possibly reverting back to whiny, younger childlike conduct. Linda said she understood and even expected that.

While still in the hospital, they'd already lined up a counselor for him in Ohio. They're hopeful he'll communicate and not shut down, which, according to the psychiatrist Ron and Linda spoke to, is the most important thing—that he doesn't bury or bottle it up. Burying trauma, she claimed, does the most damage of all.

It was a slow process, I imagined—helping your child to trust the world again—and I felt confident they would be very patient through it all. Linda and Ron planned on finding someone back home to talk to as well.

In general, the details of the case still linger. I know Ken was upset with himself for not checking the hotel alibi and the conference more thoroughly. Monty, Ali, and Herman were kicking themselves for not checking the aluminum plant earlier, with that bumper sticker right in front of their faces. But I know they shouldn't be so hard on themselves. With the plant shut down and the sticker being so old, it hardly seemed relevant. They did what any detectives would do—they checked the names of former employees.

I've concluded that Monty knows about my history now—that he looked into it and put the pieces together. He won't say it directly, but I could see it in his eyes, in the way they swam with empathy at the hospital when he looked at me, how he told me not to blame myself and that I'd already carried a load long enough. When he said he'd make sure the nurses attended me while I slept, that clinched it for me. It wasn't pity Monty expressed, though, and that was important. I couldn't bear pity. I didn't come all the way to America, to the mountains and expansive skies of Montana to live under the weight of shame or even sympathy. I know that my secret remains safe with him. I've always trusted Monty.

In a way, I've buried trauma myself by keeping secrets. But I didn't bury anything at fifteen when it happened. I railed, moaned, cried, threw up, went numb, got angry, became inconsolable, and ran through a million other emotions. I remain thankful for the help I received in Norway from both my sleep doctor and my counselors. They helped me process what I could of the ordeal and helped me hang on enough to take things one day at a time. Which is exactly what the Coreys are now forced to do. Wendy and Kyle too.

They visited me, Wendy and Kyle. They came to my house two days ago, after I returned from the hospital. I slept most of the first day: deep, peaceful sleep with no sleepwalking symptoms. I moved slowly at first. But by the afternoon, I felt better and I answered her call and invited them over. The three of us sat inside drinking tea and watching the horses huddling under a distant tree in the adjacent field through my living room window. Wendy could hardly look me in the face when I told her I was sorry that her father hadn't come out of his coma. I could tell she was not only reeling from grief, that she felt deeply crushed and responsible in some way for what happened to Jeremy and to me, even though she didn't say it. She could hardly speak at all, and Kyle actually tried to make conversation in her silence.

Because I wanted to offer her some solace, I told her that what happened to me in that plant paled in comparison to what happened to Jeremy, and that I was simply glad I could get the boy out before he ended up like the others. When I mentioned them—the other possible victims—her face went white like a snow goose, and she put her face into her hands and began to weep.

I wasn't sure how she would ever get over what her father had done, but then again you'd be surprised what the human spirit can endure. I didn't tell her that I thought she'd get through it. She'd have to figure that one out on her own. For now her life would remain a mess, with reporters hassling her and the eyes of a small community forever on her, questioning how she couldn't have known, judging her for being related to a monster. I felt her pain deeply, and all I could do to help was remind her that I was there for her if she needed anything. I couldn't share with her what I knew: the world doesn't need permission to create disaster and devastation, but that the same world will also produce limitless beauty and good.

The silver lining in the whole thing was that when they left, I watched Kyle open the car door for his mother even in the pouring rain before he walked around to his side to drive her home. To see him rising to the occasion, being strong when his mother couldn't, made all the difference. Incremental changes, baby steps. Progress.

So no, there's no heroism in any of this, and there's certainly no releasing of the albatross. There's no taking away what I did, ever. Over and over, I will see Per's blood across his pillow. I will never stop missing my older brother, never stop feeling profound sorrow not only for ending his life but for ripping him away from my parents.

I've never shared the blame with them. They couldn't have known my sleepwalking would get so serious. My counselor back then pointed out how ultimately it was their job to keep both of their children safe, including me from my own self, if they knew I had sleep issues. But ultimately I didn't buy that. They tried to forgive me, to continue being good parents to me, but in the end, the pain reflected in their eyes became a mirror too clear to view. Some wrongs from the past don't ever release their grip on the present, but that doesn't mean we can't still fight for the future.

In the meantime, I wouldn't do anything differently, really. I intended to follow my usual routines: locking myself properly in at night, taking my meds, and watching my caffeine intake. I planned to continue my jogging, enjoying the scenery of the beautiful place where I lived. I intended on getting back to work quickly, continuing to help others behind the scenes in whatever small ways I could, enjoying my coworkers, and trying to be a friend to Wendy.

I have felt a little lighter, a little happier, in the past days, as if a dam has been released, expelling a great load of powerful water. I've felt a smile on my face more often than usual and, once in a while, I've even caught myself singing to some carefree, meaningless song on the radio. I couldn't tell you the last time I did that—maybe when I was fourteen. I've also felt my emotions much closer to the surface over the past week—a common occurrence after trauma, I was told by the trauma specialist who also visited me in the hospital. Tears have suddenly welled up and betrayed me at unexpected moments, and sometimes I've felt as if they'd never stop—that I'd create a river of them that would sweep me away and carry me all the way back to the sapphire blue of the North Sea.

I guess Jeremy vicariously helped me to accept that I needed to appreciate myself more and life in general, that it's not enough simply to survive—you have to live too. I'm not sure how he helped me see that. It wasn't anything in particular that he said. It just hit me in the days following that night. Perhaps it was the way he smiled back at the nurses and squeezed their hands when they held his. Perhaps it was how he slipped his fingers around mine so unself-consciously in the hospital room and simply held them—how he understood the importance of the human connection even when he felt broken, weary in his body, his mind, and his soul.

As for Monty, I'm not going to shut him out, but I don't intend to invite trouble either. Like I said, we're all still dealing with what happened. My sleep disorder is real and must be reckoned with. I'm not going to give up living, but I'm not ready to pretend I'm normal when I'm not. I don't expect everyone to understand that, but if anyone can, it's Monty.

The sun had come up fully, returning the sky to its rightful color of clear blue and painting the fields yellow. The horses had lowered their heads and begun to graze. Just four months before, on a cool, misty spring morning, I'd seen an entire herd of elk grazing in the early dawn, steam erupting from the nostrils of the two bulls, and the reedy cries from the harem of cows reaching me before they began to head back to the higher elevations. Now the air hung crisp and still, and the grass stayed perfectly motionless.

I stood, listening to the noise of nature stirring, the groundhogs and field mice scurrying through the hay and long grass at its edges. Freshly rolled bales of hay stood in the field like golden treasure chests. A skein of geese honked in the distance and flew above, perfecting their chevron before the days of fall arrived. From a maple tree closer to my house, a flock of chickadees stirred, rising as one unit and making erratic sharp turns until they settled onto a tree on the other side of the field.

I looked out to the horizon. The brightening sun exposed everything—every bit of glory. It rose, stretching its light across the sky to turn it an indifferent pastel blue that said good-bye to the night, to the darkness, for just a little while.

Acknowledgments

With each book, my list of people to thank grows larger. Enormous thank-yous to the amazing team of publishing professionals at Atria for their hard work in seeing this novel through to publication; to my editor, Daniella Wexler, for her excellent feedback and impressive editing skills; and to Trent Duffy for catching my many repetitions and inconsistencies and helping to bring coherency to illogical sequences. Both made *The Weight of Night* far, far better than the version I submitted. Huge thanks to David Brown for his untiring, enthusiastic help in publicity, Hillary Tisman and Jin Yu for their guidance and hard work in marketing, Chris Sergio for his fabulous design work, and Haley Weaver for assisting. I continue to express my gratitude and admiration to Judith Curr, the revered president and publisher of Atria Books.

I owe endless thanks to my wonderful agent, Nancy Yost, for numerous things, but especially for her unwavering support, keen guidance, and ability to make me smile. Thank you also to Sarah Younger for being so helpful.

Once again, I relied on generous assistance from Frank Garner, former chief of police in Kalispell, and Gary Moses, former lead ranger in Glacier National Park, and cannot thank them enough for their time in explaining local law enforcement practices to a layperson like me. I'd also like to thank Commander Brandy Hinzman with the Flathead County Sheriff's Office for her insights; and Lisa Black, fellow suspense writer, latent-print examiner, and crime scene investigator, for her help with many forensic details.

I am more than grateful to my dear friend Suzanne Siegel, who always seems to find exactly what I'm searching for whenever I need information. My appreciation is beyond words for all her valuable research, reading of drafts, feedback, wise counsel, and limitless reassurance. And much gratitude to Kathy Dunnehoff, friend and brilliant plotter, who never tires of tapping into her muse to help me sort out story-line issues, or having coffee with me to keep me sane. And to Janet Vandemeer, for the enormous support in reading pass pages and for all the invaluable book-launch help.

I continue to find my way through the world of publishing with my husband Jamie's rock-solid support, guidance, and reassurance; plus, he's not a bad plotter himself when I run into a hitch. Endless appreciation goes to my parents, Robert and Jeanine Schimpff, for providing a lifetime of love, support, and wisdom, and to my dad for always knowing the answer to just about any question I have. To my brothers, Cliff and Eric, and their wives, Pam and LeAnn, for their support. To my aunts, Janie Fontaine and Barbara Dulac, for always bolstering me from afar. Much love to my children, Mathew, Caroline, and Lexie, for continually motivating me with their enthusiasm. Mathew, thank you for helping me work through this ending!

As many Glacier Park visitors and locals know, the summer of 2015 was a particularly bad fire year for the park and the surrounding areas. I used one of the actual fires in this story: the Sheep Fire, one of the three fires in the Thompson Divide Complex near Essex. For the most part, though, I fictionalized how some of it occurred for dramatic purposes and also created the imaginary Ole, Trail Creek, Desert Mountain, and Columbia Mountain fires.

Also, as in my two novels preceding this one, I formed a fictional Park Police force in Glacier. It is not meant to make light of the tremendous work GNP rangers do and the valuable services and law enforcement they provide. I also took liberties with the way the Flathead County Sheriff's Crime Scene Team is structured.

I tried but failed to get a tour of the aluminum plant in Columbia

Falls, so I went with my imagination. I'm sure I got many things wrong in trying to describe it, but I couldn't resist writing about the deserted mammoth of a place that was once an essential part of the Flathead Valley's industrial backbone. When I wrote this, the jury was still out on whether the plant would be included in the EPA's Superfund Program's National Priorities List, and it has since been listed as one of the nation's most contaminated sites.

I owe countless thanks to many more folks for their generous support in my journey as an author: some fellow writers, some friends, some readers. Many thanks, or *Tusen Takk,* to Vibecke Cates and Thomas Korsdalen for their help with information about Norway and its language. As for the rest, I couldn't name them all, but I'll throw heartfelt thank-yous to Jackie Brown, Steve Streich, Patti Spence, Mark Stevens, Shannon Baker, Ginnie Cronk, Mara Goligoski, Dennis Foley, Marian Ellison, Sarah Fajardo, Pat and Missy Carloss, Adrienne Cardan, Tony and Marci Stais, and Paisley and Diego Amaya. I thank Glacier National Park Conservancy for their kind support, all the amazing book clubs I've participated in, both local and afar, all the extraordinary booksellers out there, and, of course, all the wonderful readers! With each book, I continue to be overwhelmed and inspired by the encouragement I receive.

Any mention of landmarks, popular local establishments, or made-up establishments resembling actual businesses is done only to gain verisimilitude. Always, all errors, deliberate or by mistake, are wholly mine.